"*Reasonable Adults* has everything I look for in a rom-com: a relatable heroine, dialogue that zings, an original setting and most importantly—a dog. This is fresh, fun, feel-good fiction."
—Sophie Cousens, *New York Times* bestselling author of *This Time Next Year*

"*Reasonable Adults* is smart romantic comedy filled with madcap moments that will leave you laughing out loud. An absolute delight!" **—Trish Doller, international bestselling author of *The Suite Spot***

"A sparkling debut novel about reinvention, self-discovery, and second chances. With a memorable setting at a troubled artists' colony, a quirky cast of characters, and a double serving of romance and redemption, *Reasonable Adults* is sure to satisfy."
—Kate Hilton, author of *Better Luck Next Time*

"Smart and stylish, *Reasonable Adults* is a fresh, funny, vividly told story of one woman's journey from down and out to up and coming. A sparkling debut destined to become the must-read romantic comedy of the season." **—Bobbi French, author of *The Good Women of Safe Harbour***

"Written with humor, passion, and oh-so-much romance, this book is spell-binding. I couldn't put it down. Robin Lefler has built a world that rivals the like of all the great rom-coms onscreen and off. I can't wait to see what she does next. Her wit, warmth, and honesty shine through these pages. I will be returning to Treetops as frequently as I rewatch *When Harry Met Sally,* which is to say I will be re-reading it once a month every month." **—Ava Bellows, author of *All I Stole From You***

ALSO BY ROBIN LEFLER

Reasonable Adults

Not How I Pictured It

Not How I Pictured It

ROBIN LEFLER

KENSINGTON
PUBLISHING CORP.

www.kensingtonbooks.com

KENSINGTON BOOKS are published by

Kensington Publishing Corp.
900 Third Avenue
New York, NY 10022

All Kensington titles, imprints, and distributed lines are available at special quantity discounts for bulk purchases for sales promotions, premiums, fund-raising, educational, or institutional use. Special book excerpts or customized printings can also be created to fit specific needs. For details, write or phone the office of the Kensington sales manager: Kensington Publishing Corp., 900 Third Avenue, New York, NY 10022, attn Sales Department; phone 1-800-221-2647.

The K with book logo is Reg. U.S. Pat. & TM Off.

Illustration on p. iii by Stephanie Amatori
Images from Adobe Stock

First Kensington trade paperback printing: May 2024

ISBN: 978-1-4967-4134-9

ISBN: 978-1-4967-4135-6 (e-book)

10 9 8 7 6 5 4 3 2 1

Printed in the United States of America

FOR JARON

Where were you at 10:00 p.m., November 22, 2004?

Twenty days earlier, George W. Bush had been reelected. It had been nine days since the European Space Agency probe SMART-1 started orbiting the moon, becoming the first European satellite to do so. The war in Iraq was reaching new heights. Not ringing any bells? Let me tell you where I was, because the trauma of the night is seared into my memory.

On November 22, 2004, at 10:00 p.m. I was curled into an adolescent ball of sobbing emotion, cursing the television gods for ending the finest teen drama ever created: *Ocean Views*.

Today, dreams (mine) are coming true as the cast gathers for the first time in nearly two decades for the first table read of *Ocean Views: Turning Tides*, a limited series set to air on the Good Things Network early next year.

What one (again, me) wouldn't give to be a fly on the wall as the cast, notoriously dramatic on and off set, reunite. Not only do we have former spouses Bradley Isaksson and Libby Kim presumably forced into close proximity, but Hollywood darling turned bad girl turned enigma Ness Larkin has also signed on, marking her first credited role since leaving the series abruptly in 2003.

Reflecting the rumored generous budget behind *Turning Tides*, the show will start shooting episode one on Eclipse Island in the Bahamas (what IS the budget for this thing?!) later this week. Anyone up for a vacation and a little, uh, birdwatching?

CHAPTER 1

ASIDE FROM THE CAMERAS, THE HOTEL BATHROOM WAS NICE.

Ness Larkin tried to glare the creases out of her flimsy coral-colored dress. Sweat trickled between her freshly spray-tanned shoulder blades as she attempted to ignore the not-so-sneaky pictures being snapped by the pair of women two sinks down. She gave up on making the dress presentable and heaved her beat-up duffel bag into one of the spacious stalls.

She was wrist-deep in crumpled T-shirts, dog-eared romance novels, and a month's income worth of travel-size skin care products when her phone rang. She mashed it between her ear and shoulder, cursing herself for the ten thousandth time for leaving her earbuds on the plane. And cursing the airline for misplacing her luggage. And cursing the hotel for losing her reservation. *And why was it so humid?* Her chocolate waves had gone from (relatively) smooth and glossy to pure chaos in the two hours since she'd landed in Miami.

"Good morning, Bethany. How are you?" She stifled a creative expletive as high-heel-clad feet pitter-pattered to a stop just outside her bubble of faux privacy.

"That cat. It's doing it again."

Ness stared at the toes outside the stall, daring the woman to knock on the door.

"I spoke to them last week," she said. "They're working on it, but these things take time. It seems cats aren't easily trained."

"Did you give them the name I provided? The veterinarian who can perform the silencing treatment?"

Ness tugged a mostly wrinkle-free black shirt and a pair of denim shorts from the depths of her duffel, sat back on her heels, and pinched the bridge of her nose. She dragged the pad of her thumb up, smoothing the deep furrow between her brows, vaguely wondering if she should have gone for the fillers she'd so adamantly refused.

"I mentioned there are options they could explore." She would rather be roasted like a succulent forty-two-year-old pig on a spit than suggest poor Bixby have his vocal cords ... permanently remedied.

Bethany sighed dramatically. "I'm going to have to take this up the chain."

Bethany, a primary school teacher who dressed like an investment banker, was among the worst of Ness's tenants. Not because she had a beagle who howled like a deranged werewolf yet persisted in complaining about the cat upstairs. Not even because she refused to close her windows while maxing out the air conditioning in the summertime.

No, Ness hated Bethany because every time she had to go into that apartment to address a (usually fabricated) issue, her photo would surface, featured in *What Ever Happened To* ... articles, or upvoted on Reddit threads about celebs of yesteryear. There Ness would be, bungling her way through hanging a new door or, her personal favorite, wielding a plunger, an expression of great determination on her sweating face.

Ness pulled the phone away from her ear long enough to check the time and confirm that she was definitely going to be late. As she heaved herself to standing and started the circus act of getting changed, a phone edged under the door of the stall. Taking a split second to mute her end of the call, Ness flicked the lock and flung the door open with a bang, yanking the fresh shirt down as she went.

"*Are you serious?!*" she blurted, but the women were already halfway out of the lobby bathroom. She considered trying to catch them, or at least making a report to security, but Bethany's voice rose in pitch to a nasal whine usually associated with teenagers or nearly-dead car engines, dragging her attention to the phone in her hand.

Back in the bathroom stall, she leaned against the cool metal of the partition and closed her eyes, trying to remain calm. She muttered some choice words for Bethany, and the world at large, then unmuted.

"Bethany, I *am* the chain. You're welcome to send another formal letter of complaint if it'll make you feel better."

"Perhaps I'll send formal notice that I'm vacating instead."

Ness inhaled deeply through her nose, the artificial citrus scent of the bathroom tickling her sinuses. She couldn't afford to lose a tenant. As horrible as Bethany was, she did pay her rent on time.

"I have a two-bedroom unit available in another, cat-free house. It's being updated now." Or would be, once she got home and started the work. "Why don't we arrange for you to see it when I'm back in town in a couple of weeks?"

Silence.

"I would happily match your current rent for the first six months." And cry a little bit as she watched her bank balance creep ever lower.

"Fine. But you'll also be seeing that complaint."

"I would expect nothing less."

Ness ended the call and checked the time again: 9:54. Shit.

In the Bleu on the Sands lobby, Ness hit the elevator call button repeatedly and with unnecessary but satisfying aggression. The shiny silver doors slid open, revealing an empty car. Thank god.

She retreated to the back corner, not really believing she'd made it. A full twenty-four hours later than she'd planned—thanks to a leaking washing machine in one of her rental units, a missed flight, and a tornado warning that temporarily grounded all planes at the Toronto airport—she was here. Was she sure she *wanted* to be here? For sure. Mostly. Probably.

Ness smoothed a hand over the high bun she'd quickly twisted her Florida-humidity-accosted hair into, wishing for the hundredth time that her luck wasn't such garbage.

The hotel had apologized profusely for "temporarily misplacing" her reservation, and she'd graciously accepted their promise to coordinate with the production staff on site to get her accommodations sorted out, but she would have happily emptied her bank account for a shower. At least she'd been able to leave her duffel at the front desk instead of schlepping it with her.

She tried not to think about rolling into one of the most important days of her adult life looking like she'd run here from Canada.

Sure, the others had seen her at her less-than-best, but that was nearly twenty years ago, when she'd had the dewy skin and pep of a well-hydrated twenty-two-year-old. Now, she'd been subject to years of forehead-crinkle-inducing stress, summers spent reading on her back deck with too little sunblock, and, well, then there was gravity, which was doing her no favors.

Pulling out her phone, she scrolled to distract herself from what was about to come. Her surprise reentry into The Biz was like starting a new fitness program—it felt good, but it also hurt in surprising new ways when she least expected it.

The top email was from a publicist she'd spoken to earlier in the week, detailing her monthly rates.

Ness felt her green eyes widen in shock at the number on the screen. She choked on her own spit and let out a squeak-turned-cough as the elevator bounced gently to a stop to admit a couple so pretty it hurt her eyes to look at them.

"Are you sure we need to do this?" the tanned blond man asked the equally tanned, leggy blond at his side. She draped a toned arm over his shoulders and dropped a kiss onto his stubble-covered cheek. They smelled like coconut sunscreen and vitality.

"I told you, babes, we're just taking a quick peek. *Ocean Views* was, like, all I watched in high school. Mindy may be full of shit, but if she's right about them shooting the reboot here and I don't check it out I will never forgive myself. Ever. I will wallow for an eternity—" Her words were cut off as the man turned and planted a slow kiss on her lips.

"Got it," he said, forehead pressed to hers, big, strong hand cupping her jaw. "We're making dreams come true."

She sighed, nuzzling his palm. "You already did that, babes."

Ness concentrated on her phone and tried not to gag too loudly. Resigned to her fate, she waited for the moment of recognition, for the woman's eyes to widen in shock and excitement. The door dinged open on the hotel's top floor and the couple stepped out, heads swiveling, looking for signs of washed-up TV stars of decades past.

Looking for her.

Ness hurtled down the faux-barnboard-lined hallway toward the board-room on the top floor of the hotel. It was Miami's premier destination for those seeking a decadent, Instagram-worthy getaway. It was also the setting for the first table read of *Ocean Views: Turning Tides*, and Ness's big return to showbiz.

Her purse kept slipping off her shoulder. She was dangerously close to hyperventilating.

She could hear voices floating toward her, see PAs buzzing around like highly caffeinated bees, stacks of printed scripts clutched to their chests. Ness paused outside an unmarked door, closed her eyes, and reminded herself she had chosen to be here. She was, in fact, incredibly lucky to have this chance. She was confident. She was grateful *and* graceful. She was—

A hand wrapped around her upper arm, yanking her through the door-way into a fluorescent-light-drenched room the size of a large shower.

Ness started to scream, but a single, gel-nailed finger was pressed to her lips. Hard.

"*Shhhhh.* For fuck's sake, Agnes. They'll hear you."

"Coco?" The finger pulled back and Ness pressed a hand to her chest, sucking in air, trying to slow her racing heart. "What the *hell*?"

The woman leaned back against the door and slid down until she was sitting on the floor. Her skin was as pale as ever but shimmered with the pearlescent glow of thousand-dollar moisturizer. She took a deep draw on a vape pen, exhaling a minty cloud. The harsh lighting glistened off her perfect slicked-back, bleached bob. Not a gray hair in sight. It also crash-landed in every delicate crack and crevice carved into her beautiful face over the past two decades. Ness ignored the little spark of satisfaction that ignited in her belly.

She hadn't talked to Coco—born Kathy McGrubin, of Boise, Idaho— or any of her *Ocean Views* co-stars in two decades. Not since she'd left L.A. after . . . Well, suffice it to say she hadn't stuck around for long goodbyes.

"You haven't been in there yet, have you? It's terrible. Like a high school reunion without the dim lighting or booze." Coco inhaled again, holding her breath for an impossibly long time. Ness could feel her own chest getting tight as she waited. Finally, Coco blew out, her shoulders slumping slightly.

"Bradley and Libby are either about to murder each other with ballpoint pens and broken coffee cup shards or fuck on the table." She held up her hand, fingers extended, and ticked off each one as she ran through the list. "Ian is holier-than-thou to the extreme. Like we aren't the ones who rescued him from passing out in puddles of his own puke more times than I can count."

Ness winced at the clouded memories. Ian hadn't been the only messy one.

"And Daisy. Jesus. Daisy . . ." Coco considered her next words, looking affronted. Ness refocused her attention. Daisy Payne. Her new on-screen daughter.

Coco's voice was low. "You know when someone looks so perfect that you want to erase them from the earth because just seeing them makes you feel every one of your flaws?"

"Um. You mean murder or, like, a comically large pencil eraser?"

"Either." She paused. "Both, maybe." Coco stared at the ceiling tiles like they held all the answers to life's biggest problems.

Folded linens lined the walls, stacked on shelves from floor to ceiling. Bins of tiny toiletries were tucked into a corner. Ness checked the time: 10:10. They were definitely late. She *hated* being late. She shifted her weight from foot to foot.

"Simmer." Coco tap-tap-tapped her brown leather brogues on the linoleum. "They're still waiting on half the network bigwigs. You didn't expect this to actually run on schedule, did you?" Her plain white, ribbed tank top was tucked into loose-fitting trousers reminiscent of 1950s menswear. Leaning against the door, wrists draped over her bent knees, she could have been mid photo shoot for a high-end editorial.

Ness crossed her arms over her chest.

"If they can't start yet, why am I suddenly your captive alibi?"

Coco shot her a sheepish grin. "Old habits die hard."

Ness's lips pressed together, suppressing her own smile, despite the mild panic building in her chest. The good girl image she'd hauled along with her for years had gotten Coco out of more tricky situations than she could count, purely by association. Surely the responsible, trustworthy Ness Larkin wouldn't lie about why they were late—though eventually more than one showrunner suggested she get a new car.

She dropped her arms to her sides and ran a hand through her hair. Checked her phone yet again. Groaned.

"Fine, *fine*." Coco rose effortlessly to her feet and pocketed the vape, ran a hand down the front of her shirt as if to check that her abdomen was still completely flat. It was.

"What'd you think of the revised script?" Coco asked, hand on the door handle.

Ness's stomach flipped as she pictured the missed FedEx delivery notice stuck to her door at home. With everything else going on, she'd totally forgotten to pick it up. She breathed through the urge to crumple to the floor in the fetal position.

"Honestly, I haven't had a chance to do a full read. What did *you* think?"

Coco's eyes widened slightly. She cleared her throat. "You haven't read it?"

Ness squirmed. "It's been a wild couple of days." She ran through the flight delays and delinquent hotel reservation, deciding to skip over how she'd left hours later than planned when, shortly after she'd finished with the leaking washing machine in one unit, another of her tenants had called to report a clogged toilet. The joys of property management. She reminded herself she was "in real estate" if anyone asked what she'd been up to for her entire adult life.

"No wonder you look like that." Coco fished a key card out of her back pocket. "Here. I have a three-bedroom suite. You can crash in there. Heads up, though, I'm right next to Libby."

Ness winced.

"Yeah, well. Maybe get my assistant to make sure the coast is clear before you leave the room." She tapped her lower lip thoughtfully. "You know, maybe she's going to take the high road and kill you with kindness instead of, like, arsenic."

"Cool. Thanks for that." Ness gingerly accepted the key card. "But really, thanks, Coco. I appreciate this." She looked at the beige linoleum floor. "I wasn't sure how everyone would feel about me being here . . . You're being very, um, chill about it."

Coco shrugged. "You did what you thought was necessary. Plus, twenty years of therapy and convenient access to a wide selection of cannabis edibles have really brought out my easygoing side." She hauled the door open, stuck her head out, and looked up and down the hallway before sliding out.

"Well, at least Hayes isn't here to blind everyone with his Big Time Movie Guy shine," Ness said as she followed, forcing lightness into her voice, despite the fact that saying his name still (still!) tied her tongue in knots. Not to mention her heart and . . . other parts. It was embarrassing.

Coco's brow crinkled as much as the Botox would allow. "Mmhmm," she murmured. "Right."

Reddit

Dudes! I've heard the rumors that Ness Larkin owns a couple of houses in Toronto but I didn't realize she rents them out. Like, HERSELF?!

Went to see an apartment today and acted a complete fool when Ness MF Larkin opened the door and started showing me around. She's super cool. Also very short? I guess that's normal for actresses? Anyway. The place was nice. She seems super chill and like a cool landlord.

Bad news is rent is on par with the rest of the Danforth. Which is to say, bananas for those of us trying to survive on a single nurse's income. But Ness Larkin! *sighs* A story for the grandkids for sure. Not that they'll know who tf I'm talking about.

⇧ Vote ⇩   💬 Comment   ⬆ Share

CHAPTER 2

THEY SWEPT INTO THE SPRAWLING, OVER-AIR-CONDITIONED MEET-ing room, nabbing blessedly cold water bottles from a sideboard dotted with fruit bowls and mini candy bars. Ness's hand hovered briefly over a tiny Twix but retracted before making contact. She jammed her fingers into the insubstantial pockets of her shorts, trying to look casual as she took in the room.

Tables had been set up in a large U shape, with chairs for today's audience—primarily crew and network stakeholders—arranged in front. Giant windows presented a view of a packed beach, perfect blue skies, and pretty waves rolling gently onto the sand far below.

"We'll get started in a couple of minutes, folks!" a cheery voice boomed. Morris Wagner, producer, former model, and, if the rumors were true, all-around nice guy, standing on a chair, beaming down at everyone. "Just waiting on a couple of stragglers, but if you can start making your way to your seats, we'll be underway soon!"

Around Ness, executives and harried-looking staff were alternately chatting, frenetically texting, or shaking hands with enough prolonged force to cause lasting damage. She eyed the table, trying to pick out her seat, wondering how long it would take for the rest of the cast to notice her. Or had they banded together in collective snubbing? That would be, um, neat.

As promised, Bradley (never, *ever* Brad—at least, not to his face) and Libby were nose to nose, having what appeared to be quite a passionate conversation. Ness winced as Libby repeatedly stabbed a long fingernail into his chest for emphasis. Edging closer to the murder end of the scale than table sex, it seemed.

She wondered how many hours a day Bradley was spending in the gym to maintain his Thor-esque muscle tone. It couldn't be easy looking fifty in the eye and still making your pecs dance.

Suddenly, as one terrifying unit, they turned toward Ness across the table. Libby's eyes narrowed. Her plump lips curved into an expression of disapproving scorn. Ness couldn't figure out where to direct her eyes or what to do with her hands. She'd been expecting a confrontation with Libby but had really, *really* been hoping to put it off for a day or twenty. One didn't ghost one's (presumably now former) best friend for a couple of decades without expecting some kind of comeuppance, but she could try to avoid it as long as possible.

Bradley, seemingly oblivious to the undercurrents literally right under his nose, ran a hand through his shoulder-length, perfectly tousled curls and flexed his triceps in what could be loosely interpreted as either a neutral greeting or an oddly specific threat.

Without thinking, Ness pulled a quick Hulk Hogan double-arm flex before wincing at her own awkwardness and rotating away from the danger zone toward potentially more friendly territory. Libby wouldn't attack her while her back was turned. Right?

It was hard to believe she was actually here. Coco wasn't wrong—it did feel like a high school reunion. Awkward, exciting, and like everyone had something to prove. Ness tried to project confident professionalism and not stare like a wide-eyed newbie.

It had been impossible, of course, to fully avoid any mention of her former colleagues since she'd left L.A. She'd hear radio spots talking about their current projects, or see one of them (usually Bradley or Coco) on the cover of a fitness or fashion magazine at the grocery store checkout. Ian had been riding the fame wave after his bestselling memoir, *Just One Bump,* had rocketed to number one only a few months earlier. Ness couldn't walk past a bookstore without seeing the cover—a close-up shot of his gray-blue eyes, emphasizing the fine lines snaking out from the corners.

And, of course, every year or two she'd be driving somewhere innocuous only to be faced with a fifteen-foot image of Hayes's face on a billboard.

She'd grown up with these people. And then, when her dad-slash-manager had peaced out with her life savings and left her to fend for herself, he'd taken her dignity and capacity to trust with him. Ness had felt like an idiot. How had she not seen what he was doing? Libby had been telling her to get more involved in her finances for years.

"You're an adult now," Libby had said over more than one Sunday brunch, in the know-it-all tone usually reserved for people other than her bestie. "Don't you want to know where your money is going?" But it had felt like a tomorrow problem, and besides, it was her *dad*. Surely, if anyone had her back, it was him.

Well, that turned out to be laughably incorrect.

Ness had tried to ignore the pitying looks, but she couldn't escape the feeling that she was not only the world's dumbest human, but also that she must be deeply and utterly flawed for her own parent to turn his back so easily. She'd suddenly found herself deep in debt and entirely incapable of digging herself out. It was humiliating. After a few months she couldn't take it anymore. The collection agencies, the whispers behind her back, the lowball offers for roles she previously would never have considered.

Navigating the minefield of showbiz and media attention without the guidance of the person who'd shielded her for so long was beyond shocking. Sure, she'd wanted *some* freedom, but being thrown directly into the lion's den without even a year's worth of savings to protect her? Disaster.

Slowly at first, and then with concerning frequency, people had started pulling away. She'd given the rest a hefty shove.

Ness left and didn't look back. She wanted a fresh start far, far away from every single person who served as a reminder of what her life had been. It was ridiculous, looking back. Even completely destitute, if she'd been able to work past the humiliation she could have found doors to open and a way forward that didn't involve abandoning her life's work and the only thing she'd ever been truly passionate about.

Over the following years, it had become increasingly clear to Ness that what she was lacking, in addition to her purloined millions and self-confidence, was closure on that chapter of her life. Sprinting north had seemed like the only option then, but now, with the benefit of time to (mostly) heal and the perspective a little age brings, Ness wanted the chance to tie those loose ends into what might end up being a sloppy but emotionally fulfilling bow. She wanted to stop asking herself "what if" on repeat. She'd never know what her life could have been if she'd chosen a different path all those years ago, but she could forge a new one now. A path she could look back on and be proud of.

Seeing her *Ocean Views* co-stars online or in print had always made her heart stutter and her stomach flip. She'd spend the rest of the day replaying scenes from her past in her head and imagining scenarios in which they were reunited, sometimes in a sprinkling of happy tears, but usually . . . not that.

And now, here they were. All of them. Well, almost all. Ness wasn't sure she could make it through a face-to-face with Hayes emotionally unscathed. His inability to participate in the reboot had been the final sign she'd needed that this was an opportunity she had to take.

She took a deep breath and visualized a light switch (her therapist was really into visualizations). Then, with a quick prayer to the gods of fortune, she flipped the switch from Agnes Larkin, mediocre landlord and unblocker of sinks, to Ness Larkin, self-assured woman of the world and Extremely Prepared Actress.

When someone launched themselves onto her back, enveloping her in a bear hug to rival the attack of an actual, mid-size, largely hairless bear, she barely stifled her screech of terror.

"Nessinator! You made it!" Strong arms spun her around and she found herself face to face with a still stunning Ian James.

Ness's heart stuttered as long-buried Ian-tinged regrets danced through her mind, but she shoved them aside. If he was going to act normal, so could she. She felt her lips spread into a wide smile. "Hoooolyyyy smokes. It's good to see you."

Ian slung an arm across her shoulders, the cool silk of his pineapple-print shirt brushing against the back of her neck.

"Can you even believe this? The whole crew together again! This is going to be a blast." He steered her toward their table, head swiveling as he looked across the room. "I need to talk to Stella about the coconut water sitch, but for real, Ness, I'm pumped you came back." He squeezed her shoulder gently before bopping across the room.

Ness pushed away the burn of emotion that felt uncomfortably like happy tears and went to find her space at the table.

Coco had plopped into her seat, two folding chairs to the left of center, and was flipping through the script, smirking as she made notes in the margins.

Ness scanned the name cards propped in front of each spot. *Daisy Payne. Bradley Isaksson. Coco. Ian James. Morris Wagner. Libby Kim. Ness Larkin.* Ah. She headed toward her spot, wondering who'd had to dig deep into the archives to figure out how they'd been seated during the original *Ocean Views* readings. It was a nice touch.

Traditionally, Hayes would have been next to her. Curious, her eyes darted to the next seat down. *Hayes Beaumont.* Her heart pounded. Her stomach performed nausea-inducing acrobatics. *Ah,* she thought after a moment of panic. *It's a gesture. An homage.* She pulled out her chair and slid in, shaking her head at her overreaction.

Morris was glad-handing a sixty-something exec in rumpled khakis and a Hard Rock Café golf shirt, but he took a moment to smile warmly at her. "Ness! Welcome!" Was that relief on his face? She wasn't *that* late. She smiled back, letting some of her excitement show.

Hard Rock slapped Morris on the shoulder, making him wince, and meandered over to the coffee station. A gangly, pale man in khakis and a mint-green collared shirt that did nothing good for his complexion sidled into the now vacant space, clipboard in hand. He gave Ness an inquisitive glance, then trained his eyes on Morris, like an attentive puppy waiting for a command.

"Oh, hey, Tyler. Did you get the—"

In a practiced movement, the man freed a stack of paper from his clipboard and placed it gently in Morris's hand.

"Awesome, thanks." Morris rolled the paper into a tube and slid it into his back pocket. He focused on Ness. "This is going to be a great day." He seemed to really mean it. "You have the updated schedule for tomorrow? It's going to be a bit frantic, but it's important to take advantage of these early press opportunities, right?" His smile tightened. "And then we're off to paradise! Small change there." His eyes darted sideways. "Core cast will be going to Eclipse Island by boat once we land on Grand Exuma." He gave an apologetic half shrug, like, *What can you do?* "I think we tried to send the details to your assistant but . . ." He trailed off. "Anyway"—he nodded, scanning the room—"it's going to be epic." He drifted away from her to continue glad-handing.

Episode one had the *Ocean Views* gang reuniting for the funeral of Theo Osgoode, teen bad boy turned tech billionaire, played by Hayes Beaumont. Word on the proverbial street was that Hayes had a conflicting big-budget movie shoot and couldn't make the scheduling work. Or didn't want to. It was to be a closed casket event.

Someone on the other side of the room laughed loudly. Outside, the sun shone between scattered puffy white clouds onto the glittering water below. Ness jolted as the air conditioning kicked on, dumping cold air through the vent above her. She shivered and wondered if she should get up and try to go make conversation with someone. Her eyes drifted from face to face, but she stayed put.

She looked at the script in front of her. Running a hand over the first page, she realized this felt right. She was, despite everything, happy to be here. This was as close to time travel as she was going to get. Her very own *Sliding Doors* moment.

As Ness twisted the cap off her water bottle and got ready to read as much of the script as she could cram in before they started, someone stopped on the opposite side of the table.

"Ms. Larkin?"

Ness's gaze skimmed up the woman's toned body, clad in a cropped emerald shirt over loose boyfriend jeans that rested on her hips. Red curls were piled on top of her head. A couple of stray strands fell alluringly around her face.

"Oh my goodness, it's so great to finally meet you!" Daisy Payne gushed, smiling widely. Ness was reminded of a young Julia Roberts and, for an instant, understood Coco's displeasure with the new addition. Then she remembered she was supposed to play this woman's *mother*. It was a fresh punch to the gut.

She pulled her face into a welcoming grin, reminding herself she was an actress. She may as well practice.

"Daisy!" She stood, and the two embraced lightly and awkwardly across the table. Luckily, Daisy was nearly six feet tall in her sneakers and easily closed the gap that Ness's short body left. She was about to launch into what would probably have been a so-so "Welcome to the team" speech when she heard a collective intake of breath from the gaggle of PAs gathered nearby. A heartbeat of complete silence followed. Ness's eyes followed the trail of open-mouthed stares to their target.

"Hey, everyone! So sorry I'm late," said Hayes.

Ness tried to play it cool. She was a cucumber. Ice. Jack in the frigid water when Rose was hogging the door-raft. But when Hayes took his seat beside her and rocked gently, so his shoulder connected softly with hers? When he cocked his head and looked at her through lowered lashes and said "Hi," with an uncertain smile dancing across his recently exfoliated lips? She was a puddle. A confused, distraught, butterflies-in-the-stomach-and-other-parts mess. Luckily, as stated, she was an actress—some might even say a good one—so she was pretty sure her return smile and casual "Hi" were, at a minimum, passable. She could do this.

• • •

"You told me he was dead!" Ness whisper-shrieked into her phone. As soon as Morris had called an end to the read, she'd fled the room, taking refuge behind a stand of potted palms in the farthest possible corner of the hotel's eighteenth floor. The spiky foliage poked at her face every time she moved, but at least she was out of sight.

"I meant in the show, Agnes." She could practically hear Audrey's eyes rolling. Audrey Wilson, her agent for the past seven months, had been recommended by a friend of a friend as a strong representative for Mature Women when the Good Things Network had reached out about the reboot. Ness couldn't decide whether Audrey thought she was an idiot, or if this was her standard demeanor. Maybe she thought everyone was an idiot? That kind of made Ness feel better.

"Yes, thank you. I did understand that part." She took a breath, attempting to regulate her tone. She batted a palm frond away from her eye. "Maybe I misunderstood, but I thought you said you'd spoken to the production team and confirmed that Hayes wasn't participating. Because *his character* is dead. *So he doesn't need to be here.*" She could feel her voice creeping toward shrill.

"Yes, well, obviously something has changed."

"Yes. Obviously."

"Listen, Ness. He's doing one episode. You've got what, three, four days with the guy? Nine, max. Maybe a couple more if there are reshoots. Whatever. You had a thing. So what? It happened eons ago. Film a few flashbacks together and otherwise keep your distance. Then he'll be off in lord knows where for that space cowboy movie. I wouldn't be surprised if they've rented out Mars."

"I just—"

Audrey talked right over her, taking a bite of something with the crunch of a baby carrot, but wetter. A pickle? Ness tried to ignore it but could feel her molars starting to grind.

"Put on your big-girl pants and get to work. Heck, jump in the sack with an NDA-abiding pool boy if it makes you feel better. Then

Mr. Beaumont will be flitting off to make his millions fighting alien squids, and you'll be lounging in the Bahamas. Well, working. Probably long hours. But maybe some of your scenes will involve a reclined position." She paused, chewing. "Make sure you suck in your stomach while in repose. Save them some effort in post."

Ness's mouth opened and closed like a fish. Audrey didn't get it. She couldn't. She wasn't the one who had spent the past two hours desperately trying (and actually mostly succeeding) to ignore his freshly-washed-male scent and invasive pheromones in order to focus on the script and deliver her lines smoothly. You know, like she'd read them in advance. Maybe even practiced a little.

She'd managed to suggest some tweaks she was pretty happy with, which balanced out the sting of Hayes chatting with Coco during the breaks while being contrastingly distant with Ness. How could a shoulder go so abruptly from sweetly welcoming to frigid?! It was confusing! Hurtful! *And why was he even there?*

Audrey was droning on. Something about camouflaging upper-arm jiggle.

"Thanks for that, Audrey. I need to run. Talk soon!" She hung up and sagged against the wall, inhaling the scent of moist potting soil and her own despair.

She was fucked. Not literally, unfortunately, but definitely emotionally. She had assumed she'd be over Hayes. It had been decades. She'd figured there was a good chance he was awful now, having stewed in celebrity juices far too long. But no. No, he wasn't. The years had been more than kind to him. He'd transformed from a handsome young man to dear-god-take-me-now levels of sexy.

His sandy hair was brushed with silver. A soft green T-shirt hugged his shoulders. Worn jeans hung perfectly on his hips and showcased those long, long legs. Dark-rimmed glasses finished off a World's Hottest Professor look. And he was *nice*. Even while treating her like a complete stranger, he was so goddamn annoyingly kind and supportive and . . . ugh. Like she'd said. Fucked.

She was trying to convince her body to move toward Coco's room when Morris rounded the corner at the end of the hall, mid phone call. Tyler, his faithful lackey, trotted two respectful steps behind, clipboard dangling from a lanyard around his neck. It thunked gently against his stomach as he moved, occasionally clipping the edge of the phone on which he was speed-scrolling.

There was no casual way to exit her hiding spot. She'd either need to mosey on out, like it was totally normal to be lurking in a corner outside what was presumably Morris's room, or hide. Easy choice. She dropped into a crouch, wrapping her arms around her knees and tucking her head into her arms. She channeled boulders. Woman-sized rock. Modern statuary.

She peeked through a crack between her thigh and upper arm.

Morris's jaw was clenched so hard she could see the muscles bunching from ten feet away. His raspy baritone had lost its earlier friendliness. "But we agreed on a budget, Trisha. This isn't it." He stopped in front of a door and patted his pockets. "You wanted, and I quote, big beauty. Compete with *White Lotus*, you said. Do you know what *their* budget is?" He paused mid-stride, causing a near-collision as Tyler narrowly avoided mashing into his back.

"No? Neither do I, but I can almost guarantee we're suddenly working with peanuts in comparison. I had to pull every string in my string bank to get us to the island without going into the red." He held the phone away from his face, silently screaming at it before putting it back to his ear.

Tyler's thin lips pursed in a moue of concern. He patted his pockets as if trying to find something to offer Morris to reduce the strain of the moment.

"Christ!" Morris continued down the hall, looking around to make sure no one was in the vicinity. He seemed vaguely startled to see Tyler so close to him. "Do they know what we're dealing with here? The odds of half the cast falling apart completely or killing each other before we're halfway through the season are astronomically high. It's going to be like herding mildly talented rabid cats as it is. You're—I mean, it's bonkers."

He pulled a key card from his wallet and shoved the door open. As it swung shut and clicked behind him, Ness thought she heard him say her name. The tone wasn't encouraging. Tyler stood, unmoored, outside the closed door. For a moment, Ness worried he was going to park himself on the floor and wait for Morris to reemerge, but then a quiet buzz from his phone had him hotfooting it back the way he'd come.

Someone cleared their throat to Ness's left, just outside her cluster of protective foliage. A security guard loomed, one hand on a walkie-talkie.

"Ma'am, you shouldn't be here."

Ness stood, ignoring the creaking of her joints. She sighed.

"Yeah, I know."

Ness declined Coco's kind offer to "get shit-faced and bathe in the tears of our enemies" and instead headed to the private gym on their floor. The thought of tomorrow's flight on what was bound to be a teeny tiny island-hopper of a plane taking them from Miami to Great Exuma was making her antsy, and then there was the boat to Eclipse. The idea of being trapped in a confined space with Libby *and* Hayes? She suppressed a shudder and hoped a workout would exhaust her enough that she could get some sleep.

Lost in thought, she pushed through the door into the gym and wandered toward the cardio equipment. The black athletic mats were springy under her feet, and the vents seemed to be blowing temperate imitation sea breeze. The scent of salt and fresh rain permeated the space, which still maintained a chilly, workout-friendly temperature. Were they piping in the real deal from the beach, cooling it along the way?

Ness clambered onto a bike, paired the headphones she'd scored from the welcome basket in Coco's room, and started scrolling through the thirty-minute virtual class options. She'd follow that with some weights, wrap up with a bit of yoga, and then retreat to one of Coco's spare rooms for a night of personal reflection and regret paired with a side of self-flagellation. Perfect.

Someone slid into view in front of her bike. Ness's gaze skimmed up the toned, dewy body wrapped in matching navy bike shorts and sports bra. Daisy's hair looked just as good if not better than it had at the table read, shining healthfully with artistic tendrils skimming her neck. Her cheeks were gently flushed, as if she'd walked quickly across a small room, or felt a moment of moderate excitement.

"Drat! I just finished my run." She dabbed at her face with a pristine white towel, eyeing the bike beside Ness. Her brow crinkled slightly. "But I only did five miles. Hmm. Would you mind if I joined you?" She started toward the neighboring bike but paused before mounting, waiting for Ness's agreement.

Ness moved one side of her headphones aside, sure she'd misheard. "Did you say *only* five miles?"

"Yeah. It's usually my warm-up, but I'm wiped from the travel so I was going to slack a bit." She grimaced. There was an utterly charming gap between her top front teeth.

"My trainer has me on two-a-day workouts. I'm so lucky to be in a position to have that time, and access to places like this—did you hear the whale sounds earlier? I thought I was hallucinating—but I also miss . . . normal life? It seems irrational to work so hard for something and then complain about making it. God, I'm rambling. Sorry. Nervous habit. Kills me in interviews."

"Don't worry about it. Achieving your dreams is, well, not as simple as I wish it were." Ness shot Daisy a tentative smile. "I was going to do the 2000s pop ride."

"Perfect! I've been meaning to brush up on the music of that era, get into the zone, you know?"

"Daisy?"

"Mmhmm?"

"Please never refer to my prime years as a different era again."

"Oh. Yeah. Right. It's just, I was, like, five when *Views* ended."

Ness pointedly shifted her headphones back into place and turned her gaze to the bike's screen.

"Okay, okay." Daisy laughed. "But, you know, it's perfectly normal for kids to talk about how their parents grew up in different times. In fact, if you want to tell me about, like, riding a moose to school in the snow or something before Canada had cars, I'm all ears."

Ness flung the clean towel she'd hung on her handlebars across the aisle at Daisy, who was giggling uncontrollably.

"You're grounded."

Daisy snorted, scrolling to the right class. Her manicured finger hovered over the Start button.

"You know, I heard a lot of things about the cast." She lowered her voice. "You're not what I was expecting."

"I'm sure you did." Ness waited, trying not to look as exasperated as she felt. Would people never move on? It had been so long. She sighed. "Listen, can we save that for another day? Maybe struggle in silence for a while? Be one with the inevitable pain in our quads and/or souls?"

Daisy started the ride on her bike and the sound of "Mr. Brightside" drifted faintly into the air.

"You got it, Mom."

"How dare you!" Ness started pedaling, wondering if she could generate enough momentum to propel a stationary bike through the wall, to freedom.

Rumor has it things are already heating up on the set of *Ocean Views: Turning Tides*. Production hasn't even officially kicked off and we're hearing that sparks are flying. And not necessarily the sexy kind.

An anonymous source on the set of a recent early publicity event (why are we promoting already, *Turning Tides*? You worried?) says Libby Kim and Ness Larkin haven't let sleeping dogs lie.

"It was uncomfortably tense," our source says. "At one point Ness stormed off set, leaving Libby to salvage the segment."

Yikes! For you youngsters just tuning in, one, you need to go stream *Ocean Views* immediately, and two, the drama between Libby and Ness is legendary. Rivals turned besties turned enemies for life. We're seeing the toxicity of Hollywood, here, folks. Turning women against each other and reveling in the fallout.

Keep your eyes on this space for more updates from the burgeoning trash fire that is *Ocean Views: Turning Tides*.

NESS'S CHARCOAL-GRAY PENCIL SKIRT BARELY ALLOWED HER TO maintain her alluring position perched on the slippery wooden stool. Her lost luggage had arrived well after she'd gone to bed, interrupting what had been shaping up to be the best hour of sleep she'd get all night.

In front of her, within kicking distance, Hayes, Ian, and Bradley were lounging on a couch, comfortably manspreading. The women hovered behind on bar-height, low-backed stools that would have meant certain death to anyone a few drinks deep and attempting to sit at an actual bar.

"We're thrilled to have this unusual opportunity to speak with all of you so early in the process of bringing *Turning Tides* to life! How does it feel to be back together?"

"It's so exciting, Krista!" Ian leaned forward, resting his elbows on his knees and clasping his hands. Ness watched a bead of sweat roll down from his hairline into the collar of his shirt. "It was a bit of a case of 'you don't know what you have till it's gone.' Having the chance to be back with such a multifaceted, talented group after the past few years of hardship—which you can read about in my memoir, *Just One Bump*—is a dream come true." He beamed at the beautiful, very peppy interviewer. She fluttered her eyelashes before turning her attention to Bradley.

"Bradley, you've been diversifying your portfolio over the past few years—loving the Chateau Giselle Rosé, by the way. What was it about this project that tempted you to step back in front of the *Ocean Views* cameras?"

"This show has always held a special place in my heart. Kind of like a first love . . ."

As he droned on about his many varied accomplishments, Ness caught a movement out of the corner of her eye. Libby had pulled a pen from somewhere and scrawled "BROKE" on the back of her cheat sheet, which had been wedged under her thigh. She angled it to show Coco, who, in turn, snorted a laugh she tried to turn into a quiet cough. Ness attempted to look interested in the interview, which had thankfully moved on.

"Hayes, you were a last-minute addition to the cast of *Turning Tides.* What compelled you to sign on so late in the game?"

His broad shoulders flexed under his jacket, and Ness wished she could see his face.

"I was interested from the moment I heard the revival was under consideration, but I'd already signed on for two other projects, *Alpha Lunar* and *Meet Me at Noon.* For a while, it didn't seem like we'd be able to make the scheduling work, but with a bit of luck and some very understanding producers, here we are. Like Ian said, reflecting on our time together twenty years ago, I realized some opportunities were left on the table. I'm excited to see where our chemistry takes us now that we're older and wiser." He nudged Bradley. "Well, some of us are wiser, anyway."

Bradley chuckled cooperatively.

"Speaking of aging, can we take a moment to appreciate how great these ladies are looking?" Krista's co-interviewer, Jordan, chimed in.

Ness hoped her cringe was purely internal but feared it was written all over her face.

The men gave appreciative murmurs and nodded.

Coco piped up with, "Yeah, the guys look like trash," making Daisy choke on the water she'd just sipped.

Jordan's forehead crinkled in consternation. Krista shuffled her notes, cleared her throat, and continued.

"Ness, you've been a woman of mystery, out of the spotlight for quite some time. What brought *you* back?"

"I left acting quite young. I've built a life I'm happy with, but I've always wondered what would have happened if I'd stuck around. Maybe nothing, maybe everything." She shrugged. She'd been expecting the question but didn't like how even her PR-friendly language still felt like baring her soul.

"When I was invited back, it seemed like a chance to revisit a part of my life that's been calling to me for years. Like Ian and Hayes said—unfinished business. When you're twenty, it feels like you have all the time in the world. I know better now."

Coco barked out a laugh. "I just wanted a chance to spend a week in the Bahamas. I've been shooting in Alaska for the past two months. Give me some heat!"

Krista laughed. "Speaking of heat, we've got a surprise for you!"

Ness's stomach clenched. She hated surprises. She had actually specified to Audrey that she wanted "no 'fun' surprises during publicity" in her contract, but Audrey had convinced her the optics weren't great.

"No one wants to work with a spoilsport, Agnes." Audrey had sighed her *what have I gotten myself into with this one?* sigh. "You're coming back new, fresh, ready to take on the world—or at least that's the image we want to project. We don't want to do anything to indicate you're not 100 percent on board."

"I'm on board, just not with this one tiny facet of the whole thing."

"I'll put it in if you want, hon. That's my job, after all. Client first. But it's *also* my job to set you up for success, and let me tell you, putting up an obstacle on something this small is going to cost you in the long run."

Ness had acquiesced. Besides, what were the chances anything would actually come up? She'd be fine.

Now, Libby sat three feet away, and Ness was certain she saw the promise of death in her eyes. Between them was a table with a large, glowing red button in the middle. Ness couldn't be certain they'd been paired up to maximize drama, but based on the gleeful hand-rubbing of the sideline observers it didn't seem particularly far-fetched.

"Welcome to a little segment we call Hot Shots, where we test your memory and your ability to consume vegan hot wings *at the same time!*" Jordan was using a game show host voice that made Ness want to punch him in his smug face.

"Here's how it works. I'll ask a question about the original *Ocean Views*. The first to hit the buzzer and answer correctly gets to sip this nice frosty oat milk. But if you answer wrong, you'll need to eat a wing. They increase in spice from left to right, so with each incorrect answer, you face a greater burn! Ready, ladies? *Alright, let's gooooo*."

Libby managed to look simultaneously bored and furious. Ness thought she was probably coming off as scared and confused. Exactly what every viewer wants from their talk show captives.

Her eyes darted from the red button in the middle of the table to Libby's eyes, which, for a second, also seemed to glow red. A trick of the light, right?

Ness licked her lips nervously.

"First question! In season two, Libby's character, Vanessa, hitchhikes from the Mango Café to North Beach for a date. She's picked up by a tall, dark, and handsome police officer played by . . . which guest star?"

Ness's hand flew toward the buzzer, making contact with the soft skin of Libby's fingers with a startling *smack* as her opposition got there a split second faster.

"Libby! What's your answer?"

"Keanu Reeves!" Libby smirked. "Who could forget being hand-cuffed by *him*?" She gave a dramatic shiver-shimmy of her shoulders.

"Correct! Ness, that means you're taking the first hot shot."

It went downhill from there.

The vegan wings had the texture of a mealy pear combined with stale bread crumbs and smothered in . . . well, Ness didn't want to speculate about where the hot sauce had come from, but it tasted like it had been brewing on someone's windowsill for a while.

By the time they'd worked through five questions, Libby was leaning back in her chair looking smug, lipstick still perfect, hair glossy. In contrast, tears were streaming down Ness's face and she could feel her hair plastering itself to her forehead. This was a nightmare.

She forced a smile that she hoped wasn't showing off teeth full of soy protein and chugged another glass of oat milk.

"All or nothing for the last one, Jordan?"

"Hoo boy! Libby, are you in? Ness gets this one, you'll need to eat your entire plate of hot shots in one go. Ness, if you lose, you'll need to clear Libby's plate. Are you sure you're up to it?"

Ness's stomach roiled and she fought back a belch. She smoothed her expression to one of calm. She locked eyes with Libby and cocked an eyebrow. Her returning smirk said, *I see you're still an idiot. This is a bad idea.*

She'd built a life on bad ideas. She gave a single nod of assurance, breathing deeply.

Libby shrugged. "You bet, Jordan." She leaned forward, hand at the ready. Ness mirrored her opponent.

"Okay, then. Final question. In season four, when Ness's character, Aubrey, is in dire straits, who offers to run away with her?"

Ness's world went fuzzy as her eyes landed on Hayes, slouched in a director's chair in the background. She could feel the heat of the lights, and hear the shuffling of Jordan's notecards as he tapped them on the table. The smell of the room-temperature food in front of her was suddenly unbearable. It felt like someone had punched her in her already overwhelmed stomach.

As if she were watching from a distance, she saw Libby's hand moving to the buzzer. Suddenly time resumed normal speed and Ness's finger shot out, smashing the red button and leaving a smear of grease and sauce behind.

"It was his. I mean, Hayes's character, Theo." She smiled as her stomach revolted, and she slid her plate across the table to sit beside Libby's full one. "Enjoy."

She pushed her seat back and slid down, walking quickly off the small set. Her footsteps echoed off the hallway walls. She walked faster, her heels clicking obnoxiously. Behind her, someone laughed.

Hayes found her in the parking lot.

"Are you okay?"

The light assaulted Ness's eyes. She blinked and squinted, staring at the patch of asphalt the door she'd picked at random had spit her out onto. Cigarette butts littered the ground. A coffee can sat beside the door, overflowing with them.

She checked her watch. They had to be at the airport in two hours. The day was somehow speeding by while also feeling endless.

"I'm fine," she said, breathing in the scent of wet parking lot. It seemed they'd missed an afternoon shower. Droplets still plopped from the shrubbery. The sun shone as if nothing had ever happened. She shot Hayes a tight smile, noting that he didn't look any worse for wear.

She skirted the truth. "It's just . . . it's a lot. And I hate vegan chicken. I didn't know that until today." She started to pace but then realized how much her feet hurt in the pointy-toed stilettos. She stood still, shifting her weight from foot to foot. It didn't help.

"I'm glad you're here, you know. You're doing great." His voice was low and rumbly. Because of course he'd somehow intuited where her mind had been parked, idling, since she'd arrived, full of insecurity and self-doubt. *Of course* he was worried about her. Even when they'd been together, she'd always felt like he was everything bright and good while she was some murky gray area heading farther and farther into the dark. He kept her in the light, even if it was by association, and for some reason that annoyed the hell out of her.

"Great. Good. That's good." A seagull swooped down to swipe a soggy stray french fry from the ground.

"I didn't think you'd be here," she blurted.

He snorted, charmingly, of course, and canted his head to the right. He looked like an inquisitive canine, and Ness wanted nothing more than to take him home with her. Well, that and a toothbrush.

"You think I'd pass up a chance like this?" he asked.

"Um, yeah. I mean, it's not that big of a chance, really. It's not like you need it." Not the way *she* needed it. She ran her tongue over her teeth. "Do you have any gum?"

He shoved a hand into his back pocket, producing a pack of Triple Mint gum, Ness's preferred flavor. He held it out to her and she nodded her thanks, taking two pieces and chewing vigorously.

"Thank god." She sighed as the taste of processed soy and regret was masked by three different varieties of simulated mint. Her head dropped back in relief, face to the sky, her eyes closed.

Hayes spoke, quiet and serious. "I have my reasons for being here."

"Is this your in with Libby to invest in Kim Beauty? I hear it's going to be huge." Typical Ness, deflecting with humor.

Hayes started to speak, but the door behind them burst open, slamming back against the brick wall and making them both jump.

"There you are!" A flustered production assistant fanned his face with a clipboard. "I've been looking everywhere. We need you back on set, Ms. Larkin. Just a quick gloat over your win."

"Yeah, sure. I'll be right there."

The PA's gaze landed on Hayes and he froze. Ness wasn't even sure he was breathing. "Ohmigod," he wheezed. "Hi."

"Hi." Hayes smiled warmly, making every heart within three miles skip a beat or two. "Shall we get Ms. Larkin back to her seat?"

The PA cleared his throat and gave his head a shake. "Yes, thank you. Yes." He backed away, as if leaving the presence of royalty.

"Does that ever get old?" Ness asked quietly.

"You have no idea." And she didn't.

As they walked side by side back to set, making small talk, Ness wondered just how much of a do-over she was going to get, and how much she deserved.

Who doesn't love Hayes Beaumont? The silver fox has been charming the metaphorical pants off audiences everywhere since his time on *Ocean View*s two decades ago, encouraging comparisons to George Clooney's time on *ER* and subsequent rocket to stardom.

Well, we're hearing that these days Hayes may have made a few enemies. Or at least ruffled some feathers.

Reports are trickling in that the Georgia-born dreamboat has thrown a big wrench into the production schedule for his next film by insisting he participate in episode one of *Ocean Views: Turning Tides*.

Someone close to the project tells us, "Everyone knows he got his break with *Ocean Views* and that he has emotional ties to the show, but there are other commitments in play. This is very un-Hayes-like."

And from what we've seen, that seems true. Hayes Beaumont is nothing if not dependable. A sure box office hit, an all-around nice guy— maybe one of the last truly good men in Hollywood.

This could all be a misunderstanding, but we'll keep monitoring the situation. Only time will tell whether revisiting the passions of his youth will put a torch to Hayes's bright future.

CHAPTER 4

NESS EYED THE DARK CLOUDS GATHERING OVER THE WATER IN THE distance. The wind whipped her hair into her face, adhering carefully shaped curls to freshly applied lipstick.

They'd flown into Great Exuma an hour earlier and been driven directly from the airport to the marina with promises that their assistants, for those who had them, and luggage would be following shortly to meet them at Eclipse Island via ferry.

"Take this time to reconnect!" Morris had directed them at the airport. "I'll see you over there!"

"Why aren't *we* flying again?" Bradley asked, eyeing the puddle jumper idling nearby.

"It's full of gear! Just a scheduling thing. Nothing to be concerned about, er, budget-wise, though! All good there!" Morris had said apologetically as his phone rang in the pocket of his cargo shorts. He pulled it out, glanced at the screen and scowled. "Sorry, I need to take this. But enjoy the ride! It'll give you a chance to see the landscape and understand the journey your characters would have had to take to get out here. The travel isn't trivial. They'd have had to really commit to being at Theo's funeral. What creates that drive for each of you?"

"Kyle would have flown," Bradley called after him, shouting to be heard over the revving engine, but Morris was already halfway up the steps of his plane, phone pressed hard to his ear. Bradley wasn't wrong. His character, Kyle Everstreet, entitled party boy turned down-and-out

IP lawyer, would have chartered a private plane even if he had to sell a kidney to finance it.

At the marina, they prepared to embark on what had been billed as a short, pleasant sunset jaunt. The boat, they'd been assured, was stocked with premixed cocktails, local beer, and light snacks. Ness couldn't quite picture how they'd ingest anything without chipping a tooth as they bounced over the growing swells.

A seagull squawked from its perch atop a nearby garbage can and Ness noticed the dock was otherwise very quiet, most boats secured and unmanned. In fact, all the proverbial and literal hatches looked about as battened down as they could get. All except for their transport—a jaunty turquoise and white affair that, under blue skies and atop calm water, she could easily have found charming, if slightly (okay, much) less swanky than she'd expected.

Where she'd been picturing a fully enclosed living space, perhaps with wait staff, *Gentleman's Delight* was the type of thing she'd charter for a day with a group of friends on a budget vacation.

The cracked white vinyl-covered benches tucked fore and aft screamed "lounge on me with a frosty beverage and liberally applied SPF!" and the captain's nook (totally a nautical term) had what appeared to be teak cabinetry and paneling, popping in an aesthetically pleasing fashion against the brighter paint around them.

As things stood, however, the thirty-some-odd-foot vessel looked decidedly insubstantial against its oceanic backdrop. Ness eyed it uncertainly.

"Um, are we sure this is a good idea?" Daisy asked, addressing the group. "The weather seems a bit . . . ominous?"

"Calm yourself, my little duckling." Ian nudged Daisy with his hip. Despite the ease of his movements, Ness thought he looked tense. He bounced lightly on his toes. "They wouldn't risk the lives of the entire core cast for the sake of scheduling, right, Tyler?" He smiled fiercely, bright-white teeth gleaming.

Tyler had apparently been given the job of getting them to Eclipse Island. Ness couldn't decide if this was considered a plum assignment or if Morris just wanted to reclaim his personal space, but it seemed like Tyler was embracing his cat-herding responsibilities with great enthusiasm. He looked appropriately horrified at the idea of putting lives in jeopardy, watery blue eyes widening behind his glasses.

"Risky? Certainly not. We've consulted the appropriate environmental agencies and all signs point to safe transit, despite the storm warning. Isn't that so, Captain Dirk?" he said to the weathered, deeply tanned man whose boat bobbed with increasing intensity on the waves.

"We have life vests and the required emergency supplies," Captain Dirk affirmed, inspiring confidence in no one.

"Can I talk to you for a moment, Captain?" Tyler asked, smiling around clenched teeth. "I'd like to go over our route one more time." He steered the older man along the pier to a small outbuilding.

Coco leaned against a palm tree, vaping with great enthusiasm. Meanwhile, Libby paced the dock like she was trying to get her twenty thousand steps in before they boarded. She'd always been an overachiever. Frustration rolled off her in waves.

Bradley grumbled under his breath and went to sit at a nearby picnic table, scrolling on his phone and shoving his hair out of his face every couple of minutes.

"I'm going to see if I can find coffee," Ian announced, popping a piece of gum in his mouth before traipsing toward the main building, which housed a restaurant and café.

Hayes leaned against a low stone wall that edged the walkway leading to the docks, looking decidedly unconcerned. The wind snatched at the brim of his navy ball cap and he grabbed it before it took a solo flight down the coast, turning it backward and settling it back on his head.

Ness could all but feel her pupils dilating. Her breath hitched. It shouldn't be *that* sexy. That easy to tie her in knots. She wasn't eighteen. She was a grown woman in control of her feelings, dammit. And what kind of forty-five-year-old man sports a backward ball cap, anyway? He should look ridiculous.

His eyes drifted to meet hers and a slow smile spread across his face.

"Oh, shut up," muttered Ness, turning on her heel, determined to focus on something, anything, else. Unfortunately, as she spun, she collided with Libby's arm, knocking her phone to the ground. They both watched, horrified, as it skittered, screen down, across the gravel path toward the water.

Ness's mouth dropped open. The phone slid under the barrier, teetered for one precarious second on the cement edge. *Plop.* The rhinestone-encrusted case glittered like the scales of a tropical fish as it gently floated down and out of sight.

Libby glared at her. "What the hell is wrong with you?"

For a moment, Ness flashed back to a hazy memory of Libby saying those exact words to her in the garbage-scented back parking lot of their favorite club, Imposter. In that case, the offense had been less an unfortunate accident than a pattern undermining their entire friendship. Not that Ness had noticed at the time.

Now, Ness was certain Libby was about to send her on an unscheduled undersea expedition, but the thwacking of Tyler's Tevas saved her as he hustled back toward them. The tendons in Libby's neck strained and Ness was pretty sure she could see a vein pulsing in her otherwise perfectly smooth forehead. She moved farther away, seeking protection behind Daisy, whose comparative youth probably lent itself to quick reflexes when it came to deflecting an attack.

"Minor change of plans, folks!" Tyler called, waving everyone toward him. "Captain Dirk has been called away for a family emergency, but I'm happy to report that I am fully capable of getting us to Eclipse. So! If you'll make your way down to slip four, we'll be on our way!"

"Wait. *You're* going to drive the boat?" Ness hadn't meant to sound quite so disbelieving. She'd been aiming for mild, valid concern.

Tyler smiled brightly. "I grew up with boats. You're in excellent hands. Trust me, I wouldn't take on a challenge like this if I wasn't sure I was up for it."

"Yeah, but, um, why is it a challenge if you're so confident?" Daisy also missed the mild, valid concern mark.

"It's not a *challenge* challenge." Tyler closed his eyes for a beat and took a deep breath before reengaging. "Listen, we have to get to the island tonight. Half of you have a 5:00 a.m. call time tomorrow. Captain Dirk is otherwise engaged and no one else is available. We're on a tight timeline and I am fully capable of getting us there. But *we need to go*."

Ness shifted her weight from foot to foot, trying to keep her mouth shut and go with the flow. She failed.

"I'm just not sure this is the best option."

Tyler's smile tightened, teeth clenching. "Would Captain Dirk have given his keys to someone he didn't trust?"

Ness's eyes narrowed. For all she knew, Captain Dirk would hand the keys over to a persistent seagull if it had enough room on its credit card.

If they had all banded together and refused to go, it would have worked. What could Tyler, who looked as though his most intensive workout was carrying multiple clipboards around at the same time, do?

Unfortunately, teamwork had never been their strong suit.

"Let's just go," grumbled Bradley, striding down the dock.

"Excellent! Thank you, Mr. Isaksson!" Tyler beamed sunnily even as dark clouds converged above the marina.

"It's a quick ride, right?" asked Coco.

"Twenty minutes, max. I bet I can make it in fifteen," Tyler assured her.

She shoved hair out of her face and puffed out a breath. "Fuck, fine."

Tyler turned his gaze to Libby. "Ms. Kim?"

She looked from Ness's concerned face to her phone's watery grave and to where Bradley was sitting on a bobbing bench seat, already cracking a beer. Without a word she turned and flounced to the boat.

Daisy sighed.

"You don't have to do anything you're uncomfortable with," Ness said to her, but she could feel the moment Daisy chose not to make a fuss.

"We're probably overreacting," the younger woman said, eyes going to the whitecapped waves outside the relatively calm water of the enclosed marina. "Let's just get there. Tyler's right, we've got a painful call time tomorrow, and I'm sure everyone's taking the proper precautions."

Tyler bounced a little on the balls of his feet, clearly eager to get this show on the road. He looked around, pale brow furrowing.

"Where's Mr. James?"

Ness shrugged. "He went to get coffee?"

"Is that a question or a statement?"

"A statement?"

They locked eyes, holding on to neutral, pleasant smiles that moved toward grimace territory with each passing second.

Ness broke first.

"You know, Tyler, this feels . . ." She waved her hand through the air as she searched for the right word. "Risky."

He leaned in, lowering his voice and keeping a pleasant smile pasted on his chapped lips. "I'd heard about your proclivity for drama, Ms. Larkin, but wasn't expecting to see it so early in our time together."

Ness's mouth dropped open, her eyes agog. She started to form an appropriately scathing response when an arm draped over her shoulders.

"I'm back!" Ian announced, sounding peppy. Ness wished she'd gotten coffee too. "I see we're ready to get this show on the oceanic road." He grabbed Ness's hand and towed her along behind him. "Come on, Drag-ness. Time to go!"

Ness looked pleadingly at the rest of the group, but they were wrist-deep in the coolers of drinks and seemed to be pointedly ignoring her.

"Alright," she said, giving in. "Why not."

Coco had attempted a relaxed lounge position but was jostled into an upright, edge-of-seat-clutching pose instead. The door of the built-in fridge swung open, connecting with her shin.

"Can someone explain why we didn't get a yacht?" She kicked the fridge closed, barely missing Ness's foot in the process.

Tyler stood in the partially enclosed wheelhouse, occasionally wiping errant ocean spray from his glasses with the lower edge of his short-sleeved pale-pink button-up, inexplicably patterned with tropical foliage and cat faces. He steered them out of the inlet that housed the marina.

"This is the Bahamian standard for island hopping," he said, like that answered the question.

Coco's eyebrow rose skeptically.

The wind picked up, sending a stinging spray of water across the open rear of the boat as they cut across the waves. Ness looked up at the darkening sky and felt raindrops patter on her face, so small she could almost convince herself it was spray from the boat cutting through the water. Over the sounds of the engine, thunder rumbled. She was sitting beside a pile of black equipment cases the size of standard airline carry-ons. Tyler had said they held a bunch of backup camera gear Morris had asked him to bring along at the last minute. Ness counted seven of the hard-sided cases and wondered how many thousands of dollars of tech was snuggled inside. She hoped they were watertight.

"Uh, hey, Tyler?" she shouted from her seat at the bow of the boat. She'd put as much distance between herself and Hayes and Libby—who, along with Bradley and Ian, were tucked into the back—as she could. All told, it was about twelve measly feet. Depending on how the wind gusted, she was sure she was still catching subtle wafts of *eau de* Hayes. Or it was the horrendous up-and-down of the boat making her stomach somersault.

"Tyler!" she repeated, louder. "How much longer?" They'd been zig-zagging along, past island after island, for nearly thirty minutes.

Their pasty pseudo-captain didn't answer as he glared at the flickering GPS display panel and bopped it with the heel of his hand. The image seemed to tremble before going completely dark.

Tyler's eyes widened as he looked between the black screen and the ocean around them. He brought the radio to his mouth.

"This is pleasure craft *Gentleman's Delight*. Is anyone there?" The wind picked up, making it nearly impossible to hear any response from where Ness was sitting.

Tyler held the radio to his ear, squinting as he strained to listen. He tried again, voice shaky as he yelled to be heard over the wind.

"This is *Gentleman's Delight*. Do you read me?" He pressed buttons on the dash, turned dials, and tapped at gauges before facing his increasingly agitated and damp passengers.

"There's absolutely *no need* to worry, but it seems that the electrical panel and radio have both failed. This is okay, though. I know what to do."

He scrabbled in a cabinet beside the steering wheel and pulled out a paper chart. He held it behind him, handing it to Bradley.

"We're passing the western edge of, um, Hummingbird Cay now. Eclipse should be only a few clicks ahead, but can you find it on here just in case?"

Bradley stared back at him. "Just in case what?"

Tyler shook the chart emphatically, his lips pressed into a tight, pale line.

Across from Ness, Daisy's face was whiter than usual. She gave a weak smile and hugged herself tightly.

"It's chilly with that wind, huh?" Ness said, slipping her goosebump-covered arms into the life jacket she'd found wedged under the bench. She reached down and passed another to Daisy, who gratefully followed suit. Ness raised a questioning eyebrow at Coco, who let go of the bench long enough to make a "gimme" gesture and accept the proffered flotation device.

"Ugh. Smells like it's been steeped in stale vomit," she complained. Ness couldn't disagree.

Bradley knelt on the floor, fighting the wind as he tried to unfold the chart and keep it in place. He looked at Ian. "Hold this down while I chart a course, will you?"

Ian snorted a laugh. "Since when can you *chart courses*, Captain Highliner?"

"Since I took on the role of Ahab in the stage production of a boldly reimagined *Moby Dick*, you dick. It's called research."

"Children!" snapped Coco. "Can we save this titillating trading of insults for later and *focus on not dying?*"

A low wall of water smacked into the side of the boat, not quite coming over the edge but sending Bradley sprawling. Ian threw his hands up to catch himself against the back of the captain's chair, releasing the map, which flew like an expertly launched kite into the sky.

At the same time, the captain's chair rotated, the seat banging into Tyler's knees. He skidded sideways, slamming against the side of the boat and barely catching himself on an antenna before his weight could propel him over the side and into the waves. As he righted himself, feet hitting the inner deck with a thud that reverberated under Ness's feet, the antenna snapped off in his hand. Simultaneously, his glasses slid off his face, landing directly beneath Ian's flailing foot, where they were promptly crushed.

Lightning lit the sky as the clouds burst open, pelting them with rain.

"Ohmigod," Daisy gasped.

With no one at the wheel, the boat was at the mercy of the wind and water. They were pushed sideways, parallel to the waves, rolling up and down with sickening intensity.

Tyler scrabbled along the deck, chasing the remnants of his glasses, blood dripping from a cut at his hairline. Ian sat on the floor, his back pressed against the bench, laughing maniacally, face turned up to the pelting rain.

"Ohmigod. Ohmigod. Ohmigod," Daisy chanted.

Libby was screaming at Bradley to "DO SOMETHING!" while Coco had wedged herself into a corner with her eyes squeezed shut. Hayes slid around with an armload of life jackets, jamming people's arms into them if they didn't react quickly enough to do it themselves.

No one seemed interested in driving the boat.

Ness scooted across the floor, too unstable to stand, and grabbed the wheel, bracing herself against the padded inner wall and the base of the captain's chair as waves tossed them up and down like a toy in an over-wrought child's bathtub. Once she had her footing, she stood, squinted, scanning madly through the driving rain until she thought she could make out a dark mass ahead.

A gust of wind sent sheets of water across the bow. Behind her, Ness heard Coco swearing loudly.

"Can someone get us to a goddamn motherfucking island, please?"

"Working on it!" Ness hollered over her shoulder. She slid to the right, catching herself just short of smacking her head on the clear plastic structure that was providing less and less protection from the weather.

"Steady there, Cap." A warm body clad in a clammy, musty life jacket pressed against her back as strong arms came along either side of her. "I've got you," Hayes said, putting his mouth close to her ear to be heard without shouting. "You steer, I'll keep you upright, okay?"

Ness exhaled and fought the urge to close her eyes and melt back against him, her frantic nerves calmed by half just with his presence. Another aggressive wave brought her back to reality.

She jerked her chin to the right. "I think I saw land over there." Heaving the wheel, she accelerated, turning toward what she hoped was safety.

Hayes pressed forward to get a better look as they got closer, wrapping a stabilizing arm around Ness's waist, his fingers gripping her hip bones. Ahead of them, a wall of scraggly mangroves materialized through the mist, waving in the wind. Ness couldn't see anywhere that they could secure the boat and get to land safely. The idea of spending the night on this bobbing cork of doom made her stomach clench.

"Is that a beach?" Hayes shouted, pointing to a barely visible stretch of beige a few hundred feet away.

Ness fought the wind, getting them turned in the right direction, and started chugging toward the maybe-beach. She did a shoulder check to confirm everyone was still on board.

Tyler was laid out across the black gear cases, a crumpled fluorescent-orange rain jacket under his head. Blood dripped to the floor beside him, diffusing into a growing pink puddle. The rest of the group was quiet, straining their bodies forward as if they could will themselves to safety.

The boat surged and fought, and Ness wondered why anyone would ever choose to be a ship's captain. A push of wind rammed them closer to land just as the rain seemed to take a breath, giving them a three-second view of the island immediately ahead, much closer than Ness had thought. It also revealed the cement dock they were about to crash into.

Hayes's grip tightened on her waist and she heard his strangled gasp.

"Hang on, everyone!" Ness gunned the engine and veered to the right, barely dodging the dock and running up onto the beach.

Apparently, nobody had held on, or the landing had been worse than she thought, because when she looked behind her, everyone was lying in a heap on the floor. At a quick glance, no one seemed seriously injured beyond bruises and egos.

Ness shook her head, hoping to clear the haze of panic that had settled there. The wind whipped her hair into her face, where it tangled in her eyelashes and stuck to the super-hold brow gel that had seemed like a great idea that morning.

She dragged her attention back to the task at hand, fighting to open the stiff latches securing cabinets and storage cubbies until she found a large coil of yellow rope. She heaved it into her arms like a loopy, twenty-pound baby.

"We need to tie the boat up!" she called to Hayes, who was hoisting people to their feet and looking deep into their eyes while murmuring what she assumed were words of comfort. *Someone needs to cast him as a sexy pastor*, Ness thought, unbidden.

He pivoted, took two long steps, and plucked the heavy mass of rope from her arms like it was no more than a loaf of bread or a small dog's designer puffer coat.

"You hop down and I'll throw it to you? I want to take a better look at Tyler's head."

"Yeah, sure. Okay. Good plan." She hated the plan. She'd assumed he'd do this part, but it was fine. She was capable. She'd tied many knots in her day—if she counted the lopsided throw blanket she'd crocheted for a neighbor, one might even say she'd nearly mastered the tying of string-like materials.

Hayes was looking at her expectantly, the rain rolling across his glasses. He shoved them up onto the top of his head as she sidled carefully to the side of the boat and swung her legs over. The water suddenly looked very far away.

"Here I go!" she announced, mostly to herself. Ian, at least, gave her a shaky thumbs-up.

She jumped.

Ness hit the thigh-deep water and stumbled, falling to her knees and getting a noseful of salt water. She staggered a bit closer to shore and turned, arms extended. Hayes chucked the rope, which she did not catch and had to fish from the water in dripping lengths.

Sputtering, she heaved the mess with her to shore, trying to identify a good anchor tree through the driving rain. The water dragged at her soaked jeans and threatened to pull them down her hips. Wouldn't that be the cherry on top.

There was a tall, robust-looking option a little farther up on the beach. She pulled the trailing rope to it, feet digging into the sand for traction.

Back on the boat, Hayes had efficiently secured the other end to an anchor point. His saturated clothes clung to his body and he'd lost his hat somewhere along the way. He shoved a hand through his hair, pushing it back off his face and giving it a shake.

Ness snapped her dangling jaw shut and turned back to the task at hand. She wrapped the rope around the tree three times, tying what felt like an intricate yet sturdy knot between each loop. She finished the whole thing off with one more knot, yanking the tail hard. There.

She sloshed back to the boat, which, all things considered, didn't look worse for wear, and was hauled aboard, her shoulders popping in protest as Bradley leaned down and lifted her over the side like a sodden sack of potatoes. The others were sufficiently recovered to begin complaining in earnest.

"What now?" Coco demanded, her question aimed at no one in particular.

The rest of the group had migrated forward, pressing into her space, seeking whatever shelter the tiny wheelhouse could provide.

"Alright, everyone!" Ness yelled loudly enough to make Bradley flinch. "We need to find shelter. Grab whatever water and food you can and let's go."

They huddled together in a dark, rotting outbuilding at the back edge of the beach. Around them, trees creaked and groaned in the whistling wind. Branches scraped along the outer walls of the shed like the claws of a folkloric monster. The waves were almost deafening as they crashed onto the shoreline, rushing toward where they had taken refuge.

Ness hadn't realized nature could be so incredibly loud. The wind whistled through cracks in the worn, wooden walls. She hitched her bag higher onto her shoulder and shivered.

Hayes held his phone skyward. "Nothing," he said. "I don't know if there's no service here, or if cell towers are down because of the storm, but I can't get a signal. Anyone else?"

"I *lost* my phone," Libby said sourly.

Ness stared at the wet sand encrusting her shoes. Her own phone had disappeared into the sea while she was wrestling with the rope and her own lack of grace.

Coco's phone was waterlogged, and Daisy, teeth chattering, said she couldn't get a signal either. They turned to Ian, Bradley, and Tyler.

"I don't have a phone," Ian said breezily. "I refuse to get caught in the scrolling cycle and dark matter that is so widespread and easily accessible via technology. You know, 60 percent of people—"

"Yeah, got it, don't care," Bradley interjected. "My battery is dead." He showed them the dark screen. "Tyler?"

The rain had rinsed most of the blood from his face, but a dark gash was stark against his pale face in the dim light. He shook his head. "It must have fallen out of my pocket when I slipped."

They all looked at one another, waiting for someone to make a move.

"We can't stay here all night," Hayes said finally. "Maybe there are other buildings nearby. Or at least a more sheltered spot away from the beach." He stepped out the door and into the dark, terrifying night. The rest of them exchanged morose looks before following.

They reformed their huddle on the beach, pivoting in a slow circle as one to try to spot salvation as the rain pummeled them.

A faded *For Sale* sign was staked deep in the sand, the words washed out by time and the elements.

As if on cue, lightning zapped across the sky, illuminating a structure looming on the hillside above them. Thunder boomed, and Ness swore she could feel the ground shake beneath her feet.

"Is that a . . ." Daisy trailed off.

Coco's raspy voice rose over the sound of the wind. "It's a fucking *castle*?"

October 23, 2003

Drama, drama, drama. It's what we expect—nay, what we need—from everyone's favorite guilty pleasure, *Ocean Views*. But we're hearing that the drama isn't limited to on-screen.

"The fighting is constant," a source from the set told us. "People are always crying or storming off. It's unprofessional and totally uncool."

It's a poorly kept secret that certain members of the cast can't stand each other, despite their civil behavior during public appearances. But something more interesting seems to be bubbling to the surface.

"Now that Ness is so much more intriguing—who doesn't love a bad girl?—the men can't stop chasing her. It's making the other female cast members furious. Honestly, Ness's dad should have taken off years ago. This is the best thing to ever happen to her career. Film studios are banging on the door trying to book their next sad-eyed muse."

It's also hard to ignore that Ness has dropped some pounds over the past few months, something her friends are crediting to stress and increased exercise. We hope Ness bounces back soon, but girl, you're looking great!

CHAPTER 5

SHOULD WE KNOCK?"

Ness stood on tiptoe to peek over Coco's shoulder at the gigantic arching door. A rusty iron mermaid was mounted dead center against the flaking turquoise paint, articulated at the hips so her tail smacked down to announce the arrival of guests. Or castaways, as the case may be.

They'd staggered up a sandy path before navigating slippery stone steps set into the hill, leading them up, up, up to the building's main entrance. Bradley had led the charge with the single actual flashlight found tucked away on the boat. On either side of the overgrown path, scraggly shrubs and tall, sharp grasses waved and rustled. Lights from the remaining functional phones barely lit the path ahead, casting shadows and creating extreme horror movie vibes.

Hayes and Ian each lugged a hard-sided cooler up with them, filled with whatever drinks and snacks had been on the boat. Ness's legs burned, and she wished she hadn't shied away from the stair-climber during her workouts. And maybe taken survival training. Hindsight, right?

Tyler, still shaky and clutching his head, had slipped halfway up and grabbed the handle of Ian's cooler, trying to catch himself, wrenching it out of Ian's grasp. They'd all stood, frozen, as bottles of water, premixed cocktails, and lord knew what else tumbled into the waving grass and bounced merrily down toward the beach far, far, *far* below.

Setting the empty cooler down without a word, Ian had kept climbing.

The wind was even stronger at the top of the hill, snatching at Ness's damp hair and driving the rain into her numb skin.

"Should we knock?" she asked again, trying to keep her teeth from chattering.

"Pretty sure no one's home." Libby gripped her purse to her chest. She'd lost three of her glossy acrylic nails.

Upon closer inspection, the house wasn't a true castle. At least, not how Ness knew them from binge-watching *Outlander* and perusing the resulting Travel Scotland targeted ads.

It was a tropical approximation, formed from slate-colored concrete and limited to what appeared to be two stories of moldering turrets, battered shuttered windows, and a wraparound balcony that no doubt offered exceptional views when the weather wasn't hell-bent on destruction and mayhem.

The base of the structure was set into the hill, providing what Ness hoped was a hurricane-proof foundation. This allowed what appeared to be the main floor to take advantage of walkout access to the aforementioned balcony. Assuming the whole thing didn't crumble before their eyes, that is.

She blinked rain out of her eyes and wondered how likely it was that she was hallucinating this whole thing. Maybe she'd slipped while changing the showerhead in one of her rental units and was in a coma, enjoying high-end pain meds and full-service hospital care.

Someone coughed pointedly, bringing her back to the terrible present. She huffed out a breath. "I'd just feel better if we at least tried to make contact with anyone inside before barging in."

"Nobody. Is. Here." Libby said it slowly and loudly. Her eyes, still perfectly lined with the world's most waterproof makeup, bulged with condescension.

Ness huffed a breath out of her nose, nodding and shrugging simultaneously.

"Fine. Whatever."

"I think Ness is right. We should make an effort." Ness's head whipped toward Daisy, surprised she was weighing in after spending the climb up looking like a beautiful but morose Irish portrait. Ness had figured she'd collapse into a delicate heap of emotions once they found shelter, much as she wished to do herself.

Daisy continued, voice gaining strength. "We don't want to get shot. What if whoever's here thinks we're . . . I don't know, pirates or something?"

"I don't understand why we're standing in a fucking hurricane discussing etiquette." Coco strode forward, elbowing Bradley out of the way. She wrapped a hand around the mermaid's tail, waited two dramatic beats, then dropped the knocker and stepped back, arms crossed over her chest.

The wind howled, throwing vegetation and sandy dirt into their faces. Everyone turned, staring at Ness.

"Yeah, okay. Got it. No one home." When no one moved, she edged through the group and tried the handle, ignoring the distinct sound of scoffing coming from Libby. Locked. She stepped back, staring up at the strange face of the house. All the shutters she could see were closed tight and there were no other obvious entry points. She sighed.

"We should split up, see if there's an open window or door somewhere," Ness said, regretting the suggestion even as the words left her mouth.

"Um, no thanks," Libby said, leaning against the door. "I'll be waiting right here."

Tyler muttered something from where he sat cross-legged on the cold, wet ground. He looked as though it was taking all his remaining strength not to lie down and fall asleep right there.

"What's that, bud?" Ian asked.

"I *said*, that's a surefire way to get murdered."

"Ummm," Ness stalled. "Yeah, okay, so how about Libby stays here to make sure Tyler doesn't pass out." Libby started to protest, but Ness ignored her. "I'll go around this way." She pointed to the left, where the covered entry extended onto the wider balcony.

"I'll come with you," Hayes interjected. Ness nodded coolly, as though she wasn't entirely surprised by this announcement.

"We'll go with Ian and Brad," Coco said, looping her arm through Daisy's, whose teeth were beginning to chatter. She started walking to the right, pulling Daisy with her, and paused. "Does anyone have a cigarette?"

Silence.

"Well, shit. Alright. To our deaths, then." She strode forward, her hand sliding down to grip Daisy's. They'd almost disappeared into the dark before Ian and Bradley caught up, jogging ahead to light the way.

Hayes stepped out into the rain, then paused to look back to where Ness stood.

"Shall we?" he asked, rolling a hand out toward the balcony ahead.

"I guess." Ness steadfastly ignored his extended arm, with its ropy muscles and rivulets of water running down toward his fingers.

He held up a phone, its completely inadequate light limiting the visible area to about four feet in front of them. Ness crept on, hoping they'd come across an open side door any moment now.

Something whistled past her head and, to her left, there was a deafening crash. She let out a squeak of panic and fought the urge to run, even as her brain processed the iron bistro chair rocking on its back as it settled, then the remnants of the concrete block shattered around it.

She turned her face upward, into the rain, and tried to figure out where the block had fallen from. Her breath was coming in quick little puffs. She tried to slow it down, assuring herself there was no reason to panic and this was an entirely manageable situation.

"We should keep moving," Hayes said, settling a hand on the middle of her back. His voice came to her as if through a fog, soft and gentle. Slowly, carefully, they shuffled forward, testing the shutters as they passed. Hayes tried to pry the edges outward but came away with nothing but an impressive collection of splinters to show for it.

"Remember that time we climbed the water tower?" The words were out before she'd even decided to say them.

Hayes snorted a laugh as he tried the handle on a barred door.

"You mean the time we almost died so you could prove you weren't scared of heights, except you really, *really* were?"

"It was your idea!"

"It definitely was not."

"Was too. You said to rise above my fears! How was I supposed to know you were being *literal*."

"Oh, and your memory of that time is crystal clear, is it?" He said it lightly, but Ness felt it cut deep.

"Um, no," she said quietly, not even sure he could hear her over the noise of the raging ocean and wind.

He winced. "I didn't mean anything—"

"It's fine."

She moved ahead to deflect from a conversation she definitely didn't want to have and found a barred, locked gate over a set of wooden doors. Ness managed to sneak her hand through a gap between the bars and joggle the door handle half-heartedly. It turned, and the door flew backward as the wind grabbed it.

The door slammed against the interior wall before zinging back toward her. She jerked her hand away just in time to save it from being crushed, and held it to her heaving chest.

"Yikes," she muttered. She looked over at Hayes. "I'm fine," she assured them both. "Just startled." She wiggled her fingers, verifying that the hand was intact and functional. The inner door swung back open. *Not ghosts*, Ness thought. *Probably*.

"Any idea how to pry open a metal gate?" she asked, leaning in to get a better look at the rusty lock.

Behind her, Hayes cleared his throat. Ness turned and let out a short, startled scream at the sight of him holding the iron patio chair over his head.

"Could you scooch over there?" he asked, casually nodding to the side. She scurried out of the way and he hurled the chair. They winced in unison as it clattered uselessly off the gate and crashed to the ground.

"Huh." Hayes scratched his chin. "Well, it was worth a shot."

Ness shivered, wishing she had a jacket or, better yet, a way into this stupid, probably haunted castle.

"Oh, for sure. My go-to move is always launching heavy objects at my opponents."

"If they can't catch, that's on them."

Ness huffed out a laugh while simultaneously acknowledging that she was moments away from crumpling into a bleary-eyed heap of sadness and dismay. She'd rather do that somewhere dry, though.

She leaned back against the gate, trying to stay under the limited protection of the small overhang. Hayes stood in the rain looking like a wet golden retriever, morose and adorable.

She nodded her head at the spot beside her. "Strategy huddle?" she offered, pressing back against the metal to allow more space.

With a sudden groan and crash the gate's rusted hinges detached from the frame, sending Ness flying backward to land with a butt-numbing thump on a dusty tile floor.

"Unexpected," Hayes said, offering a hand and heaving her upright. Ness patted as much debris from her soggy jeans as she could and turned in a slow circle, trying to get a sense of the space around them.

The phone's light barely penetrated the heavy darkness, throwing strange shadows as the weak beam hit furniture and doorways. They were in a living room of sorts, if the couch and broken bookshelves were any indication.

Ness nearly had a heart attack when the phone illuminated a giant, black-framed mirror on the opposite wall, showing them their own bedraggled reflections. She cleared her throat, gracefully unwrapping herself from around Hayes's arm.

"Thought I saw a rat."

"I've heard a lot of the islands are teeming with them."

"Please tell me you're joking."

"I wish."

"I guess all creatures great and small are entitled to a place in paradise." She swiped at the water dripping off the end of her nose.

Eyes starting to adjust to the dark, Ness paused on her way to the front door to open the black sideboard positioned along one wall. She quickly opened cabinets and drawers looking for another light source, meanwhile making big noises to scare anything (great or small) that could be lurking within.

A few feet away, Hayes pried open a wooden chest that sat to the side of a large, cobwebby fireplace.

"Aha!" Ness hefted a black pillar candle into the air with one hand, flicking the lighter she'd found with the other. When the flame caught, she thought she might cry tears of relief.

Shielding the flame with her hand, she slowly moved to where Hayes was still rummaging. He tossed a couple of damp-smelling blankets onto the floor.

"I'll get the door," Ness said, eyeing the pile of faux-fur throws with trepidation.

"You take the flashlight," Hayes said, swapping her for the candle and shoving the phone into her hand in its place. "I'm going to keep looking around."

"Sure. Yeah. Cool. I can do this solo. No problem."

She exited the room through an arched doorway, heading back in the direction they'd started from. She walked quickly through a decrepit kitchen, another living space, and a dining room before making it to the black-and-white-tiled front entryway.

Ness twisted the deadbolt and heaved the door open eight tantalizing inches before the swollen wood wedged itself against the floor and refused to go farther. Wind whistled in, driving a fresh wall of rain along with it. She'd expected Libby to race past her to (relative) safety the second she was granted access, but no one appeared.

She stuck her head through the opening, hoping an errant gust wouldn't suddenly slam the door on her neck, and shone the flashlight around the low-walled area that formed what normal folk would call the front porch, but which Ness presumed the rich had an alternate name for. Her ear brushed against the mermaid knocker's tail and she flailed wildly for a moment, fending off a nonexistent spider, before she fully took in the scene in front of her. No Libby in sight, but a dark, wet form was sprawled out face down on the ground.

"Tyler?!" Ness said, trying to get the door open far enough to squeeze through.

"Hey!" she shouted. He didn't move. She swiveled her head. "Libby?!" Nothing. The wind roared, and Ness thought that if she could see the trees they'd be practically horizontal.

She pulled her face back into the foyer.

"Need some help here, Hayes!" she yelled into the darkness. Moving to the windows to the right of the door, she fought with the rusty latch, trying to get them open to access the shutters.

She wondered if it would be faster to go back the way she'd come and run around the outside. As she was about to give up, the latch turned, scraping a couple of layers of skin off her fingers in the process.

Footsteps echoed down the hall, growing louder, until a bobbing lantern came into sight. The black candle sat in a glass enclosure, the handle looped over Hayes's wrist.

Hayes dumped an armful of blankets onto the foot of a sweeping staircase and jogged to Ness's side.

"Tyler's passed out on the porch and I can't get the door open. Libby's gone. Help me with the shutters."

"For god's sake, Agnes." A dripping Coco was suddenly beside her, grabbing the phone from her hand. She shoved it through the gap, took a cursory look at Tyler's prone body, and shimmied partway through before getting momentarily stuck. She slid back out and rammed the door with her shoulder, forcing it open another few inches. Hayes wrapped his fingers around the doorknob and forced the entire structure upward, scoring enough clearance to open the door the rest of the way.

Daisy darted out, grabbed Tyler under his arms, and heaved him inside. His wet sneakers squeaked obnoxiously as the heels dragged across the floor, and Ness found herself stifling a hysterical giggle.

"Thanks for coming to get us," Ian said sarcastically. He waltzed across the room from the direction Ness had come from, taking Daisy's spot at Tyler's head. Bradley, following behind, grabbed his feet.

"There's a couch that way," Ness said, pointing down the hall. "I'm going out to look for Libby."

But before she could make her heroic, if hesitant, exit into the whirling storm, Libby fell through the door, tripping on a disintegrating carpet runner and toppling with slow-motion grace to the floor.

"Whoa, hey, are you alright?" Hayes asked, dropping to her side. He slid an arm behind her upper back and hoisted her to sitting.

Ness narrowed her eyes, skeptical.

"Where did you go?" she demanded. "You were supposed to stay with Tyler."

Libby blinked, squinting through the darkness to take in the details of the room.

"I did!"

Ness's eyebrows rose. Libby's eyes rolled.

"I mean, I obviously didn't stay *the whole time*. I was only gone a second. Tyler keeled over and I went to find one of you to help." She scowled. "I don't need to explain myself to *you*, of all people, Agnes."

Before Ness could voice any of her many questions, concerns, and hopefully witty rejoinders, Bradley walked back into the room.

"No power. No running water. No telephone on the main floor that I can find."

"Emergency radio?" Hayes asked hopefully, helping Libby to her feet.

Bradley shook his head. "I don't think so. I haven't done a thorough search yet obviously—you're welcome to help if you think I missed it." His tone had gone from cool and collected to insulted teen in the blink of an eye.

Ness took a deep breath and tried to stop the rolling of her own eyes back into her head. She was an adult, and tensions were running high. They were, after all, marooned on an island, in a castle. A castle that was probably haunted, because what good is a deserted castle if it's paranormally neutral? Just a lame-o normal fake castle.

Unsure why she found this thought disappointing, she giggled, the sound surprising her.

"Shock," she said suddenly, as if it were part of an ongoing conversation. Six faces, made pale and (*ha!*) somewhat ghostly in the beam of the flashlight, turned toward her. She pulled her face back into a less alarming expression. Acting for the win.

"What was that?" Hayes said politely, well-groomed eyebrows raised.

"I, er, said 'shock.' We're probably all in it. There's nothing more we can do tonight. Why don't we find somewhere to sleep? In the morning we can get back to the boat and either get the radio working or get somewhere with people. Or at least a phone."

"Should we split up, or sleep together?" Ian waggled his eyebrows at Daisy, who sighed heavily and stared toward the water-stained ceiling before speaking.

"As much as I'd love some personal space, doesn't it feel safer to stay together? We can take turns checking on Tyler."

Coco sniffed. "Ugh. Him. How much do we care?"

"I'd feel uncomfortable if he died in the night," said Ness.

"Fine, then. *Fine.* Onward." Coco thrust a pointing finger in the direction of the damp velvet couch that now cradled Tyler in its moldy lap before plucking the phone from Ian's hand and stalking off, assuming they would all follow. They did, of course, like moths to a fading, battery-powered flame.

During his short search for a means of communication, Bradley *had* found a number of bedrooms down a long hallway off what seemed to be the main living area. Now he and Hayes dragged four mattresses and some very slightly less disgusting blankets in and dumped them unceremoniously in a ragged arc around the couch.

Then they all stood there, shuffling their feet like preteens at a school dance.

Coco nudged Daisy to the first mattress. "C'mon. To bed with you."

The two women lowered themselves onto the mattress and Coco pulled a thin, dark quilt over them.

"Ugh. It smells like mothballs and Polo cologne." Coco coughed, but snuggled in.

Libby dropped her purse on the only twin mattress and pulled the whole thing to the edge of the room, as far from the rest of them as she could get and still be in the same space.

Ian flopped down onto a vacant mattress and patted the space beside him as he looked at Ness.

"Nope," she said, sitting on the edge of the last mattress. A bit of stuffing was falling out the side, and she wondered what had made a nest within, whether it was still there, and how much she cared. The moment she was horizontal she decided that a rabid badger could be living beneath her and she would give absolutely zero effs. She was drained.

The springs creaked and the surface shifted as someone got in beside her. The smell of mint gum, seawater, and something that was pure Hayes drifted over.

She bit back a groan.

"I can sleep . . . somewhere else," he said, already getting up.

"No!" Ness clenched her fists to stop herself from reaching out to grab him. "I mean, it's fine. I'm practically asleep already, badger and all." She gave up on the idea of wriggling out of her soaked jeans.

"There's a badger?" She could hear him smiling.

"I hope not," she mumbled.

She shifted, trying to get comfortable. Her bladder was making itself known with increasing intensity.

"Everything okay over there?"

"I, er. Well." Ness really didn't want to have this conversation. She also didn't want to wander around the pitch-black house in the dark, trying to find a bathroom. Oh god. Was she going to have to go outside?

"I need a bathroom."

There was a beat of silence, then Hayes said, "Number one or number two?"

"I really don't want to talk about this."

Hayes sat up and rubbed a hand over his face. Ness could hear his stubble rasping against his palm.

"Well, here's the thing. If we're talking pee only, you can use the bathroom, assuming it's not falling apart or infested with snakes. If it's a number two, we gotta go outside."

Outside the shuttered window, something banged loudly against the stone of the balcony. The rain pelted the house as if it was trying to break in.

"Number one," Ness mumbled.

They used 3 percent of precious battery power in Hayes's phone finding a bathroom and making sure there weren't any snakes or rats or unhinged criminals hiding therein before Ness shooed Hayes into the hallway. She vowed to wake up first and go down to get a bucket of water to flush with, then stood in front of the cracked sink wondering what hand washing etiquette was in a shipwreck situation.

It turned out she'd started a trend, and when she exited the bathroom, a line had formed. She scurried back to the relative safety and comfort of the living room, made sure Tyler was still breathing, and hopped back onto the mattress.

Hayes followed shortly after, and with the warmth of his body at her back and the promise of a day that might be slightly less awful when she awoke, Ness fell asleep.

Hot on the tail of Ferdinand, the season's seventh named storm of the Atlantic season, Tropical Storm Georgette is developing 140 miles northeast of the Bahamas. Georgette is not expected to hit the island chain directly, but residents will see substantial rain and sustained winds of up to 45 miles per hour later this week.

The National Hurricane Center continues to monitor the storm, predicting moderate flash flooding in urban areas and widespread power outages before Georgette disperses.

This August has been the most active for Atlantic tropical storms in twenty-five years, with more in store over the coming weeks.

CHAPTER 6

U MMM." NESS STARED AT THE EMPTY BEACH, TURNING IN A FULL circle as she tried to spot landmarks that might indicate they were in the wrong spot. That the boat was not, in fact, gone.

A misty rain drifted down around them, soaking her anew as she stared out at the choppy sea.

She'd woken up with a start as the gray light of a dreary morning began to trickle in the windows. After failing in her attempt to exit her shared mattress situation without being detected—primarily because there was a heavy, gently snoring man draped over her, which would have been a very acceptable start to her day on almost any other occasion—she left the others dozing and headed down to the beach, a remarkably bedhead-sexy, extremely grumpy Hayes in tow.

"You can't heave a bucket of water all the way back up here yourself," he grumbled, rubbing his eyes and trying (and failing) to clean his glasses on the hem of his T-shirt. "Do you even *have* a bucket?"

She didn't. But she did have an empty cooler, after picking up the one Ian had abandoned on the trek up the hill the night before.

Before heading down to the beach, Ness had gotten a sense of the island's layout from the balcony, and it seemed much more benign in the light of day. The chunk of land they'd washed up on was a crescent. The house sat on one of the highest points, along the uppermost curve of the island. An inland lagoon lurked, gray-green and opaque, at the bottom of the hill, visible from the cracked and crumbling hot tub.

Also visible was what appeared to be an overgrown strip of runway. A taller hill sat behind the house and blocked their view of whatever was beyond it. There didn't appear to be any other houses or buildings on their chunk of rock, and the misty rain hid any nearby islands. For all they knew, they could be doggy-paddling distance from salvation.

The walk from the house to the beach had been weird, in the way only making small talk with a former colleague-slash-romantic interest could be. But also, that colleague was now one of the world's most recognized movie stars. And had been *People's* Sexiest Man two years earlier—not that Ness had been paying attention.

And, though it was *barely* relevant, Ness was twenty years older and looked fantastic, *thank you very much,* but also . . . she was twenty years older. It was hard not to worry about what Hayes saw when he looked at her. It was harder not to think about the fact that though they had once coexisted in the same flawed ecosystem of glamor and fame and the struggle to Make It, he was now the sun and she was—metaphorically—some dusty, half-blown-up meteor stuck in his orbit.

Luckily, a great way to distract herself was to worry about the apparent disappearance of the *Gentleman's Delight.* The thing that was supposed to be whisking them away to civilization right about now.

"Is there another beach? Maybe we're on the wrong side of the island." Hayes said it about as convincingly as Ness said things like "Today I'll do a hill workout" or "That zebra print is *so* flattering!" He bent down to pick up a piece of driftwood, absently chucking it into the waves. Overhead, a bird squawked in what could have been alarm or disgust at having people on its usually solitary turf.

Ness replayed their route from the night before in her head, feeling very close to throwing up.

"Maybe? But I'm almost certain this is where we came ashore." Plus, there was a single overgrown path from the front door of the house, and it was the one they'd taken here. To this stunning, boat-free expanse of white sand spotted with broken branches and edged in seaweed and the varied debris that had washed up overnight. The tide was higher now than when they'd arrived, but Ness was nearly certain they were in the right spot.

Beside her, Hayes linked his fingers behind his head and took a deep breath. In through the nose, out through the mouth. Ness hoped he wasn't about to panic, because one of them should stay steady, and she was pretty sure it wasn't going to be her.

"Let's stay calm," he said, sounding anything but.

Ness knew this Hayes, rarely seen by anyone other than close friends and family. He was a real champ in the midst of a crisis, but after the comedown? When he'd had time to reflect and think through all the ways in which it could have gone wrong, could *still* go wrong in the future? Utter doom spiral. Throw in some interpersonal conflict and she was surprised it had taken this long for him to start fraying around the edges.

She did the only thing she could and called on her business voice. Confident, yet comforting, despite the galloping of her heartbeat and the churning in her stomach.

"Hey, we're fine. We have food and water. I bet there's more in the house we can scavenge. It might not even give us botulism."

He was pacing now. Four steps, about-face, four steps. He'd kicked off his shoes, and his bare, tanned feet were already on their way to creating a trench in the wet sand. Ness envisioned him getting deeper and deeper until only his hair was visible, bopping back and forth.

"I was kidding about the botulism." She paused. "In that it probably *will* poison us. But at least we won't be starving!" She hooked a gung-ho fist through the air in front of her and immediately felt stupid.

Ness ran a hand nervously over her hair. "Erm, rather, what I mean is, we're okay. This isn't critical yet. It's been, what, fifteen hours since we left? And the storm went on half the night. They're looking for us— they have to be. I bet crews just got out to start searching." She stubbed her toe on a branch. "Speaking of rescue, we should make a fire. Maybe a big SOS sign with all these branches once the tide goes out."

Hayes made a sound that seemed to indicate his stress was not decreasing. Ness stepped in front of him, halting his progress mid-pace. She looked up at him, holding a hand out just short of actually touching his arm. It hovered there for a moment before she stuffed it into the back pocket of her still-damp jeans.

"Want to talk about it?" she tried. His anxiety wasn't new. Needing to know the schedule, having a plan and four backups. He'd once told Ness that part of the reason he gravitated to acting was that, when he was filming, it was like being able to see the future. All the in-between parts were the tricky bits.

He stepped around her and started to wear a new trench perpendicular to the first one. Feeling stung, Ness gave up trying to talk about his emotions. She remembered how they used to be a safe haven for each other, somebody who could see the other at their worst and love them anyway. She knew those days were long gone, but some part of her had hoped he'd still feel some small piece of that security. Though she'd never admit it out loud—hell, she was barely admitting it to herself—she felt it with him.

Ness huffed out a breath of frustration and forced her mental frown upside down, going to work pinpointing which of the large mangroves was the one she'd used as an anchor point. It was somewhere among a stand of them that to the untrained eye—i.e., Ness's—appeared to be identical.

Except for the one that had a strand of yellow nylon fluttering in the wind where it was stuck in the cracks of the bark.

"Hayes?"

Nothing. Only the sound of toes on sand.

"I know you're having a hard time right now, and I want to be here for you to get through it. But . . ." She knotted her fingers together and rested them on top of her head, trying to force deep breaths into her lungs. "I think I lost the boat and I'm a little—very—worried about telling the others. They're going to kill me and say it was necessary for survival. I have very little meat, Hayes. I'm stringy, I'm sure of it. And probably bitter . . ." She was spiraling.

A warm, strong hand closed around hers, pulling her along.

"Breathe," Hayes ordered, slowing his pace but not stopping. "One, two, three, four, turn." He counted out their steps. "Breathe in, two, three, four, turn. Out, two, three, four."

Ness breathed. She paced. She didn't throw up, though she wouldn't go so far as to say they were completely past the risk of same.

"This works," she said a couple of minutes later, surprised to feel her heart rate slowing from frantic runaway horse being pursued by wolves to something more stable.

"Sometimes."

He stopped and turned to face her, taking both her hands in his and looking her in the eye. He let out a long breath. "Let's get it over with."

Hayes carefully carried the cooler full of seawater back up the hill while Ness gathered a few bottles of water and an assortment of protein and granola bars that had taken a tumble the night before. Despite how nauseated Ness felt at the prospect of confronting the others, her stomach rumbled at the sight of the shiny foil packages.

At the house, they found the rest of their contingent spread throughout the main living space of the open kitchen and living room, looking like reticent teens on day one of a forced family vacation.

Ness stood, arms crossed, shaking with nerves she liked to think the others would mistake for a morning chill despite the rising temperature, and explained their findings. In front of her, Bradley grunted softly as he executed a third set of push-ups. Where Hayes paced silently in times of stress, Bradley turned to intense physical exercise.

"This is horrible." Tyler was convalescing on a red leather daybed that sat awkwardly between the kitchen and dining room. He cradled his head in his hands and groaned.

"I know this isn't the situation we would have hoped for, and really, I can't express how deeply sorry I am, but—"

Libby scoffed. "There's always a 'but,' isn't there?"

"I was going to say that I have faith in our ability to get through a couple days until someone shows up to get us."

Daisy was doing some square breathing with vicious-sounding exhales.

"My career is over," Tyler whined, with his head now flung back over the arm of the couch, arms dangling limply. "This is the worst thing that's ever happened to me."

Ness looked pleadingly at Coco, who shrugged and went back to flipping through a 1998 issue of *Maxim*, perched on a decaying pleather stool at the kitchen island.

"Again, I'm sorry. I really thought I'd tied everything securely." She nervously rubbed her forearm, where bloodsucking miscreants had left a series of raised, itchy bites. "But we have some food and water." She chose not to add that it was enough for a day and they'd still be hangry by sundown.

"I don't know why we trusted something like this to *you*." Libby's face was pinched, her skin pale. Ness couldn't tell if she was more angry or scared.

Ian, forearms braced on the island's countertop, massaged the bridge of his nose. "Can we all take it down a notch?" he pleaded. "Morning angst really sets a negative tone for the whole day."

Tyler groaned loudly. Ness wondered if he was going to cry, which would be fine, but then she might start as well. She looked to Hayes, who was sitting on the counter, head resting against the upper cupboards. As far as Ness could tell, he was counting the cracks in the far wall.

"What do you think?" Tyler demanded suddenly, eyes opening to focus on Hayes.

"Me?" Hayes asked, startled back into reality.

Tyler stared at him expectantly.

"Erm, well. It's a challenging situation, and it's entirely appropriate to have some strong feelings."

Ness opened her mouth to leap to her own defense.

"But," he continued, looking pointedly at Ness, "like Ness said, I think we'll be fine. They'll come for us soon. We just have to avoid killing each other until then." He relaxed back again, apparently satisfied with his answer.

Libby slapped the vegan protein bar she'd been nibbling onto the counter.

"What now?"

Ness shrugged. "I guess we get comfortable."

Daisy's curls were loose and she anxiously twisted a strand of hair around her middle finger as she spoke. "We need to search the house again for a way to get in touch with the authorities, let them know where we are."

"And where are we?" Libby demanded, her grip tightening around her water bottle, making the plastic crackle loudly.

Coco looked up from her magazine, eyebrows raised. "On an island with a goddamn castle on a fucking mountain. How many of those can there be?"

"You might be surprised, actually," Daisy said.

Libby swallowed some water and glared. "Are you suddenly an expert in Bahamian real estate?"

"Do you know anything about me? Maybe that's my side hustle."

Ness's head jerked up at the sound of Daisy fighting back. It was good to hear.

"Your side hustle is probably waitressing at a low-light strip club masquerading as a burlesque bar."

"What's your problem?"

"What's *your* problem?"

The two women glared at each other. Ness wasn't sure who she'd bet on in a fight, but really hoped she wasn't going to have to launch herself between them.

"Do any of you have any survival experience?" Bradley interrupted, sounding vastly irritated, as if they should have been prepared for this.

"I'm a twenty-three-year-old woman in Hollywood. My entire life is a survival experience." Daisy's mouth snapped shut as though she hadn't meant to say it out loud.

Coco snorted and scooted her stool a little closer to where Daisy perched, nudging half a granola bar in her direction. "You haven't eaten," she said.

Daisy smiled, her cheeks flushing as she mumbled a thank-you.

"Focus!" Bradley snapped, finally giving his pecs a break and joining the conversation. "We need to make a plan."

Tyler nodded enthusiastically, then winced and held a hand gently to his head. "Exactly," he agreed, staying carefully still. "I have no doubt the network is doing everything in its power to expedite our rescue, but in the meantime, we need to pull together and take action." He looked around, then slumped dejectedly. "I lost my clipboard."

Ness glanced at Hayes, hoping he had a better grasp on the situation than she did. He looked back at her, shrugged, and put his hands in his pockets like "Not my circus, not my monkeys," except he was a monkey, and they were mid-performance.

"And what do *you* have to offer, Top Gun?" Coco asked Bradley, her fingertip marking her place in an article about how consuming two gallons of whole milk a day could increase muscle mass.

Bradley's shoulders squared and he tossed his hair. "I spent two months training with Wolf MacKenzie for *Wild Orchids*."

Ian, now pacing the length of the room, snorted.

Ness made a point of not seeing movies with people she knew in them, but she'd caught snippets of the *Wild Orchids* trailer while scrolling mindlessly. As far as she could tell, it was the sepia-toned story of a man lost in a muddy wilderness eating a bunch of slugs for two hours.

"Is MacKenzie the guy who drank moose blood to stay alive in the Canadian tundra?" Hayes asked.

"He's widely recognized as one of the foremost wilderness survival specialists and general badasses in—"

Ness chimed in. "Wait, the guy who got bitten by that monkey in

Costa Rica and then said he had to have his arm amputated, but it turned out he was hiding it in his shirt for three months?"

"That was obviously a publicity stunt engineered by the producers." Bradley's face was turning an interesting shade of red.

"The one who said he was living with a group of tigers in the jungles of Sri Lanka until he was accepted into their hierarchy as Head Tiger, but he was really taking day trips to a zoo?" Daisy asked innocently.

Ness was pretty sure she was hiding a smile behind her hand. Coco snorted a laugh and the two women locked eyes, sharing their mirth and . . . Ness watched them, intrigued. *Were they flirting?!*

As Coco fluttered her eyelashes at Daisy, Bradley plowed on.

"Again, producers! Drama! None of that changes the fact that I'm going to have to lead our ragtag group for however long we're stuck on this rock if we're going to survive. Wolf's reputation may have been tarnished—through no fault of his own, I'll add—but I learned enough during my time with him in the torrid Australian Outback that I think we'll make it." He nodded confidently.

Libby crumpled the wrapper from her protein bar and dropped it onto the floor, looking disgusted.

"Honestly, I hadn't really considered that we *wouldn't make it*," Ness said. She felt her brows drawing together in consternation and quickly relaxed her face into a neutral, wrinkle-free expression. She ran a finger lightly over the space above her nose, feeling for lasting crevices.

Hayes was rummaging in the cupboards. Every so often he'd huff out a breath of disappointment before moving to the next one.

Bradley spun on his leather-sandaled heel to face her, and she raised her hands in a "cool your jets" patting of the air motion, speaking quickly. "But now that you bring it up, I can see how there's probably some risk. Lord knows what's lurking here. Like, um, sand fleas," she finished lamely.

"Or rats!" Daisy offered enthusiastically.

Ness's nose scrunched as she remembered Hayes bringing up the same thing the night before. "Ugh. Do you really think so?"

Daisy nodded earnestly. "Oh yeah, I read something about a bunch of the islands having rat issues. I think one also had donkeys, but it doesn't look like it's this one. Unless they're, like, scrub donkeys? Particularly adept at hiding?" Her head bobbed side to side, eyes turned upward as she considered. "But, you know, it would actually be really helpful if this was the donkey island. At least we'd know where we are."

Ian had abandoned his pacing and moved on to sitting on the counter, snapping his fingers while looking around like a useful task would suddenly reveal itself to him.

"Do you know the *name* of the donkey island?" Libby tried drumming her fingers on the counter as she awaited an answer, but the effect fell short as her remaining two acrylic nails wouldn't allow the rest to hit the surface. She huffed a frustrated breath, blowing upward to flutter her somehow-not-greasy bangs to the side.

Daisy's lips pressed together.

Coco thwapped her magazine shut. "For Christ's sake, Libby, would you take it down seven fucking notches? Go see if there's a tanning bed you can lock yourself in for a couple hours."

Daisy leaned back, lips pressed together. Her eyes bounced between the two women, and Ness couldn't tell if she was alarmed by the potential for a full-on fight, or pleased that Coco was standing up for her.

Libby's eyes grew large with overdramatized emotion as she raised her hands in mock surrender. "Oh, I'm *so* sorry if my agitation is causing you discomfort. Maybe you haven't noticed we're *trapped on an island*? I have investor meetings today. Then I have meetings about the meetings. This little side trip is costing me . . ." She trailed off, teeth clenching. "You know what? Never mind. You wouldn't understand."

"Right. No one wants to be here, Libby." Ness pushed out the next words. "Maybe Bradley isn't entirely wrong." She hated admitting it, but someone had to take charge, and she very much didn't want it to be her. "We should come up with a plan to get through at least a day or two."

"Your confidence is astounding, Agnes." Bradley took a deep breath, collecting himself and, presumably, plumbing the depths of his survival knowledge.

"We need to search the house. Make an inventory. Understand our resources." Bradley ticked each item off on manicured fingertips.

"Food would be great," Tyler chimed in from the couch. "We should find some." He'd fully reclined and draped his forearm over his eyes. His abomination of a shirt had ridden up, exposing a stretch of blindingly white skin.

The mention of food snagged Ian's attention. "Oh yeah, man. Agreed. Food would be literally the best."

Ness cleared her throat. "I was thinking we should start a fire. And there are a bunch of branches down on the beach. We could make a sign for planes that might fly over."

Hayes, having emerged empty-handed from his cupboard adventure, stood casually in a spot of sunlight. A streak of dirt ran along the side of his nose. A cobweb adorned his silver hair, shimmering in the soft breeze making its way through the open windows.

"A sign seems good," he said, hands in his pockets. Ness could feel the tension radiating from him despite his casual stance.

Bradley's eyes narrowed. His nostrils flared.

"Those are . . . reasonable suggestions." His tone indicated that he thought they were asinine. "But first, we need to identify and secure any resources."

"Yeah, okay. But I've identified that we have the resource of wood. And if we help people find us, we might not *need* other things. Surely rescue is our first priority . . . ?" She tried not to sound as frustrated as she felt, or look as suspicious as she felt. Was he foiling her on purpose? She plowed on. "We're somewhere in a pretty populated chain of islands, not lost at sea in a kayak. Someone is bound to pass by soon."

Bradley placed a heavy hand on her arm and looked down his nose at her, staring into her eyes with unnerving intensity. His short-sleeved button-down was open enough at the collar for her to see his recently waxed chest, and she tried not to be distracted by a single stray hair poking out from his collarbone.

"I understand you haven't had training for this. And I see you're in a place of emotional reaction instead of critical foresight. That's okay. That's why I'm stepping in." He squeezed her arm, stopping just shy of making it painful. He looked at her pityingly before turning back to the group.

Libby let out an infuriated sound somewhere between a groan and a scream.

Bradley gave her a cautious sidelong glance and edged away. "We'll split into teams." He looked like he was about to start assigning partners, but he didn't get a chance before Ian slid off his barstool and announced, "I'm with Ness."

Ness nearly choked on the chalky mouthful of protein bar she'd taken in a half-hearted attempt to camouflage her frustration at being so fully dismissed. "You are?"

"Me too," said Tyler, swinging his feet down to the floor and trying to hoist himself upright. He wobbled as he stood, and plopped back down. "Actually, maybe I'll wait here and run the command center."

Ian shrugged. "Sure, my dude. Command center it is." He swiped Coco's half-full bottle of water off the counter, tightened the lid, and lobbed it into Tyler's lap. "Stay hydrated."

Bradley plucked the partially eaten bar from Ness's hand. "First rule, conserve our resources." He slid the cookies-and-cream-flavored rectangle into his back pocket and continued, pointing at each of them as he assigned duties. Ness's mouth hung open. She considered tackling him and taking her breakfast back by force. It tasted like stevia-coated dirt, but it was *her* dirt.

"Hayes and Daisy, you take the upper level. Libby and I will inventory the kitchen and then work our way through the main floor."

"Naaahh." Libby drew it out, sounding purposely contrary. Typical. "I'll check out the bedrooms. By myself."

Bradley pinched the bridge of his nose. "Fine, whatever. Ian and Ness—"

"We'll do a perimeter sweep. Got it, chief." Ian saluted, grabbed Ness's hand, and pulled her through an arched doorway toward the back of the house.

"I'll back up my pal Tyler here at command," Coco said as they walked away. "Something something, special ops, whatever the fuck." Ness heard a magazine page flip, followed by an exasperated sigh that could have come from anyone in the room. Coco had that effect on people.

Despite the complete dumpster fire of a situation she'd tumbled into, she smiled. It was nice to know some things hadn't changed.

AGNES LARKIN

Rating: ★★★★☆

My girlfriend wanted to get this apartment because Ness owns it, even though the view is garbage. (Literally. We're ground level and look out at everyone's bins.) I was fully prepared for the experience to be awful, but Ness is a responsive, thoughtful, and respectful landlord. Repairs can take longer than you might expect, and she does most of them herself.

Pro tip: Don't ask her to empty the trap on your kitchen sink. She spent longer trying not to gag than it took to actually do the job. Maybe also avoid having her deal with the raccoons. There was a whole stakeout situation and an attempt at an automated deterrent involving a broom and a Céline Dion recording . . . Just get garbage bins with secure lids.

If anyone wants to buy photos or video of Raccoongate, DM me.

CHAPTER 7

I HAVE A SURPRISE."

Ian kept hold of her hand as he pulled her through the hallway, stepping carefully over fallen pieces of drywall. They were heading toward an exterior door that led to the side of the house that Coco, Daisy, Ian, and Bradley had searched the night before.

Ness tried to dig in her heels, at least metaphorically. "Yeah, no. I don't want or need any more surprises."

Ian wrestled with the swollen door until it screeched open. Ness had thought it was humid inside the house, but the air that enveloped them as they exited practically condensed on her skin with post-storm dampness. They stepped onto a narrow path running alongside the house.

"You'll like this one," Ian assured her. He gave her a charming over-the-shoulder smile, his brown hair glinting red in the daylight.

Ness shook her head. Arguing was pointless. If anyone loved a ridiculous reveal, it was Ian. She was probably about to meet a wild island boar he'd somehow found and adopted over the course of the morning.

"Hey, Ian?"

"Yeah?"

"Should we be freaking out? I mean, Libby might have a point. We're on an island with no way of reaching the outside world, and our greatest hope for survival is Bradley telling us what to do. Is this the beginning of our personal apocalypse?"

Ian stopped walking and looked back at her over his shoulder.

"If it makes you feel better to vent some emotion, then sure. But honestly? Like you said, I think we'll be out of here by this afternoon. They've probably been searching since the weather cleared, and it's not like the Bahamas is a fully deserted chain of islands."

"You're saying I can continue ignoring the growing feeling of impending doom? Because I know I said those things, but I don't know if I actually believe them."

"Why not? It's a surprise vacation day! Sure, we're missing the mimosas and spa services, but at least no one's waxing my butt."

"Yeah . . . right. Okay." Ness tried to force her mind back to their current mission and not dwell on the fact that Ian had a history of lulling her into a false sense of security right before everything fell apart. He didn't do it on purpose. He seemed to genuinely believe everything would work out, and he was even more shocked than those around him when nothing went to plan.

They turned a corner and made their way along the back wall of the house. Above them, trees swayed in the now gentle breeze. Bugs hummed. Every so often a ray of sunshine managed to poke through the cloud cover.

"So, this surprise you have in store, is it a seaplane? Water taxi? Well-trained dolphin with saddle?"

"Close."

"Kayak?" she continued. "Jet pack? A bunch of people with cameras ready to yell 'Gotcha!' and reveal that this was all a terrible prank?"

They trotted down a small set of steps that led to an even narrower, cracked paved pathway that quickly gave way to gravel, then sand. The surrounding trees and vines were so overgrown they brushed the side of the house, catching at Ness's clothes and hair as she passed.

Ian brushed aside a wall of trailing vines and turned to face her, an arm sweeping out to reveal . . . a very large doghouse.

Ness looked from the wooden box to Ian. "I feel like I'm missing something."

He dropped to his knees and started opening the latches that held the door of the structure shut.

"I nearly missed it too! But check this out."

The door creaked and groaned as he heaved it open. Ness stared at the black and red machine hulking inside. The metal components were rusted. Some of the plastic was cracking. She stepped closer for a better look, hoping a snake or island squirrel equivalent wasn't about to launch itself at her face. Her heart fluttered with excitement as she realized what she was looking at.

"Is that a—"

"It's a generator!"

Visions of running water and a shower and lights ran through her head. Suddenly, the gloom seemed brighter, the humidity more tolerable. Her chapped lips turned up into what felt like her first genuine smile in days. She looked back at Ian, who was staring at her expectantly.

"So, start 'er up!" he said.

Her brow furrowed in a way that certainly wasn't helping her un-Botoxed wrinkle situation. She looked from the generator to Ian in confusion.

Ian spread his arms wide. "Listen, we get this thing going, we're heroes, right? Picture it in the headlines, because we both know the press coverage on this thing is going to be mega." He arced a hand through the air, presumably highlighting said headlines. "*Ian James and Ness Larkin Save Co-stars from Certain Death.*"

"You *just* said we'll be out of here by lunchtime, and now we're facing certain death?" She rolled her head from side to side and took some deep breaths.

Despite Ian's charm, which was plentiful, this side of him was nothing new either. Fame and recognition above all else. She dropped her hands to her sides, remembering how hard that had been to deal with when all she'd wanted was to hide her head in the sand. He'd dragged her out into the world, yes, as a friend, but the additional media coverage hadn't gone unnoticed. Whatever he had, it was never enough.

Not that they had much at the moment, but still.

"Just do it, Drag-ness. Pull the rip cord or whatever and we'll reveal ourselves as a united front. A power to be respected."

"What makes you think I know anything about vintage generators?" Ness was, much to her chagrin, actually quite familiar with them. But goddamn, it annoyed her that he would assume it.

Ian huffed and dropped his pleasant expression. "You must! How else do you stay warm in winter?"

The crevices between Ness's eyebrows grew deeper. She felt her head inch forward, neck stretching like a curious turtle. Ian plowed on.

"You need to heat your trailer somehow, right? Canadian winter isn't exactly tropical."

"I don't even . . . what are you talking about?"

"You don't need to be embarrassed. I get that sometimes we need to forgo certain luxuries in the name of survival, and Ness, *I respect that*. But I would be even more respectful if you could stop pretending you're one of us *and start the motherfucking generator*."

Ness took an involuntary step back at the sudden venom in Ian's voice.

"One of you," she said flatly. "Right, of course. What am I, then, Ian? The help?"

She watched him try to arrange his face into some semblance of kindness or empathy, and fail. His fists clenched and unclenched at his sides.

"Can you do this or not?"

"Maybe, but I'm trying to decide why I should even try. Right now, watching you all slowly devolve into something akin to normal, desperate humans is kind of appealing. Washing your hair in the ocean? No moisturizer for those wind-chapped cheeks?" She sucked in a hissing breath and shook her head. "Might be time for you to give up some luxuries in the name of survival. I'd respect that, Ian. Truly." She put a hand over her heart. "And I bet the headlines would be real attention-grabbers." It was her turn to highlight the imaginary text. "*Ian James Relapsed? Aging Star Looking More Haggard Than Ever!* You'll probably get some great roles, though. Angry grandfathers. Surly dive bar owners who die before the third act."

Even as she said it, Ness knew she was going too far.

"Right on fucking brand, Ness. Nice."

She closed her eyes and took a deep breath. The air smelled like salt water and rotting vegetation. A mosquito whined in her ear.

"Sorry. Shit. I'm sorry, Ian. I didn't mean it." Her stomach roiled with disgust directed entirely toward herself. Her anger at his words faded to barely a grumble in comparison.

Ian had taken a few steps back in the direction of the house but stopped and was staring into the trees. When he spoke, she could barely hear him.

"I know I'm a fuckup, alright? I know I've hurt people, including you. When your dad . . . When everything happened back then, you needed a friend, and I didn't know how to do that. Not properly, anyway. I like to imagine I was doing what I thought was right at the time, that I was helping you, but I was probably too fucking high to really think about it. I just wanted someone to be on the ride with me. It was how I was coping, and, well, you seemed into it."

Ness felt her face getting hot. Ian's role in her downslide had taken her years to get over—at least, she'd thought she'd moved past it. But hearing him confirm her hazy memories of him gifting her pill after pill was different.

She nodded, even though he was still facing away from her. She'd wanted a chance to confront her past, to see if there was room for a do-over. This was part of that, she reminded herself. It couldn't be a fresh start when everyone was carrying the baggage of their sordid youth.

"You know," she said carefully, toe nudging the sandy soil, "I read your book. It's really good. You should be proud." She puffed out a breath. "Neither of us was in a good place back then, huh?"

Ian snorted. "Putting it mildly."

"I don't blame you for anything. It just . . . hurts. Thinking about it *still* hurts, and being with all of you now . . ."

"Feels fresh again, huh?"

"Certainly not as well buried as I had thought."

Their eyes met. Ian sighed and gave her a half smile. Ness felt the pressure in her chest lighten.

"Is there gas?" she asked, before turning back to the generator shed.

"You'll do it? You *can* do it?!"

She turned her head to shoot him a wry smile. "I can try. And for the record, I don't live in a trailer, but if I did, I'm pretty sure electrical hookups are standard." She paused. "Aren't you from Michigan? You know Toronto is like at least a four-hour drive from there, right? Our winters are basically the same as yours."

"But the moose on the highways! The beavers making dams in Toronto harbor! Geese invading the CN Tower!" She could hear the smile in his voice as she checked the cable connecting the generator to the house. Blessedly, it looked like nothing had decided to snack on it.

"Gas?" she repeated. "This is going to be a pretty short-lived experiment without it."

"There's another shed over there." Ian pointed at the barely visible path going farther into the trees.

"Why does everything here have to be like some weird, subdued horror movie?" Ness grumbled as loose sticks and spiky weeds bit at her. "We can't just have a nice sunny day and an open space? Oh no, let's go traipsing through the rat-and-maybe-donkey-filled wilderness on an empty stomach." Out of the corner of her eye, something brown swayed toward her from an overhead branch. Her breath caught for a moment, heart thumping, scream stuck in her throat, before she realized the hanging vine was not a murder snake.

Ian forged on, oblivious to what could have been a near-death experience. "At least you're not having dehydration-induced hallucinations yet."

"Something to look forward to."

She spotted the shed ahead on her left, nestled into what must once have been a small clearing; now it looked more as if the plants were trying to consume the rusted, tin-sided structure. When Ness turned and looked back, the house and the generator shed were barely visible.

"How did you even find this stuff last night?"

"Mostly by accident. We heard a weird sound over this way, so I checked it out."

"You ran toward sketchy noises in the dark woods during a hurricane?"

"Seemed like a good idea at the time."

Ness shook her head and looked at the structure in front of them. "Open the door."

Ian pointed a finger at his chest. "Me?" he mouthed silently.

"Yeah, you. Lord knows what's taken up residence in there."

"Probably just the island scrub donkeys." Ian scratched the stubble on his cheek. "What if we open it together?"

"If I'm supposed to be the generator brains here, you're the brawn. What good are those biceps if you're not going to use them?"

He looked down at his arm, flexed, and waggled his eyebrows at her. "You noticed, huh?"

"Hard not to. Did you really rip the sleeves off your shirt?" Loose black threads dangled around his shoulders.

"It felt right. A little *Castaway*, a little *Tarzan*."

"As long as a loincloth isn't next." She jerked her head at the door. "Well?"

"Yeah, yeah. Fine. But it's on you to train the donkeys to carry my corpse back after they murder me."

"Stop stalling."

Ian's chest rose and fell as he inhaled a preparatory breath. He took a quick step forward, thumbed the latch, and flung the door open, then spun and tackled Ness, catching her head in his hands and cradling it an inch above the ground. His body hovered above hers in a perfect plank, keeping what could maybe be considered a respectful distance between them.

She stared dumbly at him as he pushed himself up to standing and pulled her along with him.

"Sweet, huh? Used that one in *Almost Gone,* and let me tell you, it gets the girls." He started to pat the sand from her lower back, but she swatted his hand away.

"Anyway . . ." He looked back at the shed, scanning for hazards. "Seems like we're safe." He rolled a hand in front of him. "After you, m'lady."

"You're a goddamn menace." Ness couldn't keep the laughter out of her voice. This was the Ian she remembered.

In that hot, musty shed they experienced their first true miracle of the day in the form of five full, tightly sealed gas cans that didn't explode while Ness and Ian jumped up and down with glee. The second miracle came when the generator actually started, grumbling to life with a roar that had Ness falling backward onto her ass in the sand as she clapped, applauding her own success.

She lay sprawled on her back, intermittent fat raindrops splatting against her smiling face, until Ian heaved her up and over his shoulder, sprinting back to the house whooping obnoxiously, his arm clamped over the backs of her legs.

He slowed only slightly as his wet feet skidded on the tile in the entryway.

"Put me down, you goon!" Ness laughed, walloping his back ineffectively. He stopped and lowered her feet to the ground with a bit less grace than she might have appreciated. She straightened her shirt and tugged her stretched-out jeans higher onto her waist.

"Why aren't the lights on?" Ian demanded. "Why aren't people shrieking with excitement and running to greet us as their saviors?" He sounded like a petulant, entitled teen. Which, Ness supposed, he was, at least in spirit. Ian James, only child of television producer extraordinaire Wilson James, could probably count the number of times he'd heard "no" in his life on one hand.

She took a deep breath and counted to five, a patented Dealing with Tenants technique, before answering.

"Um, we might need to find the breakers? Or, you know, over however long this place has been abandoned, the electrical might have developed a few effing flaws, Ian."

She reached over, flicked a light switch, and watched the gaudy black sconces on the wall cast a flickering, gothic light over the room.

"Or we just need to turn them on."

While Ness marveled at the transformation of Ian's face from anger to beaming, angelic happiness, Coco sauntered in.

"Hey, lights! Nice one." She beckoned them to follow her. "You gotta see this," she said, barely containing her mirth. "It's . . . perfect."

"Who *is that?*"

Ness stared in awe at the white marble fireplace that took up a third of the dining room's far wall. Why anyone needed a fireplace in a country where the temperature never dropped below seventy she couldn't fathom.

Hanging over the mantel was a painting of a man in a deep-purple and black brocade smoking jacket, legs crossed ankle over knee as he posed in a high-backed armchair. His eyes, behind dark, rectangular frames, resided over a rather aquiline nose. Thin lips quirked into a self-satisfied smirk. A crystal tumbler was cradled in one hand, filled a third of the way with ice and amber liquid. A large brown snake was draped across the back of the chair, its tail brushing the floor on one side as its diamond-shaped head hovered over the man's left arm. It seemed to stare out of the picture at her. In the background, slightly blurred women sprawled in various states of undress.

Ness couldn't suppress a shudder as she leaned in so close her nose nearly brushed the flaking paint.

"It's horrific, but I can't look away."

She read the small, tarnished plaque attached to the bottom of the frame. "Gustavo F. Maltravers, 1992."

On either side of the fireplace, white shelves ran halfway up the wall and met with black and red velvet-flocked wallpaper. The shelves were filled with VHS tapes, cardboard cases peeling at the edges.

Ness's eyes widened as she scanned the titles. "*Three Minutes to Heaven. Seven More Reasons to Love Mitzy. Nineteen and Naughty. Fifty Ways to Fuck a Princess.*" Her voice rose in a combination of distress and disgust. "Are these *all* porn?" There had to be hundreds of them. Her eyes landed next on the bulky TV anchored to the wall above a glass and steel sideboard. Ness tried to imagine eating a formal dinner with *Two Mechanics and Me* playing in the background.

The twelve-person dining table made of poured concrete was an immovable part of the decor. A few clear acrylic chairs were strewn around the room, most of them broken. *Who lives like this?* Ness wondered.

"Wait. Did you say *Seven More Reasons to Love Mitzy?*" Ian asked excitedly.

"I did, unfortunately."

"I know where we are!"

She scoffed. "You can't possibly."

"No, really! We're on Ginger Cay, island getaway and play place of the Modern Prince of Porn himself, Freddy Maltravers!"

Coco looked very doubtful. Ness suspected a similar expression was on her own face.

"You're making that up."

"Yeah, Ian, not funny."

"How could I make that up?!" He paced back and forth in front of the shelves, nudging clumps of dust out from the baseboards. "I swear. I read a book about the guy. Okay, an article, but it was, like, a whole feature! He inherited a molded plastics business from his dad, sold it, and started the UK's most successful adult film company of the nineties and early aughts. There were like five chapters—fine, paragraphs—about this place!" He paused, eyes widening. "We have to find the wine cellar. You guys. The wine cellar! It had millions of dollars of rare bottles in it."

"You don't think he took that with him?"

"I don't know, Coco, but he didn't take this stupid chandelier or the videos." He gestured at the hideous tangled web of black and silver dangling above them. "It's not entirely out of the realm of possibility that we could find a nice crisp white to have with lunch. Assuming there's lunch." His face fell. "Aw, man, are we going to have to go fishing?"

Fleetingly, Ness wondered how lunch wine fit into Ian's recovery.

"Hey, does anyone know how to fish?" Hayes walked into the room, a fishing pole and tackle box in his arms. He set them on the table and started unloading his plunder just as Daisy entered, hauling a heavy-looking cardboard box that clinked as she walked.

"Who magicked the lights on?" Daisy chirped. "I love it. So modern!"

Ian preened until Ness had cleared her throat with enough force and frequency to get an acknowledgment of her contribution. Hayes flashed her a smile to end all smiles, and her knees nearly buckled. From hunger. For food. Ahem.

Coco filled them in on the recent location revelation as Daisy thunked her box onto the table and levered herself up to sit beside it, legs dangling.

"Huh," she said, flipping back the flaps on the box. "I had some theories, but porn castle wasn't one of them."

Hayes shrugged. "At least we know where we are. That's a big win." He shot Ian a double thumbs-up that would have looked lame had anyone else done it. "You may have saved us."

Ian looked disconcerted. He put the copy of *Six Slutty Sisters* he'd been perusing back on the shelf and joined them at the table.

"We found a secondary kitchen upstairs," Hayes said, and Ness's hopes soared ever so briefly. "But there was nothing there except that." He nodded to the box Daisy had set on the table. "And this." He thwacked a folded map of the Bahamas onto the table.

"The stairs were a bit dicey," Daisy said, "so we probably want to avoid them as much as we can."

Hayes opened the map, careful not to tear the worn paper as he spread it out. A game of Spot the Island ensued, with Coco emerging as the winner after locating Ginger Cay on the outskirts of the island chain. Compared to the other land masses, which seemed cozily situated near their neighbors, Ginger was on its own, floating in a circle of uninhabited blue.

"Neat," Ness said. "So private. So out of the way."

Hayes flipped the tackle box open. "Okay, we've got . . . um . . . well, that's not what I was expecting."

"Oh. Oh wow." Coco peered around him. She extended a finger and poked at the contents. "How many different flavors of lube do you think that is?"

Ness moved around the table until she could see. The little cubbies where one might expect to find things like fish hooks or lures were stuffed with sample-size packets of lubricant.

"If only it had any nutritional value." She sighed, scanning the package for any sign of caloric information. "Why can't they add vitamins if you're supposed to ingest it?"

Daisy nudged the cardboard box. "We've got gin, a couple of bottles of rye . . . even some champagne, warm, but drinkable. Ah! And I also found this." She pulled a crumpled, faded tube of SPF15 sunblock from her back pocket and held it up. "Expired in 2017, but hey, it's something."

"What's more likely to give us cancer, ancient stewed chemicals or the sun?" Coco grumbled, examining some mimosa-flavored slip 'n' slide lotion.

"Hey, where's Tyler?" Daisy asked suddenly. "I didn't see him when we came through the kitchen."

Coco waved her hand vaguely. "Eh, I think he went to go find a place to empty his bowels."

"Gross. But how long ago?" Ness didn't like the idea of finding Tyler passed out with his pants down somewhere.

"A while. Actually, now that you mention it, he should have been—"

"Libby, put it down!" Bradley's raised voice drifted through the house.

"I TOLD YOU I WANTED TO BE ALONE. You never *listen* to me!"

Ness and Hayes locked eyes across the table.

Hayes's shoulders drooped. "They were doing so well, all things considered."

Daisy looked from Ness to Hayes to Coco. "What's going—"

"Get away from me!" Bradley's voice wavered. Footsteps pounded down the hall. Ness shifted away from the door just in time to avoid getting steamrolled as a wide-eyed Bradley flung himself into the room.

"She's trying to kill me," he panted. "Again."

"I was making a point." Libby glared at Bradley, her lower lip protruding in a pretty pout. She held a pale blue perfume bottle loosely in one hand.

"You know I'm allergic, Libby! My trachea could swell like your ankles after a pancake binge, and then what, hmm? THEN WHAT?"

Daisy nudged Ness and whispered, "What did he mean she was trying to kill him *again*?"

Ness waved a hand vaguely. "I'm out of the loop on the specifics, but theirs is very much a love-hate relationship, heavy on the hate." She paused, considering. "I think her attempts on his life are usually more passive, like annoying him into an early grave. Taking advantage of a little-known allergy is pretty diabolical. I'm impressed."

They'd moved to what they were calling the living room, where Bradley had flung the water-stained satin curtains open and fought with the window until it agreed to slide up, allowing fresh air to flow across their faces. He was perched on the ledge, upper body leaning precariously outward. Ness had to stop herself from gasping every time he shifted his weight, sure he was about to plummet to the dry, sad grass below.

"Let's all calm down," Hayes tried.

"You calm down," Libby shot back, lifting the bottle. "This is premium, refined essential oils. It's not my fault you walked in mid-spritz." Casually, she depressed the nozzle, sending a tiny, vaporized puff of fragrance into the air. "Oops."

Bradley's eyes rolled in his head like a panicked horse.

"It's bergamot, Bradley, not liquefied arsenic."

"It may as well be!" He jumped to the floor, braced his hands on the window ledge, and stuck his entire torso into the open air, where he sucked in deep, dramatic breaths.

Ian had opened a snack-size bag of pretzels from the boat and was working his way through them by the handful, which was actually only one handful. It was a very small bag.

"What's the deal with the fragrance?" he asked, licking salt from his fingers. Ness felt the pressure of a hunger-induced headache settling in.

"It's the signature Kim Beauty scent." Libby tossed her hair as if this was practice for her next late-night TV appearance. "I wanted to test it in real-world humid conditions and, god forbid, freshen up a bit."

Ian paused mid-chew, considering. "Okay, yeah, that makes sense." He sniffed the air. "I like it. Undertones of tobacco?"

"Can we focus on the fact that she knows I'm extremely allergic to bergamot and yet she chose not to notify me of the risk? Not only that, but she wafted the scent toward my face! It was an aggressive and uncalled-for action, Libby." Bradley crossed his arms over his chest and glowered.

"Am I on trial?" Libby studied her hand and started prying off the remaining fake nails, grimacing, which, Ness noted with admiration, had barely any effect on her forehead.

Coco leaned in. "Ohhh. Can this be like *Judge Judy*, minus the judge, and we air Libby-related grievances?"

"No one's on trial," Hayes assured Libby, giving Coco a look that he then expanded to encompass all of them. "We need to work together.

It's been less than twenty-four hours. In all likelihood, we'll be out of here tonight, but if that doesn't happen, we can't fall apart. Or incite potentially deadly allergic reactions. Please. Thank you."

"Speaking of togetherness," Ness ventured, "has anyone seen Tyler?"

Ness, 42

Property Management

Dogs over cats, beer over wine, I always read the book before seeing the movie, and if you can come up with a Ness pun I haven't heard before I'll be equal parts impressed and exasperated.

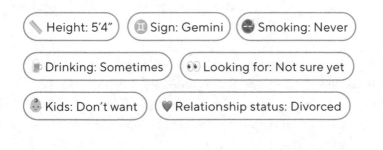

Height: 5'4" Sign: Gemini Smoking: Never

Drinking: Sometimes Looking for: Not sure yet

Kids: Don't want Relationship status: Divorced

CHAPTER 8

NESS WENT TO FLICK THE GENERATOR OFF TO CONSERVE GAS, THEN joined Hayes to look for signs of their wayward chaperone. Not because she specifically wanted to spend more time with Hayes, of course. Buddy systems were important in times of emergency. Everyone knew that.

They took the opportunity to scope out the freshwater tank at the rear of what could loosely be called a yard that sat below and to the side of the balcony, behind a screen of tall flowering shrubs. Said scoping involved walking around it in a big circle looking for holes or other damage that might have compromised the contents while the scrubby grass tickled the backs of their knees. Then Hayes scrabbled up the side like a chimpanzee and muscled the cap off. He took a moment, looking as though he was preparing for something, and peered inside. He sniffed cautiously.

"It smells okay!" he called down. "And I don't see any dead bodies."

Okay. "But do you see water?"

"Hard to say. It does look . . . moist."

Ness chucked a small rock up to him and he dropped it into the hole, ear pressed against the opening.

"Yup, sounds wet."

"Okay, so we've confirmed there's liquid and probably no corpses." Ness's head tilted. "Why were we concerned about corpses again?"

"Didn't you listen to that podcast about the girl in the hotel who disappeared and then they found her in the rooftop water tank?"

"Um, yeah, I did, actually."

"Well, since we're looking for a missing person it seemed worth checking. You never know."

Ness's face pinched at the thought.

Hayes slid down the side of the tank, landing easily on two feet, as opposed to the face-plant Ness would have expected of herself.

"It's a bit alarming that you're open to the idea of someone on this island stuffing a body into the water tank."

He grimaced. "Too many true crime podcasts lately, I guess. I like to listen to them when I travel, which is . . . constantly. I know it's not ideal to avoid my own trauma by listening to other people's, but it's also so *interesting*, you know?" He paused. "Also, wouldn't it have sucked if Tyler was in there and we kept walking past and maybe even *drinking the water*?"

"Yes, obviously. But do you really think someone here is feeling murder-y? Because you suddenly seem awfully calm about all of this." Ness looked around, peering into the surrounding trees.

"I mean, no?" He cleared his throat and tried again, with confidence this time, squaring his shoulders. "No, of course none of us are, uh, murder-y." He ripped some leaves from a drooping branch and started shredding them, watching the pieces float to the ground. "And I'm not. Calm, I mean."

"You're hiding it pretty well."

"You mean compared to this morning, when you were also the picture of tranquility?"

Ness pursed her lips, considering her words. "It did seem like, perhaps, we were having a bit of an anxiety spike."

"The spike has receded to more of a constant, low-grade mound. I think my brain might be so overwhelmed by all the potential catastrophes that it's given up thinking them through. For now, at least."

From the balcony far above them, backlit by the sun, Daisy yelled something, waving her arms to get their attention.

"What?" Ness hollered, shielding her eyes with a hand.

Daisy repeated herself, but the breeze carried her words away. Ness put her arms out in the universal pose of "I have no idea," which led Daisy to give her an aggressive double thumbs-up and beckon them back.

"I guess he's surfaced? Should we go check in?" She started back toward the house. "We could start up the generator again for a minute. See what comes out of the taps."

He slid his glasses off and wiped a hand over his face before nestling them back into position, trailing behind her. "You know," he said conversationally, "the last time I went on a date, she asked me how much plastic surgery I've had and whether I thought my kids would have *this* nose or the original. I haven't even had work done. It got broken on set a couple of years ago and I never got around to having it smoothed out again." He tapped the appendage in question fondly. "Besides, I think it adds character. Like a scar. And it helps keep my glasses on."

Ness's mind tumbled over a messy hill of feelings. The idea of him on a date with anyone was . . . uncomfortable. She'd noticed his nose at the table read and, dammit, it *did* add character. Everything about how he'd changed over the years made him better. His body didn't have the sheen of unblemished perfection it had in their twenties, but, if the fluttering in her nether regions was anything to go by, he'd only improved with age.

"It helps keep your glasses on? Are you seventy?" Ness climbed the steps to the front door and then veered off around the porch, heading for the back of the house and the path to the generator. The sun had finally peeked through the clouds and cast dappled green light onto them. Bugs buzzed and whirred in the undergrowth. The air was hot enough that even a small amount of exertion had her huffing and puffing as if she hadn't spent the last six months devoting herself to cardio, Pilates, and the consumption of lean protein on a bed of wilted leafy greens.

She sucked in a deep breath, nearly inhaling a small winged insect in the process. "Well, *my* last date took me out for dinner, canceled my wine order because at my age I need to be careful with phosphates and their interactions with free radicals, *then* asked if I'd frozen any eggs while I was still highly fertile."

"So . . . you're not seeing anyone?" Hayes asked, sounding surprised. "I thought . . ." He trailed off.

Ness choked on the breath she was inhaling as her brain raced to catch up to this new line of conversation. She coughed, recovering some semblance of a cool facade. Laughing dryly as she ducked under a low branch, holding it aside so it wouldn't hit Hayes in the face.

"The only people I see regularly are my tenants, my therapist, and the three friends who gather for our ultra-cool biweekly Catan night." She knelt to unclasp the door to the generator. "My life is the epitome of low-key these days. Although, Catan can get pret-ty heated at times."

"Huh."

"You're surprised? You try trading for bricks during an apocalyptic shortage."

"No. That I can, maybe, understand. Not that I know what you're talking about, but it sounds like a fascinating nerd subculture."

"The fascinating-est, actually. You'd fit right in."

"I'm awaiting my invitation to the next game night."

Ness's head swiveled, owl-like, to stare at him before she wrenched her eyes back to her task. It had been a throwaway comment, right? He didn't actually want to hang out with her in a non-work, non-castaway situation.

"What I meant, though, is . . . well, it's just . . ." Ness's eyes nearly rolled back into her head waiting for him to spit it out. Then, in a rush, he said, "Someone sent me a picture of you with someone a couple months ago and I thought you were together."

Ness had so many questions. Who sent the picture? Did her name come up in conversation on a regular basis with his friends? Who *were* his friends these days, anyway? Why would anyone even think he was interested in information about her dating life? Was she about to spon-taneously combust? She wracked her brain trying to think of a photo of her with anyone noteworthy. She came up empty.

"Who was it?"

Hayes shifted uncomfortably. "I don't remember," he mumbled.

Ness rocked back on her heels and stared up at him from where she was crouched, her hand frozen just above the power switch. "You do so. Is it embarrassing? For me, I mean? Is it, like, someone's creepy uncle? One of my tenants?" She grimaced at the thought. "I have one who smells like Axe body spray and Parmesan, but he also *looks* like he smells like Axe body spray and Parmesan. I really hope you didn't think I'd found true love with him. I was probably there to rake his lawn or something." She caught his alarmed look. "That's not a euphemism, by the way. Now, are you going to tell me or do I have to keep guessing?"

He studied the rotting shingles on top of the generator hut.

"Drake."

Ness nearly fell butt first into a prickly-looking bush. "I'm sorry. *What?*"

"I don't know, okay? You looked . . . close." He stared at something off in the distance, rubbing the back of his neck.

"In that we were beside each other?"

"In that you both looked comfortable and happy and . . . good. And there were rumors! Didn't you see all the gossip online?"

She hadn't, but she was extremely interested in the fact that *he* had.

"You know what, forget it. I don't know why I even brought it up."

Ness tried very, very hard to not read too much into his interest. Maybe he was a big Drake fan.

Hayes was looking so uncomfortable, a rosy blush spreading across his cheeks, that she took pity.

"One of those fascinating game nerds I mentioned? When she's not crushing my attempts at game-world domination, she's a makeup artist. She dragged me out to a party that just happened to be at Drake's house—I use the term loosely, that place is an estate. But I digress. He's a fan of *Ocean Views* and asked for a picture. We chatted about being TV kids for two minutes and then he was absorbed by a horde of models."

It had been the most innocent interaction she could ever imagine having with one of the world's biggest names in music. She'd walked away feeling like he'd been doing her a kindness, making the odd one out at a party of very cool people feel relevant, if only briefly.

Picturing herself as any more than that was laughable. In fact, she couldn't hold it in anymore and burst into uncontrollable giggles.

Hayes harrumphed and crossed his arms over his chest. "It's not that funny."

"It is. It is exceptionally funny." She flicked the generator on, wincing a little as it roared to life. Still cackling, she wiped a tear from her eye. "Drake!" she said again, shaking her head.

She straightened and reached up to clap Hayes on the back.

"Man, I've missed you."

They got back to the house to find Tyler lying on the squeaky red leather daybed, sipping a can of room-temperature diet Sprite.

"Glad to see you're not dead," Hayes said in a tone Ness couldn't quite gauge. Tyler's eyes widened behind the soda can.

"Same?" he said hesitantly, eyebrow cocked. He lifted a droopy magazine. "I don't suppose one of you would read to me for a while? I can't see a thing without my glasses."

Hayes ignored him, sliding out onto the balcony, plopping himself cross-legged onto the leaf-strewn concrete in the shade. Ness watched him watching the birds passing overhead, wondering what was happening beneath that silver-streaked hair she couldn't stop admiring. Then she remembered she had work to do. Important, not-making-eyes-at-Hayes work.

"I'll read if you can find something other than *Sports Illustrated*, *Playboy*, or *Maxim*."

Tyler pouted. "The articles are educational! I can't even see the pictures!"

She was a hero, briefly, after running the taps and confirming they had a semi-reliable source of fresh water (though she'd argue the term "fresh" was a misnomer here). She filled three relatively clean jugs they'd found in the secondary kitchen.

It went downhill when she said they probably shouldn't drink it unless absolutely necessary, and then not without boiling it. Things didn't improve when she reminded everybody they had no idea how much water was actually in the tank, so they couldn't run around taking baths willy-nilly. In fact, they should probably stick to sub-minute showers if they really, truly had to shower at all.

Ness hated that part. She'd have traded her tarnished soul for twenty minutes of steam and soap. Maybe with a cold beer at arm's reach.

"And the generator situation is just as dicey," she plowed on, as Tyler opened his mouth to contribute heaven knows what nugget of corporate wisdom or useless network guideline. She was determined to be the responsible one. "We have five jugs of gas. We'll have to conserve. I think we should turn it on only at dark, and for a short time."

The reception to this news was lukewarm at best. Actually, who was she kidding? Aside from murmured words of support from Daisy and Hayes it was a near mutiny.

Libby, who had been lounging theatrically on a mattress, a silk scarf dampened and laid across her eyes, snapped to attention. It gave Ness some small internal satisfaction to learn that even the most graceful of them couldn't roll off a floor-level, saggy box of springs and maintain an aura of svelte athleticism.

"Who put you in charge?" she demanded, clutching the soggy silk in one hand. It dripped lazily onto the floor, making a tiny puddle in the dirt.

Ness's heart jittered at the idea of yet another tiff. She wasn't built for conflict.

"No one, Libby. I'm not declaring this the Isle of Ness, just making some suggestions about how we can go about surviving."

"Sounded like orders to me." Now on her feet, Libby assumed Power Pose Number Three—they'd documented them one night, tipsy on cosmos, and it had stuck with Ness ever since. Number Three was single hand on hip, said hip cocked sassily, head thrown back as if expecting the wind machine to kick in any second. It was a classic.

"My apologies. Heaven forbid someone try to apply some logic to the situation."

"There's logic and then there's forcing yourself into the center of everything."

Ness considered throwing Power Pose Number One, a.k.a. the Wonder Woman, but dismissed it, opting for retreat.

"Fine. Use the generator. Drink unboiled water. Live your best island life, Libs."

She snagged a bottle of water and went out to turn the generator off, expecting to be locked out of the house when she got back, but no such luck.

In an attempt to find refuge, Ness offered to take first watch, a job she made up on the spot as an alluring alternative to moping around the periphery as the others shot dagger-y glares at her.

"We should have a lookout in case a helicopter or something comes by. Two-hour shifts? Great." She nodded emphatically without waiting for anyone to voice an opinion. "I'll go first."

She tiptoed cautiously up the crumbling stairs to the top floor and through a room that looked like it had once been an office, out onto a small balcony she'd spotted from below. She hadn't stopped to grab the squeezed-out and battered tube of SPF15 that Daisy had left on the kitchen counter, and she regretted that in short order. How much peeling skin could makeup disguise? Was there even any point in worrying about filming at this point? Would a partial protein bar, some water, and the teensy half bag of stale almonds she'd dug out from the bottom of her bag and consumed in guilt-ridden secrecy be enough to stave off delirium?

It was hard to remember a time when she wasn't steeping like a worry-teabag in a mug of concern and simmering anxiety. There was always something she wasn't getting done, or something she *had* done but really, 100 percent, should not have. And, she thought, reliving the day, someone she was disappointing. Or in this case, seven someones.

Sometimes it felt like she was walking around with every embarrassing moment, awkward interaction, and poor decision on her back, and it was slowly (sometimes not so slowly) driving her into the ground. She used to wonder if she'd be this way if she hadn't spent so much time being judged. Her body. Her voice. The way she walked. How her nose crinkled when she laughed. At one point or another, it had all been declared wrong. She was always falling short. Wasn't good enough. Easily replaced by any one of the hundreds of girls lined up behind her. Women who were probably keeping their lives together infinitely better than Ness had been able to.

She didn't wonder anymore. She knew that those experiences, starting when she was twelve and feeling oh so grown up, had exacerbated a part of her that had always existed. Really, she thought everyone had this little monster lurking in their heads, but some people found a way to, if not banish it completely, at least coexist.

Ness had fed her gluttonous monster until, like a goldfish in a large pond, it had grown to fill every corner of her mind. It had taken years to whittle out a space for herself and feel comfortable in her own skin. A few days back in this world and she could feel the uneasy rustling of the monster waking up, hungry and smelling a feast of self-doubt and fear.

She groaned in frustration and scrubbed her face with her hands before grasping the rusty metal rail in front of her.

Her head dropped between her extended arms in submission. With so much to worry about, why not go with the flow? She could focus her energy on learning to fish or weaving a bedsheet from palm fronds and let someone else make the decisions.

The afternoon sun had carved a path through the blanket of clouds, casting glimmering rays of golden light that danced over the island's greenery and sparkled on the surface of the shockingly blue water.

The haze had cleared out earlier, and if she squinted Ness could see the outline of another island in the distance. Much too far to swim to, but maybe they could make a raft . . . She imagined the eight of them paddling in the ocean, dropping (or, more likely, being shoved) into the water one by one until only the strongest made it to safety.

So far, no planes had buzzed overhead. No boats had passed within hailing distance.

She leaned on the cement railing, the breeze a whisper in her ear as she sweated through her once-heather-gray T-shirt. She was scared to inhale too deeply in case she smelled herself.

Clapping a hand over her mouth, she tried to stop the hysterical laugh-turned-sob that threatened to burst out. *Imagine*, she thought. *Imagine I worked up the courage to take this chance, to right some wrongs, to understand whether I made a mistake when I walked away, and instead I wound up shipwrecked with some of the most useless, aggravating people on earth, and this is how it all ends.*

I could die here.

The last time Ness remembered feeling this lost was after her divorce, twelve years earlier.

With L.A. a dark cloud in her proverbial rearview mirror, she'd landed in Toronto with just enough cash to rent a mediocre apartment. Knowing she wanted a job behind the scenes, far, *far* away from the public eye, she'd gotten a gig in the back office of a real estate company. A referral from a friend of a friend with a soft spot for a down-on-her-luck barely-adult with no real life skills.

In an even bigger twist, three years later she'd gotten married. Colin Montgomery was an investment banker she'd met when he came into the office to pick up the keys to his new Thornhill home. Seventeen years her senior, he was gentle, caring, dependable . . . all things she'd never had. Her therapist *still* loved talking about how she'd dived into marriage as a safe haven, protection from everything she'd run away from. She'd slipped into a life completely different from anything she'd ever imagined and reveled in the comfort of being taken care of.

But shortly after her thirtieth birthday Colin had sat her down with a steaming cup of milky tea, sweetened to perfection, and asked her, kindly, with tears welling in his eyes, for a divorce.

He was in love with someone else, he explained, cradling her cold hands in both of his. He hadn't been looking for it, he promised. But Abby, a lawyer he'd met at the optometrist's office, fulfilled him in a way he hadn't realized his relationship with Ness was lacking.

He said it gently, Ness remembered, with genuine regret, but the gist was that he was tired of parenting his wife. Ness needed to grow up, and the best way for her to do that was to go live her own life. He'd make sure she had enough capital to get started.

He left that day, taking a box of his favorite books and a small suitcase to Abby's house to give Ness space to pack. She had been ready to cling to the bitterness, to bathe in it until she was fully saturated, but Colin had been right, as usual.

It hadn't made it hurt any less. And now she was here, chasing down the past she'd been so desperate to escape.

Someone poked her, none too gently, in the ribs, bringing her back to the present.

"You look like I did after hooking up with Leo at that *Vanity Fair* party. Remember that?" Coco exhaled in a whoosh. "Those were the days."

She gave the railing an experimental nudge before leaning on it, her elbow touching Ness's.

"What's happening out here? Are you flagging down a rescue or having a pity party?"

Ness sniffled. "Both. I'm great at multitasking. And there's no one to flag, which might have triggered some minor amount of the self-pity."

"And you're stuck here with us."

"There's no one else I'd rather be stuck with." Ness managed to get it out with a straight face. Coco hung her head down, chin to chest, as she guffawed.

"Have you played that game where you can pick three things to take to a desert island?" she asked, still laughing. "Let me tell you, a gaggle of self-absorbed actors lacking most useful life skills has never crossed my mind. Bottomless gin and tonics? Yes. A shelter furnished with a luxury mattress and down pillows? Of course. My dogs? No, they'd hate it."

"You have dogs?" Ness couldn't reconcile the Coco she'd known with someone who could be responsible enough to keep a hearty succulent alive, let alone dogs, plural.

"Mmhmm. Olive and Pickles. They're Frugs—French bulldog pugs." Her mouth quirked down for a second. "I miss those little idiots." She swiped the back of her hand quickly across her eyes and blinked a few times.

"Being an adult is fucked up. I'm forty-four years old. Nearly half of a goddamn century. You'd think I'd have the ability to decline boarding an oceangoing vessel in the face of a storm." Coco's dark eyes locked on Ness's. Her hair was gorgeously tousled by the wind and she looked like she was filming a perfume ad.

"I don't want to be here, Ness. I have shit to do."

"Ditto. On the not wanting to be here, I mean. I have shit to do as well, I guess, but none of it is particularly exciting or important." She angled her neck to the side, trying to stretch away a growing tension headache. "I wanted to get back to acting, doing what I actually love. It seems so stupid now to have run away from it."

Ness wondered what would happen to her properties, her tenants, her own hearty succulents if she never got back. It was easy to imagine a world where things just carried on, no one noticing she'd disappeared until a washing machine leaked or the snow removal company didn't show up on time.

Well, that was depressing.

Coco sighed. "You know, some of us would trade places with you in a heartbeat."

Ness laughed—a deep, true belly laugh.

"No, really. Okay, not *all* of us—Hayes would be an idiot to give up what he's got going. But the idea of a stable income, a low-key, relatively anonymous life? It sounds kind of nice."

Ness gripped the railing and shook her head, smiling ruefully. "Didn't we get into this business because we *wanted* the fame?"

"Maybe once upon a time." Coco sounded wistful. She gazed out over the island, eyes catching on a flock of birds taking off from the beach. Pushing back from the railing she grinned at Ness. "Nah, who am I kidding? Being famous is the fucking best. Now let's find a drink."

In the aftermath of Tropical Storm Georgette, the western edge of which grazed the Bahamas yesterday before dissipating overnight, eight people are reported missing. Seven actors and one crew member from *Ocean Views: Turning Tides* were aboard a boat headed for Eclipse Island. This vessel did not arrive at its destination and authorities have been, so far, unable to locate it.

Turning Tides follows the now mature cast of the early 2000s hit *Ocean Views* as they navigate midlife and the death of one of their own. While the identities of the missing individuals have not been confirmed, sources say Hayes Beaumont, star of the Stars Blazing action trilogy as well as last year's runaway rom-com hit *Gorgeous*, is attached to this new series.

Search and rescue efforts are underway, but it seems the boat may have gone significantly off course at some point during its journey.

"I was against it from the start," Captain Dirk Henderson said today from Great Exuma. It was Captain Henderson's boat that carried the missing individuals. "I'm worried about those people, don't get me wrong, but what about my boat?"

When asked why he wasn't aboard the vessel at the time of the storm, Captain Henderson stated he was unable to proceed with the journey, but a *Turning Tides* staffer with proper training and experience had taken his place, after leaving a sizable deposit.

CHAPTER 9

AS DARKNESS FELL AND IT BECAME CLEAR RESCUE WASN'T IMMI-
nent, Ness found herself in the candlelit kitchen trying to decide
how to divide two stale croissants, three protein bars, and two
apples among eight ravenous people.

They'd piled their paltry resources on the counter that afternoon.
She'd made a list, scribbling on the back of a gas receipt she'd found in
her wallet:

- 21 bars of various kinds (ranging from protein to granola
  to date-and-nut combos that tasted like someone forgot to
  add whatever was supposed to make them taste good)
- 6 packages of peanut butter crackers
- 1 large packet of turkey jerky
- 6 apples (4 thoroughly bruised)
- 1 orange, abused
- 2 croissants, smushed
- 12 chocolate-coated granola bars, melty
- 8 premixed cocktails
- 7 bottles of light beer
- 16 bottles of water
- box of assorted scavenged alcohol
- 1 cheese sandwich

"Do you think there's a freezer somewhere in this place? I just want to lie in it for a little while," Coco whined from what had quickly become her spot at the breakfast bar.

"No. But here." Ness slid a gin and tonic in a mason jar across the dusty, cracked countertop.

Coco picked it up and rolled the glass between her hands. "This is the same temperature as my panties." She twisted the lid open and took a cautious sip. "Disgusting." She took a more generous mouthful and set the jar down as Daisy came in from the balcony.

"Too dark to see the cards anymore and the mosquitoes are killer," she said, scratching her neck. "I think the guys are just bullshitting each other now to see who gives up first." She settled on the stool beside Coco, and Ness watched, intrigued, as Coco's shoulders changed from casual slump to something she could only identify as *posturing*.

As Ness hacked at an apple with a tiny Swiss Army knife someone had produced from their bag, Hayes, Bradley, Ian, and Tyler came through the door, hovering around her like a horde of teenagers after school.

Ness batted them away. "Can you back off until I'm done? Why don't you go find the wine cellar or something?"

"Yes! Genius!" Ian headed to the table where they'd piled most of their light sources, which now included two dozen black pillar candles, three flashlights (only one of which actually worked), seven books of matches, and a battered yellow lantern with a hand crank. He grabbed a candle and went through four matches before getting it lit and nestling it into a gothic-looking lantern enclosure.

The light cast a spooky glow onto Ian's face as he hoisted the lantern in front of him. He smiled ghoulishly at them. "Who's coming?"

Bradley dropped to the floor and started doing push-ups, launching himself high enough to clap after each one.

"Pass," he said, exhaling with a grunt.

Hayes rolled his eyes and snagged another candle. "Sure. Why not?" He raised his hand to accept Ian's high-five before turning back to

Bradley. "At some point you might want to conserve energy. There aren't that many calories to burn around here."

Bradley held a plank long enough to extend one hand with a raised middle finger. "We all cope differently, Captain America," he said through clenched teeth at the top of the next push-up.

Hayes shook his head and turned to follow Ian.

"I'll come!" Tyler said eagerly, swiping the flashlight.

"Whoa, not the flashlight. We're saving that for emergencies." Hayes waited until he'd put it back down and prepped his own candle, then the three of them disappeared into the darkness of the hallway.

Libby, who had been reclining in the adjacent living room, sashayed in and surveyed the offerings.

"Is there anything less processed?"

Ness looked around. "There's a cheese sandwich." She held out the package.

Libby stared at it, her lip curling in disgust at the sight of the sweating cheddar. She sighed and pinched the plastic delicately between her fingertips. She examined the offering with disdain before dropping it back onto the counter, where Daisy's manicured hand scooped it up.

"Split it?" she asked Ness and Coco, tearing into the wrapper. Ness's hand was out to accept her third before Daisy was done shaking the sandwich out of its prison.

Bradley, who had moved on to jump squats, eyed his ex-wife with suspicion, as if she was one smooth arm motion away from spraying perfume in his sweaty face.

Libby huffed and looked like she was going to make her way back into the gloom of the living area, but she settled onto the red daybed on the perimeter of the kitchen. Not quite participating, but not entirely excluding herself.

Ness laid out their sad dinner in individual piles spread across a cracked wooden tray she'd found and wiped clean. Beside it, she arranged the remaining mason jar cocktails.

"Dinner's served, I guess," she announced, eyeing the lackluster spread. Tomorrow she'd at least *try* fishing.

Ian, Hayes, and Tyler returned as Bradley was finishing his last set of burpees. He transitioned into weighted squats, snagging an elaborate metal side table and holding it to his chest, ornate legs sticking out. He exhaled as he lifted into a calf raise with each rep.

"Idiot," Libby said under her breath.

Tyler raised an eyebrow. "I, for one, applaud Mr. Isaksson's commitment to his physique. I have no doubt you'll be in front of the cameras imminently—we can't let *everything* slide because of this unfortunate turn of events."

Libby ignored this completely, Tyler's chatter nothing more than an annoying bird chirping nearby, and went back to her perch on the daybed, having grudgingly, and in a move that Ness would never have anticipated, accepted a slice of apple and a portion of a croissant at Daisy's insistence.

The intrepid wine explorers had returned empty-handed, having failed to locate anything resembling a wine cellar, much to Ian's chagrin.

"I *know* there's one here. There were pictures of it in that article." He demolished his dinner in under a minute, still grumbling. "It was all stone walls and moody lighting. Looked like a vampire's bedroom."

"I was thinking tomorrow we should light a fire on the balcony," Ness ventured, studiously ignoring Bradley's condescending huff of laughter. "Toward the edge, obviously, and far from anything flammable, but it would make a pretty obvious signal since we're so much higher than the beach."

"It'll be even more obvious when we burn this place down." Bradley looked at the tray Ness had prepared. "These portions are too generous given our limited—"

"Resources," Ness finished for him. "Got it. But being hangry isn't going to help anything, and we should use up the perishables first.

Tomorrow, we can go fishing and then walk around the island. Get a sense of what else we can use here. We haven't even been to the far end yet. There might be another island close enough we could make a raft and paddle there."

"You're talking like you expect to be here a while," Ian said around a mouthful of orange, peel and all.

"You're both overreacting," Tyler interjected, before Ness could reply or Bradley could launch into the details of how he survived on kangaroo urine and mud pies during his time with Wolf MacKenzie. "We can make a fire on the beach, if we're not already picked up by then. Can you imagine the liability to the network if we cause damage up here? Untold pain for everyone involved. I'm sure no one wants to have civil suits brought against them." He looked at them expectantly.

"Who would sue us for trying to survive?" asked Daisy. She cradled an untouched old-fashioned in her hands.

Ness wondered if they should be saving liquor to disinfect wounds or something. Would that work with the bitters and sugar? Or would it just make them more delicious when they died and the local fauna feasted on their remains? She gave her head a small shake and set her own drink, some kind of limey tequila concoction, aside.

Tyler looked at Daisy with something akin to pity. "Who would sue us? Maybe our pal Freddy Maltravers? Or whoever currently owns this place." He tapped an index finger to his temple. "Think, Ms. Payne. We're trespassing. Regardless of the circumstances, we need to protect ourselves from all angles, legal and otherwise."

The candles flickered and sputtered. Someone coughed quietly. Ness wondered if it was too early to go to bed.

"Jeez, Tyler. Way to bring the mood down," Coco said, crunching into an apple slice. "I thought we were already scraping the bottom of the barrel, but no. Let's bring lawsuits into it. Why not? Anyway, whatever the Porn King of Wisconsin or wherever tries to get from us won't touch the out-and-out windfall we can get from Good Things for this snafu."

Ness watched Tyler's eye twitch at the mention of legal proceedings against his beloved network, but he pressed his lips tightly shut and refrained from commenting.

Coco wiped her forehead with the back of her hand. "That's what's keeping me warm at night. Well, that and the sweltering heat. I didn't know I could sweat this much through all the fillers."

Libby had retrieved a candle, which flickered beside her, casting a dramatic shadow. The couch squeaked as she shifted to put her feet up.

"While I refuse to bail Ness out if she sets the island on fire—"

Ness made a strangled sound in the back of her throat. "I'm not going to burn everything down!"

Libby made a fake shocked face. "My mistake. I thought that was kind of your thing."

"Have you considered a role as a supervillain?" Ness asked. "Or aged mean girl?"

"After this, I won't need to consider acting ever again," Libby said casually, waving a hand through the air. "Kim Beauty is about to take off. This is a final hurrah, if you will. A rather lucrative one." She sipped a glass of champagne the temperature of bathwater. "These network budgets have gotten obscene."

Ness felt a twinge of unease start to build in her chest. As far as she knew, the budget was being spent on shooting this episode on a private island. And maybe on Hayes, because movie stars didn't come cheap.

The movie star in question was savoring his mouthful of chocolate mint protein bar. The entire dinner was equivalent to a quarter of a snack on his bulking diet. Luckily, in the flashbacks for *Turning Tides,* he was supposed to be critically ill. A little weight loss would add to the realism.

"How did they get *you* here?" Ness asked him before she could stop herself. She glared at her nasty little jar of tequila and screwed the lid back onto it. "I thought you were already triple-booked or something."

Hayes leaned his forearms on the counter. The candlelight shimmered over the silver in his hair and made his cheekbones even more ridiculous. Ness suppressed an appreciative sigh.

"I wanted to be here," he said simply.

"Because of the money?" Ian asked. "I'm buying a place on the coast when this is done. I've always wanted to learn how to surf."

Ian was sipping something clear, but Ness hadn't been paying attention to the contents. Someone had broken out a bottle of vodka unearthed in the earlier search and it had been passed around enough that more than one of them was unsteady. She wondered if there was an appropriate way to ask if alcohol was part of his sobriety journey and whether they should be paying more attention. This didn't seem like the time to bring it up, but she quietly gathered the rest of the unopened jars and nestled them back into the second cooler.

"Nah," Hayes said. "I just wanted to see everyone." He was looking only at Ness. She felt her cheeks flush and was glad for the poor lighting.

"It feels like they're really taking a gamble on this," Daisy said. Her lids were heavy, head resting on Coco's shoulder. She sat upright as the group's attention turned to her. "I didn't even make this much for *Omaha Fancy*," she said, naming a dark comedy series that had been a runaway hit a couple of years earlier.

"Oh, I loved that one," Libby said from her dimly lit corner, shocking everyone. "What?" she said at their surprised looks. "It was a great show."

"How'd they lure *you* back, Ness? Must've taken a lot to make you wade back into the fray after all this time." She knew Coco meant it kindly and was trying to include her in the conversation. The sad thing was, it had taken very little to get her to sign on. Once she'd gotten over the shock of an opportunity like this even existing, she'd known she'd say yes no matter what they offered.

"I heard you really held out until the end," Ian said. "Must've bargained hard. I bet you're making the most of all of us."

Ness was not—that was a certainty. She hadn't held out; she'd been an afterthought.

"They thought you wouldn't be interested," super-agent Audrey had told her when they'd found out the show had been written without her character being included. "But then someone pointed out that you'd be a big draw, the mysterious Ness Larkin and all that, and here we are. Someone's got an angel on their shoulder, it seems."

The first offer had been disconcertingly low, but she'd been ready to sign. Audrey, freshly recruited to Team Ness (an embarrassingly small team), had held her off, gone back to play hardball and returned with an improved number. Nothing life-changing, at least not monetarily, but she'd be able to do some of the renovations she'd been putting off. If she really budgeted, she could even scrape together the down payment on another property. She'd figured her pay must have been in range of the others'. Apparently not. Not even close.

Everyone was still waiting for her answer.

"Always with the mystery, this one," Ian joked.

He looked around for another drink and came up empty. He harrumphed and stared out the window. "I'm going to stargaze and air myself out. Anyone want to come?"

"Does bourbon work as mosquito repellent?" Coco wondered.

"I think your BO is doing that already," Tyler said, his filter relaxed by the alcohol. There was a muffled "Ouch!" as Coco punched him in the arm.

Ness watched them start to trail out onto the balcony, then grabbed a candle and went to find a quiet place to fall apart.

June 2002

If there is one celebrity couple the world needs now, it is Hayes Beaumont and Ness Larkin. The longtime painfully platonic duo were spotted together Friday night leaving what appeared to be a dinner with friends at Taco-Taco. From there, they went to a much more interesting destination: a tattoo parlor that seems to have stayed open for a special appointment.

Eagle-eyed observers report each received some new art—Hayes on his ribs and Ness on her hip—before posing for a photo with their artist and leaving separately just after 2:00 a.m.

What does it all mean? Are they already filled with regret? Only time will tell.

CHAPTER 10

AFTER GETTING SIDETRACKED BY THE IDEA THAT THE REMAINING food needed to be somehow secured to keep the possibly non-existent rats away, and then turning the generator on so people could complete their evening ablutions with the luxury of light and running water, Ness walked down the hall with purpose. Her time alone in the kitchen, listening to the others laugh outside, hadn't helped her mood. She got two doors past the bathroom and decided this was as good a place as any for an ugly cry. Whatever lay behind this horrific metallic silver door would be just fi–

Hayes was lying on a four-poster bed in boxer briefs, a candle on the black bedside table. The mattress was bare but for a vintage floral pattern sheet that seemed completely at odds with the rest of the decor, which was, well, terrible.

Ness's gaze locked onto the bed, suddenly oblivious to the deep-purple walls and the mural of a dolphin straddled by a nude woman in stilettos.

The dim light flickered over a professionally maintained torso that had somehow gotten better with age. While he still sported a visibly toned physique, Hayes's abs were no longer defined into eight perfect sections. Ness had the sense that his body had settled into itself over time, becoming more solid. *Stop staring*, she ordered herself, but her eyes had landed on a small black mark at the top of his ribs.

Her thumb ran over the smooth, blemish-free skin of her hip bone as she remembered how hard she'd cried after getting the tattoo removed once she was engaged to Colin. She'd told herself she was erasing a youthful, tipsy mistake, but it had ended up feeling more like cutting the final tether holding her to her past. And it hurt. She'd always assumed he'd had his dealt with as well, but there it was, a tiny "hi" in her curly script staring her down from across the room. As far as she could see, it was still the only one he had.

It had been a joke between them, the idea that you could say that one teensy word with a million different inflections. It could mean everything from "What the hell are you doing here?" to "This is an unexpected but thrilling surprise!" to "I wish we'd never met" to "I love you." Every time they greeted each other they'd say it in a new way, trying to best the other with a mountain of (pretend, mostly) emotion behind a single syllable.

Hayes shifted, his tanned shoulders and chest flexing as he rolled onto his side to look at who had come in. His eyes widened for a second when he saw her, then focused, pinning her to the spot.

Dimly, she heard a small whimper escape her throat.

"Oh, yikes. I'll . . . I'll just . . ." Ness stammered as she backed out, closing the door as she went, still unable to tear her eyes away. *Probably some kind of science thing*, she thought. *The light's holding my attention. It has nothing to do with the man-buffet spread before me.*

Hayes swung his legs over the side of the bed and reached for his clothes. "Hey, wait a sec!"

In her final glimpse of him through the slim crack before the door shut, perhaps more firmly than was necessary, he was scrambling a little, trying to put feet into pants while also walking toward her.

She headed toward the stairs, ignoring the sound of her name being called behind her. The light from her candle-powered lantern was completely insufficient but also allowed her to gloss over the safety hazards that would have been undeniable in daylight. Sure, the wood was a bit on the smooshy side, and yeah, there were holes here and there, but she'd scamper up like a light-footed squirrel to find solitude in her metaphorical tree. Easy peasy.

She heard the bedroom door creak open and Hayes's footsteps as he jogged down the hall toward her.

She had pivoted, ready to tell him to back the hell off, when her foot went through the fourth step.

"Aw, come *on*," she moaned, trying to maneuver it back out without driving splinters of wood farther into her ankle.

"Would you *hold still*?" Hayes said, sounding as exasperated and wrung out as Ness felt.

"Would you *go away*?" she countered.

Hayes glared at her. She set her jaw and glared back. He'd put on his shirt, she noticed, and she was even more annoyed when she felt a pang of disappointment.

"No," he said finally.

"I can deal with this." She put her hands on her hips, the picture of competence. "It's no big deal. I don't need help."

He let his head drop back in exasperation. "There's nothing wrong with needing help."

"I never said there was. I said that now, in this moment, I don't need any. I'm fine. Thank you for your concern. Please return to your naked meditations."

He harrumphed.

She growled.

"This is stupid."

"You're telling me." Hayes stepped back and crossed his arms, looking at her with one eyebrow raised, like *I could do this all day.*

Ness was pretty sure she could feel blood running down her leg. Small, rodent-sized feet scrabbled nearby. She wondered if rats were attracted to blood. Beside her, the wall made a thunking sound, as though something large had bumped into the other side. The thought of larger, person-eating things made her flinch, jerking her attention back to the task at hand. She needed to get out of there.

"I can figure this out." She glared at her foot and the traitorous step.

Hayes took a deep breath in through his nose. "I'm sure you can. My point is you don't have to do it by yourself. I'm right here."

Could she just wiggle it, like . . . ? Pain streaked up her calf. Nope.

"Listen," she said, carefully bending the knee of her free leg to lower herself, sitting on the step above. "I'm strong, independent, capable." She edged her hand down the crack between the craggy edge of the board and her leg.

"No one's arguing that."

"You standing there feels like a silent argument."

"So you just want me to leave you here, stuck in the stairs?"

She wiggled one finger into the edge of her shoe and started the delicate operation of trying to pop it off her foot without flexing her ankle.

"Yes. I won't be here long." She hoped.

Hayes glared at her.

"Why are you so stubborn?"

"Why are *you* so . . . you?!" Ness bit back a frustrated scream as splinters tore her skin. "You don't have to save everyone, Hayes."

He crouched down in front of her, forearms across his thighs. Behind the dirt-flecked lenses of his glasses, his eyes narrowed.

"You don't have to be so goddamn selfish."

"Now I'm stubborn *and* selfish? You haven't seen me in a lifetime. You have no idea who I am." She pulled her gaze from his, directing her eyes to the crumbling ceiling overhead. Wires dangled like snakes through the spaces where drywall and plaster had fallen away.

Hayes let out a long slow breath and said, "I see you now, hurt, in an unimaginable situation where we all have to depend on each other. What are we supposed to do with you, Ness, if that gets infected?"

"Sacrifice me to the sea as an offering."

"This isn't a joke!" He took off his glasses and rubbed his eyes with a thumb and forefinger. "It gets exhausting taking care of you," he said quietly.

"Then stop."

With her shoe now off, ever so carefully she eased her foot to the surface and flopped back onto the stairs, panting with relief.

"I've been on my own for a long time, Hayes. You don't need to worry about me."

His eyes drilled into hers as though he was examining her soul.

"But I want to."

Ness forced a hollow laugh as her insides flip-flopped.

"I don't need to be saved."

Hayes's mouth curved into a sad smile. "Maybe I do."

Ness shifted her weight on the lumpy mattress, trying not to move her foot or think about stupid Hayes and his stupid body and how his eyes had a look she knew well from seeing it in the mirror. Feeling lost and afraid was nothing new to her, but it didn't suit Hayes.

Instead of embarrassing herself by limp-hopping into the living room with the others, she'd retreated to the room where she'd found Hayes sprawled out, pursuing the theory that being alone was almost certainly better than having to curl up next to him in the living room.

Alone was not better.

The candlelight had made the blood oozing from a gouge just above her anklebone look black. She didn't think anything was critically damaged, but man, it *throbbed*.

The night before, surrounded by the breathing, grunting, and shuffling of seven other people, Ness hadn't appreciated the quiet of the island. Now, with only her thoughts to keep her company, she tried to focus on identifying each sound.

She'd heaved the window open to allow some of the cooler night breeze to flow through, and even up on the hill where the house was perched, she could hear the waves. Leaves rustled. It would be peaceful, she thought, if she weren't so thoroughly creeped out.

If she had to describe the theme of the room it would be reflection, in the literal sense. There were mirrors everywhere. A twelve-foot swath of them covered one wall. In the corner, a set of full-length, wood-framed mirrored panels formed a kind of privacy screen. Ness had been scared to look at the ceiling for fear that another would be lurking above her head, but she'd lucked out—just a plain old ceiling, more intact than the one in the stairway.

The sheet beneath her smelled vaguely of Hayes. She put her hands over her face and groaned as she replayed the evening in her head.

She didn't want to be the one causing people stress or adding tension to an already off-the-charts dramatic situation. She was the solid one now. Dependable. Calm. Easygoing and low-key. The Ness stuck on this island was *not* the Ness of 2003 that these people thought they knew.

Except she was acting like a nitwit and couldn't seem to make herself stop.

Admittedly, she was proud of her independence, but she wasn't an idiot. She knew her limits . . . didn't she? An annoying voice in the back of her head suggested that she was fooling herself. Something she'd gotten quite good at very early in life.

She'd been a baby when her mom died in a car accident on her way to a beginner tap class for adults. A drunk driver hopped on the highway going the wrong direction and that was it. It was just Ness and her dad. It was the only way she'd ever really known it.

As an adult, she'd spent a lot of time thinking about how he coped in those early years.

A steady stream of babysitters, mostly local high school girls recommended by kindly neighbors, had taken on the majority of her care while her dad worked as an assistant manager at a bank. It was one of those girls, Mallory, a cheery, gratingly optimistic brunette, who had dragged Ness along to an open casting for the Canadian equivalent of *Gilmore Girls* when she was eleven.

In some tired-looking hotel lobby, Ness sat in a corner, reading Nancy Drew and eating chocolate chip cookies until her stomach hurt, while Mallory took her shot. She was one of the last to face the table of exhausted, grumpy casting directors and assistants and was in and out in fifteen seconds. "Not the look we're after, thanks for coming," an assistant said, ushering her out the door with a hand hovering near, but not touching, her back.

One of the people from the table came out to get some water and spotted Ness lying on the floor, legs propped vertically against the wall, while Mallory sobbed into a nearby pay phone.

The woman was suddenly looming like a dark angel with the harsh fluorescent light glowing behind her head.

"How tall are you?" she demanded.

Ness quickly stood up, sure she was in trouble.

"Spin around."

She twirled like a music box ballerina, covered in cookie crumbs and floor debris.

"Can you see without your glasses?"

This seemed like a stupid question, but Ness pulled the bright-red frames from her face and squinted at nearby signs, reciting from memory. She couldn't see a thing.

She wondered when the woman was going to call her dad and how much trouble she was in for . . . lying on the floor? Being out and about without a grown-up?

"You're perfect." She handed Ness a business card, instructing her to have a parent call as soon as possible.

And just like that, everything changed.

She'd expected her dad to be mad, livid even, that she'd been bused across the city and left unattended while Mallory chased her dreams. But as it turned out, the lure of fame and fortune was hard to resist. The next day he skipped work to go to the casting agent's office. The day after that Ness went to a go-see and was booked for a two-episode guest spot as the distant cousin of a main character in a show that was a real hit with the Canadian tween crowd.

The rest, as they say, is history. She was on a Times Square billboard for the Gap at thirteen, had a recurring role on the Disney Channel by fourteen. At seventeen she scored a lead role on an edgy new series, *Ocean Views*, about kids and their questionable choices. She was making what her dad called "real money" and paving the way for a long, solid career in the Biz. Or so she thought.

Part of surviving that life had always meant ignoring the bad parts. Pretending not to hear or see things that might rock the boat. Acting like everything was fine when it wasn't. Always putting the work ahead of herself, her health, and her happiness.

In the Hayes-scented bed, surrounded by mirrors that had borne witness to lord knows what kind of depravity, Ness made herself stay present. To enjoy a short retrospective of the day and see it for what it was—a big pile of tropical-colored shit.

She wiggled her toes experimentally. The foot didn't ache quite as much, but she'd kill for a bag of frozen peas.

Thump.

Ness bolted upright, staring at the wall of mirrors.

Thunk.

The mirrors shuddered slightly, making Ness's disheveled moonlit reflection glimmer like the surface of a puddle.

"Who's there?" Ness called, her voice scratchy and not nearly as commanding as she'd been aiming for.

She cleared her throat and tried again. "This isn't funny!" There. Appropriate anger and an edge promising retribution.

Keeping one eye on the door, she looked around for a weapon and, shuddering only slightly, doubled up a pair of novelty handcuffs from the bedside table and slid them onto her knuckles. It would probably hurt her as much as whoever she needed to punch, but it seemed worth the risk. At least the cuffs weren't furry.

A minute ticked by. Then two. Ness counted slowly to thirty, listening for any hint of movement. She slid out of bed, handcuffs still in place, and hop-stepped toward the door, her ankle protesting at the slightest flexion. She cracked the door open and peered out at the empty hallway. Easing through, she quickly hobbled into the living room, stubbing the toes of her good foot on the way.

Muffling a curse, she eased down onto the mattress beside Hayes. He mumbled something in his sleep, turning to her. His arm came around her waist and he snuggled close, his chin resting just above her head.

She tensed, then let out a breath, long and slow, feeling her body relax.

It wasn't until she was yawning, already half asleep, that she noticed Ian wasn't there.

Just One Bump

by Ian James

Preface

My fall from grace was swift. My ascension from rock bottom to a life that feels whole and beautiful and fulfilling is a continuing journey. Some days—many days—it feels impossible. It isn't, but it is hard. Harder than anything I've done in my entire life.

I'm told the work is never done, and I accept that as my fate. Part of that work has brought me here, to the place where I can share my journey with others in the hope that it will help. Is this partially a selfish endeavor? Absolutely. I need to think that this was all for something.

The pages that follow tell the story of a man with the whole world at his fingertips, but all he could see were the dark spaces in between.

THE MORNING SUN WAS CHEERY, AND BIRDS CHIRPED HAPPILY FROM their perches in the trees outside the house. Ness determined that, so far, she wasn't suffering from blood poisoning, gangrene, or anything worse than a nasty scrape. When she'd woken up, Ian had been on his mattress, drooling on the balled-up pants he used as a pillow. All in all, things were looking up.

"Today's the day. I can feel it," Tyler said as he passed around water and subdivided portions of prepackaged peanut butter crackers.

Hayes surreptitiously cracked his knuckles, smiling politely while almost certainly edging toward a mental-health cliff. He was great at playing it like a laid-back, go-with-the-flow kind of guy, but the signs were still there if you knew what to look for.

Ness looked down at her sweat-and-dirt-encrusted clothes and felt her nose crinkle with disgust. She'd taken a page from Ian's book and hacked her jeans into shorts using a dull kitchen knife and brute strength. The resulting aesthetic was certainly more temperature-appropriate, but also looked very much like she'd chewed through the denim with her recently whitened teeth. Though she was loath to admit it, the idea of being rescued and inevitably photographed looking (and smelling) like this was off-putting.

She popped her second and final cracker into her mouth, chasing it with half a mason jar of water, still steamy from being boiled during a half hour of generator use at the crack of dawn. That the electric stove functioned at all was a blessing given the state of the place. She glared at the jar, wishing for coffee. Her stomach rumbled in protest, and she eyed the tidy but dwindling stack of food on the kitchen island, sighing.

"I'm going swimming," she announced, sliding off her stool as Hayes surreptitiously performed some square breathing. *In, two, three, four. Hold, two, three, four. Out, two, three, four. Hold, two, three, four.* Maybe a dunk in the ocean would take his mind someplace less dire. She knew it would make her feel more human.

"Ohmigod, take me with you?" Daisy pranced to her side and was practically vibrating with excitement. She was very charming, Ness had to admit. If she was going to have a TV daughter, Daisy was a good one.

"Yeah, sign me up too." Coco stretched her arms over her head and yawned, coming in from the living room. It seemed that their circumstances weren't hampering her ability to enjoy a lie-in. She swiped her cracker and water allotment from the counter and downed it all like medicine. Her hair was sticking up on one side in an epic display of bedhead, and the bright morning light made her look every one of her forty-four years.

As Ness turned to see if Libby was going to grace them with her presence, she caught sight of Daisy, eyelids low, a flush creeping up her pale neck as she watched Coco move across the room.

"What's happening?" Ian asked as they made their way to the door.

"Swimming," Coco explained breezily.

"I'm in!" He yelled back into the house, "Come on, guys! Swim time!"

It was agreed that the women would swim on the beach where they'd originally come ashore, while the menfolk made their way along the white sand and rounded the tip of the island to their own patch of privacy behind a row of palm trees and other, more wild-looking foliage.

Ness, Daisy, and Coco stripped to their underthings and waded in. Ness hissed as the salt water stung the cut on her ankle.

"I'd go full skin," Coco said, "but this stuff needs a rinse anyway."

Libby had trailed after them, twisting her hair into a tidy high bun as she walked. She'd produced a silky, botanical-patterned robe from somewhere and, much to Ness's chagrin, still looked great. At first, she sat in the sand at the water's edge, toes being tickled by the waves as they washed up.

Then Daisy clambered up onto Coco's shoulders so she could cannonball into the clear blue water.

"Hey! I can see Hayes's butt from here!" she called, shading her eyes with a pruny hand.

Ness hastily blinked water out of her eyes.

Daisy smirked at her. "Must have been a trick of the light."

"Nothing I haven't seen before," Ness muttered, ignoring the heat flooding her cheeks.

Daisy shot her a look that made it clear she wasn't fooling anyone, then jumped from her perch. She knocked Coco over in the process and soaked Ness, leaving everyone sputtering with laughter. Even Libby couldn't hide the hint of a smile that cracked her crusty veneer.

Coco saw it too and waded toward her.

"Get in here, Kim."

"Absolutely not." Libby scooched backward. Ness couldn't believe it. Libby had practically lived at the beach when they were younger. She'd even learned to surf with middling success. Ness hadn't made it past their first lesson.

She'd read things online about Libby doubling down on her image—always cool and collected, rarely photographed smiling. It had started in her twenties, this chilly exterior, but with her friends she'd still been *her*. Warm and deadly funny. Ness wondered when that had changed.

"You don't want the paps to see you like this, do you?" Coco pulled a face. "Consider it an exfoliating treatment. Or an ultra-mod, niche meditation circle where the meditating looks like having fun." She kept edging closer, until she bent suddenly and grabbed Libby's ankle with both hands, dragging her across the sand and into the sea, clothes and all.

Libby screamed like she was being abducted, threatening them all with a thousand years of pain and destruction. Then, wonder of wonders, she started to laugh, scooping up water and flinging it at Coco's face.

Coco was so shocked by the sound that she froze for a second, giving Libby the time she needed to mount a full, no-holds-barred counterattack. With the agility of a snarky bottlenose dolphin, she launched herself from the sea, wrapping her arms and legs around Coco. She rocked her weight abruptly to the left, chucking the other woman into the surf.

Ness and Daisy stood, mouths agape, gentle waves lapping against their hips.

"Savage," Daisy said quietly.

Libby directed a laser-vision stare at a sputtering, snot-nosed Coco. "I. Don't. Swim," she said, voice cutting like a sword.

She was halfway out of the water when Bradley, Ian, Tyler, and Hayes came sprinting around the top corner of the island. All of them, except Bradley, were completely naked. Well, Tyler was more staggering than sprinting, pasty skin blinding in the sunlight, but the others were basically an ad for a very, *very* adult *Baywatch*.

They clutched clothes over their, um, more sensitive bits as they ran.

"Are you okay?!" Hayes yelled when they were in shouting distance. "Who was screaming?" Their heads swiveled from woman to woman, their pace slowing as they approached and it became clear that no one was in immediate distress.

"What. The. Actual. Hell," panted Ian. "We thought someone was being eaten by a shark or abducted by pirates or drowning, because that's exactly the kind of thing that would happen this week." He bent over, hands on his knees, his lump of penis-shielding clothes dropped carelessly to the ground.

Libby glared at Coco. "I was assaulted."

"You were fucking *not*." Coco swiped a hand through her short hair, pushing it back off her face.

The men looked at Daisy and Ness for clarification.

"Misunderstanding," Ness offered, keeping her gaze on some fluffy clouds off to her left.

"Yup," Daisy seconded. "For a second Libby thought she might be having fun. She panicked."

Ness snuck a look at Daisy, impressed by her sass in the face of a livid Libby. She noticed that Daisy was not averting her gaze. Then she noticed . . .

"Hey, Ian? Could you maybe, um, put some pants on?"

"Oh, like you're any better." He gestured to their soaked underwear. Admittedly, it wasn't leaving much to the imagination.

Ness sighed for what felt like the ten thousandth time in the last seventy-two hours.

"Everyone, cover thyselves!" Coco hollered.

With a great deal of strategic positioning, Ness managed to get herself to the beach, grab her clothes, and tug them onto her wet body.

"I was going to air-dry," she grumbled.

"I wasn't going to charge to the rescue, junk flopping, but here we are," Hayes said from his designated changing area a few feet away. They'd spread out a bit and turned their backs to each other for some semblance of privacy.

"Old habits, eh?" Ness said it hopefully, a tentative, easy lob of a reconciliation ball.

Hayes smiled at her as he buttoned his shorts. He looked relaxed, at least for the moment. Ness tried not to stare. Failed.

Nearby, Ian let out a frustrated growl and hurled his shirt to the sand.

"You okay, man?" Bradley asked. He slid his sunglasses onto his nose and stretched his arms over his head, grabbing a low-hanging branch and pulling himself up until his chin was above the rough bark.

"No. I'm not *okay*," Ian snapped, mood turning on a dime. "I'm everything that is the opposite of okay. I'm tired. I'm hungry. I smell like a wet dog. There's sand in my boxers. I'm *hungry.*"

Ness quickly finished getting dressed, resigning herself to sporting the distinct outline of a wet bra on her shirt. She took at peek at Ian and realized he looked . . . bad. No one looked great, but he was pale and sweating more than the nudist jaunt along the sand really warranted.

She stepped closer. "Do you feel sick?" She moved her hand to his forehead, wondering if he had a fever, but he batted it away.

"Don't. Don't touch me."

"Oookay."

Ian stomped off, heading away from the house. Libby watched him go for the length of one slow breath, then went wordlessly up the hill in the opposite direction. They all stood there, heads awkwardly swiveling, watching the two of them go.

"We should start a fire," Ness announced as Ian disappeared around a corner and the tall grass swallowed Libby.

"Ugh. Yeah, I guess we may as well," Coco agreed reluctantly. "It doesn't seem like rescue is swooping in any time soon." She froze, then stomped the sand. "*Fuck.* I'm supposed to have a video meeting with a director tomorrow."

"I'm supposed to be on set in two days." Hayes rubbed his eyes. "I already threw the original schedule out the window to be here. They're going to kill me." He looked up the hill at the crumbling castle. "If I don't die here, of course."

"Death is unlikely," Bradley said idly, dropping back to the ground and twirling a stick like a baton between his fingers. "We, well, *I* have the skills we need. We could live, if not happily or particularly well, without imminent peril, for, ohhh . . ." He cracked the stick in half and let the pieces drop. "Months, I'd say."

Ness ignored him, gathering wood from the beach. It was damp, but she figured with enough dedication they could get it lit.

The air smelled like salt water and grass, and if she closed her eyes and tuned out the noise of the others, she could imagine she was on Eclipse Island enjoying a quiet moment between takes. For most of her L.A. life, she'd loved those moments of anticipation before heading back in front of the camera to transform into someone else. So much about that life didn't live up to the hype, but there were pieces of it she'd mourned for a long, long time.

Her eyes fluttered open, revealing undulating palm fronds and their beautiful but disappointing reality.

Tyler walked slowly back and forth across the sand, picking up sticks. He was being awfully quiet for someone who had been consistently providing the most annoying commentary at every opportunity. She wondered how he felt, being marooned here with them. At least most of them had some semblance of a relationship to fall back on, as fraught as those connections may be, and Daisy seemed to be fitting comfortably into their dynamic. But Tyler was the odd man out. Was it getting to him? In his place, Ness would have felt, well, at sea. She stifled a burst of mildly unhinged laughter at her terrible joke.

When they'd gathered a waist-height pyramid of driftwood and semi-dry grass, Ness pulled a book of matches from the bag she'd brought down with her. Ian had a lighter, she knew, but she really preferred not to ask any favors of him at the moment. Also, the walk up to the house and back was killer.

She burned through five without getting any hint of a stable flame going.

Hayes held out his hand. "May I?"

Ness plopped the matches into his palm. "Knock yourself out." She paused. "Not literally, please."

She wanted to talk about the night before and apologize for being so stubborn, but she could feel Tyler watching them intently, even while he pretended to be focused on peeling bark from a stick, and she chickened out.

Hayes lit the match and gently cupped the flame with his free hand, bringing it to some tendrils of grass that stuck out from the bottom of the brush pile. He leaned in close, blowing softly on the glowing tips until they caught. He quickly struck another match, and another, performing the same magic until there were two matches left and the small sticks they'd stacked near the grass were starting to crackle merrily. He passed the matchbook back.

"For emergencies."

"Sure," Ness said, sliding it into her back pocket.

They stood in a circle, watching the flames lick at the carefully arranged wood. There was a collective sigh of relief as an impressive cloud of smoke started floating upward. They'd done it. They'd made fire. Ness felt the same sense of satisfaction she got from successfully retiling a foyer or single-handedly building a new section of fence. She smiled at Hayes. He smiled back, slowly, sexier than anyone had any business being. She felt her cheeks flush and hoped he'd put it down to the sun and heat from the fire.

"I require shade and a paltry sip of warm water," Coco said, sashaying to the path.

Bradley stared out to sea for a long moment before he, too, turned and made to leave. "I need to . . ." He trailed off as he walked.

Tyler, Ness noticed, was turning a shade of red usually associated with crustaceans.

"You need to get out of the sun," she told him.

Tyler craned his neck to get a look at his bare shoulders. "Ugh. I have the sunblock on and everything." He rambled off toward the house, hands held over his shoulders like ergonomically horrific protective armor.

Hayes, Ness, and Daisy looked from the fire to each other.

"Someone has to stay here to keep an eye on it and add more wood," Ness said, resigning herself to an afternoon with the mosquitoes that were slowly getting closer and more abundant as the shade of the trees began to shift onto the edges of the beach.

"I'll do it," Hayes and Daisy offered at the same time.

Ness looked at them doubtfully. "You *both* want to sit here cooking in the sun and being slowly devoured by the native wildlife?"

Hayes's forehead crinkled as he thought it through. "Well, no. But it doesn't seem fair that you should do it by default."

"Really, guys," Daisy said, shooing them toward the path. "I've got this. Someone can come swap with me in a couple of hours."

"Are you sure?" Ness was having a hard time not feeling guilty about leaving her there alone. She knew it was probably safe, but despite people splitting off on their own more and more, she couldn't shake a default desire to travel in pairs outside the confines of the house.

Daisy wasn't concerned. "Sure, I'm sure! This is nothing, really. I'll see if I can find some more of the stuff that fell out of the cooler, maybe go for a swim. It could be nice to have some time on my own. No big whoop."

A mosquito landed on Ness's cheek. After hitting herself in the face and delicately wiping bug remnants from her hands, she looked at Daisy, who was now propping fallen palm fronds up in the sand to create some shade.

"Okay, but I'll be back in a bit." She figured by then she'd want to escape the constant bickering in the house.

Daisy gave her a thumbs-up. Her hair was loose, falling in perfect beachy waves around her shoulders. She looked like an ad for a high-end vacation.

Hayes steered Ness to the path.

"Let's go before she changes her mind," he murmured, his breath a minty whisper across her cheek.

Ness cast an uncertain look over her shoulder. Daisy waved jauntily.

"Don't worry!" she called. "I've got you covered!"

Working her way up the hill behind Hayes, her feet sliding over the loose sand, Ness figured she may as well get an apology out of the way.

"Sorry about last night," she panted. "I was feeling . . . many things, and I didn't react well to your kind offer of help." Grabbing a handful of sharp-edged grass, she heaved herself along, eyes on the ground, while she waited for him to reply. This resulted in a rather forceful collision with his back when he stopped moving.

"Oof," Ness grunted, staggering. Hayes turned and grabbed her arm, steadying her before she could topple off the path.

"I'm sorry too," he said, his hand still resting lightly above her left elbow.

She squinted up at him. "About what?"

"I tend to push when I should let things go."

"Oh." How was she supposed to interpret *that*?

His hand dropped back to his side. "We should get out of the sun. Tyler's going to have a fit if we burn."

After parting ways with Hayes at the front door, Ness was ready for a snooze. Maybe a nice snack of, erm, room temperature water. Instead, she found herself on a scouting mission with Tyler.

"Thanks for coming along," he said, panting slightly. They had looped around the lagoon—murky and likely filled with alligators or piranhas—and followed an overgrown trail to the beach at the top end of the island. In normal conditions it would have been an easy, if buggy, hike. In their exhausted, hungry, and dehydrated state it felt more like they were running a marathon.

"I would have been happy—more than happy!—to do this alone," he continued. "But there's something about having company that makes it much more pleasant, don't you think?"

Ness wasn't sure she'd call it pleasant, but given how often Tyler's shoddy eyesight had come up, she didn't think traipsing around by himself was the safest or most productive option. With their luck, he'd fall off a cliff or disappear into the dense inner-island foliage, unable to navigate out.

They were ostensibly there to search for a means of escape, but Ness got the sense that Tyler was filling the hours until bedtime. He'd been about to head out the door solo, but Ness had volunteered to tag along. She needed time out of the house to reflect on Hayes's comment—let what (or *who*) go?—and the idea of exploring the island a bit more appealed to her. What if there was a secret food stockpile somewhere? Or, better yet, a long-forgotten but still entirely functional small yacht?

"No problem," Ness assured him, though there was, in fact, a problem. She needed to pee. Badly.

"Um, hey, Tyler?"

"Mmhmm?" His head swiveled side to side, looking for signs of hidden watercraft or a tree large enough to carve an ocean canoe for eight from.

"I need to duck into the shrubbery here for a second."

"Oh, I don't think that's a great idea. We don't know what could be lurking in there . . ." He trailed off when he saw her crossed legs and desperate shifting.

"Ohhhhhhh. *Into the shrubbery*." He all but winked at her.

"Yeah."

"Okay! Yes. You should do that. I'll, um, I'll be right here, but looking, uh, this way? Is this way fine?"

"That way is great. Be right back."

She finished her business and was heading back to Tyler when she saw the shed. It was set back into the trees, painted dark green with a dark metal roof. It blended so easily into the shadows and dappled light that she might not have seen it at all if it hadn't been for the birds.

There were about fifty of them scattered over the roof and surrounding fallen logs. Their white bodies were topped with charcoal wings and a slightly darker cap, with a long white feather trailing from the backs of their heads like the iconic rat-tail hairstyle of the early nineties. They chirruped and . . . quacked? Ness couldn't quite describe it, but they were *loud*, strutting around on spindly orange-yellow legs like curmudgeonly old men.

"Hey!" she called to Tyler.

"Yes?"

"Come here! There's a shed. And a whole whack of birds."

He edged through the low-hanging branches, managing to get hit in the face by no fewer than three of them, and came to stand beside her. He smelled like a teenage boy, sweat comingled with the stale remnants of a deodorant that probably had an extreme alpha-male name. She would have taken him for more of a fresh linen kind of guy.

"Oh wow," he said, hands on his knees, puffing slightly. "That's definitely a whack of birds. Are they . . . guarding this place?"

"Maybe they live here?" Ness said uncertainly. The shed was big. Big enough to hold a dinghy or tin boat, for sure. The door hung off its hinges, giving them a tantalizing glimpse of the inside.

"Should we get closer?" Tyler asked, eyeing the birds nervously.

"Yeah. They'll probably fly away, right?"

"They look . . . strong-willed."

Ness refused to admit it, but they were surprisingly intimidating. Each one was larger than a crow but smaller than the Canada geese she'd grown up dodging in parks. In a flock this size, that added up to a lot of bird mass.

She walked forward slowly. The birds raised their heads to track her movements.

"Maybe try running at them," Tyler suggested. "But carefully. And remember, the network isn't liable for any injuries sustained here."

Ness turned to see that he'd actually moved farther away, tucking himself partially behind a tree. She rolled her eyes and continued her cautious approach. Her avian observers puffed up their feathers but didn't relinquish ground. She was fifteen feet away from them now, close enough that any reasonable animal would have fled. Maybe they didn't know people were dangerous? Ness had read about animals like that, who hadn't had exposure to villainous humans and thus went about their business unconcerned when they were around.

Suddenly, the birds gave a collective squawk of alarm and took to the skies. Ness felt oddly vindicated. She was, in fact, a noticeably dangerous human after all. She watched them go, then strode toward the shed. After eyeing the saggy roof, she peered through the door. There was a broken lounge chair visible, along with an umbrella, its stand snapped in two. A giant gray tarp was draped over a mountain of hidden items, but she could spy a myriad of table legs and the potential for an absolute clutter of spiders. Ness shuddered as a cobweb brushed the back of her neck and draped across her cheek.

Backing up quickly, sputtering and wiping at her face, she barely heard Tyler the first time he called out.

"Ness!" Tyler hissed. "Ms. Larkin!" he said, much more loudly when she ignored him. "Stop!"

Finally registering his words, she froze.

"Look." He pointed one shaky finger at a flimsy, pale cylinder on the ground to the right of the shed. The green-tinged sunlight danced across the translucent snake skin. Ness's eyes tracked along its length, stopping when, after about ten feet, it curved around the back of the decrepit building and presumably continued on.

She spun on her toes and crashed through the trees back to the beach, dancing in place on the hot sand as she tried to shake off the heebie-jeebies making her entire body tingle.

"Uuuughhhhghhghgh," she said, pointing in the general direction of the shed.

Tyler nodded, unspeaking. His already pale face was the color of rice milk.

"Take the beach back?" Ness asked, already jogging toward the house.

Tyler followed, running to catch up.

"So," he huffed, "did you see anything useful in there before the, um, sighting? Should we go back later?"

"No." She shook her head. "Definitely not." She slowed her pace, linking her fingers behind her head and gulping air.

"Yeah. Okay. Good. That's good." Some of Tyler's color had returned. He kept darting looks back over his shoulder as though they were being pursued.

"How are we going to break this to the others?" Ness wondered aloud.

Tyler pursed his lips as he considered the various implications.

"I think stress levels are high enough, don't you?"

Feeling her heart still trying to bust out of her chest, she nodded.

"Yeah," she said, resuming forward motion, albeit at a less strenuous pace. "You're right. It's probably one of those 'it's more scared of us than we are of it' things, right?"

"For sure."

Ness was psyching herself up to do some gentle yoga that would hopefully center her thoughts and distract her from the implications of the nightmare-inducing snake skin.

Complaining about how much his growing collection of mosquito bites itched, Tyler had gone down to the beach for another swim, confident he could make his way there alone. ("I'm teaching myself to navigate based on the textures of the various plants and sound of the waves. I like to think it feels just a little Method.")

Relieved Daisy wouldn't be waiting on her to take over at the fire, Ness was now wandering from room to room, trying to decide which was the least sweltering, when she heard Libby's raised voice from upstairs.

"This is unbelievable, even for you."

Ness edged toward the stairs and eyed the freshly splintered wood with residual annoyance. Her ankle still throbbed.

"You know I wouldn't ask if I had any other options."

"You did this to yourself. I can't imagine why I would be inclined to help."

Ness could practically hear Libby's smirk. She strained, trying to catch Bradley's much quieter answer. All she heard was a low muttering, followed by Libby's earsplitting shriek of outrage. Loud footsteps stomped overhead and Ness, not wanting to be caught eavesdropping, ran on her tiptoes down the hall, into the living room, and out of sight. She turned and headed back the way she'd come at a leisurely pace, rounding the corner just as Libby steamed along the same path.

Crash.

If it had been anyone else it wouldn't have been a big deal. A quick apology and they'd have both been on their way. But, of course, it was Libby.

Ness realized this was the first time the two of them had been alone since she'd gotten to Florida. She wished someone else would walk in and save her, but no such luck.

"Sorry. I was just—"

"Why are you here?"

"Oh, I was going to see if the back room is any cooler than up here. I wanted to get some yoga in . . ." She stopped herself. "That's not what you meant."

Libby stared at her, chin jutting out.

Ness had really been hoping to avoid this conversation until they were off the stupid island. Or forever. Forever would also have been fine. The idea of reconciliation had seemed great on paper, but the journey to get there—if they could even make the trip—would be rough. She sighed and mentally buckled up.

"I'm here for the same reason you are. It's a job. A good one."

"Did you think you could just show up again and everything would be fine?"

"Honestly, I was hoping we would all be at a point in our lives where we could either discuss our issues and move on, or, if we couldn't bring ourselves to be that civilized, we'd let the past stay where it belongs and do this like professionals."

"Typical."

Ness clenched her teeth, then forced them apart and resigned herself to her fate. "What is?"

"That you only thought about yourself. I bet you didn't consider what you're doing to Hayes. To me."

"It's been so long, Libby."

Ness examined the stained grout between the floor tiles, suddenly very tired, as she tried to put the right words in place. She sat down, back against the wall, looking up at Libby.

"Why do you even care anymore? You're beyond successful. You've got money and recognition and the freedom to do whatever you want." It sounded like a dream life to Ness. "Why are you still hung up on my shitty behavior from a lifetime ago?"

It was dumb, she knew, to pretend Libby didn't have an entirely valid reason to be angry. If she'd been smart, she'd have dived into her well-rehearsed apology speech and ended on a note of groveling hope. Instead, she stayed silent.

Libby loomed over her, arms crossed.

"You're back, acting like nothing ever happened? What did you think? We'd all coast through the next few months like we have no history?"

Ness had had this conversation in her head a million times. It didn't go like this. She was supposed to be calm and composed. She would acknowledge her numerous and painful wrongdoings and forge a path forward to a reasonable coexistence not doused in hurt feelings and negative vibes. Instead, she could feel her face getting hot and tears burning her eyes as words spilled from her mouth.

"Did your parents steal everything you had? Did they max out your schedule for years on end, raking in every penny you earned so they could run off into the sunset, leaving you alone, in unimaginable debt? Did the one person you trusted with everything—*everything*, Libby— just peace out one day and never look back?"

Libby glared at her, then knelt so they were face to face.

"Do you know who I trusted with everything, you self-centered, narcissistic idiot? You. I trusted *you*. So, yes, you were hurting and heartbroken and making bad choices, but I was there for you. We were friends, Ness. You were one of the only friends I had, and you left." She let out a shaky breath. "After your dad, everything was about *you*. Your pain. Your problems. How unfair your life was. And I got that! I can't imagine being betrayed by someone you trusted with literally everything. I wanted to help you, but you blocked me out. You disappeared from my life like I was nothing. You ghosted me before ghosting was even a thing. How do you think *that* felt?"

Libby didn't wait for a response, which was good, because Ness didn't have one.

Daily News

The search continues today for seven actors and one network crew member believed to be lost at sea after being caught in a storm on their way to Eclipse Island. Hayes Beaumont, 47; Ian James, 43; Elizabeth Kim, 41; Coco, 44; Bradley Isaksson, 45; Agnes Larkin, 42; Daisy Payne, 24; and crew member Tyler Yates, 30, have been missing since Monday.

With no sign of the missing individuals or their chartered boat, *Gentleman's Delight*, rescuers have broadened their search perimeter, bringing in additional volunteers from Florida to assist with the rescue efforts.

"We're hopeful that a positive resolution is near," Trisha Jung, an executive at the Good Things Network said today. "Our missing group is made up of resourceful, capable, team-spirited individuals who thrive under pressure. We are staying optimistic and sending thoughts and prayers to the loved ones of those missing."

CHAPTER 12

THE HALLWAY TILES, WHILE APPEALING IN THEIR COOLNESS, WERE far from comfortable. Ness heaved herself to her feet, rear end numb and mind reeling. She paced the empty corridor, replaying twenty-year-old memories that were, at best, fuzzy around the edges.

Her friendship with Libby had been sparked, like so many teen connections, over a boy. Pop idol Sean-Justin Grange had the audacity to think he could date both of them without the other knowing. Schmuck. After narrowly avoiding a fight of potentially epic proportions on set, they'd bonded while plotting SJ's demise. It turned out to be unnecessary, as shortly thereafter he'd blown up his own career when he sampled "Thong Song" without securing the necessary permissions.

Ness and Libby had hung out on set and after hours, hitting the clubs and hot spots, shooting sultry looks at the cameras that inevitably pointed their way. They'd traveled the road from famous teen to famous young adult together, navigating image shifts and the often (always) unreasonable expectations of the public. But by the time she'd left, Ness had pushed Libby so far away that she thought her absence would barely register, or worse, that Libby would be relieved to see the back of her.

Her feet stuttered to a stop as she stared blindly at the peeling red-and-black geometric-patterned wallpaper. Her dad had always reminded her that they had to watch out for Number One, because no one else would. Ness first, dad second, everyone else a distant third.

She'd argued, of course, as she'd gotten older. They needed to make smart career choices, sure, but they were dealing with real people. Surely it was important to empathize? To create bonds and build relationships? It didn't seem right to keep herself so isolated.

Connections, her father had parried, were always acceptable, as long as they were with the "right" types of people. Libby Kim, young, fashionable, scandal-free, fell into this category. But in this business, no one was going to look out for you but yourself. And good ol' dad, of course. Ha.

Libby wasn't wrong. Ness had been entirely caught up in herself, her life, her goals and aspirations, and then, in a false-eyelashed blink, her demise. Her humiliation.

As an adult, it was easy to look back and say she hadn't known better. She was just a kid, dealing with an incredible family blowup in front of the world. *Of course* she didn't cope well. It was harder to admit that when Libby had reached out after Ness had moved north, Ness had made a conscious decision to cut ties.

It had terrified her how badly she wanted Libby to fly in and drag her back to L.A., wrap her in one of the giant handknit throws her mom seemed to turn out weekly, and convince her that they would get through this together. She wouldn't depend on someone so fully. She couldn't.

By the time she'd realized she was doing exactly the same thing as her father—deliberately cutting herself off from people instead of letting them in—it felt too late. She couldn't even begin to imagine what she could say to make it better and have Libby forgive her. So she'd just . . . gotten on with her new life.

But she'd never completely left Libby behind. She carried the memory of their friendship with her like a little flame proving that, at least at some point in her life, someone had truly loved her. Seeing how badly she'd hurt that person cut deep.

Ness wandered into the living room and plopped onto the sofa, wondering idly where everyone was. She lowered her face into her hands and massaged her temples.

Feet came into view in front of her. Slowly, she raised her head and looked up to find Hayes gazing at her, the corners of his eyes crinkled with concern.

"I'm fine," she assured him.

"I figured." He lowered himself to the seat beside her. "Me too. I'm great. Loving this whole experience, you know?"

Ness snorted.

Hayes spread his arms along the back of the couch and tipped his head back, baring his neck in a way that made her skin tingle.

"No, really," he continued, oblivious to her fluttering heartbeat. "I think we're bringing out the best in each other, making fresh connections, really settling into island life."

She swatted at the air, batting his nonsense aside.

"Stop," she insisted. "It's torture. Hell with a beautiful sunset. I saw Ian doing naked yoga on the balcony at sunrise. I may never recover." She didn't mention that the view of his tanned rear end hadn't sparked the memories she'd expected it to.

"Is that why you're in here trying to compress your skull?"

"Would you believe I wanted some quiet time?"

"Sure."

Ness flopped back, arms hanging at her sides, palms up. She stared at the motionless cobweb-draped ceiling fan above them. There was no point in lying.

"Libby chose today to resurrect the ghosts of friendship past."

"Ah." She felt more than saw his nod. "It was bound to happen. And you survived! Great job!"

"I am the very picture of success." She paused, then turned her head toward Hayes and found his face much closer to hers than she'd expected. They'd both reclined farther, heads lolling on the back of the couch. She could feel the movement of his slow, easy breath. He somehow still smelled of ocean air and cinnamon toothpaste instead of outright panic, but his eyes were darting around in a way that suggested he wasn't nearly as relaxed as he looked.

"How do *you* feel about me being here?" She'd said it in her head, but some horribly timed brain-mouth synapse gave the words life.

"Never mind," she said quickly. "I don't know why I asked."

He didn't shift away. His breathing didn't hitch or speed up. He stayed steady, as a tropical bird squawked outside the window. The afternoon light streamed in, glinting off the gray and white in his three-day stubble. His eyes, now focused on hers, were the same gray-flecked green that were etched in her memory, no matter how hard she'd tried to forget them.

"Ness, I—"

Outside, someone screamed.

They were off the couch and through the kitchen in seconds, bursting onto the balcony with matching wide-eyed stares. Bradley was in a fighting stance, gaze darting around as though he was expecting to engage in hand-to-hand combat with a gang of ne'er-do-wells at any second.

Hayes skidded to a stop at Coco's side and tried to get her to take a deep breath. Drink some water. Put her head between her knees.

Coco dodged his attentions and extended a toned arm, pointing down to the beach. She was doing an athletic side shuffle toward the stairs at the same time, as though she was barely holding herself in check.

They all pivoted, following the direction of her index finger.

There was a boat. A sleek white one that reminded Ness of the kind she'd seen ripping around Ibiza, adorned with barely clad models. It skirted the perimeter of the island, slowing as it approached their beach. She inhaled sharply. Rescue. Salvation. At this point she would have welcomed an inflatable paddleboard with near-equal enthusiasm.

Chaos ensued as everyone tried to sprint down the stairs to the beach path at the same time. Bradley's shoulders wedged against Hayes's at the top of the steps, and it took three long seconds of them shoving each other back and forth before they popped loose like dual champagne corks and took off sprinting.

Libby had flown outside during the commotion and had processed the situation with lightning speed. She was just steps behind the men, arms pumping as she launched herself across the sand.

Ness and Coco were hot on their heels, kicking sand into the air as they ran. From the beach, the sound of an engine brushed against Ness's ears, and she thought she might have wept if she'd had enough liquid in her body to spare.

Up ahead, Hayes and Bradley were bellowing. The engine noise got louder. Distracted, Ness got her foot looped underneath a twisting root, which sent her flying face first into the sand. She lay there for a moment, stunned, waiting for air to return to her lungs.

Hands hooked under her armpits and hoisted her up. Coco was breathing hard, sweat dripping down the sides of her red face. She gave Ness a once-over, patted her on the shoulder, and took off again.

"Come on!" she huffed over her shoulder.

Ness had fallen only a couple of hundred feet from where the tall grasses opened onto the beach. She jogged, limping slightly, wondering if anyone would judge her if she went directly into the ocean for a celebratory swim.

The breeze brushed hot late-afternoon air against her body as she emerged onto the open sand. The water lapped at the shore. The fire was little more than a smoldering pile of coals, barely a trickle of smoke climbing into the air.

The boat was already growing small as it sped away, leaving a frothy white trail behind it. One of the people onboard, a guy in board shorts and a Tilley hat, turned and waved jauntily.

"Noooo," Libby moaned, crumpling to the warm sand.

Bradley rounded on a pale, sand-coated Daisy, his hands fisted. "Please tell me there's a good reason that boat is leaving without us."

Daisy's hair was tangled and dotted with small leaves. An angry red scrape cut across her left shoulder, just beside the thick strap of her tank top. She was making "calm down" gestures with her hands while slowly backing away from the mob.

"I'll kill her," Libby said, surging to her feet and looking like she meant it.

"I'm sure there's an explanation," Bradley said, pacing. "You wouldn't just let them leave. That wouldn't make any sense." He laughed maniacally.

Ness shook herself free from the shock that had frozen her in place. She elbowed her way through the group and executed the loudest, most obnoxious two-fingers-in-the-mouth whistle she could muster. It was very good. A legacy skill from a short stint as a middle school soccer star in a made-for-TV movie.

Everyone winced and, at least for a moment, stopped yelling. Before anybody could launch into a fresh tirade of threats, Ness spoke, wiping residual sand from the corners of her mouth.

"Would you all shut up and let her talk?" She ducked her head down to catch the younger woman's eye. "What happened?"

Daisy shifted her weight from foot to foot, the picture of uneasy guilt. Behind her, Ian emerged from the trees, scratching his arm and looking, frankly, terrible. He was pale and sweating, his shirt balled in one hand. He took one look at the group of them, huddled like a swarm of angry wasps, and walked slowly, unsteadily, up the path.

"Well?" Libby demanded.

Daisy was trembling, tears welling in her big, beautiful eyes. "I went into the trees—only for a minute!" Her gaze jumped from face to face, searching for an ally.

Tyler wrapped an arm around her waist. She waited a second, then sidled a safe distance away, leaving him looking discomfited.

Daisy took a shuddering breath, steadying herself. Libby hissed between clenched teeth.

"Daisy," Hayes said gently. "What happened?"

"Well," she started, "there was a boat."

"We know that already!" Libby shrieked. Coco shushed her. They waited.

The wind rustled the leaves of the mangroves. A bird called out. Bradley growled.

"There was a boat," Daisy started again. "I was . . . busy. In the trees. But as soon as I heard the engine I ran out!" She shrugged hopelessly. "I tried to wave them down, but they just waved back and zoomed off." Looking desperately from face to face, she plowed on. "I don't think they understood. The guy had a drink in his hand, and it seemed like they were looking for a spot to hang out, saw this was occupied, and moved on."

Tyler stepped forward again, putting a hand on Daisy's shoulder. "They'll realize their mistake. They'll circle back, or notify the authorities. I'm sure of it."

"Oh, you're sure, Tyler?" Libby moved closer. "You're certain some drunk frat boys on vacation are going to have an *aha!* moment? Hm, *Tyler*?" She poked his sternum hard enough to leave a bruise.

Tyler staggered back a step, clutching the offended area as though he'd been stabbed. He glared at Libby.

"Yes, Ms. Kim. If we don't hold on to hope, what do we have?"

Bradley scoffed.

Ness was beginning to tremble like a small hairless dog without a coat as the adrenaline rush from her sprint faded away, leaving her both hot and cold. Hopeful and desolate.

Tyler surveyed the group. "Now, if there are no more questions, I'd like to gather my things. I, for one, have faith that the multi-billion-dollar corporate system that brought us together can tackle something as simple as a track and retrieve mission. We should be prepared to leave at a moment's notice. I suggest you do the same."

He walked quickly away, leaving the rest of them on the beach wondering where the line between hope and delusion lay.

MackeyMacAttack
Ginger Cay

MackeyMacAttack Buzzed by Ginger Cay today with my man
@BreezeyBob2000 in the new bateau. It seems like every time we try
to hang here, someone else started their shindig first. Like, invite us,
bro! We know how to party!
#grindhardstayhumble #norestforthewicked
Alt Text: A tropical island in the afternoon light. Dying party bonfire
on a white sand beach.

CHAPTER 13

AS THE SUN SET, NESS WENT OUT TO START THE GENERATOR, GRImacing as she nestled a second empty gas can beside the first. At this rate, they had maybe four days' worth remaining if they kept usage to a minimum. That should be plenty, right? *Yeah*, she assured herself. *Plenty.*

They all seemed to be teetering on a mental ledge since seeing the boat. One by one they'd filtered back into the house. Those with functioning phones spent some time holding them to the sky, checking for a signal and still finding none.

Despite the fact that no one other than Tyler seemed to believe rescue was imminent, they quietly gathered their things, no one acknowledging what they were doing or how futile it felt. Maybe Tyler was right: hope was all they had.

After obnoxiously plopping his bag by the kitchen door, Tyler had walked, nose in the air, out of sight, declaring that he'd take a shift— likely the last one necessary—watching for signs of rescue vessels. Ness chose not to ask how, exactly, he was going to spot anything when it seemed like he could barely differentiate Hayes from Ian across a large room. He'd skulked up the path again minutes before dusk, sunburned and scratching at what Ness assumed was an impressive collection of mosquito bites. Ness had no idea where he was now and didn't care. She briefly wondered if they could sneak off the island without him.

Now, with the generator roaring comfortingly in the background, Ness flicked on every light in the house to create a beacon for potential rescue crews. Of course, as soon as the rest of the group noticed the readily accessible electricity, it became a free-for-all.

"I'm going to shower!" Libby declared, stalking toward the bathroom. She passed Ness as though she were invisible.

"Same!" Coco said quickly. "Don't use all the hot water, Libby!"

"Fuck yoooou," Libby sang back.

"It's so nice that age has mellowed her out," Coco muttered as she speed-walked down the hall to stake her claim to another of the bathrooms.

Ness watched them go, wondering if she should follow suit. She looked exactly like someone who had been trapped on a deserted island for two days. She sniffed at her armpits and sighed. Despite their earlier swim and the communal deodorant stash that had accumulated on the dining room table—one of their best team efforts—she smelled like it too.

She resigned herself to a cold shower when the others were done. For the moment, though, she could at least air herself out.

Hayes was outside, one of the last bottles of beer in his hand. He leaned over the railing, staring at the setting sun.

Ness stopped to take in the view, locking it away in her memory as something rare and precious, before joining him. The others were scattered throughout the house, though if she craned her neck a bit, Ness could see Daisy performing downward-dog-to-plank transitions over by the hot tub.

Hayes smiled and offered Ness the bottle. She accepted, taking a swig and feeling like a high schooler sneaking vodka coolers in someone's basement. The beer was tepid, at best. She grimaced and handed it back.

"It's beautiful here," Hayes said, nodding toward the deep purple and pinks of the darkening sky. "It seems wrong to hate it so much."

"Right? In another world, a couple of days of tropical weather and nothing else to do would be a straight win. And yet."

"And yet."

The last of the evening light was extremely flattering . . . as if he needed good lighting to look fantastic. Ness hoped it was doing her the same favor. She studied his profile and wished she had a camera.

It hit her that, if all went as they (desperately) hoped, they could be leaving at any moment. This strange bubble would pop and they'd be back in the real world. With cameras and production assistants and dozens of people around them nearly all the time. Here, away from everything familiar and the constant attention Hayes's level of fame garnered, it felt as though she had a real chance to get closer to him. And, most of the time, it felt as though he might want that closeness too. Would they stand a chance once they were back in the real world?

Ness turned so her back was resting on the railing, elbows propped on the sun-warmed pebbles embedded in the concrete.

"Did you really think I was dating Drake?"

"I was dehydrated when I said that. Delirious. I was thinking of someone else." He rolled the beer bottle between his hands.

"Mmhmm. Well, to clear it up, I'm seeing no one. Very single. Happily single, mostly. Usually." She took a beat to form her next words, gathering herself. "Being here feels like we got dropped into an alternate universe. Like anything that happens here could be easily erased, if someone wanted that to happen. We'll hop on a boat tomorrow and get back to work. Aside from the sunburns, it'll be like this was all a bad dream."

Hayes had turned to face her. Their arms touched on the railing. Ness didn't remember moving closer.

"What I'm saying," Ness continued, taking a breath and rushing on, "is that if people wanted to revisit any old feelings, like a trial run, and it didn't work out, it could be easy to put it down to, um, dehydration and stress." She studied her nails and cleared her throat. "If that was of interest. To anyone." There. Easy peasy. Who didn't love a low-stakes proposition? Except, if he rejected it, as gently as he would—because he would do it as nicely as possible—it might crush her. Her therapist would argue that being emotionally vulnerable with those we care about was healthy. While Ness could agree with this intellectually, judging by the blood rushing to her face and the way her stomach was performing acrobatics, her body felt differently.

She reached out and snagged the beer, taking another disgusting sip. She could feel Hayes's eyes on her.

"Okay, then." Ness pushed away from the railing and passed the bottle back to Hayes. "I'm going to, um, go plank with Daisy. Over here."

Hayes's hand closed around her wrist, slowing her momentum. She looked over her shoulder at him, then turned to face him, her head tilted to the side as though she'd heard something interesting.

"You're infuriating," he said casually, leaning back on the railing, one hand still holding her in place.

"True. You're not always a refreshing spring breeze either."

He stared over her shoulder, eyes grazing across the house before coming back to rest on her.

"When you left, I shattered." He said it the same way Ness might have mentioned that she thought it would rain later. A throwaway comment during light conversation, as opposed to a dive into the murky pool of their mutual history.

Ness's breath hitched. She studied the wispy clouds drifting across the face of the half-moon as she tried, and failed, to come up with a response that felt sufficient. In the end, she kept it simple.

"I'm sorry. I just wanted to forget, and, at the time, the only way I knew how to do that was to leave it far, far behind me." And she was truly, deeply, eternally sorry. Not only for him, but also for herself. She'd missed out on someone who could have been one of the best things in her life. Not just her youth, but her entire life. She'd spent a very long time coming to terms with everything she'd abandoned, and sometimes she still felt the sting of loss. In that particular moment, the sting was more of a slap in the face.

She'd expected to see a storm in his eyes, a mess of feelings and words left unsaid, but instead they were as calm as the ocean.

"I put myself back together," he said quietly. "It was hard for me to understand—I still can't put myself entirely in your shoes back then. But I forgave you a long time ago, Ness."

He pulled her close, slowly, inch by inch, until she was pressed against him. She tilted her head to look up at him. His mouth curved up into a small smile.

"That being said, I do appreciate the apology."

"I'm still a mess," she cautioned.

"It's largely very charming," he said, bending so their noses were a hairsbreadth apart. His breath carried the scent of cinnamon and beer, which was an unexpectedly appealing combination.

Ness's mind raced, fast-forwarding through what could happen next. She could lift onto her toes and close the distance between their lips in the way every fiber of her being was insisting, or . . .

She exhaled and stepped back.

"There's probably enough going on without adding . . ." She waved her hand between the two of them. "I know this was my idea. God, I'm sorry. I'm a disaster." She took a deep, shaky breath, annoyed to feel tears welling in her eyes.

Hayes cleared his throat and opened his mouth to speak. Then closed it again and settled for a nod.

In the kitchen, Coco clanged something metallic in lieu of a bell and hollered, "Dinner is served!"

Ness smiled sadly at Hayes, trying to communicate a lifetime's worth of thoughts and feelings via the curve of her lips. Then she turned and went inside, wondering why she seemed totally incapable of accepting the good things that came her way.

Stars twinkled merrily in the clear night sky. The temperature had dropped to something edging enough toward cool(ish) that Ness had darted inside to grab a blanket. She parked herself on a dirty, lopsided lounger and peered out to sea, waiting for the lights of their rescue crew.

Over the course of the evening, everyone had trickled out to the balcony.

Bradley, Ian, Hayes, and Daisy were playing cards. Seven-years-expired tonic water and a bottle of gin someone had found in a bedroom sat on a nearby table in the shade. Every five minutes one of them would get up and walk the length of the balcony, staring at the dark ocean and searching for lights approaching their beach.

Daisy seemed to have recovered from whatever had gone on earlier. Color had come back into her cheeks, and, after receiving apologies ranging from wholehearted (Hayes) to nonexistent (Libby) for their reactions on the beach, she had moved from the periphery of the group back to her normal place in the midst of the action.

As Ness was surveying the veritable buffet Tyler had laid out, which, she noted uneasily, consisted of most of their remaining food stores, Coco emerged and plopped onto the lounger beside her. Her clothes were still filthy, but she smelled like vanilla and mint, and her face gave off a healthy, moisturized glow in the light spilling through the windows.

Ness wondered if it was too late to claim a shower for herself.

"I'll murder you if you tell her I said this," Coco said, leaning in close. "But I stole some of Libby's stupid-ass Kim Beauty serum and moisturizer from her bag, and that shit is gold. Look at this." She put her face close enough to Ness's that she could see the tiny, unplucked baby hairs of Coco's eyebrows. "I'm dewy. In a sexy way, not like I've been sweating out of every pore for the last forty-eight hours. I might have to . . . I can't believe I'm saying this. I might have to buy some. Jesus. I'm delirious. Kill me now, Ness. I'm too far gone." She fell back in a dramatic swoon, the back of her hand across her forehead.

Coco sat up again, eyeing the drinks on the table. She looked like she was about to go snag one, but she turned to Ness instead.

"Do you think they're going to come back?" she asked quietly. "They have to, right? They can't just *leave* us here."

"Of course they're coming back," Ness assured her, with more confidence than she felt.

Coco nodded. "Yeah, right. Of course." She stared out at the view of the island for a moment, then wrapped Ness in a one-arm hug and planted a noisy kiss on her head.

"You're right. We'll be out of here at daybreak. I can feel it." She pushed to her feet. "Now, what we need is a nice, calming drink." She sauntered over to the card game and swiped the bottle of gin from beside Bradley. She eyed Ian's glass none too subtly.

"It's tonic water," he said.

Coco continued to give him the eye. "You feeling okay?"

"Yeah. I must have had too much sun earlier."

Even from her lounger, Ness could see the cards shaking in his hand.

"Okay, man. Let us know if you need anything."

Ian's eyes narrowed. "What's that supposed to mean?"

"Nothing. It's a thing people say to friends in tough situations. You know, 'If you need something, we can help'? Surely you've had friends before?"

Ian's chair scraped against the concrete as he stood.

"Better ones than you."

Daisy was looking increasingly concerned, her lips pursed slightly, brow furrowed. She set her cards down and looked at Bradley, who shrugged and leaned back in his seat.

Coco's head cocked to one side. "I don't want to argue with you. I'm worried."

"I don't need your concern. *I'm fine.*"

They were engaged in a glaring competition when Libby came out, hair wrapped in a T-shirt Ness recognized as Bradley's. Libby looked between Coco and Ian before striding forward and shoving them both simultaneously in their respective chests.

"Break it up. You both look dumb and you'll feel worse in the morning." She reached up, pulled the shirt from her hair, and started gently squeezing additional moisture from her tresses as though nothing had happened.

"Listen," she continued, sounding bored. "I'm only saying this because I don't want to be held responsible if he dies."

Their heads snapped around to face her.

"Something's wrong with Tyler."

The Daily News

October 16, 2003. Ness Larkin, star of teen TV sensation *Ocean Views*, was arrested last night after an altercation at Bar Pietro. She was released hours later without charges.

This is not the first time Larkin, once considered a role model, has been in the news for poor behavior. Recent photos and information offered by a confidential source reveal a troubled woman, lashing out at photographers and engaging in high-risk behavior.

"Ness is spiraling," one person close to the actress told us. "Her dad leaving like he did really put her in a bad place—in life, and, like, mentally. She's a lost little girl without a parent to point her in the right direction. It's sad, really."

Robert Larkin took on the role of manager early in his daughter's career and continued in this capacity until earlier this year, when he reportedly vanished from the home the two shared. Documents from a recent civil suit filed by Agnes "Ness" Larkin against her father indicate he may have left his daughter on a financial precipice, with little recourse.

"Though the money was in shared accounts and many assets were in Mr. Larkin's name, these were purchased with money made by my client and were understood to be held for her in an unofficial trust," Ness Larkin's lawyer, Gregory Herford, said in a telephone interview today. "A girl should be able to trust her father."

CHAPTER 14

AN STAYED ON THE BALCONY TO "KEEP WATCH," BUT NESS FIGURED he just wanted some space. She wondered if someone should stay with him, but she dismissed the idea when he continued to snap at everyone who tried to talk to him. She'd keep an eye on him later tonight, she thought, after they dealt with whatever was happening with Tyler.

Libby dumped the now-soaked shirt on the couch and led them to a bedroom one door down from where Ness had tried to sleep the night before. Inside, someone was moaning.

"Um . . ." A blush spread charmingly across Daisy's cheeks. "Do we know what *kind* of moaning that is?" She lowered her voice. "What if he's using some of the, erm, *extras* this place stocks?"

Ew. Ness desperately shoved the mental picture away as it tried to form.

Hayes knocked. "Hey, Tyler. You okay in there, bud?"

The moaning stopped. "Go away. I could be contagious."

They exchanged alarmed looks. Contagious? An outbreak would really be the icing on a particularly unpleasant cake.

"What's going on in there, man?" Hayes continued, using his every-dude lingo.

They got a prolonged groan in response.

"I'll be . . . elsewhere," Libby said, already walking away.

Bradley watched her go, then stepped to the door and rested a hand on the knob.

"I'll do it. I've been immunized against thirty-six of the most common travel illnesses." He took a deep breath and his face settled into the role of Serious ER Doctor. "I'll ascertain what we're dealing with here. No one else breach the entry until I give the all-clear. Understood?"

Hayes coughed into his hand.

"Got it," Ness assured him, taking a step back to give him space.

Bradley turned the knob and strode in. He'd barely crossed the threshold before he turned and walked out again, slamming the door behind him.

"He's beyond help. It's the plague. Or measles. Possibly a severe case of adult chicken pox, but it's difficult to say without running a full panel." Bradley walked quickly down the hall. "I'm going to make sure Libby hasn't been spraying more of her poison. My throat is itchy."

Ness shoved the door open again and stared into the room. Tyler was sprawled out on the bed in his underwear, covered in red bumps. He scratched madly at his stomach and groaned again.

"Make it stooooop," he pleaded.

"No," Ness said, marveling at the number of mosquito bites on his pasty skin. "This is karma. It's your fault we're here in the first place." She coughed. "Not that I'm a petty, revenge-seeking individual."

"Of course not," Hayes said, coming in to stand next to her. "But it is somewhat satisfying nonetheless."

"Is he dying?" Daisy called from the door.

"No," Ness and Hayes said at the same time Tyler screamed "YES!"

Ness rolled her eyes heavenward and walked back to the door. She stuck her head out into the hallway and yelled, "Hey, Bradley?"

A pause. Then, from the kitchen, "Yeah?"

"Can someone die from mosquito bites?"

"Not usually. I guess malaria is a risk. Does the patient have malaria?"

Ness looked over her shoulder at the writhing Tyler. "You got your malaria shots?"

He nodded.

"Cool."

She resumed her hallway yelling. "Let's assume no on the malaria."

"A poultice of macerated leaves and healing herbs mixed with cool mud has been used by the natives of . . ."

Ness walked back into the bedroom, leaving Bradley to finish his monologue. It sounded as though he'd been waiting for the perfect opportunity to bust it out. She didn't want to rob him of the moment.

"I think I saw some calamine lotion in one of the bathroom cabinets," she said to Hayes. "I'll go grab it and some damp cloths. I don't know what else we can do." She looked at Tyler. "What were you *doing*, anyway?"

"None of your business." He groaned again and rolled to face the wall, sliding a hand down the back of his briefs and scratching enthusiastically.

"I've heard if you superheat a spoon and press it to a mosquito bite it cooks the itch right out of it," Hayes mused.

Tyler's eyes opened wide. The scratching paused.

"Calamine lotion will be fine." He clenched his fists and forced them to his sides. "See? Already getting better." He smiled, his mottled face stretching painfully around his grimacing lips.

Hayes took an involuntary step back. "I'll help you find that lotion," he said, starting for the door.

They closed the door behind them to drown out the sounds of nails on skin and pathetic whimpering.

Ness let out a breath. "Yikes," she said, heading toward the stairs. "How does that even happen? We all have bites, but nothing like *that*." She shuddered.

Hayes shrugged. "Maybe he was trying to set up a solo camp in the mangroves. Tylerville."

"Tylerburg?"

"Tylerhaven."

They reached the small, dark-purple guest bathroom. Hayes ducked into the adjacent bedroom in search of some reasonably clean linens they could soak.

Ness flicked on the bathroom light, taking a split second to enjoy how convenient it was having power, and started rummaging through the cabinet under the sink, shoving aside crusty bottles of cleaning product and spare light bulbs. *How long do we leave the generator running?* With her luck, the moment they shut everything down would be exactly when someone was trying to find them. Maybe they should revisit taking shifts and keeping a fire going on the beach.

She could only imagine how that conversation would go. *Hey guys, anyone want to spend the night on the beach, fighting off insects, peeing in the grass, and keeping the fire stoked?* That was assuming they could even get another fire going. There was a 90 percent chance she'd be the one searching for dry-ish wood in the dark, and while she was willing to sacrifice herself for the greater good, she couldn't help being annoyed well in advance that that's how it would shake out.

Finding only a robust supply of cherry-flavored All Natural, Long Lasting, Ultra Effective Aphrodisiac Supplement in the cupboard, she stood and pulled the fly-excrement-speckled mirror outward, revealing a smaller storage space and a bottle of calamine lotion (expiry date: February 2016). Ness twisted the top and peered at the contents, sniffed.

It looked pink and runny. It smelled . . . fine? She had no idea what bad calamine would smell like.

She had just turned off the light when something caught her eye. She pivoted slowly, trying to figure out what had grabbed her attention. *Probably a reflection on the shower tiles*, she thought, a mosaic of purple and iridescent colors that reminded Ness of a mermaid's tail. Along the wall opposite the sink loomed a ridiculously ornate black lacquered wardrobe. A gilded full-length mirror hung beside it. Ness wondered who'd been tasked with transporting all of this awful furniture up the hill from the beach, then pictured it being lowered piece by piece from a helicopter. She shook her head and tried to focus on her task.

Her stomach growled.

Taking one more look around and seeing nothing, she shrugged it off and started to leave. She was halfway back to Tyler's room when she remembered seeing a small bucket in the walk-in shower. It would be way easier to use that to refill the toilet tank than the larger, unwieldy cooler of seawater they'd parked in the main bathroom for flushing.

Ness trotted along the hallway yet again. Her dry throat itched and reminded her to top up the drinking water jug again before killing the generator for the night. They'd need at least enough to get them through the morning. Hopefully by then they'd be out of here, making haste to a paradise of unlimited icy beverages and professionals who could at least try to reverse the effect the last couple of days had had on her body.

Not bothering to turn the light on, Ness shoved the glass shower door along its gunked-up sliders and leaned in to grab the bucket.

She was halfway to standing, one leg still extended behind her for balance, when the rat launched itself across the shower floor, bouncing off the glass in its panic to escape and ricocheting onto Ness's foot.

Its claws were scrabbling over her bare ankle, its tiny, cool nose pressing against her shin. Her extended leg flew downward and her toes caught on one of the ornate handles of the wardrobe, pulling the door open. Something inside shifted and crashed against the inner wall. She pitched forward, her chin bouncing off the rough wall tile, teeth cracking together as her jaw was forced shut.

The rat was still clinging to her, its claws pricking her skin. Panicked, she lifted her leg, flinging it back and forth. Again, she lost her footing, and this time she landed in a split-second plank before crashing down chest first.

The startled rodent ran over her calves, out of the shower. From her position on the ground, cheek pressed to the floor, she watched it climb up the wardrobe's curved leg and disappear inside.

Groaning, she used shaky arms to push herself up and leaned back against the wall to catch her breath. She glared at the offending piece of furniture and wondered how many fresh bruises she'd have for her poor makeup artist to deal with. She hobbled to her feet, swiped up the stupid bucket that she was sure was entirely to blame for this entire incident, and walked toward the doorway, shoving the wardrobe door as she passed. Inside, movement caught her eye. Something far too large to be the rat.

She stopped then, wondering how hard she'd hit her head. She closed her eyes, opened them again, and decided she wasn't hallucinating. The wardrobe's wooden back had a sneaky secret panel, which had seemingly disengaged from its hinges during Ness's altercation with the rat. It had fallen diagonally into the storage space, leaving an opening just large enough for someone to step through with some light contorting of limbs. But instead of now having a clear view to the hideous purple paint of the wall, Ness was looking into an alcove built into a longer hallway running between the bathroom and bedroom. It was furnished with a leather love seat (of course), a red-velvet-shaded floor lamp, and a small table with a built-in cupboard. On the opposite wall was a two-way mirror, through which she could see Hayes in the bedroom next door. He was tearing bedsheets into strips like they were in a war zone.

"Hayes?" she said.

"Hayes!" she repeated, louder. His head shot up and he bundled the half-ripped sheet under his arm, making it to the door in four long steps.

He rounded the corner into the bathroom doorway.

"You okay? Why are you in the dark?"

He turned on the light. Ness continued to stare through the wardrobe, trying to make sense of what she was seeing.

"I came for a bucket." She raised said vessel. "There was a rat, and then . . ." She gestured in front of her. "Narnia, but make it porn-y."

"What? Did you hit your head?" He stepped into the room and gently took her chin between his thumb and forefinger, turning her face toward him. The lump of sheet fell to the floor. He smoothed her hair back from her forehead, still staring into her eyes.

"Hayes," she said softly, running a hand up the side of his face, taking a second to enjoy the feel of stubble under her palm.

"Mmhmm?" His gaze was on her lips now.

"Look." She turned his head so he was looking through the gap at the back of the wardrobe. She watched as he took in the hidden room, tripod, and small camera pointing into the space where he'd just been.

His hands fell to his sides and his mouth dropped open.

As they stood there, Daisy walked into the empty bedroom and grabbed a pillow. A red light on the camera blinked.

She sniffed the pillow, scowled, sighed, and carried it out with her.

The blinking stopped.

Hayes and Ness looked at each other, then back at the camera.

Hayes's shoulders drooped.

"I hate this fucking island."

Ness had hastily deposited the bucket—now filled with cool seawater—along with strips of sheet and the bottle of calamine lotion at Tyler's bedside, ignoring his pleas for her to apply the lotion for him.

Now she stood in the hallway outside the purple bathroom as Daisy, Coco, Libby, Bradley, and even Ian crammed in, staring into the wardrobe with matching looks of wide-eyed horror.

They started talking at the same time.

"This is disgusting."

"Who *was* this guy?"

"I can't say I'm surprised."

"How long has that camera been here?"

They paused, considering. Bradley broke the silence.

"Well, who's going in?"

Daisy looked at him, aghast. "Um, no one?"

"There could be supplies."

"There are rats," Ness said. "Big ones."

"What if it's booby-trapped?" Libby asked.

Ian snorted. "Ha. Booby. On the porn island."

Ness rolled her eyes.

Coco groaned. "This can't be real. I'm no saint, but I haven't done enough bad shit to deserve being here."

Dust tickled Ness's throat and she coughed into her elbow.

As one, the group turned to look at her.

"You should do it," Libby said. "You found it."

As if that made it her responsibility.

"Yeah," Ian chimed in from where he crouched in the corner, fore-arms resting on his thighs. "And you already fought the rat. It associates your scent with danger. You'll be safe . . . from that, at least."

Ness stared at them in disbelief.

"I'll go." Hayes edged into the room and stuck his head into the wardrobe. His shoulders hit both outer edges of the door. He pivoted sideways and stuck a leg through.

"Should have done more yoga," he grunted, trying to execute the world's widest squat.

"Fine. *Fine.* I'll go." Ness shoved past Bradley, grabbed the back of Hayes's shirt, and heaved until he backed up enough for her to pass. It was a spacious bathroom, but not meant for seven adults.

Before she had a chance to consider her life choices, she hopped into the wardrobe, feeling the cracked floor of it bow beneath her. Quickly, she jumped down to the other side, into the hidden room, landing in a crouch, ready to leap away from any traumatized rodents that might be awaiting her, seeking revenge.

Dust motes floated around her head, but nothing squeaked or bit her or otherwise incited immediate panic. Ness stood and looked around.

The walls were papered in dark-red and gold damask, and the well-worn black leather love seat sat against the far wall, centered on the mirror looking into the bedroom.

She turned in a slow circle and could suddenly see Daisy standing on the closed toilet seat, staring apprehensively at the wardrobe.

"The full-length bathroom mirror is a two-way," she called out, receiving a chorus of groans and expletives in response.

Ness went back to the opening, where Hayes's concerned face looked back at her.

"There's a hallway," she said, pointing toward it. "I'm going to see where it goes."

"Wait!" said Coco.

Ness sighed with relief. She didn't have to do this alone.

Coco nodded at the camera. "Can you turn that off first?"

Ness's nostrils flared, a wealth of aggressive, unhealthy feelings bubbling up. Friendship only went so far, it seemed.

She wrapped her hands around the tripod to collapse it, picked the whole thing up, and threw it into the wardrobe, where it landed with a satisfying crash.

"You do it," she said, and walked off, trying not to touch anything.

Ness followed the narrow hallway around the perimeter of the bedroom toward the back of the house. Her shoulders pressed against the walls on either side as she edged through, and she wondered how anyone larger could ever fit.

There were ornate sconces mounted high on the walls. Someone had, not surprisingly, chosen light bulbs that mimicked candlelight. They flung odd shadows and seemed on the verge of going out at any moment.

She rounded a corner and found herself at a heavy metal door. She paused, out of sight of anyone watching her go, and talked herself into continuing in a low voice.

"There's no reason to be scared. Sure, someone is maybe spying on us. And yeah, that's really creepy. But probably the only things in here are the rats, and they know you're invincible. There is a small, very small, minuscule chance that whatever hell-beast left that skin by the shed knows how to get in here, because what would secret rooms be without secret monsters? But that seems far-fetched. It would hate the smell of stinky, scared humans. I know I do. Right? Right. Now, onward. Scope it out. See if you can find anything useful. Maybe there will be candy. Not that you should eat the candy."

"Who are you talking to?" Daisy whispered in her ear, making Ness scream. She clapped a hand over her mouth and doubled over, thankful she hadn't wet herself.

"*Myself*," Ness hissed. "What are you? Some kind of stealth ninja? Jeez." She took a deep breath, collecting herself, and exhaled loudly.

"Anyone else joining us?" Ness peered around Daisy, her heart still hammering.

"Uhh, no. They're checking the other rooms for cameras."

"Right."

"So, what's the plan?" Daisy whispered.

"Why are you whispering?" Ness whispered back.

Daisy looked momentarily perplexed, then said, "It seems like a situation that calls for sneaking?"

"I refuse to sneak," Ness said at a normal volume, startling them both with how loud it sounded. She gave herself a moment to recover before continuing.

"The plan is to go through this stupid door and see what we find. If there are cameras, we'll turn them off. If there are snacks, we will eat some and then take the rest back." She took in the look of horror on Daisy's face. "What?"

"It's . . . team spirit? It feels, I don't know, criminal to eat food the others don't know about."

"Did Libby offer you any of her vegan protein gummies?" Ness demanded. "Did Bradley bring out his collection of calorie-dense bulk-up shake powders? Or maybe Ian let you sample his honey-chili-infused dried mangoes?" She didn't wait for an answer, or explain that she didn't actually know if anyone was hoarding secret calorie sources, though Bradley's seemingly boundless energy for strenuous workouts was more than a little suspicious.

Always watch out for Number One. Her dad's voice sounded in her head, making her shudder.

She continued. "No, of course they didn't. Because they're a bunch of self-centered assholes who think they're smarter and sneakier and more important than everyone else. It's our turn, Daisy. Let's be the assholes."

Their opportunity for selfish gain was cut short when the door swung open into what could loosely have been called the backyard, but only in that it was at the back of the house. There was nothing particularly yard-like about it in the traditional sense. Tall grass tickled Ness's calves. The cool breeze brushed against her face. She inhaled deeply, letting the smell of the ocean, accented with a touch of gas from the generator, start to wash away the extreme ick she'd been feeling.

The night was surprisingly dark, the crescent moon covered by gathering clouds. A heaviness in the air promised rain.

"Hey, Ness?" Daisy's voice was filled with dread.

She sighed, wishing for the millionth time she was literally almost anywhere else.

"Yeah?"

"Look."

She really didn't want to, but she did.

Along the back of the house, nestled into the overgrown creeping vines and foliage high on each window, was a ragged array of blinking red lights.

Just One Bump

by Ian James

I became an expert at hiding. Not only my drug use, but the effect it was having on the rest of my life. My best-kept secret was the fact that I was absolutely, entirely, 100 percent broke.

CHAPTER 15

THE HEAP OF COMPACT VIDEO CAMERAS SAT ON THE CRACKED GLASS atop the iron coffee table in the living room. There were different models. Some looked like security cameras, and others more like high-end adventure-capture devices. On the bottom of each one was an asset tag declaring it the property of the Good Things Network.

After making their discovery, Ness and Daisy had gone back to break the news to the rest of the group. They'd completed a search of the interior of the house, finding a dozen more recording devices nestled beneath furniture and wedged into the dark crevices that seemed to abound in their crumbling surroundings. Ness couldn't help wondering if the perpetrator was among them and had pocketed more of their own goods as they went along.

Everyone was gathered around in the dim mood lighting afforded by the collection of velvet-shaded table lamps, eyeing the pile of tech like they were trying to figure out how to defuse an explosive. A gentle rain pattered against the roof.

"Well, whose are they?" Bradley asked, cutting to the chase.

Everyone executed a perfect "Who, me?" wide-eyed look of innocence. Well, Tyler's wasn't the best, but he was also so busy trying to scratch the center of his back that it was hard to tell if he'd even heard the question. His arms and legs were coated with dried calamine, making him look as if someone had dipped him in Pepto Bismol and set him in the sun to dry.

"Listen," Ness said, perched on the arm of the couch. The wood of the inner frame dug through the remaining padding into her backside. It was still more comfortable than the current conversation. "No one likes the idea of being spied on. It's creepy and, I assume, illegal. But so far, no harm's been done. There's no Wi-Fi or cell service, so there's no way anyone was streaming footage. Whatever was captured is still on memory cards, on this island. Get rid of it, and we can all move forward with our lives." She tried not to sound as exasperated and angry as she felt, but she suspected she had failed.

Libby didn't mind sounding exasperated and angry. "Don't you think you're jumping ahead a bit? How do you know anyone here set those up?"

"They're network-owned, Libby."

Libby examined her nails, though Ness could see that her hands weren't particularly steady. No one spoke for a long moment.

"I can't believe any of us would do this," Daisy said from a cross-legged position on her mattress. It sounded like she meant she *wouldn't* believe it, because that would take an already untenable situation to a whole new level of horror.

Coco went to sit beside her, wrapping a comforting arm around her shoulders, then gave each of them a hard look. "It's tough for me to stomach as well."

Perched on the edge of the sofa, elbows resting on his knees as he leaned forward, Bradley shook his head ruefully. "Desperate times can lead to desperate actions."

"Uh-huh." Ness tried to keep her voice calm. "Listen, I might be feeling extra paranoid, but . . . should we consider whether the person who set up the cameras is also the one who 'lost' our boat?"

"Ugghhh, just admit you fucked up!" Libby snarled, hands clenched at her sides.

"But it makes sense!"

"Nothing about this makes sense." Ian had moved to his mattress as well and was sprawled out, arm resting over his eyes to block out the light. "But maybe Ness has a point."

Everyone started talking over each other, simultaneously making accusations and refusing to admit anything nefarious was going on. They all, at great volume, declared they had nothing to do with this. What could *they*—the successful entrepreneur, cop drama king, limited series darling, movie star, passionate production assistant living his dream—stand to gain from stooping so low?

"Fine," Hayes said loudly, standing. "You know what? It doesn't even matter who did it."

Ness's head jerked up. *Um, what? Yes, it did.*

Hayes continued, "Whoever's responsible, leave any additional memory cards on this table by," he checked his watch, "nine tomorrow morning."

"Or what?" Libby asked. "There needs to be a consequence, or why would anyone actually do that?"

Ness ignored Libby and looked pleadingly at the people around her. The people who had maybe never been real friends, but who had history. They shouldn't be turning on each other. Certainly not like *this*.

"This is no one's best moment," she said to them. "What's happened here, the things we've discussed and done, it's the product of a traumatic experience. An experience we're all a part of. No one benefits from sharing this with the world."

"Um, someone would definitely benefit," Ian rasped. "You know how much that shit could sell for?"

"Yeah—well, no, actually, I don't really. I assume a lot. But everyone here has something to lose if those files get out. And no one needs the cash—except maybe me and Tyler. How much do production assistants make these days?"

"Oh, virtually nothing, but my mom owns the second-largest mayonnaise company in North America. I'm good for cash. The PA thing is a passion project."

Libby looked mildly apoplectic. Even Hayes seemed shocked, but recovered faster than the rest of them.

"Leave the memory cards on the table and we'll forget it ever happened," he reiterated, ignoring the sidebar conversation.

"Why would anyone give up all that information?" Libby asked. "By now, they've got something on all of us, even if that something is just us looking like garbage on this goddamn rock in the ocean."

Coco glared at her. "Because maybe, deep down in their cold, traitorous hearts, there's a glimmer of humanity, and they don't want to be total shit-heels."

"Yeah, that," Ness said, heading for her saggy mattress on the floor and a sleepless night.

The next morning, nine o'clock came and went. No memory cards appeared. No boats, either, despite the tractor-beam gazes of the group, who seemed to be walking down to the beach or standing vigil on the balcony in a depression-inducing rotation.

The hopeful sheen from dinner the night before had been blasted away and replaced by a cold layer of suspicion, and people drifted through the house alone, looking at each other with carefully blank expressions. None of this was helped by the fact that they'd consumed nearly all their food while celebrating their certain rescue. Ness's stomach felt like it was trying to eat itself.

The cameras, thanks to a convenient sledgehammer, were now nothing but shattered plastic and metal, collected and tidily swept into a pile displayed on the kitchen counter beside the water jugs.

The thing was, they'd all proven themselves to be totally capable of shit-heelery in the past. The more Ness thought about it, the more tangled a web she wove in her mind, until she was ready to scream.

To distract herself, she surveyed the paltry remnants of their food stores and updated the list.

- ~~21~~ 3 bars of ~~various kinds~~ one kind
- ~~6~~ 1 packages of peanut butter crackers
- ~~1 large packet of turkey jerky~~ 1 piece of jerky
- ~~6 apples~~

- ~~1 orange~~
- ~~2 croissants, smushed~~
- ~~12 chocolate-coated granola bars, melty~~
- ~~8 premixed cocktails~~
- ~~7 bottles of light beer~~
- ~~16 bottles of water~~
- ~~Box of assorted scavenged alcohol~~ ½ bottle vodka, ¼ bottle rye
- ~~1 cheese sandwich~~

Ness blew out a dismayed breath and listened, hoping to hear the sound of approaching motorcraft. If no one showed up by nightfall, things were bound to get ugly.

"Pass me one of those?" Bradley sauntered across the room, sweating profusely from his second workout of the day, and gestured to the bars. Ness couldn't figure out how he had energy to do more than exist at this point, and she was appalled by his audacity, asking for what amounted to one-third of their remaining food.

"I can pass you one-quarter of one. This," she gestured to the items between them, "is all we have left." Saying it out loud made the situation feel real in a way it hadn't when the words had been confined to Ness's head.

"I don't suppose you have a secret stash in your bag, do you?" She said it jokingly, but a flicker of emotion passed over Bradley's face. Something that looked very much like guilt.

"Bradley." Ness walked around the kitchen island, her hand trailing across the counter, fingertips getting covered in the dust that seemed to gather continuously from the disintegrating drywall, no matter how often they wiped the surface. She had to stop herself from grabbing the front of his shirt and yelling in his face.

"Bradley," she repeated. "We need to work together here. If no one comes for us today, we're going to have to figure out how to feed ourselves or we'll starve." He opened his mouth to speak, but Ness cut him off before he could dive into a soliloquy about the island's natural bounty and his ability to harness same.

"I'm sure we're capable of solving that problem," Ness went on, "but it would be really, *really* great to have a more than three hundred calories worth of granola standing between us and that moment."

She looked at him expectantly. He gazed back. Sweat trickled down his temple and dripped onto the floor. Ness wondered how survival had devolved into a staring contest.

She sighed, feinted right, and then sprinted left into the living room, where Bradley's messenger bag was sitting beside one of the makeshift beds on the floor. Snagging it, she dodged his attempt to grab it, and put the couch between them. She hugged the bag to her chest and tried to figure out her next move.

Admittedly, her current course of action felt immature, disrespectful, and desperate, but Ness could own up, at least internally, to the fact that she was currently all of those things.

"Um, hey, guys," Daisy said uncertainly from the doorway. "What's going on?" She spoke casually, as though Bradley wasn't about to launch himself across the couch at Ness.

"Agnes has decided to police our personal belongings."

Ness rolled her eyes. "*Agnes* simply suggested that if people have personal stashes of food, now would be a great time to pool them *so we don't starve*."

"But . . . we're leaving today. They're coming back for us." Daisy looked hopefully out the window.

"And what if they don't?"

It was Bradley's turn for an eye roll. "We can worry about that if it happens."

"Don't you think having a plan might be better than winging it? What happened to cataloging our resources?"

"Don't *you* think you might want to avoid burning more bridges?"

He had a point. "Put the bag down."

"Do you promise to share anything you have if we're still here at sundown?"

"Do you have to make it sound so ominous?" He looped his fingers behind his neck and then dropped his arms out wide. "God. Yes, sure. If we're still here tonight, which we won't be, we'll pool personal resources."

Ness leaned over the couch and handed him the bag. He swiped it forcefully from her grasp, slung the strap over his shoulder, and stalked out of the room.

Daisy's eyes were wide. "Have you always been so good at making friends?"

At eleven o'clock, after an early lunch of water and one-quarter of a bar that was supposed to be maple donut flavor but landed somewhere closer to stevia-coated wood shavings held together by paste, Ness headed down to the beach for some time alone with her thoughts.

If this were a TV mystery, someone would have said something that sparked a Sherlockian synapse, connecting the cameras to some obscure clue and a barely remembered conversation. Like lightning, the solution would hit her. The culprit would be identified and brought to justice.

What would justice look like? Locking them up in the room full of mirrors, sentenced to watch themselves age from every angle?

She eyed an iguana that was sunning itself on a rock.

The problem—well, one of many problems—was that, as far as she could tell, *she* was the one with the most to gain from the contraband footage.

Bradley's career wasn't a blazing success, but he was working steadily. He'd never fulfill his not-so-secret dream to be the next Bond, but he also wouldn't find himself waiting tables or moonlighting as a celebrity MC at someone's wedding anytime soon.

Ian had just finished the ultimate comeback. He'd managed an epic career pivot, going from black sheep to golden boy, beloved for his willingness to be so open. A couple of months earlier he'd announced that he was donating half his book royalties to various charities dedicated to helping those who faced the same challenges he continued to overcome.

Coco was cruising through her career, scoffing in the face of anyone who said an actress's opportunities dropped off a cliff as soon as they hit thirty. If anything, she was busier than ever.

Libby had Kim Beauty, while Tyler could apparently rely on his inheritance for future security, even if it didn't fulfill his artistic passion, and Daisy's time in front of the camera was off to a dynamite start with a one-way upward trajectory.

Hayes was pure A-list. The idea of him stooping this low was laughable. Or was she blinded by lust and barely buried feelings? She kicked at the sand, annoyed at her obvious lack of detective skill.

She was finishing her third trip up and down the beach without making any great deductive leaps when Daisy caught up to her.

"Can I talk to you?" she asked, not at all out of breath and only faintly flushed, despite the unforgiving sun blasting them from above. "Is anyone else here?" She looked around, peering into the scrub and mangroves.

"Just me and my feelings," Ness quipped. "What's up?" She lowered herself to sit on the sand, with Daisy following suit.

"I think Ian's in withdrawal," Daisy said, spitting it out quickly, as if she was scared she might lose her nerve.

"But he's written a whole book about sobriety," Ness replied automatically. Even as she said it, she saw the signs she'd been so resolutely ignoring.

"He's cranky. Unpredictable. Flu-like symptoms." Daisy checked these off on her fingers. "Even back in Florida he kept taking off, disappearing in the middle of things."

"We shouldn't jump to conclusions." The leap had already been made, but Ness felt as though she had to be a voice of reason. Someone had to try to keep this roller coaster on the rails. She sighed, hearing her therapist's voice in her head. *Ignoring a problem doesn't make it go away; it gives it time to grow.*

She rubbed a hand over her face, feeling the grit of salt and sand on her cheeks.

"Okay, well, how long does that last? Maybe he's through the worst of it."

But Daisy was shaking her head. "He's getting worse. Sweats, irregular breathing. Depending on what he's been taking, he could start having seizures." Her eyes got big and tears welled. One rolled gracefully down her cheek.

"Okay," Ness said, nodding reassuringly. "I hear you. This is serious." She looked out to sea, thinking about the options they had, which were basically none.

"How do you know so much about this? Did you have a role as an addiction counselor or something?"

Daisy laughed, but with more bitterness than Ness had ever heard from her. She crossed her arms over her chest and joined Ness in ocean gazing.

"Or something," she said.

There was a long pause. The waves whooshed. The wind danced through their hair.

"My brother," she finally said.

"Your brother's an actor too?"

"My brother—my twin, actually—is an addict. Opioids. Oxy, mostly, but he'll take whatever he can get his hands on." She rubbed her hands up and down her arms. "He's had . . . trouble, dealing with things. I didn't consider how different everything would be if I, you know, *made it*. Because, come on, how many girls actually do?" She sighed. "It makes the dream a little bit of a nightmare, but it'll be okay. He's in rehab now. Again." Leaning back, she buried her hands in the hot sand, turning her face fully to the sun, eyes closed. "You know, I took this gig to pay for his treatment?"

"I'm sorry," Ness said, feeling entirely insufficient and unprepared.

Daisy blinked her eyes open and smiled sadly.

"Me too. And I know there's nothing we can do to help Ian. I tried talking to him—dumb, but I can't help wanting to fix things, especially when so much is out of control." She winced and looked guilty. "That's where I was when the boat came. In the stupid mangroves, trying to fix a problem that has nothing to do with me. Anyway, I needed someone else to know."

Another pause.

"Do you think we should tell the others?" Daisy asked.

"No," Ness blurted, imagining the fuel this would add to an already dangerous situation, while also wondering just how many secrets one person could—or should—reasonably keep. "No," she said again, more slowly. "It's not ours to tell. If they figure it out, that's different."

Daisy nodded. "Okay." She rolled her head from side to side, stretching out her neck. "I'm going to try to talk to Ian. Maybe sit with him until someone comes. It shouldn't be much longer, right?" She shielded her eyes and looked up at the sky, as if a helicopter might magically appear overhead.

"Here's hoping."

Ness had pretty much bottomed out on hope, but it seemed like the right thing to say.

Ness and Daisy stood over an unconscious Ian, eyes darting between his prone form and Libby's insolent pose.

"What?" she demanded. "He was being *intolerable*. He kept snapping at me, saying I was walking too loudly. And then," her voice rose several octaves, "*then* he accused me of setting up those cameras. Can you believe it? Like I have any—*any*—interest in the personal lives of you lot."

Ness decided not to point out that Libby had a borderline obsessive interest in Bradley's personal life, despite the fact that they'd been divorced for years.

Libby started pacing back and forth across the living-room-turned-hostel.

"You can understand, of course, can't you? As you said yourself, Ness, this is a time of trauma. A time of unprecedented strain on our minds and bodies. I had to *protect myself.*"

"*By drugging him?*" Ness couldn't believe this. Well, she could, actually.

"It's perfectly safe," Libby assured them. She caught their wide-eyed looks of complete and utter skepticism.

"What would *you* have done, then?" she huffed. "Offered him another bite of granola bar? Suggested we try to brew up some calming herbal remedy from tropical leaves and parrot feathers? Maybe record him in all his misery and then sell it to the media?" She arched an eyebrow pointedly.

Ness's mouth dropped open. "You think *I* did it?"

"Oh, come on, Ness. Of course you did. You're the one here with the least to lose and the most to gain. Even Tyler has more career aspiration than you."

"That's not very fair," Daisy tried to interject, but Libby's words ran right over top.

"And you've set a precedent for this, haven't you?"

Ness's stomach did a flip.

"What, you thought I forgot?"

No, but she'd naively thought they could avoid dissecting all her wrongdoings in great detail.

Daisy's eyes darted back and forth between them.

"Ness here is a real entrepreneur." Libby had slowed her pacing and now stood silhouetted in front of the window. She'd always been great at catching the best light. "I wouldn't trust her with any of your secrets. You never know who she'll sell them to."

Ness opened her mouth to defend herself. It had been a mistake. A mistake she'd apologized for profusely at the time. And, if anyone wanted to nitpick, *she* hadn't been the one to profit.

She'd been a drunk kid who talked to the wrong person. A down-on-his-luck model named Benji who bore a striking resemblance to

Kevin from the Backstreet Boys. Ness had always had a soft spot for Kevin. He never got enough credit.

A few vodka sodas in, she'd let slip that she was out that night with her friend, who was sad about a role she'd been passed over for—her big leap from TV to film. She'd gestured messily at Libby, who was drowning her sorrows on the dance floor.

Benji put two and two together and leaked to the media that Libby had lost her chance to play Spiderman's love interest.

It's not like the news wouldn't have gotten out anyway, but that wasn't the point. And Ness got that. She got it then, and she understood it even more now, with twenty years of additional life experience under her belt. Libby had felt betrayed by someone she'd trusted, and she was right. Ness had messed up—badly.

"You really know how to hold a grudge." Ness took in Libby's ragged nails, the sunburn arcing across her forehead, the purple-tinged circles under her eyes. "Which is totally valid."

Libby's eyes widened a fraction in surprise, then narrowed again, this time with suspicion.

"Truly. I deserve every bit of your disdain. But I didn't do this." She braced her hands on the back of the couch, ignoring the urge to collapse over it onto the cushions and stay there until someone showed up to take them away. "Believe what you want, Libs, if riding a wave of righteous anger gets you through." She walked through to the kitchen and snagged half a piece of turkey jerky from the pathetic food pile.

"Daisy, I think staying with Ian is a good idea. Someone should keep an eye on him. I'm going fishing."

July 27, 2022

Dear Ms. Payne,

Thank you for taking the time to speak with me today. We at Greenmount Haven understand the emotional toll that substance abuse and addiction can take on our clients' family and loved ones, and we strive to relieve some of this burden through our highly recommended private counseling services, which you can learn more about via our website.

However, despite the trying circumstances, we do require payment for your brother's time with us thus far. Simon has come so far in these past weeks, and he would benefit from being permitted to complete this initial full cycle at Greenmount.

I have attached the relevant invoice. Please note that, unfortunately, if we do not receive at least partial payment within seven days, and complete remittance within thirty days, we will need to consider more serious action.

Regards,
Martin P. Freehampton
Accounts Receivable
Greenmount Haven

CHAPTER 16

NESS SAT ON A BIG, SUN-WARMED ROCK, PARTIALLY SHADED BY A cluster of palm trees. Her fishing line dangled in the water. She bobbed the pole up and down every few seconds, reeled the line in, and recast.

She'd gone fishing with her dad a couple of times when she was a kid. For a while, he'd been seeing a woman who had a cabin on a sparkling lake surrounded by trees. There'd been a little strip of sandy beach, and Ness had spent hours there, playing with the kids from the house next door.

Some mornings, when the sun was barely peeking over the trees and the lake was shrouded in mist, her dad would wake her up, hand her a thermos of hot chocolate, and take her out in a little tin boat that putt-putted slowly across the water. They'd find a spot that seemed promising, drop the anchor, and spend the next hour quietly arguing about who was going to get the worms out of their little Styrofoam container, and giggling when the other person got their line hooked on an overhanging tree branch, or excitedly reeled in a tangle of weeds.

Ness never knew how to feel about those types of memories. They were sweet, and part of her wanted to enjoy them like a cat basking in a patch of sunlight. But she also wondered how far back the con went . . . if those moments were him planting seeds of love and trust that meant everything to her and little to him.

She wondered if he'd seen the news. If he knew she was missing.

If he cared.

"Any luck?"

Ness jumped, nearly dropping the fishing rod into the ocean.

"Sorry." Hayes climbed up and sat beside her, his tanned legs hanging over the edge of the rock far enough that his toes grazed the surface of the water.

"No, it's fine. My mind was . . . elsewhere." She bobbed the line some more. "And no, no luck. I might need to relocate. See if the fish are hanging out around the corner. Or maybe they just hate jerky."

"Who could hate jerky?"

"Right? Seemed foolproof. Though I'm going to be pretty disappointed if I've sunk my dinner into the sea for no reason."

"I'll share mine with you. There's a tiny portion of a granola bar up there calling my name."

She smiled at him. "How did we get so lucky?"

There was a moment, as the water lapped at the rock and the leaves rustled softly above them, when it was easy to imagine they were on a well-earned vacation. That they'd taken a different path all those years ago and ended up here, together, on purpose.

A gray cloud rolled in front of the sun, giving Ness's eyes some relief from the constant glare of light reflecting off the water. She reeled in her line and stood.

"Not that a microscopic bite of granola isn't everything I was hoping for in a well-rounded and nutritious meal, but . . . want to help me find a better fishing spot?"

They walked along the beach and around the tip of the island, trying to find something that screamed "Fish here!" Eventually they settled on the concrete dock that jutted out past the rest of the beach—the same one they'd nearly crashed into on arrival—hoping there was a reef or something in the deeper water that would draw the edible creatures in.

The wind had picked up and clouds were starting to gather. Ness hoped it wouldn't rain. She *really* didn't feel like being trapped in the house with the others. A flock of birds took off from the trees, soaring above them and away from the island. *Show-offs.*

Ness carefully threaded another chunk of jerky onto the hook and then wrapped long strands of grass around the metal, knotting them as tightly as she could, hoping the green tendrils would be attention-grabbers for those little fishy eyes. She plopped the whole mess into the top three inches of water and stared at it critically. The grass waved like alien tentacles around a salty, meaty center.

"Well. Let's hope these fish are stupid and very hungry."

Standing there with her bare feet burning on the sunbaked concrete, Ness prayed to the fishing gods, then the gods of rescue services, and finally to the gods of patience, forgiveness, and generally not being an ass to those around her.

Hayes was pacing slowly behind her on the beach, hands linked behind his back, looking for any washed-up bits of fish they could use for bait.

"Libby thinks I'm the camera culprit," she blurted, instantly regretting it. The last thing she wanted to do was sow the seed of doubt in Hayes's mind as well. *Unless that's why he's here right now. Maybe he's keeping an eye on you.*

"Huh," Hayes said. His shoes were in his backpack and his eyes were on the sand. He'd already stepped on one pointy shell and was clearly not interested in repeating the experience.

"That's it? 'Huh'?"

He looked at her. "Well, did you do it?"

"No!"

"Then don't worry about it."

Ness reeled in her line and cast again. "But I *am* worried about it. I'm a very skilled worrier. Being concerned about any and all things is one of my key attributes." A small raindrop landed on her cheek.

"How's that going for you this week?"

"Super great. There's so much to fret about. I'm building new worry muscles I didn't know I had. I'm going to try out for the stress Olympics when we get home." She walked her line along the edge of the dock from the end until she was standing in the middle of the long side, where she could see Hayes without craning her neck.

One side of his mouth quirked up in a half smile.

"There's some positive thinking, but I think I might have you beat." He turned his head, looking out at the endless waves. His broad shoulders slumped ever so slightly.

"You holding up okay?" she asked.

"Yup!" he answered quickly, and with a very suspect level of cheer.

"Because it's been a wild twenty-four hours. It would be very normal for you to have concerns."

He nibbled at his thumbnail, seemingly lost in thought, and Ness decided not to push, at least not yet.

The clouds broke open just as something tugged tentatively on her hook. She froze, water dripping down her face, and gave the fishing rod a gentle pull toward her. There it was again.

"I have a nibble," she breathed, terrified that any noise, any movement, might scare off whatever was dumb enough to want what she had to offer.

Hayes jogged to her side and stared into the water as though he was thinking about jumping in and grabbing the fish—Ness really hoped it *was* a fish and not someone's shoe or an inedible creature of the deep. This actually raised a good question.

"How will we know if we can eat it?" she whispered.

"If it's not an old tire or spewing poison from its eyes, we'll eat it."

"Fair."

Feeling more movement on her line, she took a deep breath, gave the rod a jerk, and started reeling. Her clothes were already soaked through. She blinked water out of her eyes and quickly wiped her face with one hand.

Hayes was beside her, body tensed and ready to pounce.

She'd caught something. It was still there, pulling against the hook, dragging through the water. Ness's stomach danced with anticipation.

Don't get too excited, she cautioned herself, even as her mouth started to water at the thought of freshly cooked fish. *Almost there.*

The water was pitted by raindrops and she squinted, leaning forward, trying to get a glimpse of her catch.

And then, there it was, dangling at the end of her line. A fish.

Hayes charged forward, flinging salty spray at her face as he grabbed the poor thing by the tail, took a running leap to a nearby rock, and thwacked it, hard, against the surface. The fish lay still.

"Whoa," Ness breathed, staring at her catch. Its scales shimmered in the gray light, silvery pink with a yellow stripe running along its side to fan out into a bright yellow tail. It was a bit longer than her forearm.

A grin spread across her face, mirroring the one Hayes was sporting.

"You did it!" he cried, wrapping his arms around her waist and twirling her through the air.

"I did it!" Ness's hands grasped his shoulders and she turned her face up to the rain, laughing. The spinning slowed, and Hayes lowered her slowly to the ground, their bodies still pressed together.

He looked down at her, wiping a strand of wet hair from her cheek. His thumb brushed across her lower lip, and his hand moved down to rest at the base of her neck, stroking her jawline as he went.

Ness's eyes were locked on his, one of her hands on his chest, the other resting on his hip. She hooked a finger through a belt loop and tugged him to her, then reached around the back of his neck and pulled him down until her lips could reach his. She sighed against his mouth. He growled and pulled her closer. Ness forgot about her fish.

Part of her had hoped it would be lackluster. Maybe she'd built him up into such a mythical lost love in her mind that the reality couldn't possibly compare.

Turned out, the reality was like being blasted to the moon.

Hayes kissed like he lived his life, gently, but with passion and dedication to the subject at hand. Speaking of hands . . . one of his had crept up her back to wrap in her hair while the other danced over the space between her shirt and jeans, scorching the bare skin of her lower back.

Ness's arms were draped around his neck as she pressed her entire body against his. His stubble scraped her cheek as he changed angles and dove back in. Her knees threatened to give out.

Finally, Ness convinced herself to separate her lips from Hayes's. Blood was rushing in her ears. She saw stars. They stood for a moment, her forehead resting on his, both with their eyes closed as they came back to earth.

Thunder rumbled and they broke apart, panting. Lightning shot across the sky, sending jagged streaks of light into the gray sea.

Out of the corner of her eye, Ness caught the movement of silver against the rocks. She turned her head just in time to see her fish, her beautiful, path-to-forgiveness-and-acceptance fish, being snapped up in the beak of one of the white-and-gray birds from the snake shack. The fish's tail flopped as the bird launched itself into the air and flapped away, heading inland. Ness watched it disappear from sight.

She looked from the rock, to the inner island, to Hayes, whose lips were parted in surprise as he processed what had happened.

"Well," Ness said, feeling the relief and hope of moments ago replaced by a heavy weight on her chest, "I guess we should head back." She hesitated for a moment before stepping out of Hayes's arms, giving him the chance to pull her back to him.

The rain fell harder and thunder boomed.

She looked back to where Hayes was still standing, glasses pushed up onto the top of his head, brow crinkled as though he was deep in thought.

"You good?" she called out, a myriad of questions within those two words. *Was that a mistake? Did you feel the same things I did? Why do you look like you're trying to do advanced physics in your head? What do we do now?*

He gave his head a little shake, sending water droplets tumbling from his hair down his face and neck. "Yeah." He smiled, but Ness wasn't convinced. Something in her stomach fluttered nervously. "Yeah, I'm good."

He picked up the fishing rod and started walking toward the house.

If they'd been on edge earlier, by their third day as castaways the residents of Ginger Cay were balancing on a precipice. Blindfolded. With a strong wind at their backs.

Where previously they'd naturally gathered, finding comfort in the presence of others—even if those others were often incredibly obnoxious—that afternoon Ness noticed everyone spreading out, wedging themselves into the farthest reaches of the house to find some privacy.

The last of the food had disappeared while Ness was out, and she bade a sad farewell to the idea of that granola bar.

Tyler, in a spurt of industriousness, had put as many open-topped containers as he could find outside to collect rainwater, and then he hung his wet shirt and shorts to dry in the kitchen. They dangled, reminiscent of an unstuffed scarecrow, from cabinet handles while Tyler, wrapped cocoon-like in a blanket on one of the barstools, scribbled notes in the margins of magazine pages, mumbling to himself.

"We'll have so much to do once they find us. Somebody has to be addressing the potential for a gargantuan time overrun on the back end of filming because of this snafu, but heaven knows it will need adjustment." He looked at Ness. "How many recovery days do you think you'll need before resuming work? Two?" Not waiting for an answer, he bent his head to the page, close enough that his nose nearly touched the paper, and continued his frenzied scrawling, forehead scrunched in squinty concentration.

At some point, Ian had awoken from his forced slumber and relocated to the velvet couch. He was sitting cross-legged, playing solitaire and, Ness thought, looking at least marginally better, though the cards still shook in his hand and the circles under his eyes rivaled her own, which was really saying something.

Hayes had positioned himself on the floor, back against the day-bed, and was reading a script he'd pulled from his backpack, steadfastly pretending Ness didn't exist. Meanwhile, Ness pretended she wasn't watching him, waiting for some secret signal that things were, in fact, good.

He studied the pages with increasing intensity before taking off his glasses and rubbing his eyes. The bound stack of paper fell to the floor with a *thwap*, and he bent to pick it up, slid his glasses back on, and flipped through, finding his page again.

The rain started to slow. Ness stood at the window feeling restless. Rivulets of water ran down the glass, distorting the view of the trees and ocean into something abstract and eerie.

She told herself she wasn't watching for the boat.

Maybe it was only the heavy atmosphere of the rain, but the tension in the house felt palpable. It was just past five o'clock. The sun would set in a couple of hours, and they, Ness was sure, would still be here. Once the rain stopped, she vowed, she'd head to the beach and start a fire—a big one—even if they had to sacrifice some of the precious generator gas to get it started.

A sliver of pinkish-orange sun appeared, pushing its way through the cloud cover. Ness felt a tiny lightening of the pressure in her chest and was suddenly aware just how on edge she'd been, trapped in the house with so many flesh-and-blood ghosts of her past. She'd known it would be hard, coming back into the fray, but, their setting aside, she hadn't anticipated how difficult it would be to reengage on so many separate fronts.

There was, of course, the overarching theme of Ness Needs to Apologize, but beneath that ran currents of emotion that were hard to track and address in a way that felt both effective and true. Perhaps she'd played it all out so many times in her mind that the reality of it felt . . . off.

They'd left the kitchen door to the balcony open, the entry protected by an overhang that kept the water out but allowed the marginally cooler breeze to flow through. Ness walked outside, enjoying the feeling of the wet cement beneath her bare feet. The rain stopped, leaving a hazy mist resting atop the trees below. The clouds were already parting and making way for the sunset.

She closed her eyes and breathed in the wet air. It smelled of salt and loam and that special something found only in tropical air that she'd always associated with the vague promise of relaxation and easily found moments of joy. Her eyelids fluttered open and she looked across Ginger Cay, wondering if she'd ever feel the same about island vacations.

Thoroughly dejected, Ness retreated to the relative comfort of a plastic lounger, wiped it dry with a spare bedsheet, and watched the sun sink into the waves. One by one the others emerged from their various hidey-holes, until they were all standing at the railing like sentinels, holding phones up to the sky just in case service had suddenly begun to exist. It had not.

However, their positioning meant they were in a great spot to witness Daisy striding across the lawn just before full dark hit with a trio of large, very dead iguanas slung over her shoulder.

The balcony observers turned, speechless, as she climbed the steps and dropped her bounty at their feet. She put down what appeared to be the handle of a pool skimmer threaded with looped wire and stretched her arms over her head, rolling her head from side to side.

Ness could practically see the cartoon hearts forming in everybody's eyes. Well, not Tyler's.

"What's she got?" he demanded, squinting as he leaned in. "I can't see!" He sidled closer and knelt down, then scurried backward when he realized he wasn't nose to nose with a bag of chips or an innocent-looking fish.

"I need to rinse off before dinner," Daisy announced, as if this were all totally normal. As if they should all have been fully aware of her lizard hunting prowess and not dumbly agog.

She nudged one of the iguanas gently with the toe of her shoe. The reptile was the length of Ness's thigh and had very pointy teeth.

"Someone else needs to clean them up," Daisy said apologetically. "I'm excellent with a snare, but I can't bear to butcher the poor things."

Ian found his voice first. "Who *are* you?" he croaked.

"A child of Florida, of course," she drawled, winking at him, before sashaying away into the deepening purple dusk. Ness pretended she didn't hear Coco's lusty sigh.

Once they'd collected themselves, they stood in a ragged circle around the iguanas, looking from the deceased lizards to each other. It seemed the prospect of food could, at least temporarily, override the dark creep of suspicion that had been simmering below the surface of every conversation since they'd found the cameras.

Coco slid away quickly, saying, "I'll go see if I can find some salt and pepper."

"I'll start getting some wood together for a fire," Hayes said. He popped inside, grabbed the hand-crank lantern, and set off for the beach path.

Tyler scurried to catch up. "I'll come along!"

Libby, her expression a study in indifference, went back inside without saying a word.

Ian's eyes jittered between Ness and Bradley. He swayed lightly on his feet as he tried to pick a direction to run in . . . or maybe it was a residual effect of whatever Libby had slipped him.

"Phew! It got dark so fast!" He started edging away, skin tinged green as he avoided looking directly at their dinner. "I'll go start the generator for you, Ness."

Ness glared at him. "Oh, I really don't mind—"

"No no! I can take a turn. It's no trouble!" He bounded away, breathing heavily and not bothering with a light source. Ness and Bradley winced in unison as they heard him crash into something heavy and, judging by the sound of it crashing to the ground, metallic.

A faint "I'm okay!" drifted back to them.

"This seems like just the job for you," Ness tried, wishing she could turn back time and give Bradley all the protein bars in the world. "Survival skills! Yay!"

His mouth quirked into an evil smile, made more ominous by his four-day growth of dark, patchy facial hair. She realized she'd never seen him with a beard, and now understood why. He had the coverage of a nineteen-year-old.

He shook his head. "Tsk-tsk, Ness. You of all people should know the value of learning a new life skill. What kind of teacher would I be if I did this for you? Giving you a fish instead of shoving you into the river . . . Isn't that how the saying goes?"

He started down to the beach path, the last light of the day creating a silhouette of his broad shoulders and tiny hips against the dark-orange sky. Wispy clouds drifted across the sliver of remaining sun. His hair glistened, and, aside from the rabid squirrel pelt sprouting from his cheeks, Ness could see why he was such a hit with the ladies. It still took the dregs of her willpower not to push him down the stairs.

When Ness got down to the beach, flashlight in hand and dinner still whole, she was met with a pile of wood that was distinctly lacking in flames.

Choosing a place beside a large rock with a relatively flat top, she set down her flashlight and the cooler she'd chosen for iguana transport. She delicately flipped back the towel she'd draped over it so she could better ignore what she was carrying and wrinkled her nose at the contents. After casting a hopeful look around the beach and finding everyone studiously avoiding eye contact, she resigned herself to her fate and, trying not to gag, extracted the first lizard and the single semi-sharp knife she'd found in the kitchen.

A much sharper, wicked-looking knife appeared next to it.

"Here," said Daisy. "Use mine."

Ness eyed the black-handled weapon uneasily but had to admit it would be much more effective than what she'd brought with her.

"Thanks. And thanks for the, uh, bounty." She nodded at the lizard on the rock, grimacing only slightly. "I didn't know you were into hunting."

"It's more like fishing." Daisy shrugged. "We grew up snaring iguanas near our house. They put up a real ruckus about getting caught, more than any fish I've seen, but they make for a decent meal." She picked up a handful of sand and let it run through her fingers.

"I'm out of practice. Took me longer than it should have to get these ones. But I feel terrible about the boat. This feels like at least I'm doing something useful."

Up the hill, Ness heard the rumble of the generator, and the house lights suddenly blazed to life. She looked back to Daisy.

"No one blames you, you know. It'll all work out. You've managed to get stuck with seven people with extremely diverse skill sets." She looked at the knife in her hand and scrunched her nose in consternation. "Not a lot of useful skills, it seems, but hey, we'll figure it out. How did you get this on the plane?"

"It's terrifying what a smile and a selfie will do these days." Daisy smiled miserably. Still beautifully, but miserably nonetheless.

From the direction of the wood pile, Ness heard Tyler's reedy warble of a voice, indistinct, followed by Bradley's decidedly terse grumbling.

"What's up with the fire?" Ness asked as she worked herself up to dissecting the first iguana. With only the single, underwhelming beam of the flashlight to work by, she felt like a tropical Victor Frankenstein.

"Ah." Daisy lowered herself to sit cross-legged in the sand and waved a hand in front of her face, batting ineffectually at the cloud of mosquitoes that was gathering around them. "Well, none of us had any matches or a lighter, so Tyler asked Bradley to show us the fire-saw method used by the Indigenous Australian population. I guess he mentioned it earlier? Anyway, it doesn't seem to be going very well."

Bradley's head popped up from behind the wood pile, lit by the hand-crank lantern. He'd tied his hair back into a messy bun and held a small stick between his teeth. He spat the stick into his hand, brandishing it like a tiny weapon.

"It's going fine. The wood here is very wet, which is, as I'm sure you can imagine, quite different from the fire-starting materials found in the Outback."

Ness thought of the remaining matches tucked safely in her back pocket, but she held her tongue. She appreciated the distraction from her truly disgusting work. Her stomach grumbled audibly, reminding her that there were worse things than butchering dinner. Like not having dinner at all.

"I've heard the fire-saw works better with two people," Tyler suggested, moving into the circle of light and bending down beside Bradley.

Ness braced herself and cut a line down the iguana's belly, holding her breath. She kept listening to the men as she plunged her fingers into the now accessible body cavity and started removing various unidentifiable organs.

Bradley stood and glared down at Tyler. "If you're the expert, why don't you do it, then?"

Tyler held up his hands. "I'm just trying to help."

"It would be *helpful* if you could all work to be a bit more self-sufficient." Bradley dropped the sticks in his hands to the ground and stood, brushing sand from his knees. "If you think you can do a better job, then you go right ahead." He rolled an arm in invitation and glared at everyone in turn.

Coco cleared her throat. "We don't know how, Bradley. You, apparently, do, so can you please stop whinging and light the damn fire so we can eat?" She looked over to the gruesome scene in front of Ness and shuddered. "It looks delicious," she said with a grimace. "Can't wait."

Bradley walked to the far side of the wood pile and stared out to sea. The water frothed as it washed up onto the sand, lapping over his feet. In the far, far distance, Ness thought she could see tiny dots of light, revealing the location of large ships. Man, what she could have done to an all-you-can-eat buffet right now.

"It seems, perhaps, my skills aren't as transferable as I had hoped," Bradley said, barely audible over the gentle lapping of the waves.

Ness skewered the first iguana with a stick, kindly pre-sharpened by Daisy with alarmingly casual knife skills, and moved on to the second lizard, hoping she wouldn't accidentally remove her own digits. Butchering in the dark—butchering at all, really—was not a skill she'd spent time honing, aside from a weekend getaway with friends a few years before where they'd attended a cooking class and tipsily prepared a grouse. She swiped the knife decisively, removing the iguana's tail, and pondered whether she hated plucking feathers more or less than this.

"In two months with MacKenzie, he didn't maybe teach you more than one way to start a fire?" Daisy asked hopefully.

Ness was about to offer up her last couple of matches, or suggest someone go get Ian's lighter, when Bradley turned back to them.

"No. He didn't. It turned out . . ." He let out a frustrated growl, pulled the elastic from his hair, shook like a wet dog, and bundled it all back up, hunching his shoulders. "Listen, I didn't spend months with the guy. He's cool, and, um, we made a deal. A mutually beneficial arrangement. So I can't help with this, okay?"

"What did you do for those two months, Bradley?" Libby asked in a flat voice that promised danger was almost certainly lurking up ahead.

Bradley shifted nervously and let his eyes travel everywhere but toward Libby. "I took the time for personal reflection and growth, which, if you think about it, was in the spirit of the original exercise. The studio didn't need to know. Wolf still got paid, and I got some time to decompress." He looked beseechingly at Libby. "You know how hard I've been working for the last few years. I needed something for me, just for a while."

"So you hid out for two months?" Tyler interjected. "By yourself? Man, that sounds great. Where did you stay?"

"In Cairns. I, er, wasn't entirely alone, of course." Bradley's face screwed up as if he was in pain.

If looks could kill, they'd have all been dead under Libby's nuclear stare. Ness added the second iguana to the sharpened stick. She was getting the hang of this.

Ian walked onto the beach, a flaming torch in hand. It appeared to be made of an ax handle wrapped in a towel. He seemed vastly improved, largely because, as Daisy had quickly reported to Ness, he'd raided Libby's personal pharmacy while Daisy was in the bathroom, and he was now riding a wave of Xanax-induced mellowness.

Daisy was *not* impressed and had spent a solid five minutes letting Ness know all the reasons why this was unacceptable. When Ness suggested she give the feedback to Ian, though, Daisy had looked affronted. "He's suffering! We need to support him."

Now, skin glowing in the light of his precarious torch, Ian looked a bit wan, but well removed from acute suffering.

"Why are y'all sitting here in the dark? I figured you'd have those things cooked up by now." He leaned down, touching the torch to the dry grass and small sticks Hayes had positioned as kindling. He blew gently on the tiny flames, watching them grow.

Backing up to survey his work, Ian looked around the group, finally noticing the tension.

"What'd I miss?"

"Bradley may have overstated the depth of his survival training," Tyler said with unabashed cheer when no one jumped at the chance to answer. He coughed and rearranged his expression into something more somber.

"Oh, yeah, I figured."

All heads swiveled as one to look at Ian.

"What?" He spread his arms. "I saw him in Cairns when there was all that press about him disappearing into the desert with what's his face. You were with, uhhh"—he snapped his fingers a couple of times—"Kimberley! That's her name."

Ian looked at Hayes. "You know Kimberley."

Hayes's eyebrows rose. "I do?"

"Yeah, of course. She's a location manager for Paradox Studios. Yea tall." Ian put his hand level with his chest. "Brunette, green eyes, yells at people a lot but also hugs them after? Wears that bright-pink lipstick?" He looked at Hayes expectantly but got nothing, and so he went back to addressing Bradley.

"No? Okay. Well, anyway, I tried to catch up with you guys, but you dodged me somehow, and then I had to get back on set. You didn't answer my texts, either, which was rude, but I figured you were deep in something new . . ." He trailed off, finally catching sight of Libby's face, which had gone from angry to carefully blank.

"I'm going to bed," she said, standing quickly. She stumbled a little as her ankle turned in the sand, but caught herself. She grabbed the lantern and made for the path.

There was an awkward silence as Bradley watched her go, a pained look on his face.

"Libby!" he called, springing forward. "Wait!"

Ness brought her stick of lizard parts over to the fire and handed it to Hayes, who reluctantly accepted the offering.

"Your turn," she said, and headed to the water to rinse the gore from her hands, wondering about the probability of a shark relieving her of her blood-covered arms as she submerged them in the shallow water.

Ian watched Bradley and Libby go. "More for us, I guess," he said, and took the salt from Coco.

After a surprisingly not-disgusting meal of lightly charred iguana, Hayes said he would stay by the fire a while longer. Admittedly, even with the mosquitoes and sand fleas, the infinitely fresher air on the beach made it preferable to the musty, sneeze-inducing house. Maybe Ness wouldn't mind having to sleep down there as much as she'd thought.

She went up to grab blankets and fill the water jugs while the generator ran. They were perilously close to the end of the gas supply, and she'd been filling every hole-free vessel she could find with fresh water, boiling it—which took eons in the single usable pot they'd scavenged—and setting it aside. Once the generator died, so would their access to the contents of the water tank, which would be, well . . . it would be a real problem if they were still on the island. She tried to brush the concern aside. They'd be gone before it was an issue. They had to be, right?

Ness had a habit of assuming the worst in most situations, which was probably why she wasn't surprised by the fact that their rescue was still pending. But she was, what? Disappointed? Frustrated? Increasingly perplexed by the creeping scope of concerning island goings-on? None of those felt big enough. She felt as if she was keeping her panic locked away behind a flimsy door that could give way at any moment, sending her into hysterics from which she might never emerge.

Ness hefted a container of water onto the kitchen counter and tried to decide if she should fill the bathtub as well. Worst case, they could boil it over the fire. And worst, worst case, they'd drink it straight up, bacteria and all.

The lights dimmed for a second before coming back to full strength, a sign the generator was hitting the end of its fuel. Yup, fill the bathtub.

She stifled a yawn and went down the hall to the purple bathroom. In the back corner opposite the shower sat a black-bodied, gold-footed clawfoot tub. It was filled with dust and debris from the crumbling ceiling. Ness scooped out the bigger pieces, then splashed in some seawater from the bucket beside the toilet and swiped it around before running a bit of water to rinse any remaining mess.

Upon closer inspection, the golden feet were actually cloven hooves.

"This place is so weird," she muttered.

The dirt hadn't shifted with the addition of water. She went to the wardrobe and opened the bottom drawers, hoping to find a cloth they'd overlooked earlier. No dice. She opened the door to the larger compartment that led to the viewing room, thinking she might have seen a towel bunched in a corner. She shuddered at the thought of touching something so certainly contaminated with a bounty of biohazards, but these were desperate times.

Through the open space at the back of the wardrobe, Ness saw that Libby and Bradley were in the next bedroom. Libby sat on the bed, her face buried in her hands. Bradley knelt on the floor at her feet. His hands rested on her delicate ankles.

Ness couldn't hear them and hoped that meant they also couldn't hear her. She spotted the pile of fabric she was looking for and made a hasty grab for it, anxious to leave them in privacy.

As she pulled the fabric—a Fall Out Boy concert T-shirt from 2006, as it turned out—it caught on the chipboard panel that had once concealed the opening, now leaning precariously in the empty wardrobe space. Before Ness could catch it, the whole thing fell through the opening, knocking into the camera tripod someone had put back in there (sans camera), and sending the mess of wood and metal crashing into the back of the mirror. Not hard enough to break it, but certainly with enough force to announce her presence.

Libby's head snapped up, her cheeks mottled red and tearstained. Bradley was on his feet and out of the room before Ness could fully extricate herself from the wardrobe.

By the time she had both feet on the tiled floor, he was looming over her, fists clenched at his sides. His mouth opened and closed, but he couldn't seem to form words through his rage.

"It's not what you think," Ness said quickly, edging as far away from him as she could in the tight confines of the room. She lifted the dirty T-shirt. "I was just looking for something to clean the tub with. The board in there fell and I tried to catch it, but it knocked over the tripod and then that hit the mirror . . ." Not helping.

She started again. "The generator is almost out of gas. I wanted to fill the tub with water for when the pump stops working and we can't get more." Again, she held up the shirt as evidence. "I didn't mean to intrude, and I didn't hear anything."

Libby came to the door. "Why am I not surprised?"

"I was explaining that I was here for water—"

"Right. Of course. And you just happened to choose the bathroom with the peephole? Like you just happened to find the cameras?" Libby leaned in and crossed her arms over her chest. "I don't care what kind of fucked-up childhood you had, Ness, or that you're struggling now. I don't care why you're here or what you think you can accomplish. I just want you out of my life forever."

She turned on her heel and walked quickly away, leaving Ness with Bradley.

"I just wanted water," Ness repeated quietly.

"And I just wanted to be happy," Bradley said, dropping his chin to his chest in resignation.

Ness drew in a shaky breath and sat on the edge of the tub.

He studied her for a moment before stepping out of the room.

"Be careful, Ness. Everyone's got a lot at stake here. Make sure what you're doing is worth it."

He walked away before she could argue her innocence. Not that she thought it would have done much good.

To: Agnes Larkin
From: Bethany Overholden
Subject: Deficiencies, Delinquincies, and Notice

Dear Ms. Larkin,

I understand this is a trying time for you; however, it is important that you understand how recent events are impacting the lives of your tenants. Some more than others.

Since your unfortunate misplacement, the phone calls and highly inappropriate, unscheduled visits from media have been nearly constant. When renting a property from you, I did know you had links to the entertainment industry, but at no point was I warned that this distant historical connection would affect my day-to-day life. You can imagine how challenging this is for me, especially during what should be restful evenings after days spent forming the young minds of the next generation.

At this time, my only reasonable course of action is to provide you with the requisite one month's notice that I will be vacating my unit. I expect a formal acknowledgement at your earliest convenience.

I would also add it that it is unprofessional and negligent that I have not been provided with an alternate contact who can deal with these issues in your stead.

Regards,
Bethany Overholden

CHAPTER 17

NESS HAD, AS ANTICIPATED, SPENT HER NIGHT ON THE BEACH, KEEP-
ing the fire going. She'd seen a couple of planes fly far overhead,
lights blinking in the star-dappled sky, but nothing closer, and
certainly no boats close enough to see them. While unproductive from
a rescue standpoint, she had to admit, it wasn't terrible being down
there on her own, with the sound of the waves and the breeze rustling
the trees. Aside from the circumstances that had brought her there, it
was almost peaceful.

She'd hoped that the morning would bring a renewed sense of hope
and promise to everyone. Alas, it seemed all the new day brought was
a fresh dose of angst tinged with uneasy, group-wide suspicion. And
possibly also food poisoning.

"We're going to need another bucket of water for the bathroom."

Coco emerged, clutching her stomach, and lowered herself delicately onto her mattress, where she curled into a tiny ball.

"I don't know why I bothered coming out. Next time I'm going
to stay in there. I may never emerge." She groaned and rolled onto her
other side. "Tell Olive and Pickles that I love them and they should
spend their inheritance wisely. Don't let them blow it all on liver snaps
and smoked deer femurs."

"I'm sure you'll be able to lecture them on canine fiscal responsibility yourself." Ness set a jar of pre-boiled water beside her and draped a
fresh, cool cloth across her forehead.

It was just the two of them for now. As soon as it was light, everyone else had dispersed, most not even bothering to make excuses or say where they were heading.

Tyler and Hayes, at least, had taken the remnants of the iguanas down to the water to use as bait, and she was very hopeful they'd return with breakfast. Which meant they'd have to cook. Which meant another fire.

Ness stifled a groan at the thought. Maybe she could turn on the generator, only for a little while, and cook on the stove like a real, honest-to-goodness human of the modern world.

"If those idiots manage to bring back a shark or something, don't you dare think about cooking it in here," Coco moaned, as if reading her mind. "I will die. I will spontaneously combust, but instead of fire, it will be fecal matter, and someone *will* have to burn the island down into the sea. And that will be on you." Her face contorted and she rolled quickly off the mattress, staggered to her feet, and rushed down the hall to the bathroom.

"This is it for me," she called. "It's been a real experience knowing you all."

The feeling that she should be doing something useful hung over Ness's head, but for the life of her she couldn't come up with anything. Not to mention, she was tired. Not a stayed-out-all-night tired, or worked-out-really-hard tired. This was a bone-deep exhaustion that threatened to pull her to the ground.

She'd abandoned the shirt she'd arrived in after discovering the front was dappled with iguana blood, and now she was sporting the Fall Out Boy shirt from the wardrobe. Despite being dunked in the ocean and hung in the sun to dry, it still smelled exactly like it had been sitting in the dark, damp corner of a closet for lord knows how long . . . but it was still cleaner than what she had before.

She sipped some water and wished for a peanut butter banana

smoothie dusted with cinnamon, topped with coconut whipped cream. Maybe a burger on the side. And a pizza on the side of that.

Coco came back in, sweating and pale, and toppled onto the bed.

"Give me Bradley's bag," she demanded, extending her arm blindly.

"Um, that seems . . ." Ness couldn't even land on an appropriate word. Dicey? Invasive? Suicidal? Sure, she'd tried to gain access to said bag herself just the day before, but doing it while Bradley was aware versus sneaking seemed like a key differentiator. Oh, how the lines blurred in these trying times.

Gingerly, Coco maneuvered until she could reach the messenger bag half-hidden under the couch. She snagged the strap with a finger and pulled it toward her, panting slightly.

"He's a health nut, Ness. Probably carries seven different kinds of digestion aids. I want to see if there's anything in here that will encourage my bowels to stay inside my body."

It was hard to argue with that.

Where Ness may have gone for a careful rummage, Coco upended the bag and dumped the contents onto the floor. A travel-size cologne roller clattered to the tile and was quickly overwhelmed by a growing pile of empty gum packets, empty protein wrappers, and three pairs of black briefs. A toiletries pouch plopped out on top, its contents rattling promisingly.

Coco gave the bag another shake, sending some receipt-sized papers and bottom-of-the-bag garbage fluttering through the air, then tossed it aside. It slid across the floor and disappeared back under the couch.

Coco watched it with glazed eyes.

"Oops."

She went straight for the toiletries bag, unzipping the top and dumping that onto the mattress in front of her.

"Come on, Coco," Ness complained. "Can we not be even semi-stealthy about this?" She checked the room to make sure no one else was around.

Coco flung aside a pack of condoms, sending them flying onto the cracked coffee table. "What's the point?"

"We're invading his privacy! You could be a bit more respectful about it."

"I could, I guess, but it's too late for that now. Besides, I haven't even seen him today. Maybe he's hiding from Libby, or riding a pair of dolphins to freedom, and we're in the clear. This bounty could be ours. Hey, you think we could sell stuff to the others? Like a prison barter system?"

"What do you think they're going to have to trade? You want to swap Daisy some dirty underwear for another iguana?"

Coco clapped a hand over her mouth and scrambled to her feet, sending travel-size custom-formulated moisturizer and Yves St. Laurent deodorant rolling. Soon Ness was cringing at the sounds that traveled down the hall from the bathroom.

She did a quick survey of the rest of Bradley's stuff, setting aside a bottle of Advil and some organic ginger capsules and trying not to get too rage-y over the empty food wrappers spread around her. Then she got to work putting everything back where they'd found it.

The toiletries bag was a maze of tiny pockets, elasticized holders, and satin pouches—one of which revealed a small, half-empty container of dry shampoo that explained how Bradley was keeping his hair looking so much nicer than Ness's own wild mane.

She gave up trying to guess where it all went, dumped everything into the central compartment, and zipped it closed.

The space under the couch was rife with dust bunnies, a battered copy of *Sports Illustrated* circa 2014, and the desiccated corpse of a small bird. Grimacing, Ness reached in and grabbed the messenger bag, sliding it into the open. As she pulled her arm back, something brushed against her skin from the bottom surface of the couch.

She jerked her arm to safety, heart pounding, then felt like an idiot when two folded sheets of paper fell into sight. Cautiously prodding at the underside of the sofa, she felt the gap where the pages had been wedged and pulled another free. She rocked back, sitting on the mattress—the one usually shared by Ian and Bradley—and unfolded them.

Kimberley,

The last few days have been some of the hardest of my life. Not being able to speak to you, to fall asleep to the sound of your breath, has been torture.

The way we left things hangs over me. I know you're worried. And rightly so. I've been stubborn and unwilling to accept how untenable the situation is. For that, I am so sorry. What a burden for you to carry, when you already hold so much.

I do have a plan to fix things, to correct course and provide us with a stable future. While it's not what I envisioned at this stage of my career, it is what we need. I can find pride in that.

Your spirit is with me constantly, and I wish for nothing more than to be in your arms, my head on your belly, telling the Small One about all the adventures we'll have together.

I have no doubt that someone will show up soon to sweep us away from this place and back to civilization. But until they do, I'll continue to write. Just in case.

My love for you knows no bounds.

B

"What are you doing?"

Ness dropped the pages as if they were on fire. Libby stood at the foot of the mattress, surveying the mess Coco had made.

"It's nothing," Ness said, trying to play it cool and failing miserably. She shot out a hand to grab the letter, but Libby was faster.

"Hey, I really don't think it's a good idea for you to—"

Ness watched the blood drain from the other woman's face as she read. The hand holding the paper fell limply to her side, and she stared out the window.

"We tried, you know. For years we tried. But I couldn't . . ." She cut herself off, shaking her head.

"Oh, Libby. I'm so sorry."

Libby's gaze landed on Ness, her eyes widening as if she hadn't realized who she was speaking to. She took a breath, and Ness braced herself for an onslaught, but Libby seemed to change her mind, plucking the other pages from Ness's hand and walking out of the room. A moment later, a door slammed. A lock clicked loudly.

Ness let herself fall sideways and stared up at the ceiling, the scent of unwashed male and mildew rising from the mattress.

If someone was in the business of selling ill-gotten secrets, this was a real doozy.

Vulture Magazine, September 2014

When I meet Freddie Maltravers for the first time, it is poolside at his Los Angeles home. I arrive at the wrought-iron, mermaid-adorned gates thinking the rumors have surely been blown out of proportion. The property is well maintained, and the exterior decor is tasteful, though admittedly the mermaids are exceptionally well-endowed.

I'd heard things over the years about the self-styled "Modern Prince of Porn," much of which sounded completely fabricated. That he invested 30 percent of his fortune in Sriracha. He only wears animal-based products. He pays attractive women to wheel his red velvet throne from room to room. He prefers to travel by chauffeured recumbent bicycle.

After being led through a series of corridors and rooms I can only describe as nouveau riche on an acid trip by a curvaceous brunette named Jessica (who is using this gig to fund law school), I begin to think perhaps I'd been wrong to doubt anything.

Jessica and I emerge from the dimly lit, flocked-wallpaper gloom into the blinding light of the pool deck. My guide excuses herself, transforming from demure future lawyer to burbling fountain of husky giggles, and she flounces over to join a trio of women dangling their legs in the pool on either side of . . . a red velvet throne.

Maltravers lounges there, seemingly unconcerned by the idea of water damaging his seat.

>

A cotton concert T-shirt from Michael Jackson's Immortal World Tour and board shorts the color of yellow Gatorade disprove at least one of the rumors I'm here to fact-check. He does, however, sport a great python resting over his shoulders.

"Ah, Jordan!" He greets me, accent London posh to the extreme. "Come and meet Gamora." The snake's tongue flicks in my direction.

CHAPTER 18

NESS WAS HOLDING A PORTION OF WELL-DONE, ROOM-TEMPERATURE
fish on a large, shiny leaf, trying to convince Libby to eat.

She knocked gently on the door for the dozenth time.

"Libby, you need to eat something, and the only something we have is fish. Better yet, Ian and Hayes are back down there trying for more, so guess what's for lunch?"

No response.

"You're upset, and with good reason, but maybe if you get a few calories in, some healthy fats, and hell, this green leaf that probably isn't poisonous but is certainly full of fiber, you'll be in a better position to deal with your emotions. Or plot your revenge. Whatever feels right."

From inside the room, Ness heard the rustle of blankets. She could picture Libby rolling over, turning her back to the door, intent on experiencing the full range of her negative emotions in solitude.

"Libby, stop pouting and open the fucking door!" Coco yelled from the bathroom.

Ness walked the few steps down the hall and stuck her head into the bathroom. "Is that you being supportive?"

Coco gave her a weak thumbs-up from where she was curled at the base of the toilet, forehead pressed to the cool tiles. "Did it work?"

"Shockingly, no."

"Best I could do, given the circumstances." She took a shuddering breath. "Listen, she'll have to come out eventually. But tell her to use the other bathroom. This one is permanently engaged."

Ness put a fresh jar of water on the floor beside Coco's sweaty forehead and made her way back to Libby's door.

She sat and leaned against the wall, fish-bearing leaf balanced on her knee.

"Do you want to talk about it?" she tried.

"Does it seem like I want to talk about it?" Libby snapped, voice muffled.

"My therapist says sometimes the things we most want to avoid are the things that need doing most urgently." Ness drew a star in the dust beside her with a fingertip. "She also says that some relationships are past the point of saving, no matter how badly we want to find something to salvage."

Something banged against the inside of the door. Ness winced.

"Yeah, she was actually talking about you and me, but it seems like it could be applicable to other current issues."

"Ness?"

"Yeah?"

"Go away."

"Nah. I'm all settled here. Besides, I've never been very good at listening to other people's advice. This could be my chance to win you over again."

"It is not."

"Remember how much you hated me when we first met? After they gave me my part and you thought you were out? I thought for sure you were going to be out for blood, the way you looked at me." Ness started to pick up a flake of fish, then made herself stop. "When I found out you were joining I was terrified. I nearly threw up on Ian's shoes the first day on set, knowing you'd be there."

"Hey!" Coco chimed in. "Remember that time you puked on his new Jordans at Club Imposter?" Ness ignored her. She could remember, but barely. It was all a vodka-tinted haze.

"And then we did that terrible scene with the foam party when Hayes joined the cast and 'Theo' got to town," Ness continued. "And Hayes didn't know what a foam party was, but he was trying to play it cool."

There was a snort that she chose to interpret as stifled laughter.

"Anyway, I have been a terrible friend. Not just since I left L.A., but for the entire time you've known me. I was a selfish, self-centered, entitled kid who turned into a selfish, self-centered, immature adult. Just ask my ex-husband. But, Libby, our friendship was one of the best things in my life."

"Hey!" Coco shouted again. "I was there too, you know."

"One of the best things in my life," Ness continued, tearing little strips of leaf free and letting them fall to the floor. "And I didn't treasure that the way it deserved. I stopped trusting everyone. If my own father could fool me so completely, then how could I believe what I thought I knew about everybody else? Not to mention the paralyzing embarrassment and shame I felt after everything happened. It felt like my fault."

A terrible, organic sound came from the bathroom, followed by "You're making it about you again."

"You had every right to feel hurt. You're right to think I'm a horrible person. But right now, Libby? Right now, I want to give you some food, a bottle of water, and a sounding board. You don't have to like me for that."

"Ness?" came a tremulous voice from behind the door.

She sat up straighter, hope zipping through her.

"Yeah?"

"Fuck off."

"Is she peeing in a bottle or something? Does this place have chamber pots?" Coco sipped water and leaned against the wall opposite Libby's still-locked door.

"Hey, Libby!" Coco leaned forward, extended an arm, and rapped sharply on the door. "You got a chamber pot in there?"

The fish sat cold and sad on the floor beside Ness. She was still tempted to eat it but had decided that, at a minimum, her staid resolve in saving it might win her a point with Libby. Possibly only a partial point. She'd still be farther ahead than she was now.

Hayes had returned earlier looking sullen and announced the sea was devoid of edible creatures. They'd caught the last three that morning. It was over now.

Ian, looking clammy and jittery despite his continued Xanax ingestion, heckled him into playing cards on the shaded side of the balcony. Libby had given up trying to horde her pharmaceuticals and, with Daisy, had put Ian on a consumption schedule unprofessionally designed to stave off any further withdrawal symptoms until they could access medical care.

Daisy and Tyler were practicing what Daisy called "mindful breathing and appreciation actions." This mostly seemed to involve doing endless downward-dog-to-plank transitions with an occasional one-footed balance activity.

Ness still hadn't seen Bradley. She'd heard Ian muttering to Hayes about it earlier. That it seemed like a pretty sketchy time to take on an unannounced solo expedition. Ness couldn't disagree. Part of her was still stuck on the idea that whoever had been recording them was also behind the disappearance of their boat. What if it was hidden somewhere and Bradley had just . . . left them? She thought back to the overheard argument with Libby in which he seemed to be asking for something. Then the letter to Kimberley. What if he was in dire straits for cash and this was his big move? It seemed unlike him, but given the right circumstances and an unprecedented amount of stress, anything was possible.

She was considering grabbing another deck of cards for a rousing game of solitaire to distract herself when Libby whisper-yelled her name.

"Still here," Ness assured her. "Not going anywhere. I'm ready when you—"

Libby said something in a strangled voice.

"Libby? You okay? Dehydrated?" She grabbed the bottle of water, stood, and jiggled the doorknob. Still locked.

A dull thud came from inside the room. Then another.

Ness looked at Coco, who shrugged and mouthed, "Temper tantrum?"

"This is stupid." Ness walked quickly through the hall and out the side door. The sun was instantly hot on her shoulders, and she breathed in the warm, clean air as she walked around the back of the house to where the bedroom windows had once looked over the island but were now shrouded in overgrown vines and bird poop.

She pulled some leaves aside and peered in the first window to get her bearings, then counted four down, to where Libby was holed up.

The ground was uneven, with knee-high scrubby grass that was very likely crawling with ticks.

At Libby's window, she boosted herself up onto the generous concrete ledge and heaved on handfuls of vines until they ripped away from the surrounding stucco, giving her a dirt-dusted but mostly clear view of the room.

Libby was lying on the bed, wrapped in the ugliest blanket Ness had seen on the island yet. It was mottled brown and seemed to undulate in the dappled sunlight. Ness knocked on the glass.

Libby's head snapped back so she was looking at Ness upside down. Her eyes were huge. Ness watched her mouth something.

"What? I can't hear you! Just let me in! This is ridiculous, Libby. You need water, at least . . ."

The blanket moved. Ness pressed her forehead to the dirty glass and squinted.

Libby's chapped lips moved again, and this time, Ness got the message, as a large, diamond-shaped head rose from the bed to look at her with shiny black eyes, its pink tongue flicking the air.

"Help me."

"Hooooly shit," Ness breathed, almost falling backward off the window ledge.

The snake was wrapped around Libby's body from ankles to midtorso. It was as big around as a fire hose and, Ness assumed, capable of swallowing a whole pig, goat, or petite actress.

She wracked her brain, trying to dig up any random, useful snake facts that might be lurking there. Nada.

Alright, step one: get into the room. Instinctively, it felt like a terrible idea. The last thing she wanted to do was get closer. Actually, the *last* thing she wanted to do was sit idly by while Libby disappeared into the snake's disjointed jaws. With her luck, she'd be accused of plotting a diabolical murder. Imagine possessing the kind of foresight it would take to have packed a python in her carry-on. She might have planned well enough to throw in a few rolls of toilet paper as well.

Okay. Into the room.

She pressed her palms to the glass and tried to force it up. No dice.

Digging her fingertips into the crack between the sill and the window frame didn't give her anything except more broken nails.

"*Do something!*" Libby shrieked, her voice carrying through the glass. The snake had managed another loop and was now hugging her chest. Libby coughed. The creature looked at her, its head tilted to the side like a confused dog. She froze.

Ness jumped down and kicked around in the grass, searching for anything that could break the window. Grass, leaves, a startled, running iguana, more grass. She gave a little scream of frustration, which seemed to birth an idea.

Breaking into a run, she sprinted around the house to the balcony, where Hayes and Ian lounged at the heavy iron bistro table, cards abandoned as they stared out to sea in companionable silence.

Ness grabbed the back of Hayes's chair and pulled.

"Give me the chair give me the chair give me the chair!" She heaved on the iron frantically until Hayes got up, staring at her.

She lifted the hefty chair and staggered across the balcony. God, she needed more upper-body strength.

"Help!" she shouted, her breath coming in haggard puffs. "Snake eating Libby." She jerked her head toward the back of the house.

The men stood frozen, processing her words.

Ness dropped the chair and screeched in frustrated panic. "HELP ME!"

Hayes jumped into motion first, closing the space between them in long, efficient steps and picking up the chair in one hand as he passed. Ian followed close behind.

Ness ran to catch up, leading him to the right window. She boosted herself up and looked in. Libby's eyes were closed. Ness couldn't tell if she was breathing.

"Keep your eyes closed!" she shouted, hoping Libby could hear her, and wishing they had a way to protect her from glass shards.

She jumped back down and turned to Hayes.

"Don't just stand there. Chuck it!"

He put his arm out to back her up to a safe distance, eyed the glass, raised the chair over his head with both hands, and threw it, muscles straining.

Ready to leap into action, Ness held her breath as the chair flew through the air.

It bounced off the glass and fell to the ground.

They all looked from the window to the chair and back again.

"Huh." Ian picked it up, testing the weight in his hands. "I think we need to . . ." He took a couple of quick side steps, swinging the chair like a baseball bat.

Thwack. A crack appeared.

"Again!" Hayes called.

Ian backed up and repeated the motion. The crack spread. One more time aaaaand . . . the glass shattered, pieces tinkling from the frame to the tiles below.

Ness took off her shirt, wrapped it around her hand and arm, and set about clearing as much of the remaining glass as she could to make a space big enough for a person to fit through.

She looked back at Ian and Hayes, then at the opening in the glass. She sighed and shook the shirt out. Slipping it back over her head, she felt tiny pieces of glass scratching her face and body.

"Go around," she instructed. "I'll open the door!"

She jumped back onto the ledge and started wiggling through the opening, ignoring the painful drag of sharp edges against her skin.

It was a great plan. Open the door and let the burly menfolk pry the monster off Libby.

It *was* a great plan, except it fell apart immediately.

Aforementioned burly menfolk got halfway across the room, saw what awaited them, and froze.

"Oh," Ian said quietly, and fainted. Hayes caught him before he hit the floor, lowered him gently, then dragged him to the hall.

Coco stood in the doorway.

"*Shiiiiiiit.*"

Libby was definitely too still. They were running out of time.

"Where's Bradley? Didn't he have a pet snake as a kid?" Coco looked around like she was expecting him to materialize at the sound of his name.

Ness surveyed the chaos around her, her mind oddly serene. She knew what to do. Or, at least, she knew the only thing she could think of worth doing.

She ran to the kitchen, leaping over Ian's unconscious form. She was back seconds later, just in time to see Hayes trying to work himself up to launching himself at the beast.

Shoving him out of the way, she grabbed a thin blanket from the floor and approached the snake.

"What are you doing?" Hayes whispered.

Could snakes even hear? Why was everyone whispering?

"Shut up," Coco hissed, slapping his arm. "Fuck, I wish I had a camera." She seemed to realize what she'd said and paused, looking at them uncomfortably. "And a gun. A gun seems like it would be good here."

The snake turned its gaze on Ness, its head rising to the same level as hers. She felt her heart stutter. It took everything she had not to turn and run. She started speaking, low and slow.

"Hey there, friend. Hungry, huh? Yeah, me too." If snakes could look suspicious, Ness figured this one would be maxed out on side-eye. She edged a bit closer, blanket raised at her side.

"I'm sorry things have to go this way. It's just, you appear to have murderous intentions, and we can't really have that here. We're already pretty stressed out, you know? It's been a tough week."

She was an arm's length from the bed. Raising the blanket farther, she adjusted her grip on the knife in her other hand. Sweat dripped down her back.

"Again, really, really sorry. This isn't great for me either. Ready?"

It froze, and Libby let out a rattling exhale.

"Okay, then."

Ness lunged forward, throwing the blanket over the snake's enormous head and tackling it to the bed, pressing it into the mattress beside Libby's face with her full body weight. She felt it tense, ready to fling her off and, presumably, commit a second slow-motion murder.

Ness stabbed before she could think about it too much. She watched Daisy's hunting knife tear through the thin fabric, felt it hit momentary resistance, then sink farther.

The snake jerked, once, twice, then went limp.

Hayes was at her side then, setting her gently on the floor before starting to tug the enormous corpse from Libby's body.

The top portion of the python thunked to the floor beside Ness, making her jump. Quickly, additional coils followed, piling onto the others like a gigantic, messily wrapped garden hose.

Hayes was talking softly to Libby, gently patting her cheek and making concerned tutting sounds. Ness couldn't move. Her limbs felt like they were made of jelly. Or dead snake. She shuddered.

Coco joined Hayes at the bed and elbowed him out of the way. She looked at Libby, then gave her a sharp smack across the face.

"You wake up, Elizabeth Honoria Kim, you prissy bitch. I will not have this contribute to my inevitable PTSD." She slapped the other cheek. "Wake. Up!"

Libby's eyes fluttered open and she drew in a shaky breath, wincing as her ribs expanded.

"Took your sweet time, didn't you?" she croaked.

Your Flight Is Confirmed!

Passenger: Robert Larkin
Economy Class
Leaves: Harry Reid International Airport, Las Vegas,
10:00 p.m., Thursday, August 18
Arrives: Hollywood International Airport, Fort Lauderdale,
5:31a.m., Friday, August 19

CHAPTER 19

LIBBY EMERGED FROM HER PYTHONIC COCOON IN A CONCERNINGLY good mood.

"She's freaking me out," Coco whispered a little while later, as Libby lounged on the balcony looking more relaxed than Ness had seen her in . . . ever. Libby's face was tilted to the sun, her eyes closed. A small smile played across her still-pale lips.

At the kitchen counter, Ian was prepping unappetizing pieces of leftover fish to use for bait. He followed Coco's gaze to Libby, whose toes were now tapping to unheard music.

"How long was she unconscious? Do you think she's got brain damage? One of those things where a person has a near-death experience and their brain structure is altered and they have a totally different personality?"

"She should probably see a doctor," Ness said, wincing as Coco yanked another shard of glass from her palm with needle-like tweezers and let it clink into the small pile beside them.

"She's not the only one," Coco suggested.

Ian cut pink-tinged fish into inexpert chunks. He'd been oddly quiet all day. "Should someone go . . . talk to her?" he asked, voice husky from disuse.

"Not it," Ness blurted.

Hayes was the obvious choice, in Ness's mind. Even, calm, good at the nurturing stuff. But he'd gone with Daisy and Tyler to figure out if they could butcher and cook python steaks for dinner. A thought that made Ness feel more than a little nauseous, despite the hunger gnawing at her belly.

"Where the hell is Bradley? This is his fault. It's only fair he deals with the fallout." Coco snuck another look at Libby on the balcony and pulled a face. "Creepy as fuck."

Ness hadn't told anyone about the letter, only saying that Libby had been processing some upsetting Bradley-related information.

"I haven't seen him all day," Ness said. She looked at Ian. "Have you?"

"Why are you asking me?" He sounded affronted.

"Because you guys share a mattress?"

"Yeah, no. I kicked him out two nights ago."

Coco stopped dabbing Ness's arm with the dregs of the gin and stared at him.

"What? He's a spooner, which is fine, but I kept overheating." Scooping up the fish and dumping it onto an empty coconut shell they'd found washed up on the beach—disappointingly, the Ginger Cay palms didn't seem to be in nut-producing mode—Ian said, "I think he's been bunking upstairs or something. Anyway, I haven't seen him since last night. He was doing his 'staring moodily at the night-darkened sea' routine when I turned in. I think Daisy was still out there with him, though. Maybe she knows?"

Ness felt a twinge of unease.

"Yeah, let's ask her when they're done with the . . . dinner." She swallowed her disgust.

Coco sat back and rolled her shoulders. She poured a generous shot of gin into a grimy mason jar, leaving less than an inch in the bottle, and threw it back in a single gulp.

"Medicinal," she said in response to Ness's raised eyebrow, smacking her lips. "Anyway, he's probably out there doing something dumb to prove a point. We'll find him on the beach with a raft of woven tree roots and rat tails or something, ready to sail out of here."

Ness hoped that was true, but it was hard to ignore that they were all wandering around willy-nilly and largely unaccounted for. Sleeping by the fire, Ness had spent the previous night almost entirely unsupervised, which, in retrospect, may not have been the best plan. Although, now that she thought about it, there had been an unusual amount of foot traffic on the beach through the night. Midnight walks and people "just checking in." At the time, she'd assumed they'd wanted to keep an eye on her out of consideration, but now . . . had they been *monitoring* her?

Libby shuffled toward them, moving gingerly, as might be expected of someone who had recently been an involuntary pig-in-a-deadly-blanket.

"Ness, can I talk to you? Alone?"

"Um, sure?"

Coco's bony elbow nudged her in the ribs, urging her up, as her body insisted it would be best to stay put. Maybe curl up on the floor right there and have a small snooze, avoiding all potential conflict through the power of sleep.

She slipped off the barstool and followed Libby out to a pair of lounge chairs that were still partially shaded by the house behind them.

"What's up?" she asked, lacing her fingers to stop herself from fidgeting.

"I still think you suck, and I don't want to be your friend." It was nice to know they hadn't completely lost the Libby they knew and, well, accepted, if perhaps not universally loved.

Libby stretched out her legs and wiggled her chipped-polished toes in the dappled sunlight.

"We've all gone through extremely unpleasant, life-changing situations, Ness. If we treat the people around us as if they're disposable, we're quickly left with nothing but our own thoughts and regrets."

Ness nodded noncommittally, choosing not to point out that alienating those around you with unwarranted criticism and snide remarks wasn't much better.

"But," Libby continued, "I realized some things today." She started to wrap her arms around her body, winced, and lay them loosely at her sides instead.

"It's possible I've been holding on to things that aren't worth holding anymore. And, apparently, when you grip something too tightly, you can break the parts of it that matter most." She looked at Ness, really looked at her for what felt like the first time since this whole thing started. "Did you know a python breaks the bones of its prey so it's easier to swallow?" Libby didn't wait for a reply, but Ness was pretty sure her expression communicated how little she wanted to dwell on that tidbit of info.

Libby's gaze drifted out over the island. When she spoke again, it was quietly. "I think, and maybe this is the shock talking, but I might have a tendency to be a bit of an emotional python." She smiled wryly, and shifted to pull something out of her back pocket. She fanned the air with Bradley's folded letters.

"Do you think he was going to tell me?"

Ness considered this. "I think he wants to avoid causing you pain."

"That's not an answer."

"It's the best I've got."

"I've kept some version of us—Bradley and me—in my head for so long. It never made sense. We hate each other now just as much as we ever loved what we had. I don't know why I care so much. I could have snagged a billionaire by now if I hadn't been so busy plotting my elaborate and satisfying revenge and our subsequent remarriage." She shifted in her seat and looked down at the pages in her hand.

"Turns out, being emotionally shattered and then almost eaten on the same day really gives you perspective." Libby looked at Ness consideringly. "Another thing I may have been holding on to is a slightly—and I'll stress the *slightly*—overblown sense of betrayal. You were, and I have to assume still are, on some level, incapable of facing your problems. But you *did* tackle a snake the size of Minnesota for me, so I guess I kind of owe you. Consider forgiveness your repayment. Even-steven."

Ness snorted, laughing. "Oh, good. I thought I was going to have to make some kind of elaborate gesture."

It was nice to be, if not back in Libby's good books, at least in the neutral column.

Ness could see smoke drifting above the trees from the beach. She wondered if she could make herself eat snake steak. Maybe if she pretended it was chicken . . .

They sat in silence for a moment. The sound of Ian heckling Coco drifted out from the kitchen. Ness could almost imagine she *had*, in fact, managed to travel through time, spinning the clock back far enough to let her do things differently.

They say it takes ten thousand hours to become an expert at something. If that was true, Ness had fully mastered analyzing the years leading up to her father's abrupt departure and wondering if she should have seen it coming. She wondered if, after this ordeal, she'd have mastered tackling reparations for her own wrongdoings.

"You couldn't have changed anything, you know," Libby said. She kept her eyes on the wisps of cloud passing by. The wind was making her hair dance gently around her perfect, professionally sculpted chin. "You could have maybe dragged it out, made enough money to keep him around another couple of years. But your dad? He was never going to be there for the long run. He's one of those people who are never happy with what they have. They're always looking for the next big win. I wouldn't be surprised if he ended up in Vegas and lost everything."

"That's . . . not comforting." Ness hugged her knees to her chest and tried to decide how much to say. There was something about their bonkers circumstances that seemed to encourage cagey behavior and also completely over-the-top sharing, simultaneously. She decided to embrace the spirit of the moment.

"I hired a private investigator. There was nothing the police could do. His name was on everything—all the accounts, all the investments." She shook her head, the sting still surprisingly fresh. "I don't know what I wanted. It's not like the money was coming back. But I needed to know what he traded me in for."

Ness still felt the weight of disappointment pressing down on her, even after so many years.

"He bought a thousand acres in New Mexico and opened a wellness center. They adhere to a vegan menu and pipe in canistered air imported from the Alps. There's a portrait of me hanging over the fireplace in the lobby." The photo the investigator had sent was forever burned in her memory, along with the eye-watering amount on the accompanying invoice.

"Huh. That's messed up." Libby scratched a mosquito bite on her ankle. "And you never heard from him?"

"Nope."

"I'd say you're better off, but . . ." She waved a hand at their surroundings.

"Yeah."

Daisy, Hayes, and Tyler emerged from the beach path, sunburned and smiling. Daisy and Tyler each carried one of the hard-sided coolers from the boat. They looked heavy.

Hayes held out a platter of woven palm fronds piled with white meat.

"Dinner is served."

By early evening Bradley was still MIA. With full stomachs and steadily growing concern, they split up to search the island.

Libby took the command post position, staying parked in the lounger in case he suddenly appeared back at the house.

As Ness shoved a refilled bottle of water into her bag, a large winged insect made its way across the room and settled in a high corner. Ness eyed it suspiciously, making sure it was staying put as she finished grabbing supplies and headed outside.

After consulting the map they'd found their first day and the tiny dot that represented their rock in the ocean, Ian and Daisy set out for the eastern end of the island while Ness and Hayes went west. Tyler and Coco went to search the area around the house, tasked with checking the various sheds and outbuildings scattered across the acre or so that surrounded the pseudo-castle. Ness figured there was a not-insignificant chance Coco would come back without her search buddy, based on their past interactions and Coco's increasingly low tolerance for idiocy.

An hour and countless bug bites later, Ness and Hayes reached a channel across the beach that led into the mangroves, which grew nearly to the waterline along this section of the island's edge. The water was eight feet across, and currently up to their knees. They waded through, and Ness hoped crocodiles and alligators weren't on the Porn Prince's list of imported species.

The sun poked its nose out from behind the blanket of clouds, and something in the trees to Ness's left glinted. She turned toward it, wondering if there was another shed nestled in the greenery that they should be investigating. It would be very on-brand for Bradley to have established his own settlement to prove a point.

Whatever was in there was too short to be a building. It was also too white and too purposefully hidden under palm fronds and broken branches, most of which had been tossed aside by the wind and rain. She edged closer, careful not to trip on tree roots.

There, tied to a tree and bobbing gently in the shallow canal, was their boat.

Hayes and Ness stared at each other, then at the boat, their mouths opening and closing in matching expressions of shock and confusion, shifting to joy before morphing back into a blatant "WTF?"

They ran over and tossed the foliage aside, confirming it wasn't a mirage, or some other vessel abandoned here years ago and ready to disintegrate if a heavy seabird perched on its bow.

It wasn't in great shape—the nose was scraped and dented, the sides sported long scratches and gouges—but there it was, in all its boat-shaped glory: *Gentleman's Delight*, still afloat!

Ness's legs failed her then, and she plopped down onto a convenient clump of sandy roots.

"What does this mean?" she asked, not sure if she was talking to herself or to Hayes.

He was in the boat, rummaging through the water-logged contents.

"The equipment cases are gone, except this one," he said, holding up a waterproof black box by its handle. "Which I guess isn't surprising, but it does mean there's a whole lot more tech on the island unaccounted for."

He found two bottles of Kalik Light and used the metal edge of an interior cabinet to pop one open, and then the other, before stepping off the boat and coming to stand beside Ness. The drinks fizzed lightly, catching the dappled light coming through the leaves.

Ness swatted at a bug and accepted a bottle, taking a swig of the warm golden brew.

"This is disgusting," she muttered, then chugged half the bottle. She wiped her mouth with the back of her hand and suppressed a belch.

Hayes followed suit, his Adam's apple bobbing as he swallowed. He came up for air, saying, "This is an emergency. It's for the shock."

Ness stared at the boat. "Right."

She felt light-headed and remembered that, aside from the recent windfall of island creature protein, she hadn't eaten in . . . god, forever. Good thing it was a light beer. She took another sip, rolling the bottle between her hands. The label turned to sticky mush against her palms.

"Am I thinking about this clearly? Did someone hide this from us? On purpose?"

"The other option is that we came in on this beach that first night and   misplaced the boat." Hayes finished his beer in one long swallow. "The storm could have dropped all these branches . . ." He sounded nowhere near convinced.

"Did the storm also drop the cameras onto the house?"

"Probably not."

They stared at the boat in silence as birds chirped their cheerful songs in the treetops.

"Hayes," she said quietly. "Who would do this? These are people we know and trust. Okay, well, at least trust enough to think *they wouldn't trap us on a deserted island*." A mosquito landed on her arm, and she mashed it, leaving a small trail of blood across her skin as she brushed it aside.

"One would think."

"Apparently one is wrong. Again."

"Here's the thing," Hayes said slowly, setting his beer aside. "We have the boat now." He stood, smiling. "*We have the boat now.*"

Ness got to her feet.

"WE HAVE THE BOAT!"

They jumped up and down, whooping until they were hoarse. Hayes wrapped her in a bear hug and planted a celebratory kiss on the top of her head, sending her innards into a spiral. She tilted her head back, delirious with joy at the possibility of imminent escape.

"Why did it take us fifteen minutes to realize that?" he asked, staring down into her eyes.

"We're dehydrated, among the eight of us we've had the caloric intake of a picky toddler, and I might be slightly tipsy."

"Fair." He paused, forehead wrinkling in consternation. "Listen, if someone would go this far to keep us here, what's going to happen when they know we *found* the boat?" Walking around Ness to a small clearing, he started pacing.

Ness pursed her lips, determined to remain calm. Or at least calm-ish. "Well, depending on their motive, I think it could go a couple of ways."

"It sounds like you've already thought this through," he said, looking over to her without breaking stride. He only had room to take two long steps before nearly face-planting against a tree trunk and having to turn back the way he came.

"Maybe. Kind of. Anyway, if their goal is really to sell the footage from the cameras, then I think they'd roll with it, get on the boat, and play innocent until something forces them to do otherwise. Like, say, if the police search everyone and find memory cards, or dust the camera fragments for fingerprints and that implicates one of us."

"Okay." Hayes nodded, turned on his heel, kept pacing. "That makes sense. Doesn't sound too bad, aside from the fact that someone seems to have kept us forcibly confined here for days, which, if I'm being honest, is freaking me out more than a little."

"Yes. I can tell. And if the motive happened to be something other than just cashing in on the footage . . . Look, never mind. We don't need to talk about that."

"What are you getting at? Blackmail? What?" He ran a hand through his hair, making it stick up in a way that was both entertaining and endearing. He looked like a frantic hedgehog.

"No, really, I've got nothing but wild-ass guesses."

"Ness. Spit it out."

"Okay, well . . . It may have crossed my mind that we're being kept here for some more . . . dark purpose."

Hayes stopped in his tracks. "I changed my mind. I don't need to hear this right now. You're right." He cleared this throat, rolled his shoulders back, and took a series of slow, deep breaths.

He looked at her, his silver hair shining, and stepped forward. "Shall we get our sea legs back, Captain Larkin?"

"Abso-fucking-lutely. Let's go home."

Splitting up seemed like the most efficient strategy. Ness would drive the boat around the tip of the island to the main beach. Hayes would meet her there, help tie the thing up with one thousand knots and every anchor-like item they could find. And then they'd gather everyone else and head out, aiming for whatever neighboring island the map said was closest.

The sun was only just starting to dip below the trees, the sky working its way from blue into a tie-dyed frenzy of pink and orange. They had oodles of time.

They used ropes to haul the boat backward along the channel, which was barely deep enough for it to clear the sandy bottom without getting mired, and launched it out into the open shallows. Hayes boosted

Ness onboard, waited a minute to make sure the engine started, and then jogged away, a coil of rope over his shoulder.

Ness took a moment (maybe two) to check out the view as he went.

Now, standing at the helm, absorbing the purr of the motor under her feet, tears welled in her eyes, and she rested her forehead on the steering wheel. When she looked up a few seconds later, the waves had pushed her closer to the sandbanks than she felt comfortable with. She made a smooth turn and headed for deeper water.

The last thing they needed was to get beached.

From the water, the island was picture perfect. The white sand glistened under waving green palm trees and the ever-present mangroves. Overgrown flowering bushes dotted the scene with bright pinks and reds. She'd like to come back someday, she realized, shocking herself.

Laughing, bubbling over with the unfamiliar feeling of freedom, she revved the engine and drove at what felt like a safe-but-urgent pace around the craggy tip of the island. The sun was out in its full evening glory, sending warm rays onto her shoulders and back. As she rounded the corner, she wished she had her sunglasses. She squinted and saw Hayes waving from the beach in the distance.

She mapped out the route in her head, trying to remember if she'd seen hidden rocks in the water, while also envisioning her reception once everybody realized they were saved. Their ecstatic faces, and her immediate elevation from whatever scum-of-the-earth island citizen she was now to savior.

The vibrations under her feet stopped. It was suddenly very quiet.

"No," she breathed. Then louder, "No, no, NO!" She turned the key. The engine sputtered but didn't turn over. She bashed the panel with the heel of her hand and tried again.

Nothing.

Her heart pounded. Her hands shook. Tears blurred her vision.

"Think it through, Ness," she ordered herself. "What do you know about boats?"

The answer was "very little." Just enough to get her boating license

years earlier so she could pilot her ex in their classic mahogany run-
about to their friends' places on the other side of Lake Rosseau for
cocktails and bonfires, where people discussed market fluctuations, the
price of carbon fiber, and the most interesting article in that month's
issue of *The Economist.*

She'd hated those parties.

"Focus," she said. "The basics. What are the basics?" She turned in a
slow circle.

"I have a key. The boat was on. What makes a boat turn off?" The
blood drained from her face. *Idiot,* she thought, eyes darting over the
dials in front of her. *You're such an idiot.*

The gas gauge rested on E.

When she looked back at the beach, Hayes had gotten smaller. His
waving seemed to be less excited and verging on frantic, judging by
the increased intensity. Another person was running across the beach
toward him, taking deer-like leaps through the air.

Ness tried not to panic but was well on her way to a full-blown
anxiety attack as the weight of the situation seemed to land squarely
on her chest.

She was going to lose the boat. Again.

Another wave pushed her farther out, and that's when she realized
she'd better start swimming.

I could stay here, she considered, shifting her weight from foot to foot
as she looked down at the blue water. *See where I wash up. Maybe there
will be people there. Different, less angry people. That would be nice.*

She looked back at the beach. Hayes was gone. She squinted, shading
her eyes with a hand. Oh shit. A seal-silver head bobbed in the waves.
Tanned arms sliced through the water. He was coming to get her.

"No way you are killing yourself to save me, you stupid, stupid
man." The spark of anger at his complete idiocy spurred her into
action. The last storage space she rummaged revealed one remaining
life jacket. It was faded and the orange fabric was ripped in places. It
was still better than nothing. She shoved her arms through, clipped

it shut, and clambered over the bench. The upholstery was already warm from the sun, and the metal detailing along the ledge seemed to have absorbed all the heat the weakening rays could emit, making it uncomfortably hot. She sat for a second, legs dangling, aluminum burning the backs of her bare thighs.

She tried to judge how far out she was. Three hundred yards? Four? The water looked bottomless.

"I never should have left Toronto," she said, and jumped.

The water was colder that far out. It ran over her face as she broke through the surface. A wave rolled over her as she inhaled, making her cough and sputter. She barely recovered in time to dodge the next one and get herself pointed in the right direction, positioned to ride the waves up and down.

As she swam, she tried to think of ways to save the boat, but unless they built a raft and rowed after it, she couldn't see how it was possible. A glance over her shoulder revealed that it was already a good distance away, and Ness didn't think it was because she was a particularly speedy swimmer.

She rode the next wave to the top and got a look at the island. She was slightly off center to the beach but at least heading the right way.

She searched for a sign of Hayes but couldn't see him before the water dropped her back down into a bowl of blue. She tried not to think about what was swimming underneath her or how much she might look like a tasty snack. To distract herself, she started making a to-do list.

Survival skills. Stroke, stroke, kick, breathe. *Team-building skills.* Stroke, stroke, kick, breathe. *Swimming lessons.*

This continued for an eternity, and Ness knew that without the flotation device wrapped around her ribs she'd have drowned. No question. *Send donation to whoever makes sure people have life jackets.* Stroke, stroke, kick, breathe.

She inhaled some more water, coughed it up, throat and nostrils burning, and flipped over to lie on her back and catch her breath.

Overhead the sky was turning to a storm of oranges, pinks, purples, and swirls of gold as the sun began to set.

Oh, perfect. Feeding time.

She barrel-rolled onto her stomach and swam, worry for Hayes gnawing at her like the hungry, large-toothed creatures undoubtedly eyeing her soft underside at that very moment.

Something bumped into her. She shrieked, her hands coming up in fists, ready to punch a shark in the nose.

Hayes glared back at her. He was breathing heavily, his lips slightly parted. Water ran in tiny drops down his neck as he treaded water.

"You look like a furious mer-king," ocean-addled Ness observed, before realizing why he was probably so mad. She paddled in a slow circle and spotted the boat, now half a mile away. She felt a fresh crush of disappointment.

"What the hell?" Hayes demanded, slapping the water beside him. He looked heavenward, as if the candy floss sunset could give him strength or direction.

"The gas tank was empty," Ness said. "I'm sorry. I should have checked. I should have noticed. I should have—"

"That boat can sink to a watery grave alongside basically everyone else on this godforsaken island," Hayes growled.

"Oh . . . ?"

"I didn't think there were any life jackets left on board. I couldn't get to you. I thought . . ." His eyes closed for a moment, his breath stuttered. He ran a wet hand over his face and looked at her.

"I'm glad you're not dead."

"Same."

He reached out and grabbed the front of her life jacket, pulling her to him and mashing a none-too-gentle kiss onto her chapped lips.

Suddenly, they were under water as a lazy wave rolled over them. Their heads broke the surface, both of them sputtering and laughing in a slightly unhinged how-is-this-our-life way. They struck out toward land, Hayes gliding through the water beside her like a dolphin or adorable hand-holding sea otter while Ness splashed along with all the grace of a pirate thrown overboard.

They covered enough distance that the waves began to calm around them. Ness was shivering but could feel the water temperature starting to rise as they neared shore. When they were about two hundred feet from their not-so-welcoming committee on the beach, she looked at Hayes, who was sporting blue-tinged lips. His strokes had slowed. He turned his head to check on her and their eyes met.

"I thought . . ." she began before stopping herself. In the ocean with only one flotation device was not the time to discuss feelings. Apparently, Hayes had little regard for his limitations, though, because he stopped swimming and floated there, kicking his legs and waving his arms through the water as he rested on the surface.

"You thought what?"

"I thought you regretted kissing me. Before. Yesterday. And, you know, way back when, but specifically yesterday."

"I did."

"Uh, oh. Alright." Ness squinted up at the sky. "But then it's kind of messed up you just did it again, don't you think?"

He flicked water at her and she considered shoving his head under. When he started speaking, she was glad she'd exercised restraint.

"I regretted that it took this long. I'm bummed that we're on this dumb island and, if I know you, you're wondering if I only kissed you because this is so far from real life that, once we leave, I can pretend it never happened. You're thinking I'm caught up in some fantasy of what we had and who you were instead of who you are now."

She couldn't argue with any of that and stayed quiet.

"And no, I don't know you very well anymore, but I've learned more about who you are now in the past few days than I would have in a week of filming at some luxury resort where it's impossible to have a moment to ourselves. And Ness?"

She lifted her gaze from the shimmering water to his face. Her lips were crusted with salt. Her hair was slicked across her forehead in bedraggled strands. The life jacket was too loose and, as she floated, the shoulders pushed up to her earlobes, all but enveloping her chin. She'd never felt less alluring, but the way Hayes was looking at her made it easy to believe she was an epic sex kitten.

"I have no idea what's going to happen here, but I know I like being with you. I've *always* liked being with you." His hand reached out and squeezed hers. If they hadn't been floating in an ocean, probably being eyed up for a shark's lunch, it would have been among the most romantic moments of her life. Heck, even with the shark thing it was still up there.

Ness coughed, clearing the lump that had formed in her throat.

"Ditto."

He resumed treading water and attempted to drop a kiss on the tip of her nose, but he missed and mushed his lips against her eye instead.

"When we get home, can I take you on a date? A real one? Someplace far, far away from here where the most stressful decision we need to make is how many desserts to order?"

"I would love that."

His cheekbones were highlighted by a sunburn made even more pink by the evening light. Ness could feel her heart begin to reassemble itself, preparing for a potential leap into Big Feelings territory. It felt very on-brand for her that this was happening mid-near-death-experience. Ness Larkin, unwitting queen of the dramatic life twists.

"I've thought about this, you know." She kept her voice low. "What it would be like if we met again. This . . . it's not how I pictured it."

She'd been kicking slowly, keeping herself alongside Hayes, ready to grab him at a moment's notice if he started sinking. They'd rotated so she was now facing the beach and had a clear view of how many shocked, angry people would be waiting there. She wondered if they should do an about-face and head back out to sea. It was the Bahamas, after all. There were a million tiny islands here. They'd run into one eventually.

"I'd like to get out of the water now," she said quietly, resigned to her fate.

"Yeah," Hayes said, following her gaze. He sighed. "Same."

October 3, 2003

The train wreck that is Ness Larkin continues to barrel down the tracks, folks. Photographers captured images of the good-girl-turned-wicked out on the town (no surprise there) last night with a mystery man. Yes, that's right, y'all. I'd bet my life that is NOT Hayes Beaumont, despite their rumored off-screen relationship.

Ness stepped out wearing some scandalous low-rise jeans (those things would make Xtina blush!) and a cropped tube top, finishing the look with a totally adorbs fedora. Saucy! Her mystery companion didn't even try to keep up, fashion-wise, keeping his identity under wraps with an oversized hoodie as they made their way into what sources say was a private room at Hooper's, Hollywood's trendiest new restaurant.

Now, while this could be a business meeting or dinner with friends, reports from inside the restaurant indicate things were getting pret-ty spicy, and I'm not talking about the food. Stay tuned for more!

And Hayes, honey, if you need someone to comfort you, you know where to find me.

CHAPTER 20

"I KNOW THIS IS HARD TO TAKE IN," NESS SAID THROUGH CHATTER-
ing teeth.

She shivered on the balcony as the last rays of sunlight disappeared. She wanted a hot shower, a giant fluffy towel, and three days of
sleep. Her island compatriots, however, wanted to know how she'd lost
their escape vessel. Again.

For the moment, Bradley and his still-missing status were forgotten.

So she ran through it, with Hayes at her side adding details like
"None of this is Ness's fault" and "Can we take a moment to think
about the fact that someone seems to have sabotaged us?"

Libby, certainly, did not wish to take that moment.

"I don't need to think about it, Hayes. I know who's responsible."
She stood, leaning against the balcony rail. Daisy had brought out a few
of the fat black candles in hurricane lanterns and set them on the tables.
Insects were now dive-bombing the area with increasing intensity. Ness
considered walking inside and going to bed.

"Let's look at the facts," Libby continued. "Ness brought us here."

Ness sputtered at the dramatic about-face from their earlier peace-
making conversation.

Libby continued. "Ness picked where we docked the boat."

"Do you *remember* when we got here?" Ness asked, not believing
what she was hearing. "No one *chose* anything."

"Ness has taken control of our food stores and rations our power supply." She was really on a roll now. "Most critically, Ness found the cameras." She made air quotes around "found."

Ness's mouth opened and shut uselessly. She looked at the rest of the group, hoping to see skepticism all over the faces around her. But as she glanced from person to person, those hopes crashed and burned.

Ian was stroking his chin and nodding, glassy eyes narrowed in consideration. Daisy sat quietly on a lounger, deep in thought. Coco was examining her fingernails and chewing on her lower lip the way she'd always done when she was worried.

"And now," Libby went on, "Ness has found"—more air quotes—"and conveniently lost our means of escape."

She spread her arms in a "What more do I need to say?" gesture.

A voice piped up from beside what might once have been a potted palm. Tyler had a bedsheet draped over the top of his head and wrapped around his body. He'd been moaning that his clothes were chafing against his sensitive, bite-ridden skin. He looked like the ghost of someone's slightly off-kilter gran.

"Um, Ms. Kim?" he said hesitantly, rearranging the sheet so more of his face was protected from bugs. "What about Mr. Beaumont?"

"What about him?"

Hayes looked affronted, like, "Yeah, what *about* me?"

"It's just, well . . ." He looked beseechingly at Hayes. "Please don't take this the wrong way, Mr. Beaumont."

Hayes was definitely already taking it poorly, whatever *it* was. Ness wasn't sure anyone had doubted his character in . . . ever.

Tyler tucked himself a bit farther behind the plant pot before continuing. "It's only that . . ."

Libby rolled her eyes. "Spit it out, Casper."

Tyler cleared his throat. "I don't think we can ignore the fact that in all the instances you've listed, Ness wasn't alone."

In the back of her mind, Ness couldn't help but wonder why everyone else was "Ms. Kim" and "Mr. Beaumont" and "Lord Hoity-toity" while she was still plain ol' "Ness."

"That's a great point, Tyler," she chimed in quickly. "It's not like I've been skulking all over the island *by myself.*" She shot pointed looks at Ian and Libby. "I've been with someone else nearly the whole time."

Tyler shook his head. "It would be awfully tricky to hide a boat in the way you described on your own . . ."

Hayes's mouth hung open. "You think we're, what, *co-conspirators?*"

Ness could see how they'd implicate her, but Hayes? They were entering fever dream territory.

"I didn't say that." Tyler's face scrunched up in a way that suggested he was, in fact, saying that.

"And then there's the snake," Libby added.

Ness's eyes narrowed. "You're saying me saving you from a human-eating snake was . . ." She struggled to find the right word. ". . . manufactured?"

Ian got up from his seat and relocated to the cool floor of the balcony, staring up at the sky, hands clasped on his stomach. Ness watched them rise and fall with his breath, trying to take in more air herself.

Libby brushed her commentary aside. "What better way for you to ingratiate yourself with the public? God, I'm so stupid. You probably let that thing in yourself. It was all a setup, wasn't it?"

Ness's eyes were nearly bugging out of her head. "Libby, think through the logistics of that—"

"And like Tyler pointed out," Libby continued, ignoring Ness's attempt to bring some rationality into the conversation, "most of the time you're claiming to have been supervised you've been with Hayes. And no offense, Hayes, but you've got a serious blind spot where Ness is concerned."

Ah, Ness thought. *Of course. I'm not in cahoots with Hayes, friend to all. I've bamboozled him.*

Hayes stood, glowering. "No offense? Of course I'm offended, Libby! This is bananas."

Daisy spoke from her seat, quietly. "But why would Ness, or anyone, do this?" She sat off to the side by herself, looking deeply uncomfortable, like she'd intended to go to someone's birthday party and ended up at their divorce proceedings.

"Money. Power. *Revenge.*" Libby could have been doing a voice-over for a legal thriller movie trailer.

"Or cannibalism," offered Ian. He shrugged at their horrified looks. "What? I've seen the movies. I've read the books. People hunting people? It's a thing."

Coco looked at Ness, eyebrow cocked. "Are you planning to herd us off a cliff like sheep and consume our remains?"

Ness just stared back. Libby looked as though she was waiting for an answer, which was concerning. As if there needed to be more concern.

Hayes loomed imposingly, hands whoa-ing them. "You all need to take a step back and think this through again. Ness nearly died today."

Had she? Ness wondered, replaying the afternoon. *Huh, maybe.* She felt as though she were watching the conversation from afar, listening to them discuss someone else entirely.

"I don't think we have enough facts to be making these types of accusations," Ian said, cutting Libby off before she could launch into an extended anti-Ness tirade. "But," he shot Ness an apologetic look, "there are some things that don't make a lot of sense, and maybe Ness could, ah, help clear those up. Because, looking at the information we *do* have, there are some, shall we say, inconsistencies between what Ness is telling us and what we're seeing."

She waited for indignant outrage to bubble up from somewhere deep inside of her . . . and kept waiting. Instead, she realized, she was disappointed. Sad to learn that so little had changed, and the relationships she'd been attempting to nurture into something real and healthy were apparently meaningless. These people would throw someone under the proverbial bus if that was the easiest solution to whatever issue they faced that day. They loved making a mess but would always peace out before cleanup.

Ness braced herself and waded back in. "Have you all forgotten that Bradley is completely unaccounted for here?"

"She's right," Libby said, stunning Ness back into silence. "It is *awfully* strange that after you tried to steal Bradley's personal belongings from under his nose, physically assaulting him in the process, then *actually* stole his personal belongings, *then* spied on and possibly even recorded private conversations, likely for profit . . ." Her voice had grown louder with the force of her accusations, but hitched here. She took a steadying breath and continued, more quietly, but with venom. "I heard Bradley warn you off, Ness. What happened? Did he get too close to the truth?"

"Oh my god," Tyler gasped, sheet held up over his mouth. "Did you . . . *do away with him?*"

"You've got to be kidding," Hayes rumbled, walking the length of the balcony, back and forth.

They kept arguing among themselves. Ness figured they were split: Libby and Tyler were convinced Ness was out to get them; Coco, Daisy, and Ian were sitting on an uncomfortable fence. Hayes, at least, was sticking with her. For now.

Then Coco waded into the fray.

Daisy had French-braided her hair for her earlier that evening and she looked more put together than most of them, despite the dark circles under her eyes and the jittering of her knee whenever she tried to sit still. When she spoke, her raspy voice was tinged with impatience, as though she had so many better things to be doing right now than listening to this ridiculous squabbling.

"Listen," she said. "Ness has done some shitty things in the past."

Not the stellar defense Ness had hoped for.

"But she wouldn't *maroon us on an island for profit.* Or consumption." She shot Ian a look, crossing her legs and resting her forearms on her knees. "No one here is perfect. Not one of you can say you haven't done some shady shit to get ahead."

A chorus of protests.

"Fine. You want me to list stuff?" She paused, eyebrow cocked as if to say *You did this to yourselves.* "There was that time Ian paid the bouncer to punch that guy in the face so he'd look like garbage for the casting call for that dumb superhero show."

"Worth it," Ian said, nodding. "I was the better Captain Strongarm."

Coco sighed and shook her head.

"Libby, you stole clothes from set like it was your personal shopping mall. I bet you still do."

"They're already tailored to my body! They're useless to anyone else."

Coco rolled her eyes and continued. "Hayes . . . actually, you might be the annoyingly good one, but I'm sure you've done some shit you're bummed about."

Coco went on. "Think I'm going to skip over myself? Wrong. I banged the director for *Utopia* in a janitor's closet to get that part. Twice." She shuddered.

"Ness had a crisis and handled it poorly," she said. "She fucked up. She was mean and sad and made horrible choices. I mean, why else would she have fucked *Ian*, of all people, when she could have been back with Hayes?" She glanced at Ian, who looked distinctly uncomfortable. "And then she ghosted us. But we can . . ."

Coco's face went pale in the dim light. She stopped talking. Her eyes darted from Hayes to Ness.

"Was that a secret? Shit." Her shoulders slumped and her chin dropped to her chest. Ness watched her take a deep breath before looking back to the group.

"In summary," she finished weakly, "we all suck pretty equally and should shut the hell up and go to bed." She stood fluidly and walked inside, pausing on her way past Ness to give her shoulder a quick squeeze and whisper, "It was a long time ago, Ness. No one cares anymore."

But judging by the look on Hayes's face, he did.

Memorials have been erected along the beach of the Bleu on the Sands Hotel, where the missing cast and crew of the Good Things Network's upcoming show *Ocean Views: Turning Tides* participated in their first—and potentially last—table read last week.

Heartbroken fans have gathered here, and around the world, to express their love to the actors, including movie star Hayes Beaumont, who have brought them so much joy over the years. While there is still hope that those missing will be found alive and well, the chance of a rescue decreases with each passing day.

"As you can imagine, this has been a horrendous experience," says Robert Larkin, father of actress Agnes "Ness" Larkin, who tearfully addressed the media earlier today. "Agnes and I have had our differences, but she will always be my little girl."

The U.S. Coast Guard is now working with the Royal Bahamas Defence Force to expand the search area, but the authorities are asking private citizens to report anything unusual and keep their eyes open for signs of these missing individuals.

CHAPTER 21

THINGS WENT DOWNHILL FROM THERE. NESS HAD FIGURED THEY were already at the bottom, but now they were burrowing into the ground.

Libby pretended Coco's well-intentioned speech never happened, and soon she had Daisy and Ian at least tentatively on her side. Ness couldn't help but wonder if Ian's defection was at least partially based on self-preservation, after Coco's unfortunate revelation. If he stuck by Ness, his access to pharmaceuticals might immediately become much more tenuous.

Despite the whole "Ness slept with Ian" thing, Hayes tried to intervene, but by that point it was chaos and, among all the voices talking over each other, someone suggested Ness and Hayes needed to be separated in case they were criminal collaborators.

"Go with it," Hayes told her under his breath. "They need time to think this through, and then they'll see reason." Given the deep frown lines he was sporting, and the distance he'd been keeping between them since Coco's spilling of the ancient beans, Ness was pretty sure he wasn't only referring to the angry horde.

Which was how Ness found herself sitting in the mirror-covered bedroom where she'd found nearly-nude Hayes what felt like a lifetime ago. Except now she had Ian as her guard. Libby had volunteered for the job herself, but Daisy, probably fearing for Ness's health and safety if left alone with her archnemesis (whose life she had just saved, *by the way*), had suggested Ian do it so the others would be free to search for Bradley and continue plotting Ness's demise. The not-so-subtle subtext was that Ian was in no state to traipse all over the island himself and he may as well have some supervision.

Ian didn't seem very dedicated to his new role. He was lying on his stomach on the bed, reading a battered copy of what appeared to be a historical romance novel, if the swooning redhead on the cover was any indication.

Ness couldn't settle. She paced the room, replaying the scene on the balcony in her head and inserting all the scathing remarks she wished she'd thought of sooner.

"*Ethan leaned in close*," Ian said suddenly. "*His words caressed Emilia's ear, making the center of her burst to sinful flames. She could smell the winter wind still clinging to the fabric of his heavy riding cloak and wondered if he could feel that she was burning up from within.*"

Ness stopped pacing and stared at him. "What are you doing?"

He marked his spot with a finger. From across the room Ness could see his hand trembling. "Trying to distract you. Should I keep going?"

"Please don't."

He skimmed down the page. "Are you sure? Things are about to get *very* interesting for our dear widowed-yet-still-virginal duchess."

"What's going to happen when you run through Libby's pills?"

Slowly, he closed the book and sat up. Anger flashed across his face but quickly morphed into resignation. He spread his arms and shrugged.

"Withdrawal. More of what you already saw. Mood swings, anxiety, sweating." He was ticking symptoms off on his fingers. "Maybe hallucinations, which would be really exciting here. The most convenient, though, is loss of appetite. If we're looking for a positive spin, there it is." He smiled wryly, dimple on full display.

"I can't tell if you're taking this seriously."

"*I* can't tell if *you're* planning to sell our secrets for financial gain. What if I go the way of Bradley and end up," he pitched his voice deep, "done away with?"

Ness groaned and flopped down onto the dusty but still plush area rug. "Do you think he's okay?"

"Yeah, I do. He's out there proving a point. He'll probably be back in the morning, crowing about how quickly things fell apart up on this hill without him."

Ness hoped he was right, because she wasn't so sure. She thought back to the argument she'd overheard between Libby and Bradley. Then the letters he'd written. He had a plan, he'd said. What if his plan was . . . whatever this was?

She could see it. He'd wanted so badly to make it to the A-list, but never seemed to progress past cop shows and supporting roles in movies starring much bigger names. If he could anonymously sell the footage from the island, he'd make a fortune.

But where *was* he?

She tried breathing in for a four count and out for six, exactly the way her sleep app instructed every night. Instead of settling her, though, the extra oxygen seemed to push her racing brain into overdrive.

"I thought I'd already been through the worst part of my life and this was going to be an upswing, but here we are, on a swift train heading off a cliff." She lay flat and flipped her palms to the ceiling, trying more deep breaths. A whisper of cool air made its way through the room, making Ness shiver.

"You know what's sucking the most, aside from the potential murder accusations? I thought I was making real progress." She closed her eyes, talking more to herself than Ian. "I signed on to this project for what felt like all the right reasons. The money was a nice perk—though, newsflash, it sounds like they really scraped the bottom of the barrel on my contract. But it was like the universe was rewarding twenty years of trying to patch myself back together with a do-over. I was so excited to be here, in front of the camera. Well, not *here* here." She sighed.

"And despite ending up on this stupid island, and having to fight wildlife I don't even want to see in a zoo, and being so hungry I would eat that dumb velvet couch, I still felt like this was worth it. I can apologize and make amends and show people I care about them here just as much, if not more, than if we were shooting."

She heard Ian shift and looked over at him. "I thought things were getting better."

She let her eyes fall shut again, and a wave of despair washed over her. Ian's voice cut through her morose reverie.

"I thought writing my memoir would be healing. It felt like I was finally doing some good, and by sharing my experience I might help other people. If I could show even one struggling person that there is a path forward, that would make a difference. But you know what I worried about?"

Ness's eyes were still closed. She sniffled, not quite crying but not quite *not* crying. "What?"

"That helping wouldn't feel good enough. That redeeming myself wouldn't be a big enough high. That *nothing* would ever feel like enough."

"Is that why you started using again?"

"No." He laughed, harsh and brittle. Ness opened her eyes.

"No," he repeated. "I started because it was too much. For the first time in a long, long time I was fully aware of the spotlight and the scrutiny and all these people looking up to me. For a while it was great, you know? I'd done it. I was back."

"And then?" Ness prompted. She pushed herself to her elbows, feeling uneasy about the direction this was taking. The draft she'd felt earlier was also getting stronger. She peered around the edges of the room, looking for its source.

"And then that pressure started to feel crushing. I got paranoid. Anxious. Thinking that someone was always watching and waiting to catch me fucking up again. And that's when I realized it was only a matter of time until I was a disappointment. Again. Always. Forever. I've never been able to live up to the hype. You and Hayes? You've always been larger than life. It can suck the air out of a room. Everyone else is instantly in your shadow. Honestly, it was a bit of a relief when you left."

Ian was standing now, looking out the window. Her heart began to pound as her brain threw together pieces of a rather distressing puzzle.

Ian disappearing in the night. His mood swings. He'd just come off a book tour touting redemption and sobriety while still using—if that got out into the media, Ness wasn't sure he'd get a second chance at a comeback. If Libby and Tyler had convinced him she was the one with the cameras, what would he do to make sure the footage didn't leak? How desperate was he?

Of course, there was another option. One she'd be silly to ignore. If he'd been sourcing drugs and potentially paying people to keep it quiet for months now, Ian could be deep in the red. As far as she could tell, his lifestyle hadn't changed much, which meant footing a hefty monthly bill. She assumed his book advance had been substantial. Other than some guest spots riding on the publicity of his tour, he hadn't been getting much work elsewhere. It was like the industry was waiting to see what he did next before reinvesting.

If any of them was desperate for cash, it could easily be him.

Ness got to her feet and wondered where everyone else was. She wandered casually to the door and tried the knob. It was locked.

"Wouldn't be much of a house arrest situation if the door was open, would it?" Ian had turned and was leaning against the wall, watching her. The mirrors created endless loops of the two of them.

The lights suddenly glowed brighter, then dimmed. Faintly, Ness could hear the generator starting to cycle more loudly. This would be the last night with power, then.

They stared at each other for another awkward beat, and then Ian laughed. "God, this place really messes with your head, huh?" He belly-flopped back onto the bed and started rifling through the bag he'd brought in with him. He pulled out a prescription pill bottle. Ignoring her watchful gaze, he popped the top free and shook two tablets into his palm.

"Don't tell Libs I have these. Emergency stash."

From Ness's viewpoint the bottle looked perilously close to empty. She pressed her hands flat against her thighs to hide their trembling.

"Should we be, um, conserving resources here?" She looked meaningfully at the bottle lying beside him.

He rummaged some more and produced a mason jar of clear liquid. Unscrewing the top, he took a long swallow, chasing the pills down with a final glug. He wiped his mouth with the back of his hand and offered her the jar.

She accepted and sniffed. Gin. She handed it back. "I'm good."

"Alright, then. Back to the duchess." He flicked through until he found his page, and cleared his throat.

"*'You can't hide your true feelings from me, precious one,' Ethan growled. Emilia's knees trembled and she found herself backed against the banister. The hard wood of the newel post pressed into her spine . . .'*"

By the time the duchess had experienced her first dozen orgasms and then, in a real twist, been seemingly spurned by the wicked earl, Ian was asleep, snoring loudly with his face resting on his forearms. Ness was pulling a thin blanket over him when she felt a cool breeze across the back of her ankles.

Casting a look over her shoulder to make sure Ian was still out, she slowly slid open the—mirrored, obviously—closet door and peered inside. A gust of air swirled around her, tickling her nose as she inhaled dust and mummified insects.

She crouched into a ball and pressed her face into her thighs just in time, allowing her legs to absorb a gargantuan sneeze. On the bed, Ian murmured something in his sleep and rolled onto his side. She froze, counting to thirty before getting creakily upright. Man, she missed her joint supplements.

A thin strip of light against the dark wooden wall at the back of the closet caught her attention. It was partially hidden behind a slinky zebra-print robe drooping dejectedly on a metal hook. Ness brushed the fabric aside and ran her hands over the wall, searching for any kind of lever or button.

Her fingers tangled in a silky cord that at first seemed to be a particularly garish part of the robe but, on further investigation, was actually dangling from the ceiling. Its gold-tasseled end shimmered in the light. She pulled tentatively, then harder. From within the wall there was a faint click and a latch released. Ness pushed the full-size door open.

She was in a small hallway that, judging by the angled ceiling, passed under the stairs. After a moment of indecision, she shoved the door to the closet closed.

The hallway walls were painted white and the floors were the same tile as the kitchen. Dim pot lights mounted far above in the double-height ceiling lit her way. It all seemed very . . . normal, which, at this point, Ness found more disconcerting than if she'd been surrounded by prints of lusty Viking gods. She eyed the light switch, wondering who had flicked it on, and when. Considering her options of staying in her surreal bedroom prison with Ian or forging ahead into the unknown, she continued on. Maybe her luck would turn and she'd find some kind of evidence that proved she wasn't the baddie in this particular drama.

She followed the hall a short distance and entered a small room sandwiched between the kitchen and balcony. A piece of counter and cabinetry matching those in the kitchen ran along one wall, and on top stood a camera on a short tripod, red light blinking. It was pointing out a window that looked onto the balcony—specifically, onto the defunct hot tub. Ness had spent enough time pacing out there to know that from the outside the window looked just like a trellised portion of the wall.

Ness peeked out and saw, under the faint light of the moon, Coco and Daisy locked in a passionate embrace. A faint "Awwww!" escaped her lips. It was about time something good happened here.

She pulled out the memory card and ground it under her heel, then grabbed the camera, knelt, and smashed it against the tile.

Above her head, a ceiling fan whirled slowly. At the end of the room was a heavy-looking wooden door. An ornate keyhole was above the handle and Ness half-heartedly turned the knob, already weighing her chances of getting back into her prison cell unnoticed if this was a dead end. Not that it seemed like Ian cared much.

The door swung toward her.

"Huh."

More ornate sconces with candle-like bulbs were mounted on cinderblock walls, framing a set of descending stone stairs that curved left and out of view in their flickering light.

If this were a police procedural, Ness would have had her hand on the butt of her gun. She'd have been muttering into a radio, asking for backup. And then she'd have gone down those stairs alone to save the day because time was of the essence.

She could, she supposed, go back and find someone else, but then what? *Hey, bud, want to explore what appears to be a dungeon with me?* Given the current trust issues running rampant among island inhabitants, it didn't seem like a great option.

A quiet moan came from below.

"Bradley?" she called, sticking her head through the doorway to peer farther down. They'd all assumed that he'd fled outward to tame the island and prove a point, but what if he'd been in here the whole time?

She heard what sounded like a shoe scuffling on pavement. The lights brightened and dimmed again. And again. Ness figured they had a couple minutes, max, before the lights went out for good. This would be a really great time to find some more gas. And what better place to store it than in a nice cool basement. Right? Absolutely. Not that she was talking herself into anything. This was the most sensible next step. And what if there were resources down there and she didn't get them now, while there was ample light? Then she'd have to go with a flashlight or the stupid hand-crank lantern, and it would be eighty-five times spookier, and there was the chance she'd overlook something. Plus, she could really do with a win right now.

Hey, maybe there would be wine! She perked up. She could *really* go for some wine.

Taking a deep breath that smelled of wet stone and mistakes, she nodded, psyching herself up. This was the only good option.

Before she could reconsider, she was five steps down.

"Hello?"

Her voice seemed to echo back at her.

"Okay, creepy," she muttered, one hand trailing along the cool, damp cinderblocks for balance. No one had bothered to install a handrail, of course.

Pausing at the small landing at the top of the curve, Ness leaned forward, peeking around the wall to see what fresh hell awaited her.

The staircase ended in another equally dim, breezy corridor. It was no more than four feet wide, and the floor under Ness's bare feet was cool and a bit slippery. The air smelled of the sea.

She crept along, painfully aware of the increasing frequency of the light pulses that signaled the end times for their power source.

"This is so dumb." She kept one hand on the wall, thinking that if the lights did go out, she could turn herself around and follow the wall right back out the way she'd come. Barely terrifying at all.

The ceiling changed, and now it was curved, rough stone. Soon the walls followed suit, and the cinderblock gave way to the same dark rock.

The hall had become a tunnel.

Just as Ness's independent and investigatory spirit was about to max out and send her back to the surface, the tunnel opened into a cavern.

The chamber she stood at the threshold of was maybe twenty feet across and irregularly shaped, following what she assumed were the natural contours of the space. Directly across from her was another doorway, through which more light was visible.

But it was the area in front of her that really held her attention.

Given everything they'd discovered in the past few days, she shouldn't have been surprised to find herself in an oceanic sex dungeon. And yet.

Three sets of manacles were mounted to the largest wall. A large hook dangled from a chain in the ceiling at the cavern's center. Along the far left wall were shelves lined with assorted whips and . . . Ness squinted to get a better look and immediately regretted it. Needless to say, if one were into that sort of thing, there were many options.

To her left, a semicircular pool was set into the ground. Submerged lights cast an eerie green glow. She edged closer, looking in. A trio of bug-eyed fish flicked their tails back and forth, swimming away as her shadow loomed over them. Ness leapt back, startled, then peeked again. The lights revealed a tunnel that went into the wall. As she watched, the fish made their way through the opening and out of sight.

She shuddered as a damp draft funneled through the space and wrapped around her in a ghostly embrace. Something flashed in the corner of her vision. She turned to the right, where an ornate but very rusty metal chair sat. Half-rotted leather straps dangled from the arms and legs.

On the seat, a bright, bluish light flickered.

Ness felt as if she were moving in slow motion, tiptoeing across the floor and picking up the small camera.

It was in playback mode, and she froze, watching herself wrapped in Hayes's arms on the balcony, her head thrown back so she could stare into his eyes. Their lips were a hairsbreadth apart. Apparently, the camera she'd seen on her way in wasn't the only one that had been recording the action outside.

She dropped it as if it had burnt her, sending it clattering back onto the seat.

Behind her, there was a swish of air and the rustle of fabric. Ness spun as someone disappeared up the stairs so quickly she caught only the smallest glimpse of a leg before they were out of sight.

"Hey!" she yelled, starting after them. "Wait!"

At the top of the stairs, a door slammed. The faint sound of a lock clacking into place echoed dimly off the rock walls.

To: Morris Wagner
From: Trisha Jung
Subject: Schedule

Morris,

This is a hard situation for all of us, but we're three days into this crisis with no sign of a resolution. You need to find a way forward—with or without the current cast. We're burning money here. Make it work.

T

CHAPTER 22

AT LEAST THE LIGHTS ARE STILL ON.

Of course, that hopeful thought was all it took for them to shine brightly for one final, glorious moment, searing an image of the area in front of Ness into her brain, before they went out. Not a slow fade, but an immediate plunge into the darkest dark she'd ever known.

"Oh, come *on*," she moaned. She tried to orient herself from memory. Stepping tentatively forward, she immediately smashed her knee on the chair the now-dark camera rested on. Or had rested. She heard it clatter to the ground, and when she took a teensy step to the side to try to locate it, she managed to kick it farther away.

"Son of a . . ." She rubbed her leg, took a deep breath, and tried again to get to the wall, even more slowly this time. If anyone had happened to be watching with night vision, they'd have seen something very akin to a sloth crossing a road. A very cold sloth. Ness tried to enjoy the feeling of being chilled, a novelty after days of near-constant sweating, but the circumstances weren't ripe for casual gratitude practice.

One mincing step at a time, she moved forward and to her right until her palm hit the wall, scaring the heck out of her, despite having expected it any moment. She took a steadying breath and tried to slow her pounding heart before inching along in what she really, truly, *deeply* hoped was the way to the stairs and not off some cliff she hadn't clocked coming in.

Wind whispered through the cavern, but it was impossible to pin-point where it originated, or if it was in fact simply wishful thinking. Sounds bounced off the walls and echoed back. If Ness had believed in ghosts, she'd have sworn there was a whole gang of them behind her. Actually, now that she thought about it, she wasn't 100 percent sure ghosts *weren't* a thing . . .

When her icy toes finally made contact with the bottom step, she nearly wept with relief. As she edged her way up, she prayed, against all logic and common sense, for the door to be open. Maybe whoever had been down there needed to make a sneaky getaway and was now feigning sleep with the others.

Was this Bradley's secret hideout? She had to admit, it was an excel-lent villain's lair, though she couldn't really picture him choosing to stay somewhere so uncomfortable for any length of time. He was more of a feather pillow and cold-pressed coconut oil guy.

Or had Ian somehow followed her without her noticing? She'd been pretty focused on what was ahead of her, as opposed to what might be creeping along behind. If he hadn't, what would happen when he woke up and found her missing?

Ness had no idea what she'd do once she got out, but, you know, *one step at a time.* She stifled a hysterical giggle-turned-grunt as she stubbed a toe on a riser.

The door, of course, was closed. And locked. And, obviously, no one answered her screams for help. They were probably passed out for the night, their stomachs full of python meat and spiteful rage. She wished them aggressive indigestion and eerie dreams.

Was this Libby's way of getting rid of her . . . permanently?

Do snakes like cave-dungeon-basements?

Minutes or hours or years later, throat raw and knuckles scraped from pounding against the heavy, probably soundproofed, door, Ness sat on the steps. She rested her chin in her hands, elbows on her knees, and tried to project a bored nonchalance that might convince her animal-brain that there was no reason to freak out. She was definitely *not* going to die here, never to be found because, undoubtedly, someone would tear down the house in the not-too-distant future and her corpse would be forever lost among the rubble.

She really didn't want to have to haunt the island.

And *of course* no one would believe she was a criminal mastermind, charting a course to this godforsaken island with ill intentions, who had then fled in the night to avoid the consequences of her actions. *That would be ridiculous.*

But was it? Libby had made it pretty clear that she, at least, found the idea plausible. And really, Ness could see how she got there. It hurt, but she could understand it.

Despite what her nonexistent publicist would probably call "challenging optics," she did have faith that Hayes would still believe in her and come looking. Coco wouldn't be easily swayed by Libby's and Tyler's opinions, and Ness had to hope that she could cajole and woo Daisy onto her side if necessary. It helped to believe she'd mended enough fences that the group as a whole wouldn't shrug off her sudden disappearance and move on with their lives.

She shifted her weight and tried to get the blood flowing to her numb rear end. The stone steps were far from comfortable, but the idea of navigating back down in the dark was even less appealing. And really, what was she going to do down there? Fall in the pool? Sit in the sex throne? No thank you.

Thinking back through her evening, Ness figured she'd come through the door around ten. It couldn't have been more than an hour since then. Probably less, despite her feeling like she was already turning into Gollum.

"I don't even have a precious," she muttered dejectedly.

Leaning back against the door, she tried to remember the moments when she'd first come down the stairs, searching for any clue that might reveal who had been in the dungeon with her. She came up empty.

Ian shadowing her was the easiest explanation. She groaned and pressed the heels of her hands against her eyes. This was so messed up.

And she was *so tired*. And hungry. And *how was this her life?*

Her heart galloped wildly and she tried to pry her thoughts away from, well, everything, focusing on breathing. Just breathing.

All through that night she startled constantly, convinced someone was looming over her, about to go in for the kill. Eventually, a sliver of dim morning light became visible under the door, trickling through from the outer room's window.

Ness took this as her cue to resume escaping.

She gave the screaming and door-kicking another shot, but all she got for her efforts were additional bruises on her knuckles and palms to go with her dehydration headache.

She turned to stare down the stairs into the unrelenting darkness.

There was nothing appealing about going back down there. The stairs were barely visible, and Ness was almost certain she was destined to fall and break an ankle. Unfortunately, she couldn't seem to come up with an alternative. Her breath was ragged in her ears and her pulse throbbed at her temples. The longer she stood there, achieving nothing, the faster her heart beat and the closer she came to folding into the fetal position.

A drawn-out groan escaped her lips, but down she went, reverting to the hand-on-wall method.

The cavern was only a slightly less intense shade of black, inching toward what could be labeled on a paint chip as "Wet Iron at Twilight," "Charcoal in a Darkened Room," or "Shadows of Doom." She couldn't tell where the scant light was coming from, but maybe light meant an exit.

Ness squinted into the gloom, desperate for a sign of anything that signaled an alternate way out.

She needed light.

Shuffling her feet to avoid tripping, she made her way to the right, trying to remember where the shelf of, erm, accessories had been. Eventually, she walked directly into it, bouncing her face off something firm, cylindrical, and rubbery. It thudded to the floor, and bounced.

"*Gross*," she whined, but she kept a hand on the shelf. Feeling her way across, she skimmed her fingertips over metal, latex, and something cold, damp, and furry.

Moving down one shelf, she started the process again. No flashlight, lantern, or glow-in-the-dark sex toy revealed itself, but her hand closed around a metal cylinder the size of a can of hairspray. She slid her hand to the top, felt the lip of a lid, and popped it off. With the can held at arm's length and hopefully not pointed at her face, she tested the nozzle, giving it a quick jab with her forefinger.

She heard a hiss, and the air around her filled with the scent of citrus-scented disinfectant.

"That's something, I guess."

Ness clutched the canister to her chest and found the wall again. Continuing along to the right, sliding her free hand up and down the surface, she prayed she had remembered the layout of the room correctly. It was all such a blur, like playing one of those memory games where someone shows you a tray of items—in this case, BDSM-themed—and you have to remember as many as possible.

Her nail jammed into the crack between a metal bracket and the wall, bending painfully backward. Ness fought the urge to stick it directly into her mouth and settled for deep, calming breaths instead. It was not effective.

More carefully, she slid her hand along the wall again until it hit the bracket. She grabbed the thick-handled whip that resided there. The handle tapered, wand-like, before the tail began. Ness waved it through the air, testing its strength. It was weighty but balanced in her grip, and she could see how, in different circumstances, someone might enjoy the feel of wielding it.

The leather had moldered a bit, and where the pieces flaked off under her touch, Ness could feel the wood it was wrapped around peeking through. She hoped it was damp enough for what she had planned.

Stripping her T-shirt off, she sat cross-legged with her supplies in her lap. She carefully wrapped the shirt around the top of the whip's handle, then secured it by twining the tail around the fabric and knotting it as many times as the length allowed. Balancing the whole thing on her feet, she sprayed the disinfectant in short bursts until she'd figured out where the opening was, then blasted it at the T-shirt and tried not to inhale too deeply.

Shifting to one side, she reached into her back pocket and pulled out the matchbook she'd been carrying around since the first fire on the beach. Her confidence waned. The cardboard was damp. The remaining two matches felt moist.

Keeping her makeshift torch gripped between her feet, Ness shimmied her body until the gentle, constant breeze was at her back. She ripped one match free and felt for the rough strip on the back of the package.

She held her breath and struck the match.

Nothing.

She tried again. And again. And seven more times, just in case. By that point, the flammable head of the match had completely disappeared and Ness was forced to accept that her fate rested on the nonexistent shoulders of the final, shitty match.

She sat quietly for a moment, composing herself. Looking up at the ceiling, she spoke to both no one and everyone.

"If I get out of this, I will always carry waterproof matches. I will learn to swim at a professional level. I won't care so much about what other people think. I'll adopt senior dogs and give them joyous last days." She inhaled, deeply this time, the residual spray burning her nostrils only slightly. She coughed.

"I will learn to trust people. At least, the ones who earn it." She carefully ripped the last match free. "Whoever put me in earth's butthole gets zero good vibes henceforth. Straight to the no-trust zone."

Gripping the match firmly between shaking fingers, she pulled it through the folded cardboard book.

Schnick.

A delicate flame flickered into existence. Ness drew in a careful breath and cupped her hand around the tiny spot of hope. She dragged her feet closer, bringing the chemical-citrus-scented T-shirt within reach, and lowered the flame until it was touching.

There was a drawn-out moment where she was sure that the match was going to burn out. That the shirt wouldn't catch. That she'd be right back where she'd started, in the dark with no plan.

She let out a sigh of frustration and froze as the flame dimmed to a glowing red ember. Then, with a satisfying and only slightly alarming *whoomp*, the shirt was on fire.

Ness scrabbled to her feet, gripping the handle tightly. She had no idea how long the thing would last, or if the whip tail would melt and drop a flaming piece of fabric onto her, or . . .

As she circled the panic wagon, someone coughed. The sound echoed through the chamber, making it sound as if it were populated by an army of pack-a-day smokers.

"Ahhgggghhh!" Ness staggered backward and collapsed against the wall. She'd always assumed she'd be a natural fighter in this type of situation, grappling with the enemy to the death (ideally not her own), but it turned out she was more of a "curl into a protective ball and hope they don't see me" prisoner.

Dimly, through the terror, she heard a voice.

"Who's there? What's happening?" Scuffling came from across the cavern, followed by, "What *is* this place?"

Keeping with the theme of avoiding attention, despite the flaming evidence to the contrary, Ness didn't answer. Her brain *knew* that voice, but in her current state of dehydrated, sleep-deprived near-hysteria, she couldn't place it.

The mystery person spoke again.

"Listen, we can work this out. I'm sure it's all a misunderstanding."

One tiny degree of movement at a time, Ness raised her head from where it had been pressed to her knees.

"*Bradley?*"

The clank of metal on stone rang out from the other side of the cavern.

"Ness? Thank god. Come get me out of here." A thunk now of something heavy against the floor.

She started across the smooth, dark floor, then stopped.

"What are you doing down here?" she asked suspiciously. She'd been locked in the dungeon for hours, making no shortage of noise, and this fool was just announcing his presence *now*?

"Jesus, my head is killing me. Um, I don't know what I'm doing here, Agnes. Or where *here* is." A pause. "What are *you* doing here?" His tone indicated that he thought knew exactly what she was doing here, and it wasn't anything good.

Ness crept closer until she was standing outside the second doorway she'd noticed when she'd first gotten down there, what felt like a lifetime ago. She edged forward, flickering torch aloft, until she had a relatively clear view of Bradley, backed by a wall of empty wooden racks, semi-circles cut from the planks.

Huh. Ian had been right about the wine cellar after all. Too bad it had been cleared out. The occasion really called for any and all liquid numbing agents.

She dragged her attention back to Bradley.

He was strapped to what could loosely be described as a chair. It had a metal frame with padded sections at weight-bearing points. The leg rests were separated enough for another person to stand between his knees. The real defining feature, though, was the multitude of restraints that held him in place. Wide black straps were wrapped around his upper arms, wrists, chest, stomach, thighs, calves, and ankles. There was even one across his forehead.

Ness watched as he shifted his weight to the left and then quickly to the right, rocking the entire apparatus. It slid half an inch across the floor, scraping metal against rock. That explained the noise.

He glared at her from the corner of his eye.

"This is a new low, don't you think? Kidnapping, Ness? Really?" The muscles in his arms strained as he tried to rip free.

While it seemed pretty unlikely that he'd managed to secure himself to the chair, Ness wasn't in a particularly trusting mood, and she kept her distance.

"Why would I do this?" she asked, hurt, but genuinely curious. "Actually, *how* could I even have done this? What do you weigh? Two-ten? I appreciate your ridiculous overestimation of my strength, but come on."

His eyes narrowed in consideration as he judged her upper-body musculature and found it lacking.

"Fine," he allowed, then added, "but maybe you're not in it alone."

"Ugghh. Who, Bradley? Who on this rock is jumping into criminal collusion with me? Plus, I'm in the same boat as you, friend. Don't you think I'd have something other than a handcrafted chemical torch if I'd planned this?"

The torch in question was still going strong, giving off fumes that left Ness's head pounding even more than it had been earlier.

The silence dragged on, punctuated only by small grunts of effort as he continued to strain against the straps holding him in place.

"Yeah." He sighed. "Yeah, alright. I guess it's unlikely you could pull something like this off." He shifted the entire chair structure again. "So untie me already!"

"Someone locked me in a pit," Ness explained. "You can understand why I'm feeling a little wary."

He rolled his eyes, then winced. "Ow," he groaned. "Well, that makes two of us. I was heading to bed and Daisy asked if I'd refill the bathroom buckets. I got back and was brushing my teeth when I heard a weird noise. Long story short, I investigated, found another secret passage in that bedroom of ten thousand reflections, and came down here on my own like a schmuck."

Ness made a noncommittal sound, not wanting to draw attention to her own schmuckery.

"I slipped on the stairs, hit my head, and woke up like this, which, to be honest, was pretty fucking concerning."

"You've been unconscious for twenty-four hours?" The skepticism came through loud and clear.

"No," he said tightly. "It was, fuck, I don't know. Maybe a few minutes? I woke up strapped to this . . . whatever the hell this is, and had a drink." His chin jerked slightly to the human equivalent of a hamster water bottle suspended from the ceiling by a metal rod. It was off-center now, but Ness assumed it had been directly over his face before Bradley started shuffling the chair around.

She eyed the chair in question, unsure she should even call it anything so innocent. It was as explicit a piece of furniture as she'd ever seen. How long could, uh, biological samples exist on a surface? Gloves would be so, *so* great right now. She kind of wished she'd reserved a supply of the disinfectant spray.

"And then I passed out again." He grimaced. "The water must be laced with something. It tasted terrible, but that seemed . . . not surprising. I have no idea how long I've been here." His eyes locked expectantly on Ness's, but she wasn't ready.

"What about your argument with Libby?"

"Which one?"

"You were upstairs, asking for help, and she didn't seem inclined. I don't think you ended on great terms."

"It's none of your business."

Ness gestured to their surroundings. "I think it's entirely my business if you're in some dire financial straits and have gone to some pretty dicey extremes."

"Do you hear yourself?"

Ness raised an eyebrow and waited.

"Fine. *Fine.* I made a bad investment. Put all my eggs into one basket to get a movie made and . . . it didn't work out. You'd think people would be more into a biopic about the greatest body painter who ever lived. I asked Libby for a loan."

She considered. It sounded like a very Bradley move.

He strained against the strapping again. "Now will you *please* get me off this thing?"

A wall-mounted sconce provided a convenient holder for her torch, and as Ness worked her way through the straps, she braced herself for the fallout and told Bradley about the letters, the python, and how she'd ended up in the abyss with him.

She made sure to cover the invasion-of-privacy portion first, while his arms were still tied down. It would have been easy to skip over that part until they were free, but it had been weighing on her, and she wanted to be the one to tell him what had happened. Borrow-stealing necessities was one thing (and still not a great thing), but reading something so clearly personal and precious made her stomach turn—not to mention the whole "and then Libby read them" thing.

The outrage she'd expected didn't surface. Instead, Bradley seemed relieved.

He flexed his fingers and rotated his wrists, getting feeling back into his joints and digits as Ness worked her way through the last of the straps.

"I'm glad it's out," he said. "It's a heavy thing, keeping the happiest part of my life hidden away like some dirty secret. They deserve better." He looked down at her. "Honestly, I'm pretty surprised you told me. That was brave."

Ness felt the tips of her ears burn. She was just as surprised as he was, but it felt good.

"I, erm, thought the letters meant you were behind . . . all this." She waved her hands vaguely at their surroundings. "You wrote about a plan for financial stability. It seemed to line up. What's more lucrative than holding the secrets of everyone on this island?"

He scoffed. "I'm taking over for Richard Garvey, hosting *Survive the Night.*" He pitched his voice low and raspy. "Only one thing stands between you and glory. All you need to do is *survive the night.*" He shrugged and spoke normally. "It's a steady paycheck, and the chances of them canceling it in the next few years are slim. Audiences love watching people being terrified, I guess. It's the closest I'm going to get to a normal full-time job."

Bradley setting aside his dreams of blockbuster fame to embrace a reality TV career was almost as hard to believe as the idea of him as a doting father, but the mixture of resignation and pride on his face sold it.

"You'll be great," Ness assured him, covering parenthood and career change in one fell swoop. She thought she sounded pretty believable. "And hey, I have a stellar location pre-scouted for you."

The light from the torch suddenly dimmed. Ness turned, and watched, crestfallen, as the fiery remains of the T-shirt fell from the handle, landing on the ground in a smoldering pile of uselessness.

In the last of the barely present light, Bradley swung his legs down and tried to stand, but staggered, catching himself on the chair. His head drooped, chin nearly touching his chest. His breaths were as ragged and borderline panicked as Ness's. For some reason, that made her feel marginally better.

"Whoa, there, big guy." She put a hand on his damp, sweaty back. "Take it slow."

"I think I might puke." He was slightly hunched over, hands braced on the seat of the chair as he took deep breaths. Unfortunately, the air was filled with chemical-laced smoke from the spent torch.

"As long as it's not on me. Come on. We've got a door to break down."

She looped his heavy arm over her bare shoulders and was bracing herself to take a portion of his weight when they heard the squeal of the door opening, and a *thunk* as it closed again. Footsteps echoed as someone came down the stairs.

She stared at Bradley, still visible in the dying light, wide-eyed, her mind racing. He stared back with a decidedly glazed look to his eyes.

Moving quickly, she pulled him along to the barely glowing T-shirt and stomped out the remaining embers. Then, using her now well-practiced wall-guidance technique, she moved them around the perimeter of the room until their backs were pressed to the wall just inside the doorway. If anyone looked straight in, even with a light, they wouldn't be visible.

The bright glare of a flashlight flitted across the doorway, carried on past it, and then came back. The light was now pooling on the empty chair.

There was an indistinct, throaty noise, followed by a soft thump and a man's voice quietly cursing. He came around the corner, the light bobbing as he hobbled in.

"Are you kidding me right now?" Bradley's voice was strangled, steeped in offended disbelief.

The shadowy figure jumped, letting out a small, high-pitched scream at the sound of a voice coming from directly beside him. The flashlight fell to the floor and rolled until it clanked against the metal base of the chair.

"Why is it so dang *dark*?" Tyler demanded, hand pressed to his chest, still standing on one foot like an oversized, petulant flamingo. "Nothing can ever be easy. Oh no," he muttered, kneeling slowly to pick up the flashlight.

Ness leapt forward and grabbed it first, pivoting to aim the beam directly onto his sunburned, peeling face.

He raised one hand in apparent surrender, sighing.

"It's not what it looks like."

Chikungunya facts:

Chikungunya is a disease caused by a mosquito-borne virus. First indication of illness is usually abrupt-onset fever. Severe joint pain is also common, and can be both debilitating and long-lasting. A skin rash might appear. Other common symptoms include muscle pain, headache, nausea, and fatigue. In a small number of cases, mental haze and delirium may present as the fever peaks.

CHAPTER 23

TYLER LOOKED TERRIBLE. THE PATCHES OF HIS SKIN THAT WERE visible beneath the layers of days-old calamine were covered in a bright-red rash. His eyes watered as he squinted into Ness's light, his mouth screwing up into a pained grimace. Surprising herself, she took pity and lowered the beam slightly, redirecting it to his chest.

"When you say, 'It's not what it looks like,' do you mean you didn't drug Bradley and lock us both in a sex dungeon?"

Tyler squinted at the ceiling in consternation.

"Oh, well, *no*," he said slowly. "I did do that."

Bradley huffed air through his nose in a way that reminded Ness of an angry cartoon bull. She used her free hand to make a "calm down" gesture. He stayed put, but continued to breathe menacingly, leaning forward, ready to pounce, his rage apparently quelling the nausea.

Tyler watched the other man out the corner of his eye, as though he was monitoring a poorly trained dog or sticky-handed toddler. He pulled his gaze back to Ness and cleared his throat. "Do you think you could put a shirt on?"

She looked down at her pale pink lace bra, crusted with saltwater residue and dirt, and stifled an eye roll. "You're welcome to give me yours."

Tyler's face scrunched in confusion. "But it's the only one I have."

Ness considered hitting him over the head with the flashlight. She tested the weight of the light in her hand, bouncing it gently up and down.

Tyler, still looking discomfited at Ness's lack of appropriate attire, gestured toward Bradley. "Well, as I was saying, I did, technically, do the things you said. But . . . Bradley made me do it."

Ness's eyes popped open even wider as she looked between the two of them, moving the flashlight back and forth between Bradley's bulging forehead veins and Tyler's bloodshot eyes.

"I did not!"

"Did too!" Tyler crossed his arms over his chest.

Pinching the bridge of her nose, Ness wondered if she could knock *herself* out with the flashlight to escape the hell that was her reality.

"You followed me down here! You were *snooping*!" Tyler hissed. "If you'd minded your own business—"

"Hey, Tyler?" she said, interrupting the pointless back-and-forth. "I was thinking, maybe we could talk about this upstairs? It's great down here and all—love what you've done with the place—but I could do with a bathroom break and some natural light."

She smiled hopefully.

The corners of Tyler's mouth drooped. He shook his head. "Eeeeee. Wish I could help with that, but you'll need to stay down here for the time being." He gestured to the wall where the hamster water bottle could barely be seen in the gloom beyond the flashlight's beam.

"You have plenty of water. I brought food." He patted a pocket of his cargo shorts and Ness heard the crinkle of a wrapper. Her stomach instantly grumbled. She turned her head, shifting the light to look at where the water bottle dangled. The water level was visible only if she squinted and used her imagination a little bit.

"Hey, how can you even see? What about your glasses?" He'd been squinting ever since they arrived, saying things like "If only I could see." Ness had thought he was just trying to get out of doing the more terrible survival jobs.

He laughed, and it quickly spiraled into a coughing fit. He held up a finger: *one minute.*

"They were blue-light glasses." Tilting his head up and taking deep breaths as the coughing faded, he added, "You're all so focused on yourselves, you only see what you want to. I'm a nerdy, clipboard-toting PA without his glasses. Innocent. Useless. And look where that got you."

Ness let the smile drop. "Listen, there have clearly been some . . . errors in judgment here, but it's been a tough week. No one's at their best. I really think a good option, for everyone, is to move on. Forget all this happened. Right, Bradley?" She attempted to transmit a strong "just go with it" message with her eyes.

Bradley must have missed the subtext, because he stared back, arm muscles twitching with tension. His chapped lips parted, about to launch into a list of all the reasons he would definitely not be willing to forgive and forget.

Ness donkey-kicked his shin, perhaps with more force than she'd intended, heat of the moment, et cetera. Bradley closed his mouth but maintained a steady glare.

Tyler edged farther away, Teva-clad feet shuffling across the rock floor, then focused on Ness.

"I'm afraid it's too late for that. Too much in play, far too many plans made. No." He shook his head ruefully. "We must forge ahead. It's a shame to rush it, especially when you, Ness, were proving to be such a delightful and surprising star. With all the rumors, I expected you to be horrible and, well, I think we can agree your casting in *Ocean Views* was more for your looks than any real skill. Oh, come now, don't be offended. We're all reasonable adults here. It's important to deal in facts, not dreams and wishes."

Too much in play? The idea of this limp noodle of a human executing anything close to a criminal plot should have been laughable, but the more Ness thought about it, the more it made sense.

"I don't have any facts, Tyler. I have a headache, a newfound dislike for grottoes, and very little patience. *Why are we here?*" She shone the flashlight around them, letting its beam bounce off rock faces and the gently lapping water in the pool.

Tyler sighed and leaned against the wall near a set of inset shelves, scratching his forearm hard enough that Ness could hear his nails abrading his already tortured skin.

"Do you know how hard it is to make it in this business?"

She looked at Bradley like *wtf is this guy on about?* He shrugged one shoulder and, keeping his hands close to his body, pummeled one fist into the palm of his other hand. He raised an eyebrow questioningly. Ness shook her head once, quickly. *Not yet.*

Despite the dire situation, she felt kind of bad for Tyler. He was clearly troubled, and it had been a terrible week. Maybe there was a way out of this where everyone could agree it was a time best forgotten and move on.

Tyler continued, his voice ragged with emotion. His eyes were glassy, gaze fixed on a point somewhere over Ness's shoulder. Tiny beads of sweat were popping up along his hairline, clinging to the greasy strands already glued to his forehead by calamine and dirt.

"You have to be the hardest worker in the room. The quickest problem solver. The least intrusive presence while also being there every second in case someone needs something. I'm attentive, proactive, tireless. I'm trustworthy—"

Bradley scoffed, interrupting Tyler's reverie. "Wait. Aren't you the heir to a mayonnaise empire? Why are you working so much?"

Tyler jolted, as if surprised to find someone else in the room with him. "You're not the only one who can act." Tyler raised his chin and preened. "My parents kicked me out when I was seventeen. Not that I left much behind. Dad's a mechanic. Mom waits tables at the diner. They have no vision. No aspirations! They couldn't understand why I'd want to move to L.A. Imagine choosing to stay in Kenosha your whole life?

"I've been clawing my way up the ladder for *years*, underappreciated, underpaid, dedicated to my work like no one else. I don't party. I don't fraternize. I am a model employee and I deserve to be *seen*! I deserve *my* big break. And then it fell into my lap."

He nodded to himself, face lighting up like a kid presented with a double scoop of ice cream.

Ness's arm was getting tired from holding the flashlight, and the beam shook in her grip. She shifted her weight from foot to foot, wishing she'd bopped him with the light in the first place. Based on the look of exasperation on Bradley's face, he agreed, and he looked as though he might be considering launching the chair at their rashy captor.

"The network wants drama?" Spreading his arms wide, Tyler looked around the cave. "Could they ask for anything more? I mean, this is perfect. *Beyond* perfect. I'm going to hand Morris the camera footage—we can present it as a joint effort, I don't mind sharing some of the credit—and he'll see I'm meant to be here. Well, not *here* here, but *there*, an equal, finally producing my own shows and getting the recognition I've deserved for so, so long."

Tyler continued, narrowing his beady gaze at the two of them. "Unlike the rest of you, *I* take advantage of the opportunities presented to me. While you've all been mooning around, wallowing in self-pity, utterly useless, I've taken action. Do you have any idea how sought-after this will make me?"

"Do you have any idea how much you're going to hate prison?" Bradley asked.

"Shut up," Ness hissed.

"Morris wanted all of these extra cameras—thirty-five of them!—to get behind-the-scenes footage on Eclipse. It was going to be so boring. So appallingly *average*. I was going to give you a nudge here and there, of course, to help the drama along. But here? The opportunity practically threw itself at me!" Tyler cracked his knuckles, making Ness wince as the sound echoed through the chamber.

"You all made my job so easy. Especially you, Ness. My goodness, I could never have imagined just how good you would be at making people turn on you." He cackled gleefully. "It's been a joy, truly, to work with you on this.

"And of course, being as dedicated to my life's work as I am, I've left no stone unturned. I even reviewed your contracts—again, diligence! Attention to detail! Strictly speaking, I'm not supposed to have copies, but I can't stand being unprepared. Anyway, this is all entirely in line with the expectations set forth therein."

Ness's brow crinkled. "Um, I respectfully disagree."

Tyler blinked, clearing his eyes, which were collecting some concerning goop in their corners. They narrowed as he studied the two of them.

"I can't let you ruin this for me."

"Yeah, ditto," Bradley said, striding forward to push past Tyler and make his escape.

Suddenly, Tyler reached behind him, fumbling with something on one of the shelves he'd been leaning against. His arm came forward, a cord wrapped around his hand, a heavy-looking object dangling from the end.

Ness hopped backward as he started to spin it through the air in front of him, blocking access to the doorway. She peered at the whirling mass.

"Is that a . . . lava lamp?"

Bradley dipped side to side, trying to find an opening he could dodge through without getting hit in the face with three pounds of glass, metal, and whatever mystery liquid was inside it.

As Tyler edged backward to the door, still spinning his makeshift weapon, a loud rumble sounded from above. The floor shook slightly beneath Ness's feet.

The twirling lava lamp crashed to the ground, shattering into a thousand glittering, pointy pieces.

They all stared at the mess, purple-glitter-infused liquid dripping down their shins.

"Gotta run," Tyler said suddenly, dropping the cord and spinning with surprising grace to race toward the barely visible stairs.

Bradley started to give chase before realizing he was barefoot and standing in a field of broken glass.

The slap of sandaled footsteps going up the stairs echoed back to them, followed by the door creaking open. Wind whistled. Thunder rumbled. A draft of cool air fluttered across their faces. The footsteps grew faint, and then louder again as Tyler backtracked. Ness heard something thwack to the floor.

"Organic pea protein cookies!" Tyler called, already moving away. "I'll be back—"

From the open door at the top of the stairs came the sound of something very large crashing to the tiled floor.

"Oh jeez!" Tyler said, seemingly to himself. Ness heard the frantic flip-flap of his feet on the stairs before the door slammed shut again. The lock clicked.

Bradley put his back against the wall and slid to the floor, groaning dramatically. He rubbed his hands over his face before staring at Ness accusingly.

She cleared her throat and clicked the flashlight off and back on experimentally.

"Okay, yeah, I hear you. After all that, *this* was the guy hiding food?"

Has the Internet Done It Again?!

If there's one thing the online community does better than trolling their fellow humans, it's banding together to solve a mystery. Today, we're hearing multiple reports that an innocent social media post may provide important clues to the whereabouts of the missing cast of *Ocean Views: Turning Tides*.

Earlier this week, an Instagram user shared a photo of a private beach with his 3,000 followers. The island in question, Ginger Cay, had previously been reported as checked and uninhabited by the U.S.-based volunteer search team working with the Royal Bahamas Defence Force. Further investigation indicates this may be a case of human error during data entry. Requests for additional information went unanswered.

As yet another fierce storm bears down on the region, local authorities are reportedly scrambling to reach the island to confirm whether it is, in fact, sheltering the castaways.

CHAPTER 24

THEY SETTLED NEAR THE BASE OF THE STAIRS TO EAT THEIR KIWI
oatmeal pea protein cookies and regale each other with all of the
moments they should have known Tyler was up to no good.

"Why didn't we catch on when he kept going off on his own?" Ness
said, marveling at the total lack of flavor the cookie offered.

Bradley cleared his throat, trying to force the crumbs down. "Probably
because it was so nice when he went."

"All this time I thought he was just an aggravating guy, but he was
purposely provoking us? Ugh! As if there wasn't enough going on. I
hate him." She took a final, angry bite, finishing her portion, and immediately wished for another.

"The thing he said about you making people turn on you?"

Ness's cheeks grew warm at the memory. "Yeah?"

"Garbage. You came back to this thing ready to own the past and
build new bridges, and it was working." Bradley's big hand awkwardly
patted her shoulder.

She tried to thank him, but dry crumbs stuck in her already parched
throat.

In a fit of desperation, Ness tried scooping a handful of water from
the pool, only to spit the salty liquid out onto her feet. She then went
back to fetch the hamster water bottle from the other room. Whatever
was in it, at least it was water, and they were out of options. Watching
Bradley's Adam's apple bob up and down while he tried and failed to

swallow the flavorless dust lodged in his throat, Ness took the tiniest sip she could and passed the bottle over. Bradley chugged a quarter of the contents and handed it back to her. She looked at him, aghast.

"Did you not tell me this stuff is drugged? Why are you slamming it like a frat boy at dollar shot night?"

He shrugged and slumped back against the wall. "If I'm going to be trapped down here, I'd rather not be conscious."

Before Ness could launch into the litany of reasons why that was both asinine and selfish, his eyes got bleary. A few minutes later he was passed out.

Ness, feeling a bit woozy herself, turned off the flashlight and sat in silence. She listened for clues as to what was happening above them, occasionally elbowing Bradley sharply in the ribs, but he stayed deeply asleep.

After some time spent watching Bradley snooze and questioning every single one of her life choices, Ness found something new to worry about. Cool water started to lap at her calves where they pressed against the cold, hard ground. She fumbled for the flashlight, which had rolled from her grip while she was lamenting her fate. In the darkness, she fought back the heavy panic wrapping itself around her chest. *Why is there water on the floor?*

Beside her, Bradley grunted, shifted closer into the corner, his back against one wall, head lolling against the other, and let out a gentle snore.

With soggy shorts and an even less pleasant outlook, Ness's clammy hand bashed against the wall and floor until finally closing around the flashlight. She drew in a shaky breath and clicked it on.

She groaned quietly, not quite believing her eyes.

The water in their dungeon or cavern or whatever was rising. It had sloshed out of the pool and spread across the room, filling natural depressions in the rock, and it was creeping toward the outer walls. Ness moved closer to the edge of the pool, eyeing the gray water that seemed to glow despite the lack of electricity to power the submerged lights.

Her foot plunged into a puddle that came to mid-shin, sending her staggering backward. The flashlight tumbled to the floor and rolled into the puddle, casting a flickering, watery beam onto Ness like an underpowered-yet-emotive spotlight.

She snatched the light and shook it back and forth to get rid of as much water as possible. Bradley continued to snore as she perched on the stairs and clicked the light off to avoid any short-circuiting. The pool was the brightest point in the room, and Ness considered how long the tunnel to the outside might be and whether there were any larger, more toothy creatures than the fish she'd seen lurking in the depths. It would be just her luck to have a shark wash up into their prison.

She listed sideways, feeling the cool wall press against her temple, and closed her eyes, exhausted by her own fear. Hopelessness rose up to meet her almost faster than the water.

She'd started this whole adventure to prove to herself that she was a better, stronger person now. She'd wanted to make amends. To hop back onto the shooting star of fate before it fizzled entirely. She sat up straight, jaw clenched, as Bradley muttered something incoherent about a macro imbalance.

Ness clicked on the light and pointed it at his ruggedly handsome face. The water was rising, now nearly covering his legs. She couldn't believe he was still asleep. *What had Tyler put in that bottle?*

She'd be *damned* if she was going to drown in a sex dungeon with *Bradley*, of all people. She had things to do, money to make, tenuous reconnections to nurture, and drop-dead-gorgeous movie stars to get reacquainted with *in the biblical sense*. Things that were *much* more important than being buried in a watery grave before she'd even really got started.

"Bradley."

Nothing. She tromped back down the stairs and into the water, splashing over to him.

"Bradley!" She flicked water at his face and was rewarded with nothing more than a teensy flinch.

Ness knelt, wedging the flashlight into her armpit, and cupped her hands to scoop water from the ground. She dumped it over his head, and quickly repeated the motion. It felt . . . cathartic.

"Huh? What the—"

"Brad! For the love of Botox and burpees, will you *wake up!*"

He groaned, wincing, and forced his eyelids open, holding up a hand to block the light from his face.

"What?" He shifted uneasily, feeling the water around him. "How much water did you pour on me? I feel like I'm in a hangover bath." He grimaced. "Did you call me *Brad*?"

In response, she rotated, pointing the flashlight at the overflowing pool. The gentle burbles of ingress had increased to a constant stream.

"Oh. Fuck." Reflexively, he drew his knees up, eyes widening as the dregs of sleep washed away.

Ness felt an unsettlingly warm spark of satisfaction as his eyes grew big with surprise and he hopped onto the panic bus with her.

"Yeah. You think you could finish up with your snooze now?"

"This isn't good."

"Understatement."

He stared at her, face pale, eyelids at half-mast.

"What are we going to do?"

Ness's grip on the flashlight tightened. She gritted her teeth.

"How should I know? Why is it up to me? What do *you* think we should do?" She crossed her arms over her goosebump-covered stomach and waited.

Bradley pulled his shirt over his head and held it out, gaze averted.

"Here."

Ness chewed on her lower lip, feeling like a jerk. She reached out her free hand to accept the offering. She passed Bradley the light while she pulled the shirt over her head. It smelled like sweat and laundry that had been left in the washing machine too long, but even damp it was a drastic improvement over her bra-only situation.

"There. Modesty preserved and hypothermia staved off. Can we escape now?"

Bradley held the flashlight at belly-button height, directing the beam upward so shadows fell between every chiseled ab and pronounced pec.

"With your decent problem-solving abilities and these muscles? Nothing can stop us."

It turned out something could, in fact, stop them.

"Bradley I-forget-your-middle-name Isaksson. We're swimming out of here." Ness's hands rested on her knees and water lapped at her shins as she bent over to peer into the pool. The fish were long gone and no shark snout was visible in the terrifying dim light that passed through the water from the other side. The *outside*.

He groaned and laced his fingers behind his head. He closed his eyes and took a deep breath, chest rising and falling three times before he spoke.

"I can't."

"Ha! Yes! But actually you *can* do it. Upsy-daisy!"

Bradley crouched against the wall, feet and ankles submerged. An intimidatingly sized glittery pink phallus bobbed by his knees like a penis-shaped toy boat.

"Please shut up."

"I know you don't want to do it. I'm not exactly thrilled either. But look, it's literally the only option."

"No, I literally cannot."

"That's not the can-do attitude we need right now."

Bradley looked at her. "My attitude has nothing to do with it."

"Whatever. Fine. Revel in your negativity if that's what lights a fire for you. But please, Bradley, I'd really rather not find out what else Tyler has planned."

"You don't understand." Bradley's voice, though quiet, carried easily to her ears, bouncing off the walls of the cave. "I can't swim."

Ness started to say that was ridiculous. *Of course* he could swim. He was Bradley Isaksson, domestic star of many police procedurals and medical dramas of middling success. Bradley Isaksson, whose confidence cup overfloweth.

Then she saw how his shoulders drooped. His fists were clenched in his lap.

"Oh."

She tried to conceal her disappointment but was probably failing miserably. Luckily, the lighting was so poor and Bradley's self-loathing so resolute that he wasn't really paying much attention to her facial expressions.

"Okay, no worries. We'll figure something else out." Her eyes darted from point to point in the dark room as her mind struggled to come up with a Plan B.

All she could hear was the rushing of blood in her ears and the whooshing of water around them as it continued sluicing in through the pool. The problem-solving portion of her brain had given up, it seemed.

"Alright." She clapped her hands together cheerily with the can-do energy they were sorely lacking and crouched in front of Bradley. "I'm going to swim out, then circle back through the house and set you free. Easy peasy lemon squeezy. Should hardly take any time at all if I'm right about where this thing is going to spit me out." She tried to keep her face neutral. She had zero idea where the tunnel led. It was entirely possible she was about to swim directly into death's briny arms.

Bradley slowly raised his head and reached out, wrapping his hands around hers.

"This is completely unhinged behavior."

She forced a smile while her heart threatened to beat its way out of her chest.

"Probably. But I've always wanted to go scuba diving. I bet this is really similar."

His grip tightened, gently squeezing her fingers before releasing them.

"I'm sorry. You shouldn't have to do this alone."

"Bradley? Most of my life has been spent avoiding risks and trying to keep myself insulated from anything that might hurt me. Being the world's okay-est landlord is cool and all, but I want a chance to do more. To make up for some of the time I've lost playing it safe. And you don't even have to worry. I played a competitive swimmer in that *Law & Order* episode, remember?"

"Didn't she get murdered before the opening credits?"

"You *do* pay attention to my career!"

She pushed herself to standing and stretched her arms from side to side over her head, then jumped up and down a few times to get some warmth into her limbs. Bradley sputtered as her calisthenics launched water into his face.

She tried to visualize success but saw only hungry snakes and carrion-eating birds. *Do better,* she ordered herself, and she summoned an image of pepperoni pizza and a pitcher of beer. A smiling Hayes. Libby issuing a dramatic apology worthy of a Daytime Emmy. These were things worth living for. She could do this.

"Also," Ness continued, rolling her shoulders backward and forward, "you're going to have to name that baby after me once I save your life. I like Agnes for a girl and Angus if it's a boy. Or Nestor." She bobbed her head back and forth in thought, avoiding the moment she'd have to take the (literal) plunge. "We can discuss in more detail later, okay?"

Bradley shoved to his feet, sloshed over to her, and wrapped her in a stinky, moist hug.

"You're the most capable of any of us. Always have been." He spoke into her hair. "Don't die, okay? Because my quads might be twice the size of Hayes's, but he'll kill me if anything happens to you."

Not that she wanted anyone committing murders on her behalf, but the idea that Bradley thought Hayes cared so much about her was nice. More than nice.

Ness patted his back and he released her. She passed him the flashlight and edged to the precipice, her toes hanging over the edge of the pool. The water rushed past her knees as it pushed inward, the force of it enough to make her sway back. She really hoped the current would be gentler once she was below the surface. And that the tunnel was short. And that there wasn't a grate or something blocking the other end. And that . . .

Bradley cleared his throat behind her.

"Yeah, yeah," she muttered. "I'm going."

And she jumped.

At first, the water shoved Ness back, pressing her to the wall and inciting a level of panic she hadn't known existed. She forced her eyes open and ignored the sting of the salt. For a moment she was convinced she was upside down. Or sideways. Possibly inside out.

She focused on the dim circle of light in the distance, wedged her feet against the wall behind her and *pushed*. Her body was propelled forward, slicing through the water with shocking efficiency—right up until her shoulder slammed into the side of the tunnel.

Clamping her hand over her mouth as a forceful reminder not to scream or gasp, she clenched her teeth, wedged her fingernails into a tiny gap between the bricks that formed the tunnel, and heaved herself onward.

The flow of water into the cave tugged at her, but she dragged herself along, using the walls for leverage, scrabbling with bare toes and ragged fingers. Her shoulder throbbed. Her lungs burned. And she sent wild prayers into the ether, begging for the chance to take another breath. To feel the sun on her face. To eat something other than protein in bar or cookie form. To be wrapped in Hayes's arms again.

The light grew brighter.

Is this it? Ness wondered, vision beginning to darken around the edges. *The light at the end of the tunnel? How ironic.*

Her feet shoved off in one final, weak kick to freedom. Her mouth opened involuntarily, body desperate to breathe despite the obvious lack of available oxygen.

Ness choked as salty water invaded her mouth, trickling down her throat.

Reaching out blindly, her fingers gripped a rocky ledge and she pulled, feeling another layer of skin scraped from her hand.

This is the absolute dumbest way to die, she thought, letting her eyes stay closed. She drifted gently as her body heaved, fighting for its right to access air. And then, softly, her face broke the surface, where it was immediately pummeled by a torrent of rain.

Coughing and sputtering and flailing, Ness shoved at the mask of wet hair that plastered her face, threatening to suffocate her all over again.

"Ohmigod," she wheezed as rain pelted her head and shoulders. She tried to fling a strand of seaweed from her wrist and watched as the howling wind caught it and shoved it back toward her. The water was the color of steel, pocked by a million raindrops and ruffled into frothy waves by the air swirling around its surface.

Ness rolled onto her back and floated, trying to steady her breathing. Her entire body hurt. She shifted her arm experimentally, sending shooting pains from her shoulder down to her elbow. She hissed a breath out through her teeth.

Above, the sky was a mass of sinister gray clouds. A few mosquitoes, brave or stupid enough to be out in this weather, buzzed around Ness's head. Groaning, she got herself upright and treaded water, rotating in place, trying to get her bearings.

She was in the murky lagoon—the one that, up close, appeared to be an ideal home for saltwater crocodiles and deadly water snakes—and about fifty feet from shore. The house loomed above and to her left, the uppermost level visible over the trees. Mangroves surrounded the water and made space for the inlet that fed the lagoon from the east side of the island.

Paddling closer to land, Ness squinted through the rain, searching for a sign of a path. The water had risen considerably, creeping farther back into the surrounding greenery and obfuscating any sign of a readily available point of egress. Her feet hit slimy but largely firm ground as she got closer to land—or where she hoped land would eventually reveal itself—and she nearly collapsed with relief. Her toes caught on various water weeds, and at one point something terrifyingly solid bounced off her thigh, but she pressed on, feeling like a human sponge or a particularly well-stewed raisin.

She glanced left, confirming that she hadn't gotten off course and the house was still where she expected it to be. It was. Excellent. She would cut through this small piece of jungle, scoot up the hill, and *shazam*! Bradley would be free and forever in her debt, and she would never, ever let him forget it.

Reaching out to grab a convenient mangrove root, Ness pulled herself free from the water and stepped up onto a grouping of rocks. The rain continued to douse her, but it felt so nice not to be even partially submerged that she took a second to bask and catch her breath. Swiping water from the end of her nose, she looked at the nonexistent path through the trees and wished she had her shoes.

She was about to hop down and continue on her merry heroine way when her left foot slipped down the moss-covered side of the rock and she went sprawling, off balance. She was still half crouched, muttering creative curse words, when lightning hit the house.

Goodson Home Inspectors
Report #4538—Ginger Cay

Summary:

A detailed inspection of the single-family residence and associated outbuildings located on Ginger Cay has revealed a number of concerning structural weaknesses. It is the professional opinion of Goodson Home Inspectors that the main "castle" structure should be sold "as is" or, ideally, demolished ahead of the sale of the island.

The photos below illustrate the areas of greatest risk, including the roof, main staircase, and basement. While the condition of these sections is the most concerning, and these pose the largest safety risks, damage from prolonged exposure to moisture, poorly chosen building materials, and questionable customizations are also visible throughout the entire structure.

CHAPTER 25

NESS'S FIRST INSTINCT WAS, REGRETTABLY, TO FLEE. TO WHERE? She hadn't thought it through in that much detail. All she knew was that she saw nature trying to smite them, and her brain announced it was time to go—there was nothing she could possibly do. *Always take care of Number One*, said her father's voice in her head. The problem was too big and she was too small, incapable of contributing anything worthwhile all on her own. Besides, she rationalized, while staring at the smoke curling from the remains of the roof, Hayes probably had everything under control, as usual.

Except, said a different voice—a voice very much her own—everything obviously *wasn't* under control, because she'd very recently been trapped in a dungeon. Bradley was, in fact, *still* trapped in said dungeon, waiting for her to rescue him.

Her inner voice grew louder. Did she not see what she'd already accomplished?! By signing on to this cursed project she'd reclaimed her past *and* her future in one underpaid swoop! Sure, the experience so far had been a dumpster fire of epic proportions as far as career development went, but in terms of personal growth? *Sheesh!* She'd caught a fish. Fought a woman-eating snake. Executed a glorious watery escape *without dying*. Actually stuck around to have difficult emotional conversations! She wasn't going to let a teensy act of God derail her epic comeback now.

As frustrating as they were, her fellow castaways deserved better from her. She deserved better from herself.

There was a crack of thunder so loud it sounded like the world was breaking in two. Ness took a deep breath, launched herself off the rock, and ran toward the house.

Ian, Daisy, and Coco stood outside, their backs to Ness, as she tromped up the hill with all the grace of a hangry, exhausted rhinoceros. She crossed the small clearing to join them, taking in their waving arms and snippets of an increasingly loud conversation.

"If they were 'just going to come out on their own,' that would have happened already. We need to go get them." Coco was on her tiptoes, her dirt-streaked face three inches from Ian's pale one.

He took a step back, hands raised. "Whoa whoa whoa. *Of course* we need to get them. I'm just saying we need to think it through. It's not safe in there. We can't go roaring in without a plan." He rubbed his hands over his face, wiping water from his eyes.

Coco backed off, crossing her arms. Even from a distance, Ness could see how tense she was.

She jogged the rest of the way, her movement catching their attention. Ian's eyes widened and he flung his arms open. "Holy shit!"

"Aaaaaaaggghhh! Where have you been?" Daisy demanded, diving at Ness to wrap her in a soggy embrace. Ness hugged her back, closing her eyes against the rain and enjoying the additional body heat. After so many days of being hot, she'd never thought she'd be so desperate for a fireplace and a dry sweater.

"What the hell, Ness?!" Coco punched her not quite lightly on her upper arm before planting a smacker of a kiss on her lips.

"Long story," Ness said. She gave an extremely condensed summary, raising her voice to be heard over the wind—dungeon, Bradley, flooding, bonkers escape—pausing only to assure Ian he was an excellent prison guard; she was just a better escapee. She glossed over the details of the "Tyler purposely marooned us here to further his career and possibly sell footage of our private moments to the media to pad his bank account" part in case Coco decided to kill him accidentally on purpose before they'd rescued everyone. "Tyler's the bad guy, will explain later" seemed sufficient for the moment. In a situation where it was seven against one, she couldn't imagine he'd pose much of a threat, especially in his current state. Based on how ill he'd looked in the dungeon, she'd be surprised if he was still standing.

Of course, everyone had a million and one questions, which, Ness assured them—mostly via hand gestures and one-word answers—would be addressed in due course.

"I'm glad you're back," Daisy said, giving her hand a quick squeeze before going back to staring worriedly at the house.

"Bradley's still down there?" Ian asked, face crinkled in concern.

"Unless he's found another way out in the twenty minutes since I left, yeah." Ness eyed the house. The roof had stopped smoking, but she could swear a crack in the concrete exterior was looking more like a giant fissure.

"Where's everyone else?"

"Libby and Tyler are . . ." Daisy trailed off, nodding at the house. She exhaled loudly, shaking her head. "They were arguing about whether to go looking for you and Bradley when the lightning hit. Coco and I had just come out here to try to get more of the shutters closed." She shuddered, and Coco put an arm around her waist, pulling her close.

"Then the lightning hit." Coco picked up the story. "And Ian came running out, yelling about structural integrity."

"Hey!" Ian protested. "It's a valid concern!"

"And then we waited for them to come out," Daisy said. She leaned against the wind, which was picking up more strength with every moment they stood there.

"But they haven't." Coco glared at the house like it was to blame, and maybe it was.

"Hayes?" Ness asked, voice a bit shaky.

"He went to look for you a couple of hours ago," Ian said, pointing down toward the beach. "He's probably huddled in one of the sheds until the storm lightens up."

Ness looked down over the island. The long grass was bent horizontally, pressed close to the ground by the still roaring wind and driving rain.

"He's fine," Coco assured her.

"Yeah," Ness said faintly. She coughed and gave her head a little shake, trying to clear it. "We need to get Bradley and Libby." She started toward the front door.

"And Tyler," Daisy added, falling into step beside her.

Ness huffed out a breath. "Right. And Tyler." She cleared her throat. "Do you all . . . um, *not* think I set all this up anymore?"

"Did you?" Ian called from behind her.

"And tie my future success to *Tyler*? No!"

"Okay," Coco said, hauling the door open against the wind.

Ness couldn't believe it could be that easy. "Okay?"

As they stood dripping all over the foyer, Coco turned to her. "Look," she said, "maybe you *did* put together this wildly elaborate scheme with some random assistant with the personality of a deranged house cat. And maybe you both trapped us here on purpose and recorded us at our most vulnerable and tried to make a snake eat your frenemy for additional publicity. But—and I mean this in the nicest possible way— you're not a good enough actor to do all that and still pull off being so clueless the rest of the time."

And that was that.

With half of the shutters closed, the main floor of the house was shrouded in gloom, but it was blessedly dry. Above, the wind whistled through the upper level in a way that suggested, at a minimum, they'd lost some of the windows in the lightning hit.

The plan, if it could even be called anything so formal, was for Ness and Ian to get Bradley while Daisy and Coco located Libby and Tyler. They'd regroup outside and figure out next steps together.

In the foyer, everything seemed quiet, if dark. As a single, dripping unit, they edged along the hallway and into the kitchen and living area. No one spoke.

Scorch marks ran across walls, and the air smelled of ozone and burnt plastic. The house creaked as if it had aged fifty years in a few hours.

"If the house collapses on us, can we sue?" Coco whispered.

Ian glanced back at her over his shoulder. "Sure, as long as you don't mind being paid in vintage adult films and taxidermied exotic pets."

"Can we focus?" Ness said sharply. She wanted to get this done and get out. "Where were Libby and Tyler last time you saw them?"

"The kitchen," Coco answered. "Libby looked like she was about to chop Tyler up for a stringy stew."

"Okay, gross." Ian's mouth turned down in disgust. "But accurate. She was *pissed*."

"I think they went upstairs," Daisy added. "I came back in for a second and I'm pretty sure I heard voices up there."

Ness grabbed the precious emergency flashlight from the sideboard and headed toward the hallway that held the bedrooms, intent on getting Bradley and getting out. Ian, Coco, and Daisy scurried behind her.

She cupped her hands around her mouth. "Libby?" she shouted. "Tyler?"

Ian looked at her, aghast.

"What?" she asked. "How were you planning to find them? By scent?"

"The slightest disturbance could bring this whole thing down around us and you're in here hollering like we're looking for your bestie at the club? Jesus take the wheel!"

But Ness wasn't listening to him. "Shush!" She smacked his chest with the back of her hand as his mouth opened to continue his tirade. "Did you hear that?"

"You mean the sound of the beams breaking free from their moorings to crush us into elder millennial pancakes?"

"No, you drama queen. *That*." Distantly, there was a rhythmic clanging. Coco quirked her head to the side, listening. "Upstairs?"

"Let's check it out," Daisy said, walking toward the decrepit staircase.

Ness's ankle throbbed with remembered pain. "Careful on there," she cautioned.

"Yeah, Mom. Got it."

"That's still not funny."

As Daisy and Coco disappeared up the stairs, Ness looked at Ian. "Ready for *Operation: Heroes*?"

"Lame title. Yeah, let's give'er."

She walked into the bedroom where, hours earlier, she'd listened to Ian's animated sex scene narration. It seemed like a lifetime ago. Entering the closet, she let herself through the secret panel.

"This place is so creepy," Ian said, eyeing the door with distaste.

They jogged down the hall, the floor of which was covered in jagged pieces of drywall and ceiling panels that had been knocked loose. Dust and small pieces of debris adhered to Ness's still-damp bare feet. The smell of burning plastic was stronger here. It tickled her nose and made her head throb. She'd read something once about lightning traveling through wiring and plumbing to get to the ground, and assumed she was inhaling the gaseous remnants of some vintage electrical work.

Skidding to a stop at the door to the dungeon, Ness flicked the deadbolt and heaved. The door screeched open and the sound of lapping water echoed up at them, accompanied by a smell Ness could only associate with pirates, peg-legged ghosts, and her newly formed fear of dark, enclosed spaces. Seawater, wet rock, moss, and despair.

Ian froze, taking in the dark staircase and the scent of the air swirling around them.

"Is this . . . Davy Jones's locker?"

Ness pushed past, flashlight beam bouncing as she pattered down the steps.

"Bradley! Salvation has arrived!"

There was no response. At the fourth from last step, her foot dropped into cold water. She sloshed the rest of the way, playing the light across the room. Ian had caught up and was right behind her, lightly gripping the back of her shirt.

"Where is he?" Ian cupped his free hand to his mouth. "Bradley? Brad? Bradster?!"

Ness waded down to the bottom, shivering as the water brushed against her thighs.

"I hate it here," she said to no one in particular as she walked the perimeter, dreading the moment her foot would collide with a submerged Bradley. She stubbed her toe on raised rocks and nearly tripped on waterlogged debris, but she didn't discover anything obnoxious-actor-sized.

Splashing over to the smaller back room, she solved the mystery. Bradley was passed out on the same chair she'd found him on the first time, his chest rising and falling in slow motion. He wasn't restrained and had presumably chosen this perch for its relative dryness as opposed to comfort. The water bottle was on his lap. Empty, Ness discovered when she picked it up.

"Idiot!" She didn't know if she was angrier that now she had to schlep his unconscious bulk upstairs, or that she'd left him alone here for so long that he felt the only way to cope was by drugging himself yet again. *Or* that he was willing to risk drowning to avoid dealing with the situation instead of toughing it out and waiting for her. She didn't want to think about what that said about his confidence in her making it back.

Looping his giant, beefy arm over her shoulders while Ian did the same on the other side, she decided to be mad for all the reasons at the same time. Maybe burning anger would give her the strength to actually lug him out of there.

From the upper hallway came a loud crack, followed by an even more concerning thud. Two beats later, the yelling started.

"We should go," Ness said, locking eyes with Ian across Bradley's waxed chest. She'd wedged the flashlight into her armpit and prayed it would stay put long enough for them to get to the stairs.

It did, barely. At the foot of the staircase, having dropped their unconscious passenger only once, Ness wondered if her karma would be evened out after this. She had to hope that a pretty hefty number of bad deeds were being erased from her cosmic record this week.

"You want heads or tails?" Ian asked. They'd deposited Bradley onto the steps, where he now sprawled, moaning softly. Ness put her hands on her knees, trying to catch her breath, and glared at the sleeping man.

"What do you think the chances are we can wake him up so he can walk?"

Bradley burped and curled into the fetal position, stair edges cutting into his side.

"Probably about as good as the chances Daisy will ever date me," Ian replied.

"Well, shoot. I guess I'll take his feet."

After three failed attempts and nearly concussing Bradley multiple times as they dropped various limbs, they got creative.

"We'll wear him like a donkey suit," Ian declared.

Which is how Ness found herself with her face six inches from Ian's ass and Bradley's body balanced atop them. He was face down, chin resting on Ian's left shoulder, while Ness took the weight of his lower half, holding his legs under the knees as though she was giving him a piggyback, except she was doubled over and, as stated, face to buttocks with Ian.

Twenty stairs had never felt so unconquerable. Not to mention the fact that the sounds of chaos from above hadn't tapered off. If anything, they'd gotten worse, with more frequent apocalypse-like creaking, crashing, and the occasional scream to punctuate it all. The sound of roaring wind and impending doom increased in volume with every step upward.

"Ian?" Ness croaked out.

He grunted in response.

"This sucks."

Ian groaned out a laugh. "No shit, Nessinator. No. Shit."

"Hey, Ian?" She paused. They'd pretty much hit rock bottom here— no pun intended—so why not dig a little deeper?

He grunted.

"Can we talk about . . . that night?"

"Which one?"

"*The* night."

She stared at his ass, willing his face to start talking. It did not. They struggled up another step.

"The night we . . . you know."

"Oh," he finally said. "*That* night."

"Yeah, that night. I'm glad you found it so memorable."

Ness shifted Bradley's weight, wondering how bad it would be if she dropped him.

Ian glanced quickly over his shoulder (and Bradley's, as it were). "How much of it do *you* remember?"

"Um, essentially nothing. But, you know, I was doing a lot of . . . well, everything then. There are blanks where some of my more regrettable actions should go."

"Okay, so try not to be too upset, but, nothing actually happened."

Ness stared at him—well, part of him—and clambered up some more stairs. Her foot slipped off the edge of one in a particularly painful way, but she barely noticed.

"We were at Imposter," she said, squinting her way back in time. "Hammered, as was my usual state, and you offered me a ride to your place. I woke up in your bed. My clothes were on the floor."

He was nodding. "All true. Except, I think you made some errone-ous assumptions that I"—he coughed—"didn't correct."

"We didn't have sex?"

"No."

"Tell me." She couldn't believe she was having this conversation here, now.

Ian broke it down for her. "We got back to my place and you were, as you say, hammered. I was, oddly, not. I had a casting the next day for that thing with Claire Danes, remember? With the bomb in the hotel? Did pretty well at the box office, but I think it could have—"

"Focus." Bradley's leg dropped to the ground and she scrabbled to get it back into her grip. Ian paused, waiting for her to get organized.

"Right, okay. So, you? Blackout drunk. Me? Sober and grumpy as hell. Starving, mad at myself for losing some part, and primed to make dumbass decisions. But it felt . . . wrong. You didn't want me."

Ness had the leg back under control now and they forged on, as did Ian's recap.

"You wanted something else to help you forget real life. And, no offense, but I didn't want you, not really. I wanted a distraction. Maybe some validation that I was as sex-symbol-y as I needed to be for the next day. I put you in my room with a glass of water and a bottle of Advil, then slept on the couch."

"My clothes?"

He shrugged. "I guess you didn't want to sleep in them."

"Huh."

"Yeah. When you woke up and thought we had . . . I rolled with it. I figured since I'd been so chivalrous the night before, I deserved to use the situation to my advantage." He extended a hand back, holding it up beside his butt to silence her protests. He listed to the side, and the hand jerked back as he righted himself.

"I know that's a bullshit move. I was wrong and I still took advantage of you, just not in the way you thought. *That's* what I want to apologize for."

Ness took as deep a breath as she could, which wasn't very. She was relieved, but also realized it didn't actually matter that she hadn't slept with Ian. It mattered that she had gone home with him, woken up believing the deal was sealed, and done nothing about it. She hadn't been with Hayes at the time, but it had been just freshly over. She'd wanted to go back to him so badly that she'd done the only thing she could think of to drive him away forever. And it turned out that not only had she not actually done it (no credit to herself), he never even found out.

"Alright," she said, after gathering her thoughts and regripping Bradley's thigh. "Thank you."

"You're not mad?"

"I don't think so." She checked in with herself again. "No, I'm good. I appreciate you telling me."

Three hundred years later, they staggered onto the landing.

"I gotta put him down," Ness panted, convinced she'd never stand up straight again. Her arm still throbbed, and her mouth felt like she'd been chewing on a bag of cotton balls.

Water dripped onto the floor around them, making the dusty terracotta tiles even more of a slipping hazard. Through Ian's legs, she could see pieces of wood and larger sections of drywall and pieces of curved tile she was fairly sure hadn't been there on the trip in.

Unceremoniously, Ian crouched and shifted, rolling Bradley off his back and onto the floor.

He pressed his thumbs into his spine and whined softly as he tried to straighten. "He'd better make me best man at his wedding. Or buy me seven cases of that stupid organic water that's thirty bucks a jug." He nudged Bradley with his toe. "Wake *up*, dude!"

Ness had taken an alternative route, lowering herself to join Bradley on the floor, where she reclined, ever so slowly, until she was flat on her back. Eyes closed, she stretched her arms over her head, feeling her spine elongate and the gentle patter of raindrops on her face. With the speed of an elderly tortoise, her brain caught up, and her eyes fluttered open.

"Hey, Ian?"

"Mmph?"

She reached out and grabbed his ankle, making him jump.

"Where's the roof?"

The short answer was: gone. At least, in part. The section that had once covered the vaulted ceiling of this secret corridor had collapsed, sliding mostly onto the patio while also littering their escape route with interesting new challenges. Ragged edges loomed overhead like a monster's toothy jaw where the rest of the structure hung by what Ness could only assume was a construction-themed thread and her fervent prayers.

The wind seemed to have calmed itself from raging gale to a breeze punctuated by frustrated gusts. Rain no longer dumped by the bucketful, but instead pattered onto their heads, sounding like one of those ambient-nature apps.

Ness would have felt some sense of relief at this turn in the weather if it hadn't been for the imminent threat of being pancaked by an imitation castle.

After realizing how bad the damage to the house was, Ian hopscotched over the pieces of fallen wood and various house-building components to check on the others.

"I'll be speedy quick and bring someone back to help schlep Sleeping Beauty!" he assured her, tripping over a two-by-four studded with nails and tetanus.

Bradley chose this moment to rejoin the party by vomiting with great force and in distressing volume, waking himself up in the process.

Ness pressed back against the dungeon door to stay out of spatter range.

"It was probably the cookie," she said, trying not to inhale too deeply. "Or, you know, the *Big Gulp* of lord knows what drug cocktail you casually threw back, you *imbecile!*"

Hunched over, knees resting on the hard tiles, Bradley wiped his mouth with the back of his hand. His hair fell over his face, but from what Ness could see, his skin was the color of questionable milk.

"I hope Nestor has a better attitude than his namesake." His voice was hoarse and wobbly.

"I hope he's less of a selfish asshole than his father." Ness paused, alarmed by the wave of emotion rolling over her now that Bradley was conscious. She was horrified to feel her eyes filling with tears, and swiped at them with the hem of her (really his) shirt.

Before she could decide whether to hug him or push him down and pummel his stupid perfect nose, there was movement outside. The vine-covered trellis that had camouflaged the window was dangling drunkenly from one side, giving her a clear view to the balcony and the person staring open-mouthed at what remained of the roof.

"Hayes," she squeaked. Then she cleared her throat and tried again. "Hayes!" she yelled, clambering over rubble to get to the window. She raised her fist to bang on the glass but tapered it back to a gentle tapping with her nails when she saw how big the crack running across the pane was. She fought with the painted-over lock, suddenly desperate to be in his arms and feel safe, if only for a moment.

A shadow fell over her battered hands and she looked up. A bedraggled Hayes looked back at her. His silver hair was tangled with leafy pieces of tree and spiky brambles. A deep scratch ran from below his right eye to his jaw. He put a hand flat against the window and she raised hers to press against it. Her head drooped forward, forehead resting on the cool glass. There was a gentle thump as Hayes mirrored her motion. Ness took a deep, shuddering breath and felt the tension in her shoulders ease ever so slightly.

Behind her, something crashed against the floor.

As she spun, a gust of wind whooshed into the space, bringing a monsoon of roof tiles with it.

With one arm over her head, she grabbed Bradley's hand with the other and looped his arm over her shoulders. "Time to go! Use those quads you're so proud of and *stand up!*" She grunted and stood, dragging him with her. Finally, he got his feet under him and at least tried to participate, taking some of his own weight.

A tile smashed down onto his bare back, and down they went again.

"Dammit, Bradley!" Ness swore as she got back into position to try again. Not that it was his fault, but it kind of *was* his fault and she needed somewhere to direct her anger. She felt useless.

There was a sound of breaking glass, and then Hayes was at her side, gently moving her out of the way.

"Wait!" Ness said, putting a hand on his chest.

He looked at her, brow furrowed.

"I didn't sleep with Ian."

"Okay?" Water ran down the lenses of his glasses and he pulled them off, using the hem of his shirt to dry them. He took a quick look through and dropped them in disgust. They dangled at his chest from a cord made of braided grass and frayed rope fibers.

Ness plowed on, fully aware this was a stupid, impractical time to be having this conversation but desperate to get the words out before she caused him any more pain.

"But I thought I did. I meant to. I wanted to hurt you, to do something so heinous you could hate me and burn every memory of us from your mind. I didn't want you to miss me. I wanted you to thank god I was out of your life, and I'm so, so sorry for that." Ness looked in his eyes, terrified of what she'd see.

"I could never hate you." He kissed her gently, then rested his forehead against hers for the length of a deep breath. She nearly burst into relieved, delirious tears.

Another tile pirouetted through the air, crashing onto a pile of rubble beside them.

"We need to go now," Hayes said, looking pointedly at the destruction around them. He gave her hand a quick squeeze.

Ness nodded. "Yeah, right. Obviously. Life, death, et cetera."

He got in front of Bradley, crouched, and somehow hoisted him onto his shoulders in a fireman's carry.

He stood and tried to smile at Ness, but it ended up as more of a grimace as Bradley squirmed. Blood dripped down Hayes's forearm and onto the floor.

"Your shoulders are so bony," Bradley groused. "Put me down! I'll walk!"

"You had your chance," Hayes said, bouncing in place to get him repositioned.

A section of the upper-level interior wall started to peel away from its joists, dropping pieces of soaked plaster around them.

"Window or door?" Hayes asked.

Ness looked from the broken glass to the door that led farther into the disintegrating house.

Ian stuck his head through the closet door. His hair had dried into a wind-tousled swirl and he looked as exhausted as Ness felt. His face lit up at the sight of Hayes.

"You're back! Awesome. Can you come tell Libby not to push Tyler off the roof?" He ducked back out, leaving the passage open.

"So, door, then."

They plopped Bradley into the tall grass, well clear of the house, before plunging back into the dark hallways and mincing up the staircase. If it had been a safety risk before, climbing it now was a full-blown death wish.

Wind buffeted them, shooting down from the upper level and making their hair whirl around their heads. Ness could swear the entire structure was swaying beneath her feet, and she clung to the railing, like that would save her in the event of a collapse. She had never desired a hard hat, or shoes, so ferociously.

At the top, they discovered that Libby wasn't in fact threatening to send Tyler plummeting off the roof. Her preferred escape hatch was a gaping hole in the wall of what used to be yet another gaudy bathroom, complete with a red, heart-shaped jacuzzi tub that now lay shattered on the steep hillside below. It looked as if the entire corner of the room had simply . . . dropped away.

"He did this," Libby announced, prodding Tyler in the chest with a single finger. She'd backed him up to the very edge of the remaining floor, his heels mere inches from open air. He had his splotchy arms spread for balance. Water dripped off the end of his nose.

"He trapped us here. He filmed us. He lied and schemed and didn't know how to drive the fucking boat, and this is all. His. Fault. And then!" Her voice took on a tone of shrill indignation. "*Then* he asked me to help him! To *assist*! He offered me a cut of the proceeds from the sale of any surviving footage. Like *I* need the money! Like *I'd* stoop so low!"

Libby's lower lip trembled. Her clothes, like everyone's, were soaked through, and when the wind slithered through the remains of the room, she shivered, wrapping her arms around herself.

"It was an *accident*," Tyler whined. His demeanor had taken a sharp turn from the jubilant delinquent Ness had seen earlier. His eyes were darting back and forth. "Admittedly, I took advantage of the situation, but surely you can understand how desperate I was. You've all been there! You know how hard it is to make a name for yourself. Heck, some of you are nearing retirement and *still* haven't succeeded!" He directed this at Ness, which seemed a bit below the belt. "Don't tell me that you wouldn't have done the same thing if you were in my shoes!"

He looked pleadingly at her and mouthed, *Do something,* as if she were on his side.

Ness pointed to her ear, shaking her head and shrugging. *Can't hear you!* she mouthed back.

He screwed up his face, dropping any attempt to get the others to sign up for Team Tyler.

"None of you have vision. You can't recognize genius when it's staring you in the face. Literally!" He threw his head back, laughing maniacally, which quickly devolved into a coughing fit. "You should be thanking me," he wheezed, bent double, hands braced on his knees.

Coco stepped toward Tyler, looking as though she'd happily join Libby in her journey to the dark side. "Did you bring us here on purpose? Bribe the boat captain? Hell, did you knock him out in the clubhouse and steal his keys?"

Tyler's eyes widened. He put a hand to his chest, whether because he was affronted by the accusation or because his lungs were attempting to vacate his body, Ness couldn't tell.

"I told you," he wheezed. "I made the best of a horrible situation. These are *unprecedented times*. Morris trusted me to get you to Eclipse on time. He wouldn't give that job to just anyone. This was critical! Obviously a test I had to pass. We're talking career-making opportunities here! So did I provide the captain with a moderate cash incentive in order to keep us on schedule? Yes. I'm sure any of you would have done the same."

"Um," Ness started to disagree, but Tyler pressed on.

He sniffled, wiping his nose with the back of his hand. "No one appreciates how *hard* I work." Glaring at each of them in turn, he pointed a shaky finger at the group. "I'll make you famous beyond your wildest dreams. You're so *shortsighted*."

Now that the calamine was gone, Ness could see just how pale he was. A gust of wind made him sway, pushing him closer to the spot where the floor disappeared.

"We're shining a light on truth," he said weakly, legs folding as he crumpled to the floor. "Exposing the darkness that lies within," he mumbled. "It's only what you deserve. *Better* than you deserve."

The rain had turned to a gentle mist and, in the distance, sunlight tried to poke through the blanket of clouds. Coco and Daisy stood off to the side. Daisy's lips were pressed together into a thin, pale line and her eyes narrowed with concern. Her hand clenched Coco's, keeping her in place.

Hayes had made his way to Libby's side and, with the tactics Ness usually associated with calming spooked horses or stray dogs, moved her farther into the room, away from Tyler. He murmured into her hair as she turned into him, collapsing against his chest. Ness felt a tiny spark of jealousy that she shoved away. *Stupid*, she thought, as Tyler suddenly lurched to his feet and shoved past her, bouncing off the walls as he stumbled down the stairs.

One at a time, Ness, Hayes, Libby, Ian, Coco, and Daisy made their way back down the stairs—which were now *definitely* swaying—through the house, and out the front door. No one spoke. Immediate murder-crisis averted, they still had to make it out of the house before it collapsed around-slash-directly-onto them.

Bradley had managed to get to his feet, and he staggered toward them. His face was covered with sand and he was dragging his hand across his tongue, stopping every few steps to spit.

"That little turd!" He wiped at his eyes with his other hand. "I tried to grab him and he threw sand in my face! It's scratching my corneas as we speak. My mouth feels like a litter box. What is this doing to my veneers?!"

Ness patted him on the shoulder and kept walking. "Glad you're feeling better."

They slumped down to the beach and collapsed into the sand. Hayes laced his fingers through hers and listed sideways, resting his head on her shoulder.

"Should we start another fire?" she asked, not wanting to move a muscle but also yearning for the dry heat.

"We could burn the house," Coco suggested. She was lying flat on her back, arm draped over her eyes.

Daisy had plopped down beside Coco and stretched out her legs, propping herself up with long, tanned arms. Her hair had started to dry into natural beachy waves that glinted copper in the weak sunlight.

"What about Tyler?" she asked.

Ian looked out at the gray ocean, where the waves were still choppy and angry-looking.

"Where's he going to go? I say we leave him. We have enough to worry about. Like where are we going to sleep and how long can we survive on iguanas and, shoot, do we even have water?" He started to sound panicky.

"Hey, guys," Bradley interrupted. "Am I hallucinating or is Tyler riding a giant flamingo out to sea?"

Ness jolted to her knees and spun around, shading her eyes with her hand.

"Son of a . . ."

By the time she'd staggered to her feet, Hayes had already taken off down the beach, clumps of wet sand flying behind him. He disappeared around the corner at the tip of the island while Ness was still a couple hundred feet behind. She rounded the bend in time to see him dragging another paddleboat across the sand and into the water. Huffing and sweating, she reached him in time to hop on board.

Their vessel sported a toucan motif. Hayes's brow was furrowed in concentration and he pedaled frantically. Unlike the flamingo, the toucan was built for (comparable) speed. Instead of a long, gangly neck, the nose of the boat itself was the beak. The rest of the vessel made up the head.

Tucked back into the trees, its contents strewn across the ground to the beach, were the fallen remains of the snake shack.

Tyler's rash-covered knees pumped furiously as he pedaled his way toward freedom. He looked back over his shoulder, and when he caught sight of them, he rammed a celebratory fist into the air, then extended his middle finger.

His lips moved as he yelled something, but Ness couldn't make it out over the wind.

She cupped her hands around her mouth. "I can't hear you, you absolute moron!"

His lips pursed, and then, slowly, the flamingo made a one-eighty and started back toward them. When he was within shouting distance, he leaned slightly over the edge and called out, "I said, 'See you in the tabloids!'"

He raised a plastic bag with one hand and rattled it. One of the corners was ripped, and a black cube fell out, plopping into the water.

"Shit!" He chased it, circling frantically in slow motion before giving up.

"I have hours of footage! Days! Not only will I be the most in-demand director of the decade—century!—I'm going to be Malibu rich!" He attempted an evil laugh but started coughing uncontrollably. His legs were still pedaling and he kneed himself in the face. When he looked back, blood was dripping from his nose. He swiped at it with the back of his hand.

"It's amazing how the artistic vision morphs over time. At the beginning I thought small. But you're all so gosh darn insufferable. Do you even see yourselves? Your lives are shells! Meaningless! You suck the joy from everything. Well, just you wait. If nothing else, this"—he rattled the bag again, more carefully this time—"will give you a lifetime of regrets to wallow in. You'll love it. You're welcome. Must be going now!"

Ness watched his ridiculous escape. The thought of pursuing a giant fiberglass waterfowl into open waters seemed one step too far. Maybe he'd get eaten by a giant squid or an oversized, hungry albatross. She had to trust that justice would find a way.

Hayes, it seemed, did not agree.

He was seated within the toucan's beak in the pedaling position, hunched behind the sportscar-style windscreen. Ness stood behind him and gripped the back of his chair. The ocean breeze whipped her hair across her face, making it feel like they were going much, much faster than the reality, which was . . .

"Does that say three miles an hour?" She squinted at the instrument panel, which was made up of the—totally unnecessary—speedometer, a compass, and a peeling Metallica sticker.

They bounced over the low waves. A sleek, dark head poked out of the froth beside them. The dolphin kept pace for a few moments before streaking off, leaping playfully as it went.

Ahead, Tyler's frenetic pedaling had slowed. The gap between the two boats started to close.

"This is it!" Ness bounced on the balls of her feet and slapped Hayes's shoulder excitedly. "Let's get him!" She leaned forward, willing the toucan to accelerate. She glanced at the speedometer: four miles per hour. Back on the beach, the others had gathered, presumably cheering them on, though she couldn't hear them.

Hayes flicked a look back at her. "What do you mean 'get him,' exactly?"

Tyler stopped pedaling completely and stood to face them.

"God, I hate you!" he yelled, following the proclamation with a throaty, desperate yell. Fishing a hand into one of his cargo pockets, he pulled out something orange and, to Ness's dismay, distinctly gun-shaped.

"Oh my god," she moaned. "How many pockets do those things *have*?"

Ness rose to her tiptoes and cupped her hands around her mouth. "Stop being such an asshole, Tyler!"

Hayes muttered, "Don't antagonize him!" He'd stopped pedaling and watched Tyler through narrowed eyes.

"But this is absurd! Where does he think he's going to go in that stupid flamingo, anyway?"

Hayes glared and she stopped talking.

"We can work this out," he called, the picture of calm.

Overhead, a small plane buzzed by, then slowly circled back. After days of waiting for exactly this moment, Ness couldn't spare it a second thought. *Now* there was joyous screaming from the beach.

Tyler put a foot on his boat's seat and rested his elbow on his knee, trying to steady his aim. The flare gun shook visibly in his hand. He looked about thirty seconds away from passing out.

The waves pushed them closer together. Hayes surreptitiously steered the toucan so it was perpendicular to the flamingo's body.

"You're sick, Tyler. We need to get you to a doctor, pronto." He pedaled gently forward, closing the gap even more. Ness bent and extended her legs, limbering up, and watched the space between them shrink. Sweat poured down Tyler's face.

"You're hurting. You've been through hell this week."

Tyler nodded in agreement. His face crumpled as he started to cry.

"No one recognizes my effort, you know?"

Ness quirked her lips down in sad understanding. "I do. We all underestimated you, and it's easy to see now that we were so very wrong. Look at everything you pulled off! Right under our noses!"

He sniffled and wiped his nose with the arm that held the flare gun.

"This was my big chance to show everyone what I can do!"

Ness tried to look sympathetic. The boats had rotated so that what little sun there was shone directly into her eyes. She squinted, trying to keep a clear view of her target.

Hayes maneuvered closer. The toucan's beak bumped the flamingo, sending Tyler staggering.

"Hey!" The flare gun came back up, aimed directly at where Ness had been standing, but she was already in motion. Bracing herself on Hayes, she jumped onto the edge of the boat and skirted the windscreen, landing on the top of the toucan's beak.

It was more sloped and much slippier than she'd anticipated. Her toes tried to grip the surface, but the boat was sliding away from under her. Behind her, Hayes was yelling.

Tyler moved the flare gun slightly to the right and pulled the trigger. A bolt of heat shot past Ness's left arm as she launched herself across the bow and wrapped her arms around Tyler's ribs in the most vicious tackle she could manage in the tiny, wobbly space.

He fell backward, mouth a shocked *O*, and landed butt-first on the floor, sending the flamingo rocking merrily back and forth. The flare gun went skittering across the floor of the boat and slid off the rear swim platform. It bobbed happily in the water.

The toucan floated into view. A melted spiderweb of cracks radiated out from where the flare had struck the windscreen. The mottled shape perfectly obscured the area where Hayes's face had been moments before. Luckily, the man himself seemed fully intact and had resumed his role as silver-haired mer-king, swimming toward them with strong, sure strokes.

Ness watched Tyler struggle for a moment as he tried to regain his footing, then cocked her arm and punched him directly in his annoying, shit-disturbing face. She was considering a bonus round when a dripping Hayes grabbed her elbow.

Faintly, she heard Coco's exuberant string of expletives carry across the water.

"Shhhhh. We're good. You got him." He pulled her to her feet. "Look." He nudged the smaller man, none too gently, with his toe to prove he was, in fact, unconscious. Which was great because, now that she thought about it, punching someone really hurt.

Production of the ill-fated revival *Ocean Views: Turning Tides* is reportedly on hold indefinitely. Only days after seven cast members and one crew member were rescued from an uninhabited island in the Bahamas, discovered in a situation that can only be described as stranger than fiction, we're now hearing that Morris Wagner and the Good Things Network have parted ways.

While the real reason may never be revealed, Hollywood's whisper network is practically screaming that Wagner walked after repeated budget cuts and GTN's subsequent lackluster response to its missing employees.

The Good Things Network declined to provide an official comment, but a corporate source who asked to remain anonymous said, "The stakes were always high with this project, and with the unforeseen delays and uncertainty around when filming can actually begin, it was decided that it was in everyone's best interest to set *Turning Tides* aside for now."

Trisha Jung, an executive at the Good Things Network, is reportedly the subject of an internal investigation following allegations of undisclosed behaviors "unbecoming of a GTN employee."

>

While our collective heart is broken at the idea of missing out on catching up with our favorite early-aughts crew, we're thrilled to know they're back to civilization, safe and (mostly) sound.

The lone crew member on the island, Tyler Yates, has been arrested by the Royal Bahamas Defence Force and charged with assault, forcible confinement, and a litany of other transgressions.

CHAPTER 26

NESS STRETCHED OUT ON THE PRISTINE WHITE SHEETS OF HER KING-size bed at a hotel on Great Exuma. Smelling of sandalwood and vanilla, wrapped in a robe so soft and fluffy she felt like a human cotton ball, she wondered what she was supposed to do now.

Outside, gray clouds covered the sky, promising a mid-morning shower, which, from her current clean, dry, fed, and hydrated position, didn't seem so bad. Four stories below, the ocean lapped lazily at the sand, where waitstaff delivered brightly colored drinks with paper umbrellas to vacationers who refused to give up their beach time because of a little rain.

They'd been holed up there for three days, talking to the authorities, avoiding the seething horde of media camped outside, and, in Ness's case, trying to escape from what seemed thus far to be an unrelenting mental haze.

Rescue had arrived as they'd beached the flamingo boat and were trying to figure out how to restrain a near-apoplectic Tyler, who had regained consciousness on the way in. Libby had been lobbying for hitting him on the head with a rock when the snappy blue and white boat zoomed in carrying a number of concerned members of the Royal Bahamas Defence Force. Libby had quickly abandoned the rock.

Tyler, Ian, and Bradley had been transported for medical attention at a local hospital, while Hayes, Ness, Libby, Coco, and Daisy were assessed and declared to be in "surprisingly good health," if a little dehydrated, and were administered IV liquids in the comfort of their hotel rooms. Daisy credited yoga. Coco named gin as the real savior.

Libby sported bruised ribs, courtesy of the python, and had flown in an assistant to her assistant the same afternoon to make sure that all of her needs would be taken care of as expeditiously as possible while she recovered.

At first, Ness had reveled in the ability to shower in endless hot water and sleep in a clean bed and eat precisely cubed fruit salads and steaming oatmeal dappled with fat raisins, doused in real Canadian maple syrup. She devoured pepperoni pizza and sipped on frosty beer, loving the feeling of the pre-chilled glass against her hand and the richness of the food, even if it gave her some horrendous stomach cramps later. Then, slowly but surely, reality had crept in.

They were on their way out of the bubble now, heading into the real world. Hayes's mom and sister had been waiting for him at the hotel. They'd flown in as soon as he'd been reported missing and had been out on volunteer boats helping with the search every day since.

They'd greeted Ness warmly, which had surprised and delighted her. Given everything that had happened between her and Hayes, and knowing how close he was to his family, she hadn't been sure what to expect.

Since then, Hayes had been in phone meetings and on video calls almost constantly, assuring everyone he was okay and working to get filming schedules back on track. It seemed to Ness that he was quickly forgiven for any inconvenience he may have caused, but Hayes was determined to go above and beyond to make it up to everyone. In between, though, he was with her. In her room. In her bed. Her shower. Testing the strength and soundproofing of the walls. As with all his performances, he put in 110 percent.

If Ginger Cay had been a bubble of unreality, this was no better. If anything, Ness might argue, it was worse. Outside of planning how to get home and what to do when she got there, her days were wide open for luxuriating in Hayes's extremely skilled embrace. It was impossible for things to continue like this once they left. They were insulated here. Protected—literally: there was an army of security personnel keeping reporters and the nosy public at bay. Their personal employees (not that Ness had any) and the hotel staff were treating them with kid gloves, giving them time and space to process the last week. Her time with Hayes barely felt real.

At first, Ness was concerned she'd had unrealistic expectations. Years of pent-up yearning and regrets, combined with the stress of the island and subsequent rescue, had her body screaming for physical release.

Hayes had come to her room that first night, when the police were done with them for the day, and their clothes had been on the floor within moments of the door locking behind him. But despite how much Ness knew she wanted him, had wanted him seemingly forever, her brain wouldn't cooperate.

He was doing all the right things. Saying everything she'd dreamed he would say in that sexy, husky voice that made her tremble. Touching her exactly where she wanted to be touched. But while years of books, movies, and television would have her believe she should be well on her way to orgasm central after a single thrust, she seemed to have misplaced her ticket for that particular ride.

When she'd told him she wasn't going to be entering O-Town that night, instead of doubling down and trying to prove her wrong until she was forced to fake it to wrap things up, he'd ordered them a six-pack of beer and run a bath. They'd stayed in the steaming water until midnight, stewing themselves, sipping the ice-laden beverages they'd been dreaming of for the past week, and seeing who could make the other person laugh harder with endless, increasingly ridiculous stories from the time they'd been apart.

Ness had been an exhausted prune when they had finally gotten out. Hayes had tucked her into bed, closed the curtains, and asked if she needed anything else. She'd pulled him under the covers alongside her and, listening to his steady breathing, fallen into a dreamless sleep.

At first light she'd awoken, extremely content in her little-spoon position. As his hand had trailed slowly down her ribs and dipped between her thighs, she'd discovered that, lo and behold, O-Town was open for business.

Their time in limbo was coming to an end, though. Hayes would be flying to Hawaii the next morning. Ness thought this was lunacy. He needed to sleep for two weeks and eat a wheelbarrow of carbs each day and, most importantly, stay with her. But she'd known this would happen, hadn't she? Somehow, living it was different.

Part of her was looking forward to getting home. *Turning Tides* wasn't happening for the foreseeable future, if ever. It was time to get back to reality, even if it wasn't the reality she'd been hoping for. If nothing else, she told herself, she was coming out of this mentally and emotionally stronger than when she'd entered it. Acting had waited this long; she could figure out another way back in if she still wanted one. Plus, think of all the fodder she had for therapy now! New topics! Her therapist would be thrilled.

There was a knock on the door.

"Room service!"

Ness rolled from the bed and tightened her robe. She hadn't ordered anything, but Hayes had taken to having things delivered to her throughout the day when he couldn't pop in himself. Yesterday she'd received a tray of chocolate croissants with a steaming pot of tea on the side, then an enormous bouquet of flowers, and, finally, a stack of romance novels that ended up being from Ian, who had been released from the hospital and immediately checked himself back into rehab.

She swiped a hand over her hair to smooth the worst of the flyaways and opened the door. A man stood in the hallway, his sandy gray hair brushed to the side. He wore tidy khaki shorts and a royal-blue golf shirt with a repeating pattern of small embroidered birds flapping across it.

He smiled.

Ness blinked, dumbstruck.

"Dad?"

• • •

"I had to see you in person and make sure you're okay. I've been sick with worry ever since your disappearance was on the news." He sat in the small living area of her hotel room, leaning forward on the pristine white love seat, forearms resting on his knees. Ness had taken the armchair and schooled her face into some semblance of calm while her mind short-circuited.

She'd come very close to slamming the door in his face, which, she felt, would have been warranted. But even as she'd started to do so, she knew she couldn't. They hadn't spoken, not a single time, since he'd left, and while logically she knew hearing his side wouldn't change anything or make what he'd done hurt less, some part of her hoped it would let her finish healing and finally, truly, leave him behind. And, maybe, a tiny part of her still thought he might show up with a valid reason, or at least real remorse.

"Well, I'm fine. Thanks for coming by." She stood, employing the universal signal for *Now you can leave*. He didn't play along.

"I know you're probably angry with me."

"Why would you think that?" She put every drop of sarcasm she had behind it.

He waggled a finger at her like she was a naughty child.

"Now, Ness. It was time for you to be in charge of your own destiny. I coddled you, as hard as that is to admit. It was so hard after your mom . . . Well, it was important for you to start seeing the consequences of your actions and get your head in the game. With me around taking care of every little detail . . ." He lifted his shoulders and let them drop. "You were becoming a bit of a spoiled brat, if I'm being honest."

"And your solution was to steal my money and abandon me? You didn't consider something a little less dramatic? A conversation? Maybe taking a step back from the business side of my life and, oh gosh, this sounds silly, but *being my dad*?"

She watched as he puffed up like an indignant bird.

"You're forgetting that I'm the reason you got those paychecks. Do you know how hard I worked to get you to the top? I gave up everything so you could pursue your dream!" His face flushed. His fists clenched at his sides.

She tilted her head and kept her voice even.

"It was your dream too. And it was my money. I earned it. For years and years, Dad, I earned it while you had drinks on the golf course and shopped for new cars so you could look the part. This wasn't a business relationship! I was a kid and you were my father. You were supposed to watch out for me."

"You knew I was entitled to a percentage as your manager."

"How's the wellness center?"

The abrupt change in topic made him pause. He took a deep breath and reached out to pour a cup of coffee from the carafe on the table. He'd gotten old, she noticed. He'd had enough work done on his face to hide the worst of it, but his hands gave him away. They were mottled with age spots, the skin thin and brittle-looking.

"It's under new management."

"Ah. Why are you here? Really?"

He sat back, leaving the coffee untouched. Tenting his fingers, he looked her up and down, all business.

"You're going to need help. Have you been outside? The media are circling like sharks tasting blood in the water. You have a real opportunity here. I'm talking book deals, exclusive interviews. The public is dying to hear about what happened on that island. You've never been good at advocating for yourself. You need someone on your side. Someone you can trust."

She stifled a laugh, disbelieving, as she tried to find words powerful enough to express how unbelievable this was.

He narrowed his gaze. "Tell me you have the tapes."

"I don't know what you're talking about."

"Come on, Agnes. It's all *anyone* is talking about. Do you know where they are?" There was a hungry look in his eyes that made Ness feel sick. She paused, taking a deep breath. She was done.

"You should go now."

"You can't do this alone. You need me."

"I haven't needed you in twenty years and I won't be starting now."

"I'll sell my story. I can do this with or without you." He sounded desperate. Ness wondered just how far in debt he was these days.

"I'm sure you'll do what's best for you."

"You won't see me again, Agnes. Not ever," he said threateningly.

Ness walked to the door and held it open, certain she was doing the right thing. It felt good.

"I'm counting on it."

Hayes did, in fact, fly to Hawaii the next morning for three months on the set of *Alpha Lunar*. After hearing about the visit from her father, he'd offered to stay. Then he'd offered to hire a private investigator to dig up some dirt (because there had to be some) and have him arrested so he couldn't bother Ness again. And, finally, when she had assured him time and time again that she would be okay, that he needed to go, that they'd known this was going to happen, he had kissed her and promised they would make it work this time.

Ness woke up to an email from his assistant, asking that she let him know when she was ready to go back to Toronto and whether there were any dietary preferences the staff on the private jet should know about. She left that afternoon, mourning her contribution to global warming while sipping champagne and wondering how long this could last.

After a tearful reunion with friends and dealing with a laundry list of tenant issues over the next couple of weeks, her time on Ginger Cay began to feel like nothing but a bad dream. Except, then Hayes would FaceTime her, asking about her day and whether she was ready for a Hawaiian vacation yet and telling her she was beautiful in the blue light of her phone screen when she'd been up since four that morning dealing with noise complaints and overflowing toilets.

It was hard to reconcile.

Coco had checked in a couple of times, as had Daisy. Though they'd reached out separately, Ness could have sworn they were in the same New York apartment, but she wouldn't pry. Not yet, at least. Both were back at work, having quickly booked gigs to replace *Turning Tides*, and while they kept talking about the three of them getting together, Ness wasn't confident it would happen anytime soon. They'd get there eventually, though, and she *was* looking forward to that.

Autumn had begun to descend on Toronto. It was Ness's favorite time of year, when the leaves were turning fiery orange and deep red but the temperature during the day still hit something well above freezing. This was the season for last hurrahs on charming neighborhood restaurant patios and breaking out cozy sweaters to fight off the evening chill.

Ian, much to Ness's surprise, kept in touch, sending reading recommendations and asking her when she was going to book an acting gig instead of digging dryer lint out of blocked vents.

Audrey, agent to Mature Women, was asking the same question. Weekly.

"You should go to this casting. They asked for you."

"Ehhhhh, I don't know if I'm ready," Ness would answer, scrolling through an Excel sheet of her monthly cash flow, trying to make the number at the bottom turn green. Maybe if she cut protein from her diet . . .

She could all but see Audrey throwing up her hands in frustration.

"You're missing the wave, Ness. It's time to hop on the surfboard and take a ride to Employment Beach."

"I'll think about it."

In the end, Libby made the choice for her, showing up at her door on a cloudy October morning with a script in one hand and balancing a Kim Beauty–branded rose gold case against her hip.

Her long, glossy black hair was shinier than ever before. Her bow-shaped lips glistened with an autumnal shade of deep umber that suited her perfectly. She smelled like bergamot with undertones of vanilla and money. She thrust the metal box at Ness, gliding past her into the apartment.

"What are you doing here?"

"Meetings." She waved her manicured hand vaguely and turned in a circle, taking in Ness's humble abode.

"I come in peace," she continued, while staring disdainfully at a print of the city skyline. "That"—she nodded to the case—"is my apology gift."

Ness flipped open the top and was greeted by what was very likely thousands of dollars' worth of Kim Beauty products.

"Um, thanks?"

Libby lowered herself carefully onto the worn gray couch, thwacking the script onto the table.

"This"—she pointed to the stack of bound paper—"is the second part of the gift."

Ness, head spinning, picked it up and dropped into her favorite armchair.

Gallivant

Written by
Morris Wagner

"Did Audrey send you?"

"No one *sends* me. I've been in therapy since . . . everything happened. I'm making amends. I may have, er, misstepped on occasion while we were on the island."

"Remember that time you declared me guilty of trapping everyone there and recording private moments *and then you locked me in a room after I saved you from a person-eating snake?*"

"Vaguely."

"How does this"—Ness waved the script back and forth, the paper flopping—"make up for *that?*"

"Stop whining and read it."

Ness didn't stop whining, but when she was done sharing her feelings and listening to Libby's, she showed her out, feeling like they were back on even, if tentative, footing. Then she poured herself a generous glass of wine and read.

And fell in love. It was a pilot for a dark comedy about a woman in her forties who's trying to get back into dating after her husband's untimely passing. But, unfortunately, her dates also keep turning up dead.

She called Libby the next day, after a sleepless night weighing her options and realizing she had nothing to lose.

"Great, we're even, then."

"Why did you bring this to me?" It was the question Ness couldn't let go of.

There was a lengthy pause.

"This may surprise you, but I don't have a lot of friends. I was hoping we could . . . do that."

Ness's forehead creased in consternation even as her lips started to turn up in a smile. "You want to be friends. With me."

"It's probably a terrible idea. You're still a train wreck." She sighed. "But I'm in a giving phase."

"Alright," Ness said, trying not to laugh and failing miserably. "Why not?"

Beauty & Fashion Today

Kim Beauty is the little engine that could. Elizabeth Kim, CEO, has sold the young company to beauty behemoth Garth Mackie Cosmetics for an undisclosed sum. Kim will be staying on in an advisory capacity and is excited to see her first start-up venture hit such an exciting milestone.

"Garth Mackie has been such an inspiration to me over the years. Having this chance to join the GMC family is a dream come true, and will allow Kim Beauty to expand into international markets much more quickly than I had hoped. With GMC's aligned vision and dedication to using only the highest quality, responsibly sourced ingredients, Kim Beauty is just getting started."

ONE YEAR LATER

COME ONE STEP CLOSER AND YOU'RE FINALLY GOING TO FIND OUT what it feels like to die," Ness said menacingly. She raised the wooden stake, tightening her grip, as the biker-turned-vampire launched at her with a hiss, fangs bared. Without hesitation, she executed a flawless spinning kick, flinging her undead opponent to the ground and staking him through the heart in one fluid motion. His body twitched violently and his hands came up as if to wrap around her throat, but it was too late. He went limp.

"Aaand, cut! Amazing work!" Ian clapped as he came forward. Life behind the camera seemed to be agreeing with him. *Gallivant* hadn't been picked up, but it had done what Ness had needed—gotten her back in the game.

She held out a hand to help Jamie, the ill-fated vampire, to his feet.

"You okay?" She dusted him off, jokingly checking for injury.

"Sweet kick. I thought you were going to take my head off."

Daisy, still in costume, came over from where she'd been watching. The worn leather jacket and grimy jeans were her character's trademark look. Ness, however, got black athleisure tights and a loose-fitting knit cardigan. At least she was comfortable.

"All the yoga helps," Daisy explained. "Otherwise, it's tough fighting supernatural baddies at her advanced age." She draped an arm over Ness's shoulder, exaggerating their not insignificant height difference.

Ness elbowed her. "Shut it, short stuff."

"Are you insulting my girlfriend again?" Coco, who, judging by the watermelon scent traveling with her, had been vaping outside, sidled up. She'd just wrapped the first season of an edgy legal suspense drama and flown in that morning. She looked exhausted, but happy.

"Your girlfriend can defend her own honor, I'm sure," Daisy said, leaning down to kiss Coco. "Have I mentioned how happy I am to see you?"

Coco pulled her closer and wrapped her arms around Daisy's waist. "I'd listen to you say it again."

"Let's call it a day, folks! Great job!" Ian kicked off another round of enthusiastic clapping.

Crossroads, a supernatural crime-fighting series focusing on a mother-daughter duo played by Ness and Daisy, had been filming for four months. A full season release was scheduled on the Good Things Network in a few weeks, and test screenings were suggesting they might have a hit on their hands.

Ness was having the time of her life.

Her dad had been right about the endless opportunities to monetize her time as a castaway, but she hadn't taken them. Instead, she'd signed a book deal to write about her early life in show business, her subsequent fall from grace, and how she'd learned from that experience. *That* story, she had realized, she had no problem profiting from.

The advance had allowed her to hire a property management company, and she was enjoying being a hands-off landlord. She'd considered selling out of the business entirely but couldn't bring herself to do it. At her age, nothing in entertainment seemed certain. Well, nothing except the constant offers of fillers and a light tummy tuck.

Her assistant—yes, her very own!—Kyla-Mae joined her on the walk to her trailer, passing Ness her phone and a takeout container of salad.

"Audrey called. Drew Barrymore wants you on her show three weeks from Thursday. And Bradley and Kimberley want to confirm you're attending Agnes-Hope's baby welcome thing." Kyla-Mae paused, waiting for Ness's reply. She nodded a yes, wondering what one gifted one's namesake.

"And . . ." Kyla-Mae paused just outside the door to the trailer and smiled. "There's somebody waiting for you." She waggled her eyebrows and walked away, already texting furiously.

Ness pushed into the trailer. When she saw who was sitting in her makeup chair, that smile turned into a full-on grin.

Hayes spun to face her, radiating giddiness.

"Ready?"

Ness did not like helicopters. They were loud and bumpy, and this one smelled like someone had lit a scented candle to cover the smell of other people's fear.

Hayes caught her hand in his and gave it a squeeze. The setting sun reflected off his aviators. She could see herself in them and, she noted, she was looking *great*. Not just physically, though she was pleased with that too, but she looked happier than she could remember being . . . maybe ever.

Hayes's crackly voice came through her headset.

"Almost there." He pointed.

She looked out the window and, as always, the beauty of the island stole her breath. It hadn't taken long for it to steal her heart as well. The water sparkled, supercharged deep blue against the dark green of the trees and gray-brown of the rocky cliff faces.

It was a quick ride, thankfully, from Vancouver to Galiano Island, and a simple trip to Seattle or L.A., which had made it an easy choice when they'd started looking for a place to call home.

The helicopter bumped through a patch of turbulence. Well, a relatively easy choice.

Hayes had suggested buying Ginger Cay so they could tear everything down and build a place to make happy memories to replace the creepy, near-death-experience ones, but Ness had taken a hard pass, unwilling to commit to relocating an unknown population of snakes. She'd consider a flyover, or a one-day picnic situation, max.

As they landed on Galiano on a flat patch of land between forest and ocean, Ness surreptitiously pinched the skin on the inside of her forearm, making sure this wasn't all a dream.

Their bags unloaded, the helicopter took off again, leaving Ness and Hayes standing at the bottom of the stairs that led to a house nestled in the trees. *Their* house.

The lights had come on, timed through some new-age technological magic to coincide with their arrival. From where they stood, Ness could see the towering fieldstone fireplace and newly renovated kitchen waiting for them. It looked perfect, but she wasn't ready to go in yet.

The sun was a sliver of orange on the horizon. Cold wind rustled their jackets and hair. In the water, a pod of orcas glided past, barely visible in the quickly fading light.

"Welcome home," Hayes said, leaning his head to rest on top of hers.

And, maybe for the first time in her life, Ness knew without a single doubt that she was exactly where she was supposed to be.

AUTHOR'S NOTE

MY MAIN CHARACTERS TEND TO SHOW UP FIRST AS A NAME, AND THEN I kind of toss different careers at them until something feels right. Ness Larkin arrived in a slightly different fashion during the summer of 2021. I was walking my dog (a must-have accessory for those of us prone to prolonged procrastination) and meandered past a house with a pristine late-1980s Jaguar parked out front. I wondered how the people who lived there came to have it. Was it a recent purchase? If so, why *this* car? What made it so special? Or had they held on to it for the past thirty years? And if so, again, what made it so darn important?

I mulled this over for a couple days and then, while Charlotte, my senior doodle, sniffed a tree in front of the same house, found my own answer. *Obviously a teen actor got it from her father when he absconded with her life savings, leaving her heartbroken and destitute, but with his beloved luxury sedan. Because he wouldn't abandon her with nothing. She'd hold onto the car, not knowing whether it made her more sad or angry, but would definitely sell it by the end of the story. Or it would explode. Who doesn't love a good symbolic car explosion?*

And then, of course, being shipwrecked with her castmates and forced to confront her past while also embarking on a survival expedition came naturally. Just kidding. That happened months later. For a good long time, Ness was a semi-successful business owner on Long Island, providing landscaping services to the rich and richer.

Writing is a real journey, y'all.

While the car didn't make it into the final draft, much of the emotional baggage Ness has lugged along to her present stems from her father's inexcusable actions.

I still don't know anything about the neighborhood Jaguar, but maybe one day I'll ask.

ACKNOWLEDGMENTS

THANK YOU TO SUPERAGENT CLAIRE FRIEDMAN, WHO IS ALWAYS AND forever making dreams come true, providing an embarrassing (for me) number of pep talks on demand, and Doing the Business Things with awesome skill and efficiency.

I shudder to think what this book would be without the editing prowess of Julia McDowell and Elizabeth Trout. Thank you both so much for your unwavering support, incredibly insightful feedback, and seemingly bottomless wells of patience.

One billion thank yous and enthusiastic high-fives to everyone at HarperCollins Canada and Kensington. Your expertise, attention to detail, and excitement for this story are invaluable. I'm so lucky to have you.

The online bookish community—both authors and readers—continues to blow me away with its kindness and generosity. It makes a potentially very lonely job feel like part of something so much bigger. A particularly heartfelt thank you to the Claire Hype House for being a safe, supportive, and thoroughly exciting group.

To the Tarts: *dissolves into heap of blubbering emotion* I wouldn't be here without you.

And, of course, my family, who got to live with me while I was, perhaps, not my best self during the drafting of this book. Thank you for the space when it was required, the hugs when I needed them, and the endless enthusiasm for this wild ride.